ROYAL TOUR

Also by Amy Alward

The Potion Diaries

☙ THE ❧
POTION DIARIES

ROYAL TOUR

AMY ALWARD

SIMON & SCHUSTER BFYR

NEW YORK   LONDON   TORONTO   SYDNEY   NEW DELHI

SIMON & SCHUSTER BFYR

An imprint of Simon & Schuster Children's Publishing Division

1230 Avenue of the Americas, New York, New York 10020

Text copyright © 2016 by Amy Alward Ltd

Published by arrangement with Simon & Schuster UK Ltd

Originally published in Great Britain in 2016 by Simon & Schuster UK Ltd

First US edition October 2016

SIMON & SCHUSTER BFYR is a trademark of Simon & Schuster, Inc.

For information about special discounts for bulk purchases, please contact Simon & Schuster Special Sales at 1-866-506-1949 or business@simonandschuster.com.

The Simon & Schuster Speakers Bureau can bring authors to your live event. For more information or to book an event, contact the Simon & Schuster Speakers Bureau at 1-866-248-3049 or visit our website at www.simonspeakers.com.

Jacket design by nicandlou

Interior design by M. Rules

The text for this book was set in Goudy Oldstyle Std.

Manufactured in the United States of America

10 9 8 7 6 5 4 3 2 1

CIP data for this book is available from the Library of Congress.

ISBN 978-1-4814-4381-4

ISBN 978-1-4814-4383-8 (eBook)

For Lofty—one day, every day

CHAPTER ONE

www.WildeHuntTheories.com/forums/
THEKEMIFAMILY

Welcome to the Wilde Hunt Theories forums—
home of all Wilde Hunt discussion on the World
Wide Web. Rules are simple: no anonymous posting, no revealing any personal information, and no
unverified links. Mods' decisions are final. Thank
you—the WHT Mods.

**NOTE TO ALL NEW MEMBERS: This sub-
forum is for the exclusive discussion of the
KEMI family and their history as relating to the
Wilde Hunt. Any posts relating to ZOROASTER

CORP, the PATELS, the CRUICKSHANKS, the MENZOAS, or any other alchemists in Nova will be moved to the appropriate subforum. Respect all the forum members and HAPPY HUNTING.**

63,341 readers; 740 here now
7506 posts; 51 new since last visit

[STICKY POST] **AlchemyRox21 asks:** What is the greatest KEMI accomplishment? Please be prepared to back up with historical evidence.

563 replies

[Most recent] **Conspirator2561 says:** I get all your points but I still don't think we can dismiss Cleo Kemi outright. Her journal might be missing but primary sources from that time confirm she has a strong history of innovating potions.

[STICKY POST] **OrdinaryRelicHunter asks:** Does SAM KEMI have a Royal Commission? Could there be more to her friendship with the princess . . .

398 replies

[Most recent] **PixiDust3 says:** Whether she's getting help or not, don't we feel like the princess should be married by now? Any sympathy I had for her following the last Wilde Hunt is evaporating the longer she willingly keeps the country in danger.

[NEW POST] **KemiObsessed88 says:** SAM KEMI to appear on *Good Morning Kingstown* at 08:00, alongside Princess Evelyn and Zain Aster. Don't miss it!

[NEW POST] **OrdinaryRelicHunter says:** BREAKING NEWS. A source in Zambi has claimed that Emilia Thoth has escaped from her holding cell while awaiting trial. (Mods, feel free to move or delete this if it is irrelevant.)

CHAPTER TWO

"READY?" PRINCESS EVELYN SQUEEZES MY hand as she leads me out of the makeup room and toward the studio. The setup is a cozy living room: two pale pink crushed-velvet sofas are angled slightly toward each other, a low mahogany coffee table in front of them, all perched on top of a richly knotted oriental carpet. If it weren't for the array of cameras facing the sofas and the bright lights, I could have been round for tea at someone's house. A very rich person's house.

Evelyn's hand slips from mine as she extends it toward the presenter who comes forward to greet us. I wipe my sweating palms on my cotton dress. I wish I'd been allowed to wear my jeans.

Chamomile and valerian tea—a calming potion to relax the nerves, boost confidence, and soothe anxiety.

My second wish? That I could run home and take some calming potion now, but it's too late for that.

The presenter turns to me, and I swear her eyes have actually morphed into stars after her close encounter with the princess. She looks dazed as she focuses on me, but maybe it's me who is not seeing straight—I can't believe that I'm actually meeting the people I've watched almost every weekday since I can remember. Their morning cast has become part of our daily routine, as comforting as a cup of coffee and a bowl of honey-nut cereal. Except now they want to interview *me*. Well, me, Princess Evelyn and Zain. I picture my family all squished around our kitchen table, angling for the best view of the television. It's pretty surreal.

"So nice to finally meet you, Sam!" says the female presenter. Up close, she has the bounciest blond hair and the whitest teeth I have ever seen.

"Thanks for having me, Ms. Carter," I reply, trying my hardest to calm my shaking fingers.

"Call me Annie! How are you feeling? Any nerves?"

"Maybe a few . . . ," I say, but I'm interrupted by the male presenter, Mike Evans. My first impression is surprise: He is so much shorter in real life than he looks onscreen. I tower over him by a good head-and-neck.

"Nervous? This girl, who faced down enemies of our country and came out a winner?" He claps me on the shoulder. "Impossible."

Someone behind us calls out "thirty seconds," and there's a mad rush as we all get into place. I'm sandwiched onto one sofa between Evelyn and Zain, while the presenters take up their position opposite us.

"Remember," Evelyn leans over and whispers to me, "focus on the presenters, not the cameras. This is just a normal conversation. Act natural. And cross your legs at the ankle, not the knee." I adjust my legs, and before I know it I hear "Three . . . two . . ." and Mike turns to the nearest camera and begins his introduction.

"Princess Evelyn hit the headlines this year when she fell gravely ill, initiating the first Wilde Hunt in Nova for over fifty years. After a nail-biting and often dangerous search for the cure, the hunt was won by young Samantha Kemi, an apprentice alchemist from right here in Kingstown. The two of them join us now, alongside Zain Aster, who was runner-up in the hunt along with his father, Zol Aster, CEO of ZoroAster Corp. Now, Your Highness, first of all, how are you feeling?"

"I'm pleased to say that I'm one hundred percent better, thanks to my friend Sam," Princess Evelyn says, angling her head toward me. She sits with natural grace on the sofa, her head held high. I straighten my spine in response, trying not to slouch. The muscles in my back and shoulders twinge. My normal position is hunched over a mixing bowl—or maybe my laptop—not rod-straight in front of a television camera.

As Evelyn and the two presenters continue to chat, my eyes dart around the studio. The lights shining down onto the sofa are so bright, I can't see much beyond the cameras without squinting. Except I know that scrunching my face up live on national TV is probably not the best way to present myself. I try a more neutral expression.

I feel a small but purposeful pressure on my big toe and I frown—but then I catch Annie Carter's eye. She's looking at me expectantly, like she's waiting for something from me.

My brain kicks into gear. *A question! She asked me something* . . . but I can't quite remember what. Why haven't I been paying attention? *Nice work, Sam, you're about to embarrass yourself on national television.*

"She's better at mixing potions than answering questions," Zain quips, taking the attention away from me. It gives me enough time for the question to pop into my consciousness. *So, Sam, what are you going to do with the prize money?*

"Oh, wow!" I say with a laugh. I hate how forced I sound, but everyone is smiling at me in encouragement. I take a deep breath. "A lot of it has gone into our family store, Kemi's Potion Shop, and some has been tucked away for me and my sister's education and my parents' retirement . . ."

Mike laughs. "It's all so serious! Come on, tell me something you've bought that's a bit more fun." He leans in as if we're co-conspirators and I'm about to share a secret with him. A secret that millions of people will hear.

I frown as I try to think of something wild that I did with my money. I'm not really that "wild," ironically enough. If I had my way, I'd have spent all the money on books. "Well, I am going to buy a ridiculously expensive dress for a ball—"

"Not just any ball," interjects Evelyn. "Sam is going to join me on my Royal Tour, and part of that involves the annual Laville Ball in Pays—only the biggest party of the year!"

"That sounds so glamorous!" coos Annie. "So I take it you three will remain friends after the noise about the Wilde Hunt dies down?"

"Of course we'll always be friends," Zain says. "An experience like the Wilde Hunt changes you. You can't go through something like that without coming out so much stronger on the other side." He puts his hand over mine and I feel the blood rush to my face.

"I think two of you are a little more than friends," says Mike with an exaggerated wink.

I can't even imagine what shade of red I am at the moment. Beetroot, most likely.

"Apart from the prize money, it looks like you won a new boyfriend and a best friend in the princess," Annie says with a laugh. "What else would you say you gained from the hunt, Sam?"

I pause for a moment. An answer springs to my mind but I don't know if I should say it. But when else am I going to get this kind of opportunity? I wriggle in my seat and talk before I can change my mind.

"Well, Annie, I gained a lot of respect for how amazing ordinary people can be. Growing up without any magic, I always thought there was a limit to what ordinaries could do, compared to Talenteds, but I don't believe that's true anymore. Take my great-grandmother. I had no idea that she was the first woman to scale Mount Hallah until I saw her picture there."

"That *is* impressive," says Annie, her eyebrows waggling. She is Talented—she can channel magic—but she doesn't look offended by my statement. "Did your family not tell you about that?"

I shrug. "They didn't know either. Even though, at the time, she was the world's greatest alchemist, a lot about my great-grandmother's life is a mystery."

"But it's not a mystery that she lost her Wilde Hunt, right?" Mike says with a sly smile.

I nod once, briefly, clamping my lips shut. It's not a part of history that my family enjoys reliving, and I instantly regret giving him cause to bring it up.

Mike continues, "Well, since Zoro Aster won that particular Wilde Hunt, wouldn't that make him a greater alchemist than her?"

Now my face feels heated again, but this time it has

nothing to do with embarrassment. "My grandfather says she created the most powerful potion ever made! If she hadn't lost her diary the world would be a completely different place."

"I'm *sure* that's right," says Mike, not hiding the skepticism in his voice. "Zain, wasn't it by winning the Wilde Hunt over the Kemis that your family could launch ZoroAster Corp?"

Evelyn jumps in, ever the diplomat. "From rivals to friends—amazing what can change over the course of a few generations!"

A bright red light flashes above the camera, saving me from further outbursts I know I would regret. It's the presenters' cue to wrap up for a commercial break.

Naturally, they turn their attention to the princess to close out their segment. She's magnetic in her pale yellow dress, her perfect blond curls dipped at the ends with a bright gold glamour. It's a new style and the media have gone crazy for it. "Are you looking forward to your Royal Tour, Princess?" asks Mike.

"I can't wait. And with my two best friends by my side . . . I couldn't ask for anything more."

"All the best wishes for safe travels," Annie chimes in. "And better luck finding your true love this time around."

"Now, over to Helen for today's local weather and traffic news . . ."

CHAPTER THREE

"DID THAT REALLY JUST HAPPEN?" I SAY, before letting out a huge groan.

We're ushered straight from the living room set and into the greenroom. I hadn't been in the greenroom yet, as I arrived late and was rushed through to have my makeup done. Even my best attempt at eyeliner isn't good enough for a national newscast.

Now that we're safely ensconced in the room (which isn't even green, I'm disappointed to note), Zain pulls me into a kiss. "You were great," he says.

"No, I wasn't."

"Hey, at least you made it! When you weren't here by seven I thought you weren't going to show," he says, his face still close to mine. Then he slumps onto a bright red sofa, dragging me down with him.

"I overslept. There was an emergency at the store last night," I say with a shrug. "Someone came in needing an urgent mix for this morning and Granddad and I were up all night working on it."

"Are you okay, Sam?" Evelyn asks, waving away her assistant. She shuts the door behind her so that the three of us are alone.

"I think I just brought a whole bunch of ancient Kemi history back into the light, only for it to be dragged straight through the mud again. The forums are going to go *nuts* for this."

Evelyn frowns. "I don't think it was *that* bad . . ."

The tone of her voice doesn't do anything to reassure me. "Remind me not to do live television again," I say. My stomach shifts uncomfortably, and I can't help this niggling feeling in the back of my mind like I've just betrayed a huge Kemi family secret. It's the feeling I get when I realize I've forgotten to do an important task for Granddad and I'm about to get a big telling off when I get home. I'll have to watch the interview back when I get a chance. If I can get through it without cringing.

"Well, no need to worry about that as this was your last publicity commitment for the Wilde Hunt!" Evelyn high-fives me and then Zain. It's been a whirlwind of press and interviews and photoshoots since the hunt ended. It maybe would have been all right if it was just Nova that was interested, but the story seems to have captured the world's imagination—not just our country's. It's not a life I'm used to at all. The only time I've ever sustained this

level of scrutiny is when my best friend Anita used to grill
me about boys. More specifically, about Zain. I'm glad it's
the summer holidays. I hope when I get back to school in
a month, everything will have calmed down and I can live
my normal, boring life again.

"Please tell me you're ready for the tour, Sam?" Evelyn
stands with her back to the door. I can see that someone
has thrown a jacket over the only mirror in the room.
The princess still can't stand to look at herself, not since
she accidentally took the love potion that made her fall
in love with her own reflection and instigated the Wilde
Hunt.

"Err . . ."

"Sam!" she says, exasperation tinging her voice.

"What, I still have a week! Besides, I've been busy . . .
We've been busy," I add hastily, throwing a look at Zain.
He rolls his eyes at me but I can see there's a little smile
pulling at the edges of his lips: He's not mad at me for
implicating him too. He picks up my backpack and passes
it to me. I reach inside and pull out a large map, spreading
it out over my knees. "I've been doing some research and
we've narrowed down a possible source of the more potent
yellow ark flower not far from Kingstown. While you're
preparing for your Princess-y duties, Zain and I will hunt
down the ingredient."

"And that should help?" she asks.

"Without a doubt," Zain says. "Sam's research shows

that it's the best alternative in the synth or natural world to use to boost the formula."

I shoot Evelyn a sharp look. "How long does one dose last at the moment?"

She turns away from me and swallows. "I had to wake up in the middle of the night last night for another."

"In the night?" I look over at Zain, who's doing a quick calculation on his fingers. But I do this sort of math all the time for Granddad's clients at the store. "So we're down to less than forty-eight hours a dose." I stand up and grab Evelyn's hands. It's then that I realize she's shaking. "Don't worry, we'll make it stronger."

I hope that what I'm saying is true. The potion we're trying to mix is as unique as the person we're making it for—so original it doesn't even have a name yet—although to call it a challenge would be putting it mildly. Princess Evelyn, with royal blood running through her veins, is an immensely powerful Talented—so powerful she doesn't need an object, like a wand or a pair of gloves, to control her magic. Using magic comes as naturally to her as breathing. However, since she turned eighteen, her magic has grown so powerful it threatens to overwhelm her. Our potion helps her control it—but the traditional solution is marriage, so that she can share her magic with her partner. According to Novaen laws, ancient as they might seem, she needs to find a husband—and soon.

She nods. "I know you will." She lifts her hands from mine and looks down at a delicate rose-gold watch on her wrist. "I have to head back to the palace now . . ."

Zain raises an eyebrow. "Really? I thought you'd be staying in the city longer." He turns to me to explain. "Normally whenever they let Evie out of the palace you have to drag her back. Palace or prison—right, Evie?"

She smiles weakly. "Palace or prison, exactly. I don't want to have one of my *episodes* while I'm down here. And besides . . ." Her voice trails off but a blush rises in her cheeks.

It's unusual to see Evelyn anything other than perfectly composed. "Okay, Evie. Spill," I say.

"They haven't reinstalled the mirrors in your room again, have they?" Zain says. I hit him on the arm as I sit back down, and Evelyn's dreamy gaze turns into a glare.

"Very funny. No, if you must know . . . I've met someone. Or, I should say, I knew someone, but then I saw them in a different light." Her blush grows deeper as she speaks.

"That's so cool, Evie! Anyone we know?" I ask. I'm not really big on gossip, but even the hint of a crush for the princess is too exciting not to care about.

"Problem solved then, you can marry him!" says Zain. "Ow!" He glares at me as I hit him in the arm again. "What? If she's found someone she likes then what's the big deal? Better than marrying some bozo prince from the back end of nowhere."

"*Liking* someone is not the same as *loving* them. She doesn't have to marry someone just because she has a crush on them. This isn't the middle ages. What if they turn out to be a jerk?"

Evelyn laughs. "Thanks, Sam, my mighty defender. But Zain's right in a way. If they were suitable, I probably would just marry them. But alas, they're ordinary."

"Oh," say Zain and I simultaneously.

"So some kind of bozo royal it will have to be," she says wistfully.

I shake my head. "No, it's not right. There must be a way to change that dinosaur of a law." I pause, then reach into my bag and pull out my potion diary. "I have a theory."

"Go on . . . ," says Evelyn, her eyes opening wide.

"It's a long shot, and marriage is such a simple solution I don't think an alternative has ever been properly investigated before, but there must be a way to siphon off the excess power and store it permanently. Like some kind of magic battery."

"Do you think you can really do that?"

I shrug. "Maybe. I want to try."

"Oh, thank you, thank you, thank you!" Before I can move, she's thrown her arms around me and is squeezing me tight. "You are a star. Now, I really must go. See you two tomorrow?"

"See you," says Zain from next to me.

"Bye," I say. She gives me another big squeeze and two light kisses on the cheek and then, in a crack of electricity mingled with her rose-scented perfume, she's gone. I'm still not over that trick. Her disappearing act reminds me how different the princess is from me. I'm ordinary, and she's a different league of Talented.

I turn back to Zain and, now that it's just the two of us, I can't help but smile. He's not looking at me—he's staring at the screen of his tablet—but he's doing that cute thing where he bites his bottom lip while he's concentrating. His normally wild black hair has been tamed for TV, but only just.

Rogueish charm—that's how my mum described it after Zain attended his first Kemi family dinner.

His deep voice snaps me out of my creepy staring.

"You're right, Sam."

"Always," I say with a little smirk. "But about what, this time?"

He spins his tablet around. I groan as soon as I see the page that he has loaded up onscreen. I put up my hand to block it out. "No, not the Wilde Hunt Theories forums! I thought I told you to stop checking those!"

I'd placed a *proper* block on my laptop to prevent me from doing just that. After the Wilde Hunt win, people online couldn't stop talking about me and my family, dissecting our every move, and it became almost impossible for me to stop looking. I was an addict, constantly refreshing the page and reading the new posts and replies as soon as they were up.

Once, I'd called Zain in the middle of the night in tears about something they'd written insulting my dad (it's not his fault that the Kemi mixing gene skipped his generation!) and that was the last straw. No more forums for me. I'd been proud of myself for not looking for almost two whole weeks and now I'm a bit mad at Zain for making me break my self-imposed forum exile.

The truth is, it scared me how wild some of the theories were—but even scarier was how close to the bone they came too.

Like the post about the Royal Commission. It was pinned to the top of the forums so I couldn't miss it. The princess's potion was supposed to be top secret, even from the palace. How did they figure it out? Also irritating was the stuff they wrote about Zain and me. It's hard enough being in a new relationship without the weight of thousands of anonymous usernames watching you.

"You're going to want to see this, though."

I sigh and take the tablet from his outstretched hands.

[NEW POST] **OrdinaryRelicHunter says:** Anyone see Sam's appearance on GMK? What about her reference to Cleo Kemi's "Most Powerful Potion Ever"? What could it be?

64 replies

"Sixty-four replies?" I gasp. "It's only been, what . . . ten, maybe fifteen minutes since we've been off air?"

"You guessed it would happen." He moves to take the tablet back, but I stand up and spin it out of his reach. I open the thread of replies, scanning the multitude of theories about what my great-grandmother's powerful potion could have been. The hunt-obsessed *love* this kind of stuff.

Permanent mutation writes one person. *It has to be.* I almost laugh out loud. *Mutation* is the most famous alchemical potion—turning base metals into gold—and it's actually quite easy if I do say so myself. I had to prove I could do it before Granddad even let me into the lab. The tricky part is the *permanent* bit. Mutation is dead easy to detect and only lasts a few hours at most. I doubt my great-grandmother figured out how to make it permanent, otherwise we'd all be rich beyond our wildest dreams—or locked up in a Novaen prison cell somewhere.

Other theories are even crazier. A potion to give magic to ordinaries? Wishful thinking. To make animals talk? Oh, that's a suggestion from someone called *KittenLover3000* so maybe that's not so surprising.

One theory is emerging as the most popular, and the first time I see it, I bite my lip so hard I feel like I'm about to draw blood. Then there's a sharp zap on my hand and the tablet floats out of my reach, into Zain's waiting hands. I rub the top of my hand and frown. "Did you just use magic on me?"

"Desperate measures, Sam. Thought you were about to bite a hole through your lip."

Unusually for me, I don't have the energy to argue. I slump back against the wall, a million possibilities swirling in my head.

"What is it? What's up? I'm sorry for showing you that stupid forum . . ."

"The aqua vitae," I say.

Aqua vitae. Water of life. A potion that can cure any disease, deformity, and illness. Origin, ingredients, and recipe unknown. A potions legend and a fool's errand—like the philosopher's stone.

"It's their most popular theory. It's just as impossible as any of the others, but if any mixer could do it . . . my great-grandmother could have."

Zain's jaw drops. "No way," he says when he recovers. "You really think so?"

I nod.

There's only one thing for it. I need to get back to the store as quickly as possible.

Granddad has some questions to answer.

CHAPTER FOUR

WE LEAVE THE GREEN ROOM, PASSING through the series of sliding glass doors that protect the set from noise. A crowd of selfie-loving tourists are gathered outside the studio to get their faces in the background of the cast for their fifteen seconds of fame.

We pass by a huge poster advertising the princess's Royal Tour finale parade, which is to be held in the center of Kingstown after the tour is over. *BE THE FIRST TO SEE THE PRINCESS AND HER BETROTHED* reads the billboard. *Who will it be?* is written in the scrolling text beneath. It twists my stomach to see it.

Zain must have been thinking the same. "You shouldn't give her false hope about a permanent solution to her problem," he says, interlacing his fingers through mine. I've been practically speed-walking in my haste to get back to the store, but then I remember how little time I'll have with him today and I slow my pace.

"What, you don't think I can do it?"

"I *know* you can do it." He squeezes my hand tightly as he says it. "If I thought you had a few months and unlimited resources, you could absolutely do it. But at the moment, Evie is breaking Novaen law by not being married. You have until the end of the Royal Tour to find a solution. Maybe. And that's if we're still able to mix *our* potion successfully." He pauses for a moment. "Do you think the natural yellow ark flower is going to work? The synth version didn't make much difference."

I wrinkle my nose. "Of course it didn't."

He gives me a gentle nudge with his shoulder. "Hey, we're on the same side here, remember?"

"Oh yeah," I say with an exaggerated sigh.

He's right, we are on the same team now. Evelyn didn't trust going to the palace doctors, but she did trust us. I still remember asking her why. "Because they've had years to find me a solution, and now I'm asking you to try. You won the Wilde Hunt! You saved me," she'd said. "If anyone can do it, you guys can."

I couldn't really think of an argument against that. Plus, the princess can be *very* insistent when she wants to be. How could I refuse a commission so big? It feels like I'm a Kemi of old. I had to tell Granddad about it—I'm still the apprentice and he's still the Potions Master after all—but I swear there was a little smile on his face. And he's not showy with emotion.

Zain and I are a pretty good team, it turns out. Between us, we managed to put together a formula that sort of worked—after weeks of nonstop mixing and testing and remixing. But the princess's power was getting stronger and less stable by the day, and that meant finding more and more potent ingredients to add into the mix. One of those ingredients—the ark flower—was rare and had to be mixed *just before* administering the potion. Luckily Evelyn came up with the ruse of inviting me and Zain on her Royal Tour, enabling us to hunt down the ingredients and mix the cure without raising any eyebrows.

"Well, that's good then. And there's something else I've been meaning to ask you." Zain stops in the middle of the pavement, moving me to one side to let some people pass us by. My heart beats so loud, I swear he can hear it. "Will you do the honor of accompanying me to the Laville Ball?"

It takes me a second, and then I break out into a huge smile. "Of course, you goof. But I thought you didn't want to go? That it was some meaningless royal party and now that you have your studies to concentrate on then why would you bother . . ."

Zain grins. "You, my dear, have a memory that is far too good. Besides . . . I have a reason to go now. I need to see you in a ball gown."

I shudder. "Don't go expecting too much! I might wear jeans underneath."

"Evelyn will know and have your head."

"You're probably right."

"Anyway, you have to be formally escorted, you know," Zain says with a wink.

"Well, thanks for not leaving me hanging," I say, scrunching up my nose at the thought. "In fact, you're not allowed to leave my side at all during the ball."

"What, Sam who faced down enemies of our country, dangerous creatures, and saved the world is afraid of a little dancing?" Zain says in his best imitation of Presenter Mike.

I laugh. "Trust me, hanging out with a bunch of exceedingly posh, extremely wealthy, insanely Talented members of Princess Evelyn's circle is far more terrifying than a flock of vampire bats."

"Or a raging abominable."

"Or being engulfed in eluvian ivy." I shiver despite myself. "Okay, maybe *just* as scary as being engulfed in eluvian ivy. So, is this a proper date?" I add quickly.

He laughs. "No. *This* is an escort to a ball. One day we will have that proper date."

"One day," I echo back. It's been a running joke between us since our night on the mountain, when he first asked me out to a movie—a typical, normal date. So far, we haven't been able to manage it.

The high street is steadily filling up with morning foot traffic, and the market stalls that line the road are busy setting out their wares. I crane my neck as we pass, looking at the array of shining gemstones and charms, the worthless but pretty magic ornaments that sell for a couple of crowns each. We pass a stall with a giant hot plate, and the smell of delicious street food hits my nostrils. I already grabbed some toast this morning but surely an additional doughnut wouldn't hurt?

A tug on my arm leads me away from the sugary goodness, and we head down one of the narrow side streets. I love the side streets of Kingstown, with the wonky stone buildings leaning precariously toward each other, barely letting in the light. Royal Lane is a steady incline rising up toward the castle, so all the side streets lead to a series of staircases that offer shortcuts down the hill. Kemi Street, where Kemi's Potion Shop is located, is down one of these staircases, in a long-established alchemical neighborhood. The whole street's had a bit of a revamp since the Wilde Hunt, what with the influx of tourists who are flocking to the streets to see my home. Yet another thing to look forward to once all the post-hunt publicity dies down: being able to walk down my own street without fear of being photographed. I hunch my shoulders, wishing I didn't stand out so much. That's my height's fault—and Zain's. It's impossible to stand next to him and not be checked out.

Shroud powder—a mix of chameleon skin and rosewater, strained through the cloak of a wandering ghost (the cloaks of stationary ghosts just aren't billowy enough). Rub vigorously on skin to become less noticeable in a crowd.

"Oh crap," says Zain, pulling up short.

"What?"

But he doesn't need to explain. I can see for myself. Outside our store is a sea of reporters—some being trailed around by cameramen—and a crowd of people far bigger than the one outside the newscast studios.

I grip Zain's hand tightly. He moves so his shoulders are in front of mine, his body acting as a shield. I appreciate the gesture, futile as it may be.

I give it three . . . two . . .

They spot us. "Sam! Sam! How do you respond to reports that your ancestor hid the aqua vitae from the world?"

"Is there still a recipe in your archives?"

"Think of all the lives your family could have saved!"

"Come on," Zain says, though more to himself. He needs the confidence to clear a path through that crowd.

Targeted white-striped skunk bombs—mix no more than four drops of concentrated skunk juice with tree sap to make it extra sticky. I could clear a path through these crowds in an instant.

My body's immediate response to stress: Think about potions. It's not helping me now.

I spot a break in the crowd and I push Zain forward. "Now!" I say.

Someone shouts at him too: "Zain! If there's an aqua vitae recipe out there, doesn't that put ZA out of business? How do you feel about sleeping with the enemy?"

Zain picks up speed after that. He shoulders his way toward the door and it opens as soon as we step on the doormat. Dad yanks Zain through, then me, then we slam the door behind us and lean up against it.

Dad is the first to step away.

"Sam . . . what did you do?"

CHAPTER FIVE

WE DECIDE TO OPEN THE STORE DESPITE the crowd, and Zain leaves to head back to the ZA lab.

It's a big mistake. The store soon fills with people, and none of them are our regular customers. I make eye contact with one man and he shoulders his way through to the front to talk to me. He has a really sad story about his wife, who has a terrible disease that no one—alchemist or synth—has been able to cure.

"Look, sir, I'm really sorry." Heat rises in my cheeks as I wish I had better news. "Although we can treat some of the symptoms with one of our specialized mixes, there is still no cure for your wife's disease . . ."

His eyes dart between me and the wall of ingredients behind me. I know that look all too well. Desperation. My heart aches to help him. He leans forward on the counter, squeezing between the people who are crowding in on either side of him. His voice drops to a hushed whisper. "But I heard on the news this morning that you have an aqua vitae."

I shake my head. "I'm sorry . . . ," I say again.

"If it's a question of money, I can pay." He grabs his wallet, and I reach out to stop him.

"I promise you, we don't have a cure-all potion. It's a legend . . ."

"And you are the legendary Kemis! Surely if anyone can turn myth into reality, it's you," he interjects, attempting flattery. When I shake my head, he pounds his fist on the wood. "I need it! I know you have it."

"Sir, step back." My dad rushes up beside me. "As my daughter explained, we don't have the potion . . ."

"You're lying," he snaps. The other people in the store—and those in the line that already snakes out of the door—gather round, giving him courage.

"Give us the cure!" shouts someone, and the man who's been arguing with me agrees. He raises his fist. "Yeah, give us the cure!"

"Sam, get behind me," says Dad. I do as I'm told. Fear grips my throat, watching the underlying tension rise to the surface like lava through a volcano. At any moment, it's going to properly explode.

The crowd surges forward, and the man—emboldened by the mob—lunges toward me. But as soon as his outstretched hands cross the counter, a rain of sparks pours from the ceiling, cutting us off from the public. The man cries out and snatches his hand away.

Welder sparks—to create an impenetrable barrier. Specially altered so as not to ignite wooden surfaces.

The next second, a piercing wail fills the air and I slam my hands over my ears.

Banshee wail—for the most ear-splitting sound, collect on a full moon near a graveyard.

It's our security system in action. Dad throws me a pair of magically-enhanced noise-canceling headphones, which just about manage to make the banshee's cry bearable. The mob clears out of the store as fast as their legs can carry them. Once the last "customer" is gone, we lock the door. I don't think we'll be opening again soon.

I feel sick to my stomach. All those people . . . all that hope. I curse myself for mentioning my great-grandmother on national television, I curse the forums for coming up with a ridiculous theory about her most powerful potion, and I curse the media for blowing it out of proportion.

The wailing and the curtain of sparks cease at the touch of Granddad's palm. The security system is the only bit of magic he permits in the store and it's now extra potent thanks to the dose of Royal Talent we won in the Wilde Hunt.

"I'll go let your mother know we won't be opening again today," says Dad, his brow furrowed.

"Well, at least the alarm works," says Granddad,

dusting off his hands as he finishes resetting the system.

"Granddad . . . ," I start, but I don't know how to finish. *I'm sorry* is what I should say, since it's all my fault. But instead I ask, "Is it true?" The words slip out before I can stop them. Granddad casts his eyes down, suddenly looking every bit of his seventy-eight years. I can't help myself; I'm as hungry to know as the wolves at our door.

"Aqua vitae." He spits the words out. "You really think any Kemi worth their pestle and mortar would keep that kind of discovery to themselves? We're far too proud for that."

I think about it for a split second, then I shrug. He's right. Who would hide that? It would be the greatest alchemical achievement.

"But . . . ," he continues, and the word hangs in the air like a loaded weapon. He sighs. "Come on, let me show you something."

He takes me into the library, to the shelves that house the collection of Kemi potion diaries. Some of the diaries date back hundreds of years, though there are a few gaps where diaries have gone missing or been damaged. Granddad walks straight to the end of the shelf, where his own diaries are. One day I'll add mine to this shelf too.

His fingers quiver over the spines until he finds the one marked "1948." The year of the Wilde Hunt before mine. And the year that my great-grandmother's diary went missing.

He slides the diary down off the shelf, then passes it to me. I hold it as if it were made of crystal and might shatter in my hands at any moment.

It feels wrong; taboo—even though he's here with me. There's something sacred about another alchemist's journal. I get twitchy when someone picks up the bag that holds my diary—let alone the thing itself. It's like my mind outside of my body. It's full of my private thoughts—my questions, observations, experiments— all intensely personal. I'm nearly coming to the end of my first one, filling every page with my neat, round letters.

"There," he says. "Everything I remember about her missing diary is in there. I warn you, it's not much."

I nod. I place the diary on one of the wooden trestle tables in the center of the library and sit down on the long bench. I open it to a random page.

The altitude from her trip to Mount Hallah has taken its toll, but she has brought back the glacier water the potion requires. What lengths must she have gone to to get it? At least she wasn't on her own—Mr. Pringle accompanied her on the arduous journey.
She's off already, to hunt down whatever is next.
I am running the glacier water through the essence of spiderweb to prepare this part of the mix. I am learning, even if I do not know exactly what she is

trying to do. I sense there might be more to this potion
than even she realizes.

Mount Hallah. Of course—I think back to my own experiences at the base camp of that mountain, and how I saw the picture of my great-grandmother Cleo hanging on the wall of the lodge where we were stationed. My heart still swells with pride at the thought. I used to think being a Kemi meant staying cooped up in the lab, studying books, following tradition. Cleo showed me it could also mean being adventurous and exciting. It could be cutting edge. It could be different.

But Cleo also suffered for her adventures. She lost her potion diary. She never mixed again. No wonder Granddad hadn't been keen on me joining the Wilde Hunt—not when it destroyed his mother so completely.

I look up from the page. Granddad has taken the seat opposite me, but his eyes are closed; he is lost in thought. I was not prepared for the words to be quite so . . . diary-like.

Could my great-grandmother's diary have been lost on the mountain? No, that can't be right—Granddad would have mentioned it in the passage. I flick through the next few pages.

The mix for the Wilde Hunt is looking thirsty—it
is ready for the next ingredient. I don't know where
Mother has gone—to Runustan or Zhonguo or some

far-flung place—she refuses to keep me informed. I
feel certain that if we could work together, we would
figure the recipe out more quickly. But no.
No matter, when she comes back, I will look over her
journal and figure it out for myself. She will allow me
that, because that is the only way I will learn.
Wait—someone is outside. It might be her.

The ink changes color, and his handwriting turns even
more scrawl-like and slanted—written in a hurry.

I've never seen her like this. Wild-eyed and wild-haired—
I've hardly ever seen her anything less than pristine,
even on weekends! She looks as if she has aged fifty
years—her hair is all streaked with gray. I will record
the conversation now, quickly, so I don't forget
anything.
"Mother? Are you all right?"
She stares at me as if seeing me for the first time, then
shakes her head—not in disagreement, but as if to
shake cobwebs from her mind. She runs her hands over
her hair, to smooth it. "I'm fine, Ostanes. And please,
you know—in the store, it's Master Kemi."
I expected to see more luggage—or at least catch sight
of Mr. Pringle. But there is no one, and nothing. I
close the door. Something about her demeanor makes
me lock it too.

There is a loud crash. I race from the front of the store, through the door and into the laboratory. Mother has pushed the entire mix for the Wilde Hunt into the sink. Smoke rises as the acidity of the potion warps and melts the basin. I cover my mouth with my apron, then grab her back from the noxious fumes.

"Master Kemi, what are you doing? What about the Wilde Hunt?"

"It's over, Ostanes. We are out."

"Out? How is that possible?" Nothing she is saying seems to make any sense. How can we be out of the hunt? "Is it something to do with the mix? Are you stuck? Show me your diary, maybe I can help . . ."

"You can't," she says, roughly pushing me aside.

"Why? Why can't I help you?"

She turns back toward me, her body silhouetted in the doorway. "I'm done." Her voice softens. "But at least they are saved."

"They? Do you mean the queen?"

"Of course I mean the queen," she snaps. Her mood changes in an instant.

"Somebody else won?" I say. I can scarcely believe it.

"Not yet. But soon."

"Soon means there's still a chance for us!"

Her face darkens. "There is no hope for us."

"But why not?"

"Because my diary is lost."

35

My heart sits in my throat as I read, hardly allowing me to breathe. This is the moment . . . and yet, there's no indication of where Cleo has been. The next few pages don't help either. They document Granddad's attempts to get Cleo to mix again, and her stubborn refusal. I take several deep breaths.

"You see?" he says. He opens his eyes, blinking slowly.

I shake my head. "I don't understand. You always told me that my great-grandmother had created the world's most powerful potion, but since her diary was lost it could never be confirmed. You don't mention that anywhere here . . ."

He tugs at his beard and I clench my fists under the library table. He won't catch my eye, which makes me even more nervous. "When she came back, she couldn't even mix the simplest of potions. Even a cup of calming tea eluded her! I couldn't understand it. Then I remembered a legend I once read that said some potions are so powerful, they destroy the mind of the alchemist who dared to mix them. I told myself that she must have mixed one of those, because I couldn't admit to myself that she was embarrassed to lose the Wilde Hunt and simply lost her touch. That's all it was."

"So it was a lie." A lie I spread on national television. My great-grandmother hadn't created the world's most powerful potion after all. It was just another way for us to keep our family pride.

That cursed Kemi pride. It will be our downfall.

"I'm sorry you had to find out this way. She was, and still is, the best Kemi alchemist there's ever been."

"Better than you?" I ask. It's almost unfathomable to me.

"Oh, much," he says with a chuckle. "I wish you could have known her. She would have been so proud of you. You are the one who will surpass her, my dear Samantha. That much I know."

My heart swells and I can't help it: I fling down the diary, run around the table, and give him a big hug.

"Just keep your head down and study the old books." He pats my head with his hand. "Alchemy rewards the scholar—not the explorer. You would do well to remember it."

CHAPTER SIX

TODAY IS THE FIRST DAY WE'VE BEEN ABLE to open in the week following my disaster of a morning television appearance, but when I return to our store from picking up a few things for Mum from the supermarket, it's practically empty. The only occupants are my granddad and a woman with a frown so deep you could abseil down into it. "The Kemi diaries have never been shared outside of this family, and that's not going to change now," says Granddad. "Hold the door, Sam. Ms Slainte was just leaving."

Tension fills the air as Granddad and the mysterious Ms Slainte stare each other down. I know who is going to win that war. The woman purses her thin lips and the frown gets even deeper, but her clipboard snaps up and under her arm. "Don't think this is the end, Ostanes."

"It's Grand Master Kemi to you."

As she passes, she gives me a small smile, inviting me to join her in eye-rolling at stubborn old alchemists with long-held grudges. I don't accept. I give her my best stony glare, and she scuttles out of the door.

"Who was that?" I ask, locking the door behind me. It's clear we're not going to be open today, after all.

"Some government stooge," Granddad says. "On about some kind of petition . . ." He waves his hand, dismissing the notion.

I roll my eyes for real this time, then bring the groceries through to the kitchen.

I'd almost, *almost* been able to forget about the petition. "MAKE THE KEMI ARCHIVES PUBLIC" is the title, and it picked up a few thousand signatures in the aftermath of the aqua vitae speculation. It was started by the *Nova Mail*, a newspaper that seems to be aiming for the complete-and-total annihilation of our family. I swear one of their reporters has nothing better to do than to scour the Wilde Hunt Theories forums until a newsworthy story pops up.

But it's *insanity*. An alchemist's diary is his life's work and protected by Novaen law—the Alchemy Secrecy Act. Like Granddad told the government woman: There's no way anyone is getting their hands on our family's diaries that contain thousands of unique recipes dating back hundreds of years, especially not to search for a cure that doesn't exist. Not surprisingly, the *Nova Mail* is sponsored by synth money. What is surprising is that they've managed to get the government involved. My heart sinks.

"They can't make us, can they?"

Granddad snorts. I take that as a no.

My phone buzzes in my pocket. Once I've dropped the bags off on the kitchen table, I take it out.

Weathering the firestorm? It's Evelyn.

Barely, I reply. Someone from the government came here to try and get us to open our archives. Not. Going. To. Happen. So I guess for now we'll stick to being "Nova's most evil family."

WHAAAAAAT?! Who said that????

I'll give you one guess.

The Nova Mail?

Yup. They said if we'd been hiding a universal cure all these years then we should be tried as murderers.

I shiver just thinking about it. My sleep has been plagued with nightmares—visions of death by millions of flashing camera bulbs and long lines of newspaper print that wrap around my neck like a python, squeezing the life out of me. I quickly head up to the sanctuary of my bedroom.

By the time I get there, Evelyn's replied.

Ouch. Well, don't worry, it'll die down soon enough. They'll move on like they always do.

Yeah. But it's been a *week* already. Can you be spotted out in public in a dress you wore once last year or something?

:P

How's the mystery crush?

Still mysterious ;) But seriously, glad you're okay.

Just about.

As long as you're ready for the tour tomorrow . . .

I hesitate for a moment. The truth is that I haven't even started packing yet. It's been way too hard to focus on anything except the scandal that's been swirling around us. I've barely been able to leave the house, and the only time I've seen Zain or Anita has been when they've been able to brave the crowds to get to me. I'm not so sure that going on a Royal Tour and abandoning my family to this madness is fair.

As if she senses my reluctance, Evelyn sends me another message.

> Trust me . . . this will all go away soon enough.

I text her a thumbs-up emoji and vow to pack ASAP.

I sigh and slump down on the bed. How do you even begin to pack for a Royal Tour?

Before I can answer my own question, my little sister Molly comes flying up the stairs. "Sam, Sam, come look at this!" Her flushed face appears in my doorway, her braids flying out behind her.

"What is it, Mols?"

She doesn't reply, just gesticulates wildly for me to follow. I take the stairs two-by-two, racing down to catch up with her. When we reach the kitchen, she points to the TV.

SECRET LOVER FOR THE PRINCESS? HOPE FOR THE KINGDOM OF NOVA AT LAST!

Accompanying the headline is a grainy video of Evelyn locked in an embrace with a mystery person, shrouded in the shadows. My heart jumps into my throat and I feel a rush of gratitude. Our story doesn't even make the scrolling headlines below. Only Evie could have leaked that video.

I take my phone out.

Thank you, I write.

It still feels inadequate, and I wonder how I will ever pay her back.

42

"Did you know about this?" Molly asks.

"About what? That Evelyn was going to leak THE news story of the century to take the heat off us?"

Molly rolls her eyes. "Uh, no, silly. About the fact that the princess is in *love*. For *real* this time."

I raise an eyebrow. "One kiss doesn't automatically mean 'love,' you know . . ."

"But it could!"

"I don't think so."

"Aw, spoilsport," says Molly with a pout. But then her eyes light up again. She sidles up to me. "Why? What do you know?"

I hold my hands up. "Hey, patient-alchemist privilege!"

"She's not your patient anymore though . . ."

When I don't answer straightaway, Molly's jaw drops. "Don't tell me, you're working on *another* potion for the princess?" I try to think up an explanation, but Molly's brain moves even faster than mine. "That means the forums were right after all!"

I shake my head. "Wait, you know about the forums?"

"You're not the only one who knows how to use the Internet," she says, before flouncing off.

I stare after her in disbelief.

Then it comes to me. I remember exactly how I can help repay the princess. And I might just have time to do it before the tour starts.

I text Zain.

CHAPTER SEVEN

[MOST RECENT POSTS]

[NEW POST] **FinderFace says:** Zain and Sam spotted leaving Kemi's Potion Shop together. Any speculation they're finally going on a real date?

3 replies

[Most recent] **SantaClara says:** Anyone considered this might be related to the "secret" Royal Commission? Maybe the first ever synth-ordinary collab?

[NEW POST] **OrdinaryRelicHunter says:** KEMI SIGHTING—Ostanes Kemi heading toward Kingstown City Hall. Anything to do with the petition do we think?

8 replies

[Most recent] **Parzie33 says:** Nah, your source is probably wrong.

CHAPTER EIGHT

"ALMOST THERE," SAYS ZAIN. WE'RE IN HIS car, heading straight out of the city to a small village at the edge of the closest Wilds. His wand is sitting on the dashboard, glamoured to point us in the right direction.

"Perfect," I reply. I secretly cross my toes inside my boots. I really hope my source is correct. For once it would be nice to just show up and buy an ingredient rather than having to hunt it down in some obscure corner of the globe.

Not that that isn't fun, but, you know. A girl needs a break.

When we pull up in front of a ramshackle cottage, I have my doubts. Once it might have been called cute— back when the thatched roof wasn't rotten and patched up and the rose garden wasn't so overgrown it looked like a nest of thorns. There's even a tree growing out through the middle of the roof, where a chimney might have been.

I double and triple check the address on my phone, but this is the right place.

"Uh, how about I go check this out and you wait here?" Zain puts his hand over mine and squeezes it tight.

"No. If he's anything like other Finders I know, he won't be happy to have the heir to a huge synth corporation on his doorstep."

Zain grimaces, but doesn't move to get out.

I squeeze the tips of his fingers back, then get out of the car before I lose my courage. Resisting the urge to look over my shoulder every five seconds, I walk purposefully toward the cottage. When I knock on the door, it creaks open, and I regret all the horror movies I've watched with Anita in her parents' basement. They all seem to begin like this.

After I take my first step, curiosity overtakes fear. The room would be almost completely dark, were it not for the sunshine streaming through the hole in the roof where the tree has sprouted. As my eyes adjust to the light, more details emerge. It's kind of how I imagine the store might look if I didn't organize it religiously every week. Every space is crammed with jars and containers, stacked haphazardly on top of each other, spread out across the floor. I could spend hours picking through the collection if I had the time.

Maybe this guy got so addicted to the thrill of Finding, he needs to hide ingredients just so he can search for them again.

Personally, I couldn't work like this. The longer I stay in here, the more I want to start tidying up.

Oh dragons. I really am becoming my Granddad.

"Who's there? Stay back! I have salamander powder and I'm not afraid to use it."

I can't see the speaker in the murky light and I throw my hands up in surrender. "I'm Sam Kemi!" I shout into the semidarkness. "We spoke by email? You have yellow ark flower? Please don't use salamander powder on me!"

"Hmm," he says, but his tone's no longer menacing.

"I have the money we agreed," I say tentatively, still unable to make out whom I'm speaking to.

There's a rustling in the leaves of the tree, and when a face appears in between the branches I scramble backward, tripping over a stack of glass jars behind me. They tumble to the ground with an enormous crash and I wince. "I'm so sorry!" I pick up the jar closest to me, but I have no idea where it goes.

"Oh, just leave it," says the face. Its owner swings down and out of the tree, then extends his hand. "John McGraw, at your service."

"Sam Kemi," I reply, shaking his hand. He stares at me and I feel like I'm taking an exam I haven't studied for.

I must pass, because he hands over a small paper bag. I slip my finger underneath the seal and smile as I see three fresh bright-yellow ark flower petals. They will be perfect to boost the effectiveness of the potion we are making for the princess. I quickly fold the top of the bag over again, then hand him the small envelope containing the largest amount of money I've carried around with me in my entire life. No wonder I was feeling jumpy.

He snatches the envelope and flicks the notes inside, counting them like a pro. "Nice to do business with you, Kemi—"

The front door slams open and Zain barges in. Both Mr. McGraw and I freeze and the color drains from my cheeks. "I thought I heard a crash," Zain says, to our stupefied faces.

Mr. McGraw turns tomato red with rage. "SYNTH SCUM!" he roars, and without warning he reaches behind his back and throws a handful of orangey-red dust directly at our faces.

"Run!" I yell to Zain.

But he remains rooted in place, instinctively reaching for his wand. His calm demeanor turns to panic as he realizes it's not there. It's still on the dashboard of the car.

I slam into him, knocking us both to the ground. If the powder settles on our skin, we're done for. I scramble along the floor, picking up jars and throwing them against the shelves. As they shatter, I hope one of them is the one I'm looking for.

Crushed activated charcoal dust—acts as a neutralizer to several toxins, including salamander.

Black powder fills the air, sizzling as it merges with the orange dust. It gives us just the seconds we need to find our way back out of the door, not stopping until we reach the car, breathless and heaving.

Zain turns to me once we've recovered our breath, his eyes downcast. "I'm sorry—" he starts to say, but then I start giggling. I can't help myself.

"The look on Mr. McGraw's face when you walked in . . . ," I say between laughs.

It must be infectious, because Zain joins in. "When I reached for my wand . . ."

"And it wasn't there . . ."

"I thought we were goners." Zain shakes his head, but he's grinning widely at me. "You always know just what to do." He leans over and pulls me into a kiss that turns my giggles into tingles.

"I'm lucky I'm so nosy," I say when we come up for air. "I saw the charcoal when we came in and thought how useful it might be." Movement from the cottage window makes my heart skip a beat. "Come on, let's get out of here before we cause any more trouble."

"Did you get the ark flower?"

I lift up the bag. "All there."

"Great. And I know just how we can celebrate. Ice cream."

That boy knows the way to my heart.

* * *

High Park is an enormous swathe of green space at the bottom of Kingstown—and the busiest place in the city on a beautiful and hot day like today. Ice-cream vendors and hot-dog stalls line the gravel pathways, and the lake is packed with push-pedal boats floating on the inky black water. I love the park because it's a place everyone can enjoy—without needing any magic.

One of my favorite places in the park is the petting zoo, where my parents used to take Molly and me in the school holidays. They have tiny baby goats and lambs in the spring, and in the summer they even showcase some of the tamer Wild animals—little prancing kelpies in the water that grow stronger with the laughter of human children.

There's a nice breeze down by the lake, and that's where Zain and I walk, making a beeline for one of the ice-cream trucks.

"What can I get my rescuer this time?" he asks.

"Surprise me," I say, sitting down on one of the benches. As he walks off, I lean back, close my eyes, and let the sun catch my face. In my head, I picture slicing the ark flower petals into delicate strips and feeding them into the potion. Since we don't yet have a name for it, ideas for that swirl around my head: *Talent Tamer, Royal Rescue, Magic Constraining Potion.* I wonder if it could have other applications too. I would feel safer if dangerous Talented criminals like Emilia Thoth had their Talent constrained.

Zain snaps me out of my daydream by sitting down next

to me. He has two scoops of brightly colored ice cream in a cup.

"Close your eyes," he says.

"What?" Instead, I open my eyes wider, trying to guess the flavor he's bought me.

"Just do it."

"Okay." Tentatively, I close my eyes. He puts the plastic spoon to my lips and immediately I recognize the taste. "Mmm, chocolate," I say. "My favorite."

"Wait," he whispers.

I wait for a second and then there's a small series of explosions in my mouth, bursts of flavor that flood my tongue with delicious surprises. I laugh in delight.

"What did you taste?"

I open my eyes and see Zain looking at me eagerly. "Tropical fruits," I reply. "Like mango, passionfruit, and lychee. It is so good."

"That's so weird." He takes a scoop himself, waiting a few seconds for the flavor explosions to kick in. "I get other things, like apples and cinnamon and maybe a hint of caramel."

"Are you serious? What is this stuff?"

Zain winks at me. "It's called Flavor Faves. You get all your favorite tastes in one hit—I think it's new for this summer. Now I know that the key to your heart is chocolate, followed by tropical fruit."

"Hmm, and yours is apple pie!"

Zain places his hand on his chest. "I'm just a down-home boy at heart."

I laugh. I lace my fingers into his, leaning my head on his shoulder. I never thought that it could be this way with a Talented, and especially not with Zain. My reaction to him should be more like Mr. McGraw's—although maybe slightly less dramatic than throwing pain-inducing powder in his face. I should hate him. But I don't. In fact, the total opposite.

"You're itching to go, aren't you?" he says as we finish up our treats.

"The ark flower . . ."

"I know, I know. You have that need to mix."

I nod. I can't wait to see the reaction in the potion when we add the new ingredient, and to see its effects on Evelyn.

"Come on, then," he says, standing up from the bench. "We can eat and walk at the same time."

We walk out of King Canut's Gate, the closest one to Kemi Street. We can't hold hands because of the ice cream, but we walk so close together our shoulders bump as we move. "When we get to Laville, I'll take you to the best chocolate shop in the world," he says.

I smile. "Will that be a real date?"

"Hmm . . . no, that's more like a city tour," he says with a wink.

"One day, then."

"One day."

We turn the corner to the bottom of my road. The street is bustling and I hope that means our store will be busy too. With *actual* customers this time around, not people looking for a miracle we can't provide.

"Have you found something to wear yet for the Laville Ball?" Zain asks.

Before I can answer, a female voice shouts "Help!" from further up the street. "Somebody help me! We need an ambulance."

Zain and I both turn to look. There's a crowd of people in front of us, but through a gap I catch sight of a figure slumped against the low stone wall.

My heart stops. I recognize that figure—or at least the shock of white hair that has come loose from its cap. I see the cap with its faded olive-green checked pattern, lying discarded on the floor beside him.

"Granddad," I whisper.

"What?" says Zain, his voice raised with alarm, but I tear out of his grasp and race up the road, sprinting as fast as my legs can carry me.

By the time I reach him, a man is shaking his arm. "Sir, what's your name?" he says.

"I don't remember," he replies, then his eyes roll back in his head, his chin falling against his chest.

"Granddad!" I scream this time, and dive down to hold him. The man steps back, giving me space. "Are you all right? Granddad, it's me, Sam. Can you hear me?"

He comes around, but instead of words he is muttering something indecipherable. I whip my head around, still holding on tightly to Granddad's arm. "What happened? Did anyone see?"

The man closest to me frowns. "I'm not sure . . . but there was a woman here before who called for help. She would have seen the whole thing."

"Sam?" comes a feeble voice from beside me. My heart almost bursts with happiness that he recognizes me.

"It's okay, Granddad," I say, pulling him close to me. "I'll get us some help."

"I don't need any help, I'm fine," he says, though his voice is weak. I check all his vital signs and although his heartbeat is fast, it's still strong. My own heartbeat slows to a more normal rhythm. I look up—we're only a few meters away from the store.

"Zain, can you get my granddad's other arm?"

He nods, and loops Granddad's arm over his shoulder. I take the other side and thank the man for his help. The crowd gathered around us gradually disperses as they see he's okay. I breathe a huge sigh of relief.

As soon as I step forward, into the spot where my granddad had fallen, a stench hits my nostrils. It's acrid, sharp, and so metallic it makes my eyes sting.

I'd recognize that smell anywhere.

Emilia Thoth.

CHAPTER NINE

WE STUMBLE INTO THE KITCHEN. "MUM? Dad?" I yell into the house. There's no reply.

Beside me, Granddad grimaces. "No need to shout, Samantha."

"Oh, sorry, Granddad." Between us, Zain and I lower him into one of the chairs.

"I'm absolutely fine. Just took a little tumble, that's all. Nothing to be concerned about." He moves to stand up but I keep my hand on his shoulder.

"It looked like more than that to me. Zain, can you see if Mum is in the store? I'll make a cup of calming tea for Granddad." I busy myself at the stove, trying to stop my hands from shaking. My senses are still reeling from the shock of seeing Granddad on the ground, and that awful stench that hit my nostrils . . . then disappeared just as quick. But it couldn't be Emilia. She's locked up in a cell in Zambi awaiting trial. Just my overactive imagination at work again.

Granddad stands up. "I have mixes to finish off in the lab."

"I can do that! You need to rest."

"Who is the master and who is the apprentice here? I will finish off my mixes for today and you can help your mother front of store and *then* I will rest. I won't hear any more arguments about it." He storms across the kitchen, moving faster than I thought possible for his age.

"Sam, what's going on?"

Zain's brought Mum back in. Her face is lined with concern, and she keeps looking over her shoulder at the shop door. It must be busy in there. "Granddad fell outside the store and I'm worried he might have hurt himself," I say.

Her eyes go wide. "Where is he now? Does he need to see a doctor?"

I nod toward the door to the lab. "He said he was fine and he's already gone back to mixing." Zain and I exchange a look and I shrug. What can I do? Chain him to the chair? "He's going to rest when he's finished."

"Well, all right then. I could really use your help out front, you know."

"I'll be out in a second."

Mum wipes her hands on her long skirt and then pushes her way back into the store. With two large steps, Zain is by my side and pulling me into a big hug. I allow all my shock and fear to dissolve in his arms. Then he stands back, puts his hands on my shoulders, and looks me deep in my eyes. "He's going to be okay."

"I know," I say, though I hate how small my voice sounds. My granddad is my entire world. I don't know what I'd do without him. And the shock of thinking for even one single second that I might lose him . . . it's undone me completely.

"I'd better go. Sounds like you're needed in there."

I nod. I wish he didn't have to leave but he has his own family business to get back to. He's doing an internship with his company, ZA Corp.

As if reading my mind, he says, "At least we have the Royal Tour tomorrow. Two whole weeks we'll get to spend together with no work to worry about." His fingertips brush down my arm until they reach my hands. He gathers them up and kisses my knuckles. "Until tomorrow?"

"See you then." We kiss properly, then I wave him good-bye at the door.

There's a high-pitched whine as the kettle on the stove comes up to boil. Rather than let it go to waste, I make a cup of coffee for Mum—I know she will appreciate it. Just as I pick up the steaming mug to head into the store, my phone buzzes in my pocket. I fish it out and see that the message is from Evelyn.

> OMG!! I just heard from Z. Hope everything
> is okay?

All okay, I type back. **Apparently he just slipped . . . need to keep an eye on him but he's already back at work! Typical Granddad.**

Good to hear it. Still on for tomorrow? I need you!

Of course :)

Great. Be in touch soon.

I close my eyes and take a deep breath, the last remnants of a crazy morning swept away by the comforting scent of coffee grounds. Back to earth once again, I head into the chaos that is the store.

I can't help but smile. Everything is back to normal. Or at least, the *new* normal around here—which still takes some getting used to. The store is packed with customers picking up mixes or dropping off prescriptions. The wall of ingredients that stretches the entire height of the building—almost three stories in total—is totally rammed with new ingredients, merpearl sitting side-by-side with Merlin's beard, unicorn horn with unicorn tail. More boxes of ingredients arrive every day to replace our sold-out stock, sent to us by our ingredient Finder, Kirsty. We finally have what we've always wanted: a thriving, growing apothecary. The downside is it's so busy, I can't leave Mum to add the ark flower to Evie's potion. Reluctantly, I place the petals into a clean jar and put it on a low shelf, ready for me to mix in as soon as I have a spare moment.

"Sam, do you have the mixes for Mr. McDonough?" asks Mum. I rack my brain for knowledge of the mix.

Air of Apollo—heat thyme stalks, yellow river tea leaves, and Pegasus feathers over a hot brick and bottle the fumes. Helpful for asthma sufferers or for other breathing problems, including persistent cough.

Granddad approved the formula last night.

"Should be finished—I'll grab it from the back," I say. I dance around the line of people waiting at the counter and into the lab.

The lab possesses its own kind of busy industriousness. Concoctions bubble away on the stove, steam rising and curling into the otherwise still air, while bright red liquid does loop-the-loops through a rollercoaster of clear plastic tubing. All the mixes in progress. I don't see any sign of Granddad, but that doesn't mean he's not working away behind all the contraptions.

In the far corner I spot the brown paper package containing Mr. McDonough's Air of Apollo. I grab it and rush back into the store.

I find Mr. McDonough and hand over the cure. He smiles at me gratefully. "Your mix is the finest I've used—

much better than my synth medication. I have no idea why I never came here before!" he says.

I know exactly why: because he was scared off using our potions by the huge antipotion campaigns orchestrated by ZoroAster and the other synth corporations over the years. I don't say that though, I just smile and say, "Well, I hope you come again," like Mum tells me. No point getting all political with the customers—they're proving their loyalty with their money.

"See you soon," I add.

We work this way in a steady, comforting rhythm until well into the afternoon.

A bell rings behind the counter—the signal that Granddad needs me. I excuse myself from helping Mum and head back into the lab. There's no sign of him. "Granddad?" I raise my voice above the sound of the bubbling and boiling.

"Over here." I hear his voice from a far corner of the room.

I duck around a large wooden counter (that I've bumped my hip on more times than I can count) and automatically pick up any spare ingredients I see lying around, replacing them neatly in their rightful spots as I pass. A *messy lab means messy mixes*—one of Granddad's many reminders sweeps through my mind.

When I see him, I let out a gasp. There are twenty or thirty little brown bags, filled with mixes, waiting to be picked up. Prescriptions ready for their customers.

"Don't just stand there. Go take these to your mother before the afternoon rush."

I pick one up and turn it over in my hand. "These are all completed mixes?"

He doesn't reply, merely grunts. I swallow down my shock. He must have been working in double—triple—quick time in order to get all these mixes done.

"We missed a valuable morning, so I had to pick up the slack."

I nod, not quite trusting myself to speak, and load the bags of mixes onto a large tray. I carry it carefully back through to the store.

"Can you believe this?" I whisper to Mum as she comes over to stand beside me. "He's been working non-stop all morning. Just look at all these mixes."

"Oh, this is perfect." She grabs one of the bags and hands it to a client. "Here you go, Mr. Talbort. I told you it wouldn't be long."

Mr. Talbort looks like he's about to explode with gratitude. "Thank you, Katie. My daughter needs this mix straightaway and since you've been closed I was running out of options." He takes the bag and rushes out of the door.

Mum and I exchange a smile. This is the best part of our jobs: when we can really see what an impact our cures have on the community. And no one is asking about the aqua vitae nonsense.

Mum's smile gently turns into a frown. "Shouldn't Granddad be resting?"

"You try telling him that."

"I suppose so." Mum hands over another bag, exchanging it for some crisp notes. The till is almost full to bursting. Mum turns to another customer and I start filing the mixes away in alphabetical order beneath the counter.

When I finish, I look up as a familiar face walks into the store. It's Moira Grant—one of our most loyal customers but also one of our most devious. I'm sure that she takes advantage of my mother's generosity and kindness, and that she owes us several months of back payment for her prescriptions. Of course, now that we're successful, Mum wants to forget about the back payments—we don't *really* need the money now—but it just doesn't seem fair for her to keep getting away with it.

"Good morning, Mrs. Grant," I say with a smile. I want to take my time so that she can take *her* time—getting her money out of her wallet. "Let me check your prescription for you to make sure we have everything."

She throws me a scowl that suggests she knows exactly what I'm doing, and I suppress the urge to stick my tongue out at her. Instead, I open up the paper bag marked *Mrs. M G* in Granddad's spindly handwriting and peer inside.

I frown.

"What is it, dear?" she asks, her tone sickly-sweet but with iron underneath.

I reach into the bag and pull out the mix. Something about it doesn't look right. Moira takes a special cream for her arthritis.

Sunlight-infused devil's claw leaves, mixed with aloe plant and red ochre—for help with arthritis, lubrication of the joints, and smoothing of knuckles.

One of the key traits of the cream is its distinctive red color. When he was younger, Granddad worked out a way to make the red disappear upon contact with the skin, but for a long time the potion was known as "scarlet fingers." Having the telltale crimson skin was especially damaging for women who used to work in factories, sewing delicate garments or working the big machines. Using the cream helped the pain immensely—but it also gave employers an excuse to dock pay.

But the cream in this tube isn't red. It's a murky brown.

"That doesn't look right," says Moira, her eyes alight with the opportunity to make a complaint and maybe get her medicine for free.

"No, it doesn't," I say.

I pick up another bag and open it. On the front reads *PENNYROYAL FOIL* but once again, what's inside looks nothing like I expect. Pennyroyal foil should be wafer-thin slices of coppery leaves that melt underneath the tongue, but these aren't copper—they're silver. They look more like mercury foils, which perform an utterly different task.

My heart rapidly sinks into my stomach. All these potions, these mixes, are wrong. I look down at my watch. It's maybe only been half an hour since I brought out the new mixes Granddad made. How many of them have gone out? How many . . .

Moira coughs sharply, staring at me over her thick tortoiseshell glasses. "Is there a problem?" she asks.

I hope I haven't gone as white as I feel. One mix every five minutes, that might be . . . six customers affected. And more by the moment. Mum hands over another prescription and I can't help it. I cry out to stop her.

Mum frowns at me, her eyebrows knitting together. "What is it, Sam?"

I snatch the brown paper bag out of the customer's hands. I gather as many of them up into my arms as possible. "I, uh . . . I just have to check something with my grandfather. I'll be right back."

But there's no time for a "be right back." There's a shriek from the street outside, and someone flings our door open. It bashes the inside of the room, sending the jars on the shelves tingling.

"You almost killed my daughter!" Mr. Talbort stands red-faced in our doorway. "The mix I gave her sent her into a fit of hives. Instead of her epilepsy medication you gave her honeysting!"

Honeysting for allergic reactions—not at all for epilepsy, and can cause an allergic reaction in itself if taken by the wrong people.

"We've had to take her to the Kingstown General Hospital where she's getting proper treatment for *your* mistakes."

"I . . . I'm so sorry, Hank," my mum says. "I don't know what to say . . . Ostanes had a fall this morning . . ."

"And yet you let him make mixes? It's beyond irresponsible. That's why, I'm sorry, but I had to go to the authorities."

Someone steps out from behind him. She's wearing a sharp pinstripe suit with her Talented object—a gold wrist cuff—deliberately on show. Behind her are two large men, also in suits, their arms folded across their chests. I recognize her as the government woman who was in our store the day before.

The woman walks straight up to my mother. "Are you Katie Kemi, manager of Kemi's Potion Shop?"

My mum tries to draw up some height and gain an air of authority, but in her hippy headband, potion-stained white shirt, and long skirt, she doesn't quite pull it off. "Yes, I am."

"My name is Agnes Slaint, from the regulatory board of Potions and Synthetics of the Novaen government. Within the boundaries of regulation 13.4 of the Potions Safety Act, without a viable master supervising the mixing of potions it is illegal to keep an apothecary open to the public." She looks over at me, her hooded eyes filled with something other than sympathy. It's a look I haven't seen for a while, but when I recognize it, the hurt comes sharp and quick, like a snake bite. It's pity. "I'm very sorry, but we're going to have to ask you to close your store. You have until five p.m. this evening to comply—otherwise we will have to close you by force."

CHAPTER TEN

WE MANAGE TO GET EVERYONE OUT OF the store and convince Mr. Talbort, the other customers, and Agnes Slaint not to make the news of the store's closure public . . . for now. I know it won't be long until this hits the forums, though.

"We could say we're taking a family vacation," says Mum from one side of the kitchen table. Her fingers dig at a knot in the wooden surface and she keeps throwing worried glances at the shop door.

"Too obvious," replies Dad, who's returned from his errands to chaos—though his first priority was not the store's closure, but Granddad's health. "He's resting," he adds, reading my mind as to my next question.

"Did you tell him about the . . . mixes?"

Dad nods, running his hands through his hair. "At first he didn't believe me, but when I showed him the proof, even he couldn't argue. We're going to go to the hospital. He looks so tired. I'll get some things together."

"Clearly things are much worse than we realized," Mum says.

Dad nods.

"Who's going to the hospital?" My parents spin around in their chairs and I look up. Standing in the doorway with a handmade paper kite in her hand is Molly. Her long dark hair is tied up in two braids that fall to her shoulders, and she's flushed from the walk home from day camp. Her eyes are still bright and happy, but the quivering of her eyebrows tells me she knows that's about to change.

Mum stands up abruptly and takes Molly's hand, sitting her down at the table with us. "It's Granddad, honey. He had a bad fall this morning and we thought he was going to be okay, but he needs to go to the hospital."

Her lips quiver. "Is he okay? Can I see him?"

"He's asleep at the moment, sweetheart. How was day camp?"

As Molly hesitantly recounts her day, I switch off, feeling sick to my stomach. This is so much worse than the fuss over the aqua vitae.

Granddad has *never* gotten a mix wrong before. Not like this. Something must be seriously wrong. If he doesn't get better . . . what's going to happen to the store? I'm still years away from my apprenticeship being over. Even with the Wilde Hunt victory, I'm not ready to run the store on my own. Granddad was ready at sixteen, but he'd already left school. I still have my high school diploma to get, and I wanted to go to university, maybe do a bit of traveling . . . all before I officially become a potions master.

We need Granddad, or else the potions board will keep the shop closed indefinitely.

"I know he's asleep but—can I go and see him?" I ask, abruptly interrupting Molly's story.

Dad hesitates just for a second, but then nods.

"I'll come with you," my sister says quickly.

"Please just give me a moment, Mols? I just have to talk master-and-apprentice stuff, okay?" I pause—I want to speak to Granddad alone. But I know the expression on her face. It's a mix of wide-eyed innocence and steely determination that Molly has absolutely perfected.

"One moment?" I plead.

"Okay," she relents. I dash from the room before she changes her mind.

Although I storm through the lab, when I reach Granddad's room, I walk on my tiptoes. To my surprise, I can see a light shining beneath the door, and his shadow as he paces back and forth across the room.

I rap my knuckles gently on his doorway. His shadow stops. "Samantha?" he calls out.

I take that as an invitation and I push his door open. "Yes, it's me, Granddad."

His white hair is in disarray, the expression in his eyes wild. His bare feet tap against the carpet, his slippers discarded beside his bed. "Granddad, you'll catch a cold like that!" I reach down and grab the slippers, dropping them in front of his feet.

"It's here . . . it's here somewhere." He lurches away from me, turning toward the windowsill, where he has a series of old potion diaries lined up against the glass. He tugs one out and the rest topple, spilling out on the floor.

"Granddad!" I cry out in alarm.

He flips through the diary, moving so quickly he tears some of the pages. "Help me, Sam. It's been taken."

"What has? What's been taken?"

"Grand Master Cleo's diary."

It takes me a few moments to process his words. "Great-grandmother Cleo's diary? But that's been gone for years . . . decades. Remember?"

He stops and looks up at me. For a moment, he doesn't look any of his seventy-eight years. He looks like a young boy—wide-eyed and confused. "It has?" The diary he was flicking through slips from his fingers onto the floor. I reach out and put a hand on his arm, guiding him toward the bed.

I sit down next to him, and he puts his other hand on top of mine. Then, in a flash, he grips it tight. "You must find it," he says, his eyes as clear as his voice. "You must find it before she does. It holds the key."

"The key to what?"

His voice breaks, and his eyes cloud over again. "I . . . I can't . . ." I worry he's going to think himself into oblivion. He almost does. He shakes with the force of trying to remember, and even as I try to calm him, to hush his thoughts, he falls back onto the bed, releasing his strong grip on my fingers. "Find it," he whispers, before he passes out.

I can't help it—I let out a cry and I fall toward him. I put my fingers against his neck and I sigh with relief as I can feel his pulse—rapid and uneven.

"Is he okay?"

I whip my head around—it's Molly.

"Molly, please . . . we need to get Granddad to the hospital, now. Tell Mum and Dad."

To my surprise, she lingers in the doorway. "What do you have to find? You know more about what's wrong with him, don't you?" I open my mouth to protest, but she keeps going. "No, you promised after what happened in Zambi that you wouldn't leave me out of the loop. I'm not just anyone, Sam. I might be young, but I'm your sister. I can help too."

"I know you can." I reach out my hand to her, and she takes it. "I promise you, I don't know anything yet. I have a suspicion about something but . . . I need to talk to the doctors, and to Mum and Dad. I don't think Granddad had an ordinary fall. I think someone did this to him. But do you promise not to tell anyone until I know more?"

"I promise, Sammy. You can trust me," she says. "But as soon as you figure anything out about Granddad, I want you to tell me. Don't keep me in the dark again." My sister might not be an alchemist, but she's a Kemi through and through.

CHAPTER ELEVEN

> Hey, it's me . . . I came by the store after
> work but you weren't there? Everything
> okay with your granddad? Text me back,
> I'm worried.

I read the text from Zain but don't have time to reply. I
shove the phone back into my pocket.

"I'm telling you, Mum, Emilia Thoth has something
to do with this."

Mum, Molly, and I are waiting in Kingstown General
Hospital's intensive care unit. The wall opposite us is
covered in pictures of wildflowers: a mural of bright primary splashes of color. I can imagine whoever designed
it wanted to make the people sitting in the waiting room
feel cheerful and optimistic. I know the colors should
have an effect on me, the same way I know from potions

mixing that certain smells and tastes bring calm.

Chamomile leaves steeped in water; a pillow of lavender; a mug of thick hot chocolate. None of them are *potions* exactly, but they can have the right effect.

But not for me. Not right now. Everything I put in my mouth seems to taste like ash and the mural of flowers makes me want to gag. *Someone thinks a picture of a stupid flower will make my pain disappear? Who came up with that?* I pace around the room, restless.

Mum takes my hand and tries to pull me down into a hard plastic seat. But there's no way I'm going to sit down. I've been trying to explain to anyone who will listen—Mum, Dad, the doctors—about Granddad's last words to me and about the smell I noticed back when we first found him on the street. I silently curse myself that I didn't speak up before. Now, we're in the intensive care ward and dread hangs around my neck like a noose.

She sighs as I yank my hand away. "Honey, I know you are feeling a lot right now, but we are all upset for Granddad."

"But no one is listening . . ."

"No, you are the one who is not listening," she snaps. Her tone pulls me up short. She almost never loses her temper with us—Mum prefers the gently-gently method of parenting and usually leaves any disciplining to my dad. But I can see that this outburst has pained her: Tears glisten in her eyes. "The doctor says he is deteriorating rapidly. There's nothing we can do."

"But what about what he said about Great-grandma Cleo . . ." Even my voice sounds small and far away. My persistence is waning.

This time, Mum really isn't listening to me. She's looking up at Dad, who's just come in with another status report.

"He seems to be stable at the moment but they're going to keep him in overnight at least," Dad says, pinching the bridge of his nose. "They don't exactly know what it is—but what it boils down to is that Granddad is old. These things happen as people get older."

Like a jack-in-the-box, my persistence rears its head again. "Have they tried everything? I'll go back and research some cures. There must be something in an old Kemi diary somewhere . . ."

Dad shrugs. "Maybe if we had an aqua vitae . . ."

"But there's no such thing," says Mum. "And I don't think false hope is going to do us any good either," she continues, resting her hand on my dad's forearm.

"We can light a candle for Granddad, right?" says Molly.

"Of course we can, honey."

While they talk, I pick up my backpack, which has slid down onto the floor. Mum looks over at me. "Where are you going?" she asks.

"If he's stable for the moment, I'm going to go and see Princess Evelyn before she leaves for her tour tomorrow.

I'm going to tell her in person that I'm not going to be able to go with her."

"I think that's a good plan. Don't be back too late, okay?"

I nod. The soles of my shoes squeak on the sickly-green linoleum as I walk out of the hospital. I feel a soft breeze, the early evening air still warm. I pull out my phone and text Zain quickly: **Granddad much worse. I'm going to see Evie now—meet me there?x**

But even as I hit send, I have the sudden urge to see someone else—not Zain or the princess.

I want to see Anita, my best friend in the whole world.

Are you free? I text her.

Yes!! Where are you?

Meet in the Coffee Magic by Kingstown General Hospital?

You got it.

Five minutes later, I spot her cycling furiously toward the coffee shop, her long black hair streaming out behind her. I smile, despite everything, but by the time Anita reaches me, the smile has dissolved into a flood of tears. Before I know it, Anita's arms are wrapped around me and we stand together in the doorway of the coffee shop until someone coughs loudly behind us to try to get in.

Anita steers me inside and sits me down in a huge red leather armchair that engulfs me on either side. She orders me a hot chocolate with double whipped cream and when she returns with the drinks, everything spills out of me in a stream of words I can't control. "It's all been such a blur—he was fine when we left to collect the ark flower this morning, but then seeing him after his fall, and all those mixes . . . He never gets those wrong. *Never.* Now he's in the hospital. I don't understand what's happening."

Anita leans forward and grabs my hand. "Sam, I'm so sorry."

"And there's nothing we can do."

"What did the doctor say?"

"She thinks it's old age. There's no potion in the world that can help—or so she says."

Anita stares at me, her brown eyes searching my face. I cast my eyes down and take a sip of my hot chocolate. But the normal sugary goodness just turns sour in my mouth.

"You think the doctor is wrong though, don't you?" she says. It's not a question; she can read my face like a book.

I nod. "This is Granddad we're talking about. He's . . ." I want to say *invincible* but saying it out loud makes it sound so wrong. I know deep down that he's not invincible, that he is growing old and that one day he won't be in my life. But never in a million years did I believe it could happen so soon. And never in a million years did I believe that I would start to lose pieces of him like this.

It's too soon.

"He *is* old, Sam . . . ," says Anita, tentatively.

"You think I don't know that?" I snap back.

"I'm just saying—you know I lost my great aunt to Alzheimer's. There's just no cure."

"There's a cure for everything. It just hasn't been found yet."

"Maybe."

Anita doesn't deserve my curt tone. I know that she's only trying to help. But my gut churns—something doesn't feel right. *There's a cure for everything*, I think again. That has to be true. I know it in my alchemist bones. I can't believe that just as things were going right for my family, we've been struck down again.

"There's something else . . . ," I say. I'm hesitant to talk about it with her, as I know that she's only recently recovered from the ordeal of the Wilde Hunt. "I thought I smelled something rotten—metallic—at the place where my granddad fell."

Anita's face drains of color and her hand starts to tremble. She quickly puts down her coffee cup to try to disguise it, but I notice. "You can't mean . . ."

I shake my head rapidly. Seeing her react so strongly

reminds me that I can't just throw my assumptions around without consequences. "It must have been my imagination. She's in prison. I guess I'm just looking for anything to explain what happened."

"Do you want to crash at my place? We could put on a movie and eat popcorn?" she asks, quickly changing the subject.

"No, sorry, I promised Zain I'd see him tonight—and I have to let Evelyn know I'm not going on her tour."

"Oh, right," she says quietly. She's not used to me having Princess Evelyn for a friend—and even less used to me having a boyfriend. I'm not used to it either. I've surprised myself by how much I like him. The night I spent on the mountain with Zain, I thought we were going to die. Surviving that brought us close together far quicker than I could have imagined, and now . . . I find myself thinking of him when I should be concentrating on something else. It's as if he's taken up permanent residence in my brain where my rational thought once lived. I used to roll my eyes at the lovesick characters in my favorite casts. But now I get it.

Still, as much as I fancy him, I know he's not my best friend. That role is Anita's. "You're still the first person I want to talk to whenever anything happens," I say.

"Make sure it stays that way!" She winks.

"Always," I say with a small grin. "Walk me up to the castle?"

But before we get out of our seats, a couple of men dressed in black suits and sunglasses walk into the coffee shop, stopping just inside the door. They look around the café, and when their eyes lock onto mine, they make a beeline for our table. I grab Anita's hand and immediately look around for something I can use to defend myself. All I have is my hot chocolate mug. I grip it tightly in my fist.

"Samantha Kemi?" asks one of the men.

I nod, hesitantly. All eyes in the coffee shop are on us. Whoever they are, they won't try anything here. Will they?

The man flips open an ID badge, which is embossed with the seal of the princess.

"We have orders from Princess Evelyn to escort you to the palace immediately. Come with us, please." He extends his hand out to me.

Anita stares at the men. "I guess it must be important," she says.

I nod, then take his hand.

With a flick of his other wrist, he opens a large screen and I gasp. It's a portable Summons. I thought it was just a rumor that they existed.

But there's nothing of a rumor about the way an arm bursts through the Summons, grabbing me—and pulling me directly into the palace.

CHAPTER TWELVE

THE PALACE IS THE MAIN RESIDENCE OF the royal family and its location is top secret. Even Zain doesn't know where it is, exactly. All I know is that it hovers somewhere above Kingstown and is totally invisible from the ground.

My hot chocolate swirls uneasily in my stomach—I think I'm about to be sick (a common side effect of transporting). After allowing me a couple of deep breaths in the large hall I transport into, the men guide me toward a separate living area—this one far less formal than the other rooms inside the palace. There's a large TV on the wall for playing casts, and the biggest, most comfortable sofas you could imagine. It's where me, Evelyn, and Zain hang out most. I smile when I see Zain, but when he looks up at me his face is pale. He looks almost . . . guilty.

"There you are, Sam!" Evelyn is up off the sofa in a flash, pulling me into a hug. "Thank you, gentlemen.

You're dismissed," she says to the two men behind me.

After they leave, several things happen at once. I hear a click in the door's lock behind me, the lights dim, and the air suddenly feels ten times thicker, like I've been plunged into a bowl full of honey.

"There. Now listen—I have something important to tell you," says Evelyn.

My eyes flick between her and Zain. "Have you just . . . ?"

"Sealed the room? Yes. We cannot be disturbed. What I'm about to say is extremely classified information."

I swallow hard and nod. "Okay. Is this to do with my granddad?"

"Yes." She takes up both my hands and her ice-blue eyes bore into mine. "Emilia Thoth has escaped from Zambi."

My legs turn to jelly, giving out from underneath me. Magic rushes past me, sliding one of the sofas into place to catch my fall. I slump into the soft cushions, but I barely feel their comfort. "What?! How is that possible?" My mind is simultaneously processing the news and blocking it out. It can't be true.

"I'm sorry, Sam . . . I didn't want to worry you," says Zain.

His words, combined with his guilty look, click into place. "Wait, you *knew?!* For how long?"

"Someone posted it on the Wilde Hunt Theories forums but I didn't want to worry you over some unproven rumor."

"So you just hid it from me." Anger is replacing the

shock in my veins. A small voice tells me the anger is misplaced, but I tell it to shut up. "That woman *hates* my family. You put us all in danger."

"If you're going to be mad at him, be mad at me too," says Evelyn. "He told me straightaway and I went to the NSS."

"The NSS?" I ask.

"Novaen Secret Service. They confirmed it. And they thought they were close to recapturing her—"

"But they haven't caught her. Or have they?" I interrupt. She can't look me in the eye. "No."

I let out a cry that is half-groan, half-scream. "So does this have something to do with Granddad after all? Why would she come after him again? There's no Wilde Hunt this time."

"That's true, but you know all too well that until I am married, I'm still a threat to this kingdom. Even the potion you and Zain are making me is not a permanent solution. Emilia still wants my throne. She knows I'm vulnerable."

"Okay . . ."

Now she stares me at me, her eyes locked with mine. "Sam, I'm going to come straight out with it. Did your granddad know how to make an aqua vitae?"

My mouth drops open and it takes me a moment to recover. Then my brain kicks into gear. "No! Of course not. No one does."

"What about your great-grandmother?"

I swallow hard. "I thought she might have. But Granddad told me it was a lie he made up to hide the fact that Cleo had just lost her touch." Granddad's words from this afternoon haunt me. *Find it.* Maybe the lie had been a lie to stop me searching for the cure?

Evelyn nods. "Well, whatever the truth is, Emilia thinks your great-grandmother's diary is worth searching for. It is the NSS's belief that Emilia needs an aqua vitae in order to reverse the horrible changes the dark potions have wrought on her body. They're going to visit your granddad today to confirm if she used a memory extraction potion on him."

Memory extraction—an extremely complicated combination of spell and potion that can be used to take memories from a person's mind. A variation of it was used on me, Zain, and all the Wilde Hunt participants so that we'd forget the illegal recipe for love potions. It was one of the conditions of entering the Wilde Hunt.

The thought makes me frown. "But I thought memory extraction was only used if you want someone to forget something—not if you want to find something out. There's no way to 'view' someone else's memories."

Evelyn shrugs. "No way that *we* know of."

"Holy dragons," I say.

I think back to the horrific black veins, visible beneath Emilia's translucent skin. The lengths she went to, in order to become Talented and an alchemist. The more terrible her magic, the more terrible her appearance. An aqua vitae could reverse all that . . . without reversing the effects of the potions. She would still be powerful. Powerful enough to overthrow the current king and queen?

Maybe.

I blink several times, willing my mind to work faster.

Find it. Find it before she does. Granddad's words ring in my memory. Is the diary what he meant? If Emilia believes in the aqua vitae so much that she'd risk attacking my granddad in broad daylight, maybe there's something to it after all. I think of all those people in the store, desperate for a miracle cure. I could be the one to mix it. I could save so many people. I could save my granddad.

I release a long breath and crack my knuckles. "I need to get to Cleo's diary before Emilia. But I'm going to need help."

"I'll be with you every step of the way," says Zain. I hesitate for a moment, then nod. He's forgiven. If I'd read about Emilia on the Wilde Hunt forums, I wouldn't have told my family either. So many unconfirmed rumors fly around those websites. I give him a small smile, and I see his shoulders relax.

"I will help you in any way I can too," says Evelyn, "but we *must* keep this a secret from everyone else, okay? There'll be mass hysteria if news about Emilia becomes public. The NSS don't know that I'm telling you."

"What? Why don't you tell them?"

"Because if it's true that Emilia got to your grand-dad, that means she's been able to slip through our best defenses. She got to Kingstown and *this close* to the palace. So somewhere in Nova, someone is helping her. I can't trust the NSS—but I can trust you. I want you to have the best chance possible. I need you to think about where to search first. Then when we go on the first leg of our tour tomorrow, I can arrange to transport you wherever you need to go."

The reminder about the tour hits me like a punch in the gut. "The tour! I was supposed to tell you that I can't come anymore, because of Granddad."

"That's crazy, you have to come. The tour will be the perfect cover. Can you get your parents to change their minds?"

"I'll try." I can already picture Mum's face when I tell her. She will not be happy.

"Just remember: not a word to them about why."

"Kirsty!" I blurt out. "I'm going to need Kirsty. She can be discreet . . . just look at the Wilde Hunt."

Evelyn hesitates for a moment, then nods. "A Finder will be good to have by your side. You can tell Kirsty."

"Okay, good." I relax, knowing that Kirsty will be there.

Then Zain asks a question that hasn't even crossed my mind. "But Evelyn, what about your potion?"

My stomach turns. We were supposed to be heading

on tour with Evelyn in order to mix *her* potion. Finding my great-grandmother's journal might be a matter of life and death for me. But the potion is equally as important for Evelyn. If I can't find a way for her to store her excess magic, then she will have to get married.

She'll be stuck within a marriage of convenience, not of love. My heart aches for how unfair it is for her.

My cheeks prickle red with guilt. Thankfully, the princess scoffs at Zain's question. "What about my potion? This is bigger than me. This is about stopping Emilia once and for all—and saving Sam's granddad."

"Thanks, Evelyn. And I won't forget about your potion, I promise." I turn to Zain. "What are you going to tell your dad? He *cannot* know about this."

Zain rolls his eyes. "My dad won't know anything's changed. He's not exactly father of the year, is he?"

"Great," says Evelyn. "It's settled then. I'm going to lift the seal on the room or else my family will start to get suspicious."

The air immediately becomes clearer and I take a deep breath. "I'd better be going. I still have so much to prepare . . ."

"I'll pick you up at noon tomorrow. We can go shopping and then I'll take you to the plane," says Evelyn.

"Do I still have to?" I say. I hate how whiny I sound but dress-shopping isn't my favorite activity even at the best of times.

"We have to keep things looking as normal as possible. We can't let Emilia know you're on her tail."

"Okay, sounds good." I force a smile.

Evelyn laughs. "Aw, c'mon, it'll be fun. I'll make sure of it."

"If you say so." This time I don't disguise my grimace. Shopping. I hate it.

"Oh, before I forget, I keep meaning to give this to you but things keep getting in the way . . ." She hands me a package wrapped in elegant silver paper and a bright red bow. "This is for Molly. Can you make sure she gets it?"

"Of course! She'll be thrilled. Thank you, Evie. See you tomorrow."

"See you," she replies.

"Text me later?" Zain asks.

"Definitely." I reply. He smiles and we kiss good-bye.

I grip the package tightly as I walk back to the hall with the ornate gilt-framed mirror that will serve as my transport back to the store. It's nice to have something beautiful to hold onto in the middle of all this. It's only just dawning on me that I'm about to go up against Emilia once more. And this time, I have to stay one step ahead of her.

She's come after my family, and I'm not going to let her get away with it.

CHAPTER THIRTEEN

WHEN I GET HOME, MUM IS LEANING ON the kitchen counter. She looks bone tired, as if it requires all her energy to remain upright.

She was never that tired before the Wilde Hunt. We might have been down on our luck—but we'd been getting by. We might have had only a tiny customer base—but at least they'd been loyal. And we might not have been the great Kemi alchemists of old—but at least we'd been safe.

"Hi, Sam." Mum looks up when she sees me and manages a smile.

"Hi, Mum," I say. My hands are shaking. I don't want to upset her further by telling her that the Royal Tour is back on for me. I shove my hands inside the pockets of my jeans. Mum doesn't seem to notice, but Molly— sitting at the kitchen table—eyes me suspiciously. I try to give my best *nothing-to-see-here* gaze.

"I'm glad you're here. Your dad's decided to stay over-night at the hospital . . ."

"Is everything okay?"

Mum nods. "There's been no change—and the doctors think Granddad's stable for now. But that's why . . . well, your dad and I have had a chat. We've agreed not to pull Molly from her summer camp. She needs her life to continue as normal. And you do as well. While the store is closed, there's nothing for you to do here, and you know what your Granddad says . . ."

Idle hands make muddled potions. Another of his old adages.

She continues: ". . . so we think you should stick with your plan of touring with Princess Evelyn. It will be a good learning experience for you. And if anything happens to Granddad, I'm sure the princess will help you get back here as fast as possible."

Even though Mum's just given me exactly what I wanted, I can't help but feel sad. "But what will you and Dad do about the store?"

She smiles, but it doesn't reach her eyes. "That's for your father and me to figure out. And we will. But you two need to concentrate on your futures. And don't you have a dress to find tomorrow, Sam? It's good that you have something to look forward to. I know I would've died for the opportunity to go to the Laville Ball." Now her smile widens and her face lights up.

The Laville Ball excites Mum and Molly far more than it does me. "Now, who's tired? I think it's early to bed for all of us . . ."

We head upstairs together. As I step into the bathroom to brush my teeth, Molly sidles up beside me. "Anything you want to tell me?" she asks as she squeezes bright green toothpaste onto her purple brush.

I shake my head and continue to brush vigorously. In the mirror, I can see her eyes narrow at me—as if somehow she'll see the truth better in my reflection. I lean over the bowl and spit out the toothpaste. "Oh, I forgot—I have something to give you." I run into my room and find the present from Evelyn. I dash back to the bathroom. "Here, this is for you."

Her eyes widen at the sight of the expensive-looking silver paper. "Is this from who I think it's from?"

"If you mean Evie, yes. Open it!"

We move into her bedroom and I close the door behind me. I grin from ear to ear as her face lights up with a huge smile. Inside is the finest pair of pure white gloves that I have ever seen. They almost seem to glow in the dim light, as if they were woven from starlight.

"These are for me?"

"They sure are."

As Molly turns over the gloves, a note flutters to the ground. I pick it up and begin reading:

Dearest Molly,

I'm sorry that it's taken so long for me to get these to
you, but I promise they are worth the wait. These gloves
are made from strands of unicorn tail that naturally shed
throughout their lifetime. Only one or two pairs of gloves
exist like these in the world. But you are one of the few in
the world with a proven affinity to unicorns, and I know
you will perform great magic with them one day.
I hope you accept these gloves as just a small token
of my gratitude for your role in saving me.
Yours ever after,
Princess Evelyn of Nova

The wrapping paper falls to the floor as Molly brings
the gloves out into the open. She slips her hands into
them as quickly as she can. She flexes her fingers.
"They're perfect!" she says.

I enclose both her newly gloved hands within mine.
"I'm so glad."

She smiles. "You know, you can't distract me that
easily. Even with the best present in the entire universe."

I nod. "You're right, I do know more about Granddad
than I can tell you. I can't tell anyone. But I do need
your help. I need you to look after him while I'm away.
Keep an eye on him. The gloves will help."

Frustration and understanding flicker through her
face. "But . . ."

"Molly, I promise . . . if I could tell you, I would."

Finally, she nods. "I can do that," she says, her voice soft.

"Thank you," I say.

"But as soon as you can, will you tell me first?"

"It's a deal. Now get some sleep," I say. "It's been a long day."

She pads over to her bed and lifts the covers. Just before getting in, she turns around to me. "Is Granddad going to be okay? I'm scared, Sam."

I run over and squeeze her tight. "Of course he is," I say. "I'll make sure of it."

"I know you will."

I sit on the edge of her bed until she's crawled under the covers and wait there until she's fast asleep. It doesn't take her long, and I envy that easy rest.

Back in my room, I sit at my laptop and, after opening a couple of tabs for Connect and OnlineCast to switch to in case Mum or Dad comes in, I search for aqua vitae recipes and legends.

I find one from Pays that involves a potion base of water from a magical waterfall, which you can only access if you are guided by lights from fairies known as will-o-the-wisps. Just acquiring the base is hard enough—no one knows where the waterfall is, or how to get the fairies to guide you. Next I read a Zhonguo legend that involves a phoenix living near a monastery, guarded by an ancient order of monks. Another Ruso legend says that in order to know the recipe for the water of life, you must first have been brought back from the dead.

It all seems to belong firmly in the land of myth. There must be a reason no one has discovered it before. Hating myself a little, I log in to www.WildeHuntTheories.com and search the forums. But there's nothing new there except a bunch of posts speculating about why we've closed.

I shut my laptop with a snap and my head falls down onto my desk. I groan.

I'm never going to get anywhere without an actual lead.

There's a soft knock on my door.

"Come in," I say.

Mum's head pokes around the edge of my door. "You all set for tomorrow?"

I nod. I've thrown my clothes into a suitcase. The top layer looks normal—a few nice sundresses (apparently jeans are not appropriate attire for a tour with the princess of Nova), freshly pressed blouses, and floaty skirts. But hidden underneath is a layer of Finder's clothing for every eventuality: dark gray combat trousers with lots of zips and pockets, vest tops, and thermal underwear—lots of layers in case we need to go somewhere cold. "Just need my ball gown now."

"Are you *sure* I can't come shopping with you?" Mum asks, coming into my room and perching on my bed.

I smile. "It'll be a surprise!"

"Even from your dear mother?"

"You know I would show you, but it's one of the princess's requests . . ."

"Okay, okay, I understand. I can't believe my little girl is going off to a Royal ball!" Her eyes fill with tears.

I jump forward and hug her. "No crying!"

She waves her hands in front of her eyes. "I know, but it's nice to have something good to cry about."

I shift awkwardly, the tips of my sneakers pointing toward each other. "He'll be okay."

"Sometimes I wish for a crystal ball," says Mum. "But there's no magic potion here—no centaur's eye to help us see the future."

"Centaur's eye?" Something in my memory jogs. During my great-grandmother's Wilde Hunt, it was the one ingredient that the Participants couldn't find. According to the history books, Zoro—Zain's grandfather—managed to create a synthetic eye, which helped him finish his potion and save the queen. There's even a model of a centaur's eye in the center of the ZA headquarters' lobby. Except that's just the public story. Zain told me the truth, when we were trapped on Mount Hallah. It had been my great-grandmother who had really created the synth.

Mum must see something in my expression, because

she reaches out and grabs my hand. "Are you okay?"

I laugh it off. "Oh, I got distracted by thinking about Zain . . ."

"Ah, young love," Mum says, clasping her hands beneath her chin.

My reply is a deep yawn. Mum pats my bedcovers. "Come on, now. I know you're sixteen but you still have to listen to your mother. Time for bed."

I don't argue. I crawl under the duvet.

"Have fun tomorrow," Mum says, tucking me in like I'm six years old again. "I mean it. Don't let what's happening to Granddad and the store stop you from living your life. We will figure it out."

"I know." *And I'll figure it out too*. I have a lead now.

CHAPTER FOURTEEN

THE HOSPITAL'S VISITING HOURS ONLY run for an hour in the morning but I'm there from the moment they begin to the moment I get kicked out. For the majority of the time, I'm not alone—so when the nurse tells us that our time is up, I linger behind.

"Granddad . . . if you can hear me, I'm going to do this for you. I'll find it before she does." I squeeze his hand tightly, and I swear I spot his eyelids flutter. "If you remember anything that might be helpful . . . tell me straight-away. But I'll do everything I can. I won't stop. I promise."

"Samantha, it's time to go. No special privileges." The nurse pops her head around the door, her eyebrows raised. I give his hand another squeeze and reluctantly get up. Even though I'm determined to find him a cure, I don't want to leave him. I wish I could tear myself in two, one part of me staying by his side and the other going off to find the diary.

My parents have gone to the bank for scary meetings

that they don't want me to worry about—even though their hushed conversations and deep frowns make me extremely nervous.

Outside the hospital, I call Zain.

He picks up almost immediately. "Hey! Everything okay?"

"Are you at work right now?"

"Uh . . . just arriving."

"Can I meet you?"

"Aren't you supposed to be meeting Evelyn?"

"Not for another few hours. Please? It's urgent."

"I can probably come to Coffee Magic in, like, two hours?"

"No, no, I'll come to you."

"What, to ZA?" The surprise in his voice doesn't surprise me. I've only been to the ZA headquarters once, back before Zain and I were dating. I've avoided it— there's enough speculation about a Kemi-Synth collaboration that I don't need to add fuel to the fire.

"Yeah, is that okay?"

"Of course! Just buzz me when you're here and I'll let you in."

Two buses and a train later, I arrive at ZA headquarters. Zain is already outside, ready to meet me. He's leaning casually, one foot up against one of the tall pillars that guards the entrance. He's more dressed up than I'm used to seeing him, in dark gray trousers and a light blue shirt that brings out the blue in his eyes. Only his hair is as wild as ever, black strands falling haphazardly across his face. How can anyone look so gorgeous doing absolutely nothing at all?

He smiles when he sees me, and chastely kisses me on the cheek. We are outside his place of work, after all—I guess a full-on make-out session wouldn't *quite* be appropriate. "What is it?" he asks. "Do you have a lead?"

"I do. But I need your help. Can we go inside?"

"Sure."

I follow him through the big main doors that open with a small *whoosh* as air-conditioned air rushes out to meet the summer heat. Goosebumps break out onto my arms as I walk in, although whether from the chilled air or from awe I'm not sure. The inside of the building is hollow, stretching up above me over eighty storeys high.

Zain stops by a set of sleek, modern black leather armchairs. But I walk past him to the center of the lobby. Seemingly suspended in midair on a white marble pillar is a large round orb. The color is impossible to describe, shifting from amber to bright gold to rusty bronze as I stare at it. Looking closer, murky clouds seem to bubble beneath the surface, swirling in the unseen currents. I'm not sure I've ever seen anything so mesmerizing. Only the touch of Zain's hand on my shoulder breaks the spell.

"I find that thing really creepy," he says.

"Your grandfather—he wanted to be an alchemist more than anything in the world, right?"

Zain stiffens. I probably should have started with some small talk, but when I'm on the trail of a new potion I can only cut straight to the point. "Right, but what does that have to do with anything?"

"Well, if he really wanted to be an alchemist then he must have kept a diary."

Zain nods. "He did. It's all been digitized and stored in the ZA archives."

Hmm, digitizing the family archives. That could be useful for us, I think. Then, *Focus, Sam!* "Don't you see? Your grandfather *knew* Cleo. Maybe there's a clue to her last known whereabouts in his journal."

Zain's eyes light up. "You could be right, you know. Come on, I can take you to the library now." He drags me away from the giant replica centaur's eye and toward the elevators.

"Will they miss you in the lab? I don't want to take you away from your last day of work before the Royal Tour. You could just show me where it is . . ."

"Nice try, Kemi. Don't think I'm leaving you with our family secrets either," he says with a wink. We step into the elevator and he presses a button close to the top: level 78.

The elevator has a window and the view over Kingstown is breathtaking. I gasp in awe, looking out over the industrial zone, where all the synth companies are based, toward the city proper, the twisted streets leading up to the castle, perched high on the hill like an eagle's nest.

No wonder Zol feels so powerful from his office at the very top of the building, inside a giant metal letter Z. From this high up, you could imagine you own the entire world.

The elevator doors behind me open straight into the library. I spin, but then I frown.

There's not a single book in sight.

Instead, an enormous painting stretches the entire length of the wall, the biggest piece of art I have ever seen.

"Wait, is that . . . ?"

Zain nods.

"And it's . . ."

"The original? Yup."

"Woah." I'm no art buff, but I recognize it straightaway. Da Luna's *Grimoires of a Gergon Alchemist*. Maybe the most famous painting featuring an alchemist in the world. We have a print of it hanging in our downstairs bathroom at home.

In Da Luna's work, huge bookcases stuffed to the brim with thick leatherbound tomes disappear into shadow at the edges of the painting so they look like they go on forever. Even the stools and the tables are made of books—it's a book-lover's dream. The only figure in the painting is hidden away in a corner—an old man, his dark skin lit by a single candle, hunched over an open book. Though the man is from the thirteenth century, I know that look of concentration all too well. An alchemist researching a recipe.

I scan the painting for something else I know is there. A mistake. In the alchemist's hand is an ingredient, which the book in front of him labels as *Feather of a South Unis Macaw*. But the shape of the feather is all wrong—it curves inward where it should be straight; the color is a murky green where it should be bright crimson.

Some critics derided Da Luna for his error.

But Da Luna was an ordinary painter. He used no magic to create his masterpiece, no glamour to smooth out the rough edges—the places where the paints didn't quite mix, where a few hairs of his paintbrush came loose and lodged themselves in the canvas. Magic would have made it perfect.

But people are not perfect—not even Talented ones, Da Luna had said. *Humanity exists in the flaws and imperfections. That is what I paint.*

What a legend.

A cough from Zain makes me tear my eyes from the artwork. He's sitting at one of the six laptops perched on a sleek marble-top counter that runs beneath the painting. "Everything in our library is digitized," he says, switching on the computer. When he spots the (totally unintentional) grimace on my face, he smiles. "Just wait. You'll love this." With a couple of clicks, he finds his grandfather's diary. One more click and a projection pops up on the counter in front of me—a perfect hologram of the original thing. Except that when I touch it, my hand passes straight through.

"Wow!" I exclaim.

Zain laughs. "Yup. Cool, huh? And you can even turn the pages like an actual book. Try it."

My fingers slide into the projection again, and I mime turning the page. It's weird because although I don't feel anything, the page obediently turns. "That's epic," I have to admit.

"And I can also do this." He types *Cleo Kemi* into the search bar.

After a few seconds, the computer says: *Zero results found.*

Zain frowns. "That's weird."

"Try searching for centaurs."

24 results found.

"Bingo!" I say.

The hologram flips forward to the first results page. Zoro Aster's entries are much shorter than my granddad's.

08:02 Arrived. No other Hunt Participants here yet, as far as I can tell. Cal Shackleton thinks we may have a chance with the centaurs yet.

"Cal Shackleton was my grandfather's Finder," Zain whispers in my ear. It might not be a real library, but there's still something about the room that makes you want to keep the noise down. I carry on reading.

10:14

"Wow, your granddad was precise, wasn't he?"

Cal put off by rumors that the centaurs are suffering from some kind of plague. Don't know if it's catching, or how it will affect the mix if we do manage to acquire an eye. Doubled his rate and he agreed to continue. Damn greedy Finders.

10:21 Was wrong. Another Participant was here. Just seen the tire tracks. Dragonfire and trollblood! Told Cal to step on it.

"Another team!" My eyebrows rise almost into my hairline. "That could mean Cleo, right?"

I don't wait for Zain's answer, just turn the page again.

"Oh dragons," I say, as the next entry appears in front of us.

Zain leans in closer. "I can't believe it."

"You mean you've never seen this before?"

He shakes his head. "No . . . I've never read his diaries."

That shocks me into silence. I've read *all* the Kemi diaries—except the majority of Granddad's, of course, but while he's still alive, his are a work in progress and therefore off-limits unless by his express permission. I couldn't resist reading them. If I had the opportunity, I'd read all the Aster diaries too.

"Why would I read them?" continues Zain. "He told us the real story on his deathbed. Whatever's in here isn't the truth."

I think back to Granddad's stories about Cleo, which I'd once taken completely as fact. But now I know better. "Memories aren't fact," I say softly, putting my hand over his. "We've all changed a story to give it more impact, or to protect our loved ones. It's not just your family, trust me. And his words can still help us."

Zain stares at me for a moment, then nods. I focus back on the entry. The moment Zoro Aster "discovered" his synth.

09:00 Mark this day. Today, the world has changed forever. Today, I have made history.

I eye-roll at Zain and he gives me a small smile. But in a way, Zoro Aster wasn't wrong. He *did* change the world from that moment. He just left out the fact that he didn't do it alone.

After meeting with the centaurs, I could never in good conscience use a natural eye. Their population decimated, their families torn apart by grief and disease, I could not be as ruthless as those other Participants, even for the sake of Queen Valeri II. I fired Cal on the spot when he suggested we continue on our Hunt. Those that did continue failed, and brought the wrath of the centaurs upon them.

But of course, I could not abandon my queen in her time of great need. For years I have been working on a way to simulate an ingredient's effect without the need to harvest it. A way to progress beyond our old, tired methods—that so often result in the harm, or even the destruction, of our most precious resources.

And now, history will show that I have done it. With my synthetic—but potent—centaur's eye, I have mixed the antiseizure potion the queen needs.

I travel to the palace from Lake Karst in Runustan, to deliver the mix—and to save the queen's life.

This is a new start for Zoro Aster. This is a new start for Nova.

Zain and I look up from the diary at the same time. "Wow," he says.

"And now we have our first location," I say, a smile creeping across my face. "We need to get to Runustan. Fast."

CHAPTER FIFTEEN

"I THOUGHT I SAW YOU SIGNED IN HERE, Zain. Aren't you supposed to be down in R & D?" Zol, Zain's dad, steps out of the lift, his tall figure—immaculate in a tailored blue suit—casting a long shadow into the library. He stops short when he sees me. I steel myself to get yelled at and thrown out of the building.

What I'm not prepared for is for him to break out into a wide smile. "Miss Kemi! How nice to see you here!"

I jump out of my chair. "I was just leaving."

"Nonsense! Come now. I've not had a chance to congratulate your family on the success of the Wilde Hunt—no hard feelings, of course. Now that we're not rivals on the hunt—only in business!—you're welcome here any time. I hope my boy has been treating you well . . ." Then, disturbingly, Zol winks at me. I have to stop myself from shuddering.

"Dad!" Zain looks as panicked as I feel, his eyes darting from his dad to me and back again.

I just feel mega-awkward. "Err . . ."

"What? Can't a father check up on his son? In fact, Miss Kemi . . ."

"*Samisfine,*" I say quickly.

"*Sam,* then, it's a good thing you're here. I heard the terrible news about your granddad . . ."

"*Dad!*" Zain says again, but this time as a warning. Zol ignores it.

". . . and I really think that ZA can help." Before I know it, he has one arm around my shoulder.

All I can think is: *What. Is. Happening.* I didn't realize Zol was so chatty.

"Zain didn't want me to tell you about it because I know your granddad has a no-synth rule on his medical charts—very old-fashioned in my opinion—but I'm *sure* you would want to know if there was synth medication out there that could help your granddad get better."

Zol's jumping from topic to topic leaves me bewildered—is this how CEOs run a business, by thinking about a million different things at once?—but eventually his words sink in. "You have a cure for my granddad?" I blink several times, not willing to let myself feel any hope.

To my immense relief, he removes his arm, then looks me dead in the eyes. "Why, yes, Sam. I think we might."

My heart flutters. Then reality hits. I shake my head. "No, he would never allow it."

"Ah! It appears my son knows you well after all. It's a shame, because although the synth is brand new it is *very* promising. Our tests have come back showing 98.9 percent effectiveness in reversing memory loss and returning the patient to active health. It passed the Novaen Synth Trials with flying colors. We're going to put it on the market within the month, we're so confident in it. But I'm sure you'll find another way."

I nod, but his words are registering. *98.9 percent effectiveness.* That's high for a synth. *Passed the trials.* Even if it wasn't a total cure, it might stabilize Granddad and give me more time to search. *But it's a synth*, my sensible Kemi voice tells me.

The other voice speaks up again. *So what?*

"Have you shown her yet?" Zol asks Zain.

Zain lets out a groan. "No, Dad, honestly—we don't have time. Sam doesn't want to see."

Now I'm curious. "Show me what?"

Zol's face lights up, and for a split second I see Zain in his father. It's kind of disturbing, because before this, I went out of my way to avoid Zol. I thought I *hated* him. But then again, the last time we met, we were competing in the hunt. Is he actually okay in normal life? "Come, Sam, you'll love this."

We crowd back into the elevator, and I'm sandwiched

awkwardly between Zain and his dad. Thankfully it's only a couple of floors.

The doors slide to reveal a large open-plan office, where hundreds of ZA staff sitting in cubicles are working away on their computers. "This is our main sales floor," says Zol, striding out in front of us. I fall in step behind him. Zain is behind me, but he's dragging his heels. He keeps trying to get my attention, but now I really want to see what Zol wants to show me.

Curious eyes flick up at me from behind the low cubicle walls. My skin crawls with the sensation of so many eyes on my back. Maybe this wasn't such a good idea after all. A small click makes me snap my head around. Did someone take a picture of me on their phone?

This is not good. Not good at all.

Thankfully, we leave the crowded office and head down a hallway. We pass a few unmarked doors until Zol comes to a stop. "Ta-da," he says. He points to the door. Etched into a little brass plaque is the name *Zain Aster*. Underneath it reads: *Head of Synth-Natural Potions Studies*.

Zol opens the door.

I look up at Zain and he shrugs, looking miserable. "Not my idea," he mumbles.

"Your own office? But that's so cool!" I say. Zain shrugs again.

The office itself is huge. There's a bank of computers on one side ("These are all connected to the library, so Zain won't have to leave the room to access our archives," says Zol.) and a bookcase with actual paper books on the other ("For those works that just haven't made it to the digital age," he says with a laugh.). In between, there are three desks. One of them has Zain's name on it.

"So who are the other two for?" I ask.

"Well, now this is the really good part. As you've already seen, one of the desks is reserved for Zain when he's finished his studies. He's the one who inspired this whole division—Synth-Natural Potions Studies." Zol claps his son on the back. "One of these desks is for Arthur Menoaz. You know him, don't you?"

I do. He's another well-known alchemist in Nova, although he's not based in Kingstown. He was a staunch anti-synth activist for a while, so I wonder what has happened for him to change his mind. Then again, he didn't win the Wilde Hunt, so he didn't have the influx of cash and fame that we had. I still remember the times before. They were tough.

"And the other is reserved for our new fellowship student. Don't think ZA as a company didn't learn from losing the Wilde Hunt! The loss was not great for our image, as our head of PR was quick to point out, but I knew how to turn it around. We're not a proud company—we're about innovation. If learning more from natural potions is the way to go, then so be it! Let's open a department dedicated to it. So ZA has sponsored a fellowship for any student wanting to break ground in this new area. We'll cover the full costs of the course and guarantee a full-time job at the end. It's been highly competitive already. Of course, it would be even better if someone like *you* were interested."

I almost laugh then. So *that's* why Zol brought me here. And under any other circumstances, maybe it would be tempting. But right now?

"Thank you for showing this to me, Mr. Aster, it is really fascinating." I hold out my hand.

He shakes it, a small frown flitting across his face. But it's gone almost as soon as it appears. "No problem at all, Sam. And like I said, you are always welcome. Oh, and Zelda will be furious with me if I don't ask you to dinner with us. She cooks a smashing roast."

"Uh . . . maybe after the Royal Tour?"

"It's done! We'll have to break out the baby pictures, won't we, son?"

As Zol laughs, Zain lowers his voice. "Can we please get out of here now?"

I nod. We back away toward the door.

"Oh, and Sam?"

Reluctantly, I stop. I look up at Zol, whose expression has changed from jolly to the deadly serious, tight-lipped frown I am *much* more familiar with. "Don't forget what I said about your granddad. We *can* cure him. Don't let your family pride get in the way."

CHAPTER SIXTEEN

www.WildeHuntTheories.com/forums/
THEKEMIFAMILY

[MOST RECENT POSTS]

ValleeGurl says: *BREAKING NEWS* OSTANES KEMI admitted to Kingstown General this afternoon at 4:46 p.m. Looking for a source inside the hospital to confirm diagnosis. Anyone? **ETA** Sam seen arriving at ZA headquarters. POSSIBLE SYNTH CURE FOR OSTANES???

OrdinaryRelicHunter says: Nurse inside Kingstown General says he's in for treatment of rapid onset memory loss. Does this seem to fit with what we know of OK? History with CK of alchemy skill disappearing overnight. Could be a chronic disease? As for SK curing OK with a synth . . . Any proof for that statement? More likely that SK is being offered the Zol Aster Synth-Natural Potions Studies Fellowship and has arrived for an interview.

ValleeGurl says: That scholarship theory is nonsense. I can confirm 100% that it went to Arthur Menoaz.

Vitaminas3 says: Sam can't be going on the Royal Tour now, right? She would never leave her granddad alone.

CHAPTER SEVENTEEN

THE DETOUR WITH ZOL MEANS ZAIN AND I only have a few minutes until I'm due to be picked up by the royals to meet Evelyn for shopping.

"Your dad is quite . . . something," I say as we head out through the ZA lobby doors to wait for the car.

"Yeah. He's been on my back so much lately, but I don't wanna talk about it now. Hey, what are you going to do about getting to Runustan?"

I make a mental note to talk to him about his dad later. Clearly there's something on his mind, but I've been so wrapped up in my granddad and the diary that I haven't noticed. Bad girlfriend. "Get in touch with Kirsty and see what she has to say. Actually . . ."

I dig in my bag for my phone, but by the time I find it, a car pulls up to the entrance. The window slides down. "Samantha Kemi?"

"That's me," I say. I lean to give Zain a kiss good-bye

on the cheek, but he pulls me into a full-on kiss, right in front of his office. I don't complain.

I slide into the backseat, my knees weak. Ordinarily I would be awed by the rich, dark leather seats and the tiny lights embedded into the ceiling, but I hardly notice any of it. I watch Zain through the darkened windows until he disappears inside the lobby and we turn the corner, out of sight.

I take a deep breath, then I text Kirsty: **What do you know about centaurs near a place called Lake Karst in Runustan?**

While I wait for her reply, I think about what *I* know about centaurs. Not a lot.

Centaurs—nomadic creatures that roam around the Great Steppe. They travel in small herds, and their population has been in rapid decline. Once one of the closer creatures to human civilizations, the centaurs became more and more isolated as humans modernized. Use of their body parts has been phased out of potions but their eyes are said to be key ingredients in potions to aid seizures (especially those with accompanying visions) or to help find things that are lost.

A few taps on my phone brings up a map of the Great Steppe. It's a vast swathe of grassland interspersed with mountain and desert that stretches from the eastern edge of Gergon, right the way through to the western border of Zhonguo. It would take years to search it all for a herd of centaurs. I hope they still live near this Lake Karst. The map shows a huge lake in the middle of the Steppe that's as good a place to start as any.

I finally lift my head and look out of the window. I hardly ever venture into this part of town. Here, huge mansions cost millions of crowns—even a parking space is worth more than the average Kingstown home. Although they are all beneath the castle, the buildings lean up toward it, as if they can gain even more riches by bowing to the royals. It's also home to Morray Street—or *Money* Street, as Anita and I nicknamed it. My family never comes here. Mum would rather sew her own skirt out of old curtains than drop a thousand crowns on a designer version.

The one time I did head down to Money Street was just after my fifteenth birthday. I'd seen a newscast detailing how Lieb & Jacobson were harvesting dragonskin from a distant part of Zhonguo to create their latest designer handbags. The skin made the bags shimmer and sparkle in the light, and was virtually indestructible—a bag built to last a hundred lifetimes. An heirloom piece. At real heirloom prices . . . among the Talenteds, it was a real statement of wealth to own one. There were even rumors that money or gold kept within a dragonskin bag would be impossible to steal. Potential robbers would be burned by the scales, the dragonskin sensing that they were not the rightful owner.

Still, as beautiful as the bags were, it was highly

unethical to use skin from an endangered species. I hap-
pily held a picket sign: DRAGONS BELONG IN THE
SKY, NOT ON YOUR ARM, and hundreds of people
chanted and campaigned until the Lieb & Jacobson store
had to stop selling the bags.

The names above the shop doors speak of luxury, class,
and *expense*. But the one we stop outside makes my heart
stop. It's the most luxurious shop of all. House of Perrod.

"Okay, Miss—here you go. The princess told me to let
you know she's already inside."

"Thank you!" I practically skip out of the car. Never
in a million years did I think I would own anything from
House of Perrod.

To my surprise, there's the flash of camera bulbs. I
instinctively lift my hands to my eyes to shield them.

"Sam, Sam, are you working on a potion for the
princess?" asks one of the photographers, still snapping
away.

"No comment," is all I manage, before running
through the doors.

Once I'm inside, I slow down and take it all in. The
shop is designed to emulate a grand palace ballroom. A
huge chandelier hangs from the ceiling, each lightbulb
surrounded by a delicate gold filigree casing that looks
like the wings of a butterfly. The floor itself is aged white
marble, inlaid with streaks of dark amber. As I walk over
them, tracing my toe along the lines, I realize they are

spelling out *Perrod* in sweeping, curved letters. In a far corner, two mannequins are glamoured to waltz together, the twirls and spins of the dance showing off the flow of the fabric. These dresses are *made* for being swept around a ballroom. I watch them, mesmerized by their beauty. One-two-three, one-two-three.

"Well, at least I won't have to teach you how to dance," Evelyn says with a laugh. I've been swaying in time to the dancers without realizing it. She crosses the sweeping foyer to see me, surrounded by assistants. I spot Renel—Evelyn's stern, beak-nosed advisor—in the far corner, and her bodyguards melting into the dark edges of the room.

I blush and stop moving. "Oops . . . yeah, we learned some ballroom dancing in gym class this year. Our teacher was a bit obsessed with that show *Dancing with the Talent*."

"They asked me to be on that this year. Well, they ask me *every* year. I wouldn't be surprised if they ask you, being a big celebrity now and all."

Now I really feel my face turn red. "Oh no, I don't think so."

"How's your granddad?"

I sigh. "No change. But," I lower my voice. "I think Zain and I have found a lead . . ."

Evelyn shakes her head, her eyes wide. I get the message: *not here.* "Well, great news! They've closed the store just for us—I can't *wait* for you to try on your ball dress!"

"Do I get to see yours too?"

Evelyn rolls her eyes at my ignorance, but it's playful rather than mean. "My dear, my outfit has been designed and ready for months. I have to make one last-minute adjustment since I believe it's in ivory—a color for a newlywed, not someone who isn't even engaged." Apart from a slight lift of her eyebrows, she doesn't betray any hint of emotion, even though it must pain her—both to know most of Nova thinks she's failing her duty, and that unless something drastic changes, she's *still* going to have to marry someone she doesn't love.

I put my hand on her arm. "I haven't forgotten, you know."

She gives me a small smile, but I spot a crack in her perfect foundation. Her eyes dart behind me, and I catch wistful longing in her gaze. I spin around but I'm too late: All I see is the trailing coat tails of a guard's uniform disappearing into the shadows.

Before I can think about it any more, she takes me by the arm and together we stroll across the foyer.

"Of course, the designer's not going to like it if I change the color," she continues, as if nothing has happened. "But what can you do?"

She walks through the place as if she owns it (she probably could, if she wanted to) and leads me into one of the back rooms where, hanging on a polished brass rail in front of me, are a selection of the most beautiful dresses I have ever seen in my life. My eye is drawn to a floor-length dress that's a waterfall of molten silver. I reach out and touch the fabric, expecting it to be heavy—but it's as light as air.

"I sent your measurements across to Jacques—the head designer—before we came."

As if on cue, Jacques steps into the room and performs a small half-bow for the princess. Then he turns to me. "I'm sorry, these were all we could find at the last minute. We are dressing many of the Novaen guests for the Laville Ball, and we cannot have any two people wearing the same style." He eyes me up and down critically, and suddenly I don't feel like a human being—more like a blank canvas he's about to turn into a masterpiece.

"She may be too tall even for some of these longer dresses." To my distress, he pushes the silver dress away, banishing it to the far end of the rail. "She is also so young, she needs something . . ."

"More fun," finishes Evelyn.

"Yes, exactly."

He dances his fingers along the rail and eventually stops at a shorter dress, made of the same silver waterfall-like fabric, but overlaid with beaded strands that swing and tumble like an old dress from the forties. It's stunning, and far younger and cooler than the long one. Right now I can tell that Jacques is a genius.

Evelyn clasps her hands together and squeals with delight. I don't often squeal, but I know what she's feeling. I don't think I've ever had something so beautiful to wear in my entire life. I think I'm squealing on the inside.

I take the dress from his hands, holding it by the curve of the hanger as if one wrong move might vanish it away.

"Try it on," he says.

The changing room is bigger than my bedroom and covered in gold-leaf wallpaper. As I slip off my shoes, my toes sink into the deep burgundy carpet. There's a huge full-length mirror hanging on the far wall, edged all around in a gold frame as wide as my hand. I turn away from the mirror before I start undressing, but just as I do I see a figure slip from behind the frame, and before I can cry out, a hand clamps down over my mouth.

CHAPTER EIGHTEEN

"SHH, DON'T CRY OUT, IT'S ONLY ME," whispers a familiar voice. My body relaxes, and when she feels the tension leave my shoulders, she lets me go. I spin around and give her a huge hug.

"Kirsty? What are you doing here?" I try to keep my voice down, but I'm excited to see her. She looks well. Winning the Wilde Hunt has done wonders for her reputation—and her bank balance.

"You wanted to talk to me, didn't you?"

I laugh. "I did, but I thought we could just arrange to meet like normal people . . . or maybe just pick up the phone. I didn't realize you were in the city!"

"What, me, miss the opportunity to sell fabulous trinkets to the biggest gathering of rich Talenteds of the season? You're kidding, right? Trust me, the market for jewel bugs at this time of year is sizzling hot. I've spent the past week deep in the Cortez jungle looking for the best specimens, and I'm going to sell every one. Sneaking into House of Perrod is just part of the plan . . . that way I get to preview people's dresses so I can show up with the perfect accessory." That's Kirsty, always one step ahead of everyone else. She looks over at the dress hanging up on the wall. "That is gorgeous! You're going to knock everybody dead. I might even have a bug for you." She winks.

Jewel bugs—flying insects with brightly colored carapaces, which can be ground down for dyes. They can also be trained to fly around their owners or even to carry the trains of long dresses as ornamentation.

I shudder. "No, thank you." I don't need a jewel bug flying around my dress. Luckily, it doesn't have a train.

"Sam? Do you need any help?" Evelyn's voice floats through the door.

"Er, just a second!" I shout out.

"Okay, so I got your message," says Kirsty. "Centaurs, eh? They're a pretty tricky species."

I lean in close, and lower my voice. "Do you know if I might be able to speak to one?"

Kirsty frowns. "Does it have to be Runustan? I have centaur contacts in some of the neighboring countries . . ."

"It *has* to be Runustan. Why, is that more difficult?"

"Well, according to my research, no one has been in contact with the Runu centaurs in the last fifty years. They lost huge numbers from a disease and after that, they kind of sealed themselves off from human contact."

"Oh," I say. That does not sound good.

"Not to worry though. I have an old friend who's working in a village in Runustan."

I smile. "Of course you do . . ."

"Who says she can help. It's not a guarantee but it's as good a place as any to start. How soon?"

"I want to go tonight."

Kirsty raises her eyebrows. "That soon? It'll be expensive. This must be some potion . . . and don't you have the Royal Tour to go on?"

"I don't have time to explain right now—but I will."

She bites her bottom lip and looks off to one side. "Well, I was supposed to be running my market stall tomorrow and I had some appointments lined up . . ."

I grab her by her upper arms. "Kirsty, I promise you. I will make it worth your while."

She nods. "Okay, Sam, just for you. If you can make the flights happen tonight, I'll be there." She gives me a quick smile, then slips back behind the mirror. I'm left on my own.

I wriggle out of my clothing and put on the dress. There's an impatient knocking on the door. "Sam?" Evelyn says.

"Coming! Can you help me with the zipper?" I open the door to the changing room and let her finish doing up the clasp. As the dress falls into place around my body, I can see how pretty it looks reflected back at me. Evelyn looks over my shoulder and into the mirror. She studiously avoids her own gaze, as always. "You look amazing!" she says. "Come on out so we can see you properly."

I step out into the back room, where Jacques has set up a little pedestal for me to stand on.

"Zain's not going to know what hit him," says Evelyn.

"You don't think it's too short for a ball?" I say, praying it's not. Normally I hate dresses that show off my knobbly knees, but as I twist on the pedestal, the dress flares out around me. Even for the least girly girl on the planet, the sight of such lovely material on *me* gives me a little thrill. The hanging strands feel smooth as silk between my fingers, and they're crafted in such a unique way that they don't get tangled up as I move.

"Are you kidding? Maybe it would be too short if you were fifty, but you're sixteen. It's perfect. Jacques, can you have it sent up to the palace?" He nods. "Great. C'mon Sam, let's get moving."

I stick my tongue out at her, but I do as she says. Evelyn can be so bossy sometimes. Must be a product of not only being an only child, but being an only *princess* child.

"I'm going, I'm going!" I slip back into the changing room and out of the dress, terrified of damaging it. Putting my old jeans back on just feels wrong now. I suddenly get a glimpse of why people fall head over heels for designer clothes.

Before I leave the changing room, I sneak a look behind the mirror, pulling it slightly off its angle so I can see where Kirsty disappeared to. But to my surprise, there's just the regular wallpaper that's everywhere else in the room. I run my hand along the edges, searching for a seam, but I can't find one.

Weird.

When I emerge, Evelyn pulls my hand toward the large three-way mirror. "We're just going to transport back to the palace, okay? If you hold my hand, it will make it ten times easier."

I grab her hand, and allow her to pull me through. Transporting is something I thought I would never get used to. The idea is that two streams of magic are connected by mirrors, and Talented transport technicians help to pull you through if you are either an ordinary, or a Talented who has never visited the place before. But transporting with Evelyn is another matter entirely. Her magic is so strong, we make the journey in an instant.

As soon as we land and Evelyn and I are safe from listening ears, I turn to her. "Evie, I need your help. You need to get me to Runustan, tonight."

CHAPTER NINETEEN

THE NEXT FEW HOURS ARE A WHIRLWIND of activity as Evelyn makes the necessary preparations. When she wants to be, Evelyn can be as fierce as a hurricane, and I'm grateful that I'm standing with her in the eye of it because otherwise I'd be blown away. By the end of it, she's rearranged her Royal Tour so that we start in Samar, the capital city of Runustan, citing a desire for a cultural exchange and to see a part of the world she has yet to visit. It throws her staff into a huge commotion—not to mention what must be going on at the other end, in Runustan itself, but everyone is making it work for the princess. Of course they are. She's probably the most famous face in the world.

Zain and I travel together to the airport, while Evelyn travels in her own separate car—but instead of the normal Kingstown International Airport terminal it's a private aircraft hangar on the outskirts of the city.

Even though Evelyn has the ability to transport herself instantly around the world, she always travels by air to her public engagements. The grandeur of arriving by private jet, the photo ops as she descends the steps, the hordes of screaming fans—it's all part of the spectacle.

I grip Zain's hand tightly as we walk up to the plane. In his expensive blazer, crisp white shirt, and tailored trousers, he looks like he belongs—my scruffy rogue cleaned up for the Royal Tour. I've put on my nicest cotton sun dress, but only because I know I can change into something more comfortable on the plane.

The Royal family's private jet is as big as a regular commercial airliner, but decorated with the same plush fabrics and luxurious materials as their palace. Zain (who has traveled with Evelyn before, the lucky thing) gives me the guided tour. It's nothing like a normal plane, and I'm shocked by how much space there is inside. At the back of the plane there are four decent-sized bedrooms, each with a super-comfortable double bed. There are even proper stand-up showers in their ensuite bathrooms. There's a chef's kitchen (no salty, soggy plane food here) and a fully stocked bar with a dining table and sofas. At the very front of the plane, there is a section for the media, where a group of journalists relax in comfortable, fully-reclinable chairs. I'm not sure how I'm going to go back to cattle class after this.

We head back to the middle of the plane, where Renel

is sitting at the polished wood table, going over the guest list for the ball with Evelyn. There are so many different names and faces and factions that I have no idea how Evelyn is going to keep it all in her head.

"I still don't understand why we have to make this . . . *detour* to Runustan, Princess," he says.

She stares at her fingernails, examining them for chips in her nail polish. "I told you—because I want to. Renel, if I *have* to find a husband somewhere, I'm going to do it on *my* terms. That's what my parents said, isn't it? Wherever I want to go, whatever I want to do. I'll keep my end of the bargain, so they must keep theirs."

I hear a tiny click from behind me, and I spin around to see a journalist emerging from one of the bathrooms. He'd also been lingering to listen to the princess's conversation. I can tell by the grin on his face that he's got a good scoop. I can see the headline now: *WHY? BECAUSE I WANT TO: PROFILE OF A SPOILED PRINCESS.*

That's the problem with the media. As much as they love Evelyn, they also love to tear her down. I shoot him my most evil glare and he shrugs, then disappears back into the media section of the plane. I bet he works for the *Nova Mail.*

"Come with me," Zain says. I take his hand and he leads me into one of the bedrooms in the back.

Zain checks down the narrow hallways before shutting the door. He stares at me for a second, and my face turns bright red. I'm still not used to having boys—especially one as hot as Zain—look at me that way.

Like I'm something *extra*ordinary.

He tilts my chin up so I can't avoid his gaze. His fingers linger on my jawline. All at once, I can't take it anymore. I throw my arms around his neck and press my lips against his.

Any shyness I feel disappears as we kiss. Instead I could melt right through the plane floor and float all the way to the ground. We tumble onto the bed, our legs intertwining. Zain's kisses take on an even deeper urgency, his hands caressing the space between my shoulder blades, making my skin come alive with delicious shivers.

A sharp rap on the door makes us both jump. "Tea, coffee, orange juice?" asks the perky voice of the flight attendant. We break away in a fit of giggles.

I roll over on the bed and open the door. "No, thanks," I say. "We're good."

The flight attendant gives me a smile but deliberately pushes the door wide until it locks into an open position. Zain gives me a wink that almost makes me descend into giggles again. The flight attendant turns on her heel and leaves.

"I suppose we should do some research anyway," I say when we're sure she's gone.

Zain sighs dramatically. It makes me smile to see that he looks flushed too. "I *suppose* so." He pulls his tablet out of his bag and his expression turns more serious. "The little digging I did last night doesn't make the situation look good. It's not just that the centaurs cut off contact with humans. They actually hate them."

I grimace. "That's not good at all."

"But on the other hand, centaurs have much longer lifespans than humans, so in all likelihood at least one of them will have known your great-grandmother."

"Fingers crossed. How about you keep reading about them and I'll focus on my granddad's diaries? Teamwork."

"Deal," he says.

I sit back down on the bed and put my backpack at my feet, pulling out the diary. I've covered it with plastic and wrapping paper so that it looks like one of my school reading books. I didn't want anyone accidentally flipping through it, so I try to make it look as irrelevant and unnoticeable as possible.

I flip to a new section, further along.

Mother returned yesterday. I fear she may never be the same again. She has lost her diary—and without it, she is not the same. I have tried to get her to copy down sections of it from memory, while it is still fresh. But she is refusing. It's like she's given up. I have never known her to give up.

I turn the page.

Today I plucked up the courage to ask her if we should go looking for it. The diary, I mean. No one has won the Wilde Hunt yet—maybe there is still time for us. We could retrace her steps. She is adamant that it was not stolen but is genuinely lost.
If that is the case, then it can be found.
Maybe if we start in ▆▆▆▆▆▆▆▆▆▆

I groan. I suddenly have a flashback to the start of my own Wilde Hunt, when I searched through the old recipe books for a hint of how to make the perfect love potion. There had been a global ban on love potions, resulting in the magical censorship of any and all printed recipes. All that was left were thick swathes of black obscuring any relevant words, or pages where the letters huddled together, jumbling into a mass that was virtually unreadable.

This is not *quite* the same as that. This was done by a deliberate hand. Granddad has taken a black marker to the page and crossed out the locations.

It's frustrating, but the sight of it speeds up my heartbeat. It means that Granddad knew someone might come looking through his journals. It means that he's worried something might be found.

It means he doesn't believe it's been destroyed.

Obviously, neither does Emilia. For the first time, I sit back and think about what confronting Emilia again might mean. She's utterly ruthless, I know that much. She thirsts for power. She's managed an incredible feat—a Talented becoming an alchemist, who knew?— but only by creating terrible dark potions that have wreaked havoc on her body. She's desperate. Evelyn is on her Royal Tour to find a husband. If she does, it will make it much harder for Emilia to destabilize the throne.

But if she got her hands on an aqua vitae?

She'd be strong.

Rich.

Powerful.

And practically immortal.

The Novaen throne would be under threat from her, whether Evelyn married or not.

I have to stop her.

A knock on the door jolts me awake, and I sit up bolt upright from where I'd slumped down on the bed. I see that Zain has fallen asleep too, his head in my lap, a tiny dribble of drool pooling on the open page of my granddad's diary. Oh dragons, he's never going to forgive me for that. I quickly wipe my own mouth, then shake the cobwebs from my mind. "Hello?" I say.

The sound of my voice causes Zain to stir and he sits up just as Evelyn sticks her head around the open door. She laughs and rolls her eyes. "Wow, you two are so romantic. Asleep over books? I don't think I've met two nerdier people, better matched." She winks. "Anyway, we're about to land so you need to move to a seat you can strap in to. We'll get the media and staff off the plane first, then I'll leave, then you can go last and meet Kirsty. That way you'll miss the paparazzi. I'll only be here for a couple of nights and then we'll be flying to Pays for the Laville Ball. You need to be back for that in order for this cover to work. Good luck."

I grip Zain's hand tightly.

Suddenly it all seems real. I'm on another Hunt.

I really hope I'm on a winning streak.

CHAPTER TWENTY

AS WE WALK THROUGH THE TERMINAL in Samar, we can see evidence of Evelyn's presence— the starry-eyed look of fans that have just come within breathing distance of their idol, the journalists frantically writing notes, the airport staff dismantling the temporary barriers. We manage to pass through unnoticed, inconspicuous now that we've changed into our grungy Finding gear, and head down toward arrivals, where Kirsty is waiting at the bottom of the escalator. She pulls me into a big hug. "How was your flight? Not too grueling, I hope?"

I shake my head and smile. "Hardly! We were traveling in style, remember?"

"Oh yeah, I forgot that you don't have to slum it like the rest of us!" Kirsty twists her back in an exaggerated stretch and grimaces. Then she looks over my shoulder at Zain and her nose wrinkles. "Ah, I didn't realize we were going to have company."

I feel bad for not texting Kirsty about Zain—but everything's been happening way too quickly. Kirsty wears her emotions bare on her face, and it's clear she disapproves of this arrangement. She is the kind of ordinary that resents Talenteds like Zain intruding on "our" territory.

"Two alchemists are better than one," I say.

"One alchemist and one weird synth, you mean," she shoots back.

Zain puts on his most charming smile. "Nice to see you again too, Kirsty."

"I suppose an extra pair of hands never hurts. Just make sure you spend more time watching and learning than distracting my Sam, okay?"

"Don't worry," I say. "I'm in the zone."

Kirsty claps her hands together. "Right, might as well get a move on then. We've got quite the drive ahead of us."

"Is this the last time we'll have signal?" I ask. "I need to call my parents to find out how Granddad is." We were on the plane for over twelve hours, and I can't stop thinking about what could have happened by now.

"Yeah, I think so. Be my guest. We need to load up on a few more supplies, anyway." Kirsty nods to Zain, and they head toward a nearby snack kiosk.

I retreat to a quieter part of the airport to call my folks. The guilt of leaving Granddad is already hanging round my neck like a chain. I wish I could tell my parents why I'm really here; I'm not used to lying *quite* this much.

Mum picks up within a few rings. "Hello?" she says, a cautious edge to her voice. We've all grown weary of strange numbers, in case it's a journalist on the other end of the line.

"Hi Mum, it's me," I say.

"Oh, Sam!" Her voice brightens. "Great to hear from you. How was the trip on the private plane?"

"It was amazing! So fancy. How are things over there? How's Granddad?"

I can almost hear Mum's frown down the phone. "The doctors are concerned and—well—your dad didn't want me to tell you but we found out that some specialist doctors had come to visit him as well. Your father wasn't very happy about that because they didn't ask for our consent, but the specialists only confirmed what our doctors have been saying, which is that it's most likely complications due to memory loss. We wanted to take him home, but they won't let us. They want to do more tests . . ."

Specialised doctors? Those must be the secret service agents that Evelyn mentioned to me. I think back to Zol's offer. Even though I know there's more to Granddad's illness than meets the eye, I wonder if the synth medicine would help. I'm just on the verge of telling Mum when she changes the subject.

"Anyway, make sure you take a lot of photos of Runustan to show us. You're so lucky to be able to travel to all these places. Oh, before you go, here's your sister. Be safe, sweetie. And call us often. I know you're with the princess, but you know we always worry about you."

"I know, Mum."

"Sam?" Molly's voice comes on the line.

"Hi, Mols, how's it going?"

"Not so good." I hear a shuffling down the line, followed by the click of a lock. "I haven't told Mum and Dad yet, but the gloves Evelyn got me are *amazing*. I just touched Granddad's hand while I was wearing them and . . ." Her voice drops to a whisper I have to strain to hear. "I think I know why he's so sick."

My heartbeat speeds up, and I struggle to keep my voice calm. "What do you mean?" I didn't realize my sister's magic was so advanced that she could use the gloves to diagnose illnesses. She thinks it's the gloves, but I know better. A powerful object can't amplify a weak Talent. It's all Molly.

"Well, it's not what the doctors are saying. Memory loss sort of describes it, but it's more like something's missing from his mind."

Everything inside me screams to tell her, but I can't. Not yet.

"It's like a piece has been taken from him. Do you know anything about it?"

I shake my head, but I'm on a phone. "No," I choke out.

"Whatever it is, he's getting worse, fast," Molly says,

her voice curt. "If you were here, you'd probably see what I mean. But you're not. Have fun on your posh tour." She hangs up.

The guilt isn't a chain now, it's a cage—and I can't escape it. I stare at the phone in my hand for a few moments, until Kirsty calls my name.

The only thing I can do to ease the guilt is to do my best to help Granddad from here. I run and catch up with Kirsty and Zain. "Did you have any luck with narrowing down the centaur position?"

She sighs dramatically. "Oh, you know. Maybe down to the nearest few thousand acres." She cackles as my face drops. "Trust me, in an area as big as the Runustan Wilds, a thousand acres is good progress." She strides through the terminal toward the car.

"We should be able to isolate their position once we're in the Wilds, right?" asks Zain.

"Well, they're not tracked in the same way as some of the other creatures. But once we reach my contact who lives on the edge of the Steppe, then we'll be on the right track."

"Wait," says Zain, before we get in the car. "Since this is Emilia we're dealing with, I want to check there aren't any bugs—mechanical or magical—on the car. You can never be too careful."

Kirsty rolls her eyes. "There aren't any," she says, getting in the car anyway.

Zain removes his wand and whispers a few words too quiet for me to hear. An eerie blue light rushes from the wand, surrounding the car. After a few seconds, as the light doesn't change color, he puts it away. "Good to go," he says.

"No kidding," replies Kirsty. She's already strapped in the driver's seat and consulting a large map. "There are ordinary ways of checking for bugs, too—not that you Talenteds take any notice. I did a sweep before you arrived."

"An hour before you picked us up."

"Guys," I put my hands up. "Please, let's try and get along, okay?"

Kirsty takes a deep breath. "You're right. We've got a long drive ahead—Zain, do you know how to sit still for a few hours? I know Talenteds often get bored without magic to entertain them." She blinks innocently but her tone is laced with sarcasm. Awkward.

"On the plane, Zain was telling me something about centaur gatherings?" I chip in.

To my relief, Kirsty puts her professional hat back on as she starts up the car. I climb in next to her and Zain camps out in the back. "Yes—and we're in luck tonight as we should be able to find a gathering. Sam, do you know why?"

Apparently I should. "No?"

"What time is it?" she asks, as a prompt.

I look down at my watch, and something on it catches my eye. There's an alignment that I haven't seen before, something that must have happened during the timezone change. "Woah, I thought I had to wind my watch."

"You do, everywhere except for here. I know they teach us in Nova that we are the center of time, space, and the universe, but you should know better than that by now. Runustan is where time began. The peculiar magic of this country affects all our timepieces. Your watch will never be more accurate than it is right now."

"Wow," I say, staring at my watch as if it's a foreign object.

"The Runu people have always preferred to live in the Wilds as much as possible, even the Talented ones. So their magic is much wilder too—their objects look basic to our modern eye, but they're powerful. Their people once ruled over a huge stretch of the continent, but once the Talenteds began pooling their magic into cities, the Runu way of life diminished. You'll see the divide between city people and Wilds people."

I look out of the window at Samar, and it looks like many other cities I've been to: big, wide streets, imposing high-rises, statues of important people. I cry out as we pass by a statue that looks like a centaur—but then I realize it's just a man riding bareback on an enormous horse which is breathing fire from its nostrils. Wreaths of bright yellow, orange, and red carnations have been wrapped around the iron flames.

Zain looks up. "Tonight's the festival of the Fire Horse. That's what you meant by a gathering."

"Exactly," says Kirsty. "So you have been doing your research after all. It's good for us because the centaurs should be easier to find. But it also might make things more . . . interesting."

I don't like it when Kirsty says "interesting." That normally means "dangerous."

"So did you bring an offering, Kirsty, or do we need to stop along the way?" Zain asks. I catch his eye in the rearview mirror and he raises his eyebrows.

"What do you think I am, some kind of amateur?" She jerks her head toward the back of the car.

Zain cranes his neck to look in the back. "Oh wow," he says.

"What is it?" I ask.

"Two huge barrels . . . and maybe what looks like a box of fireworks?"

"Um, are we bringing the centaurs beer?" I look over at Kirsty.

"Of course not!" says Kirsty. "Whiskey."

"Oh," I say, as Zain nods his head in approval. "And the fireworks?"

"Now, those are just in case we need to make an entrance."

CHAPTER TWENTY-ONE

THE MAIN HIGHWAY OUT FROM THE CITY leads straight into the Wilds—the last refuges of natural magic, and home to most of the creatures and plants that form the basis of our potions. Without the Wilds, alchemists wouldn't have any ingredients to work with—and the shrink of natural land to make way for cities has partly led to the rise in the popularity of synths. ZA argues that synths save the Wild land, but I think they give the world cause to undervalue it.

Thanks to the princess's connections, both Zain and I were issued new Wilds passes, so we breeze through the security checkpoints.

"Here goes nothing," says Kirsty. "On to the Runustan centaurs."

"What if we fail with this herd?" I sit on my hands to stop biting my nails. I'm so nervous.

Kirsty shrugs. "Then it's about two thousand miles to the next closest sighting."

"Oh right, so no pressure then."

"None at all." She grins. "We'll manage."

Zain leans round my headrest to talk to Kirsty. "Have you ever met one?"

"What, a centaur? Nope. Not much demand for centaur-related ingredients and besides, they have very long memories. No centaur has really forgiven humans since the Wilde Hunt fifty-odd years ago called for a centaur eye."

"Did a Participant actually kill one of them, then?" I ask, horror in my voice. Murdering a creature for its parts is not in a Finder's—or an alchemist's—remit.

Kirsty nods, her forehead lined in a frown. "Yeah, we think so. No one's owned up to it, of course. The international Finding community launched an investigation, in cooperation with several governments—including Nova's—but there wasn't much that could be done. As you well know, the Wilde Hunt is governed by its own laws. Even what Emilia was doing to you in the hunt was not technically illegal. And anyway, fifty years ago the final cure . . ."

"Was made by synthetic ingredients," I finish, the pieces of the story connecting in my head.

"Exactly. So that poor centaur's sacrifice was *completely* in vain. They really hated us after that. It destroyed the reputation of alchemists *and* Finders in one swift kick," says Kirsty.

"So what makes you think the centaurs are going to talk to us now?"

Kirsty shrugs. "I don't think they will. We're looking for a particular centaur called Cato. As far as I can tell, he's the only centaur who was around when your great-grandmother might have visited the herd. But he's also the herd leader. I bet we'll be booted out of there before we can open our mouths."

Great. I slump back in my seat.

"We've come this far, so we're going to try," says Zain. I could kiss him for his optimism but instead, I settle with a smile.

It was a long time ago, but—as Kirsty said—centaurs have long memories. I just have to cling onto a tiny thread of hope. Because if this fails, I have no other leads. Back to square one.

A few hours into our drive, something beeps on the dashboard and Kirsty's head whips toward it. She flips open the center of the dash to reveal an old-fashioned radar, like the ones I've seen when Dad drags me out to look at old war submarines. There's a blip on the very outer edge, and then it disappears. The atmosphere in the car is tense—but the machine doesn't beep again.

"What's that for?" I ask.

"Look at the sky—can you see anything?"

I stare out of the window. The sky is piercing blue, without a cloud in sight, and the grass beneath it stretches for miles. It looks like a child's painting of the world: green grass and blue sky meeting in a straight line at the horizon. It's desolate and vast—whatever is on that radar screen, I can't imagine it just creeping up on us.

"It's a dragon-o-meter," Kirsty says.

Dragon's tooth—used in potions to settle disagreements. Also for boosting confidence (in correct dose).

My jaw drops, and I plaster my face against the window again. "Dragons? Like actual-real-life dragons?!"

"Yeah. They're rare but you can't take too many precautions out here."

"You're kidding me!"

"'Fraid not. But that bleep is still miles away. If it doesn't come back, we'll be all right."

I try to ease the tension in my shoulders by tilting my head from side to side. I thought I'd be used to all this adventure after the Wilde Hunt, but it still doesn't sit easily with me. It was only blind luck that saved me before. Luck . . . and a bit of knowledge. This time, I plan to be armed with as much knowledge as possible.

"How long until we arrive?" I ask Kirsty.

"Oh, we'll be driving for several hours yet."

Plenty of time, then. I reach into my backpack and pull out a giant tome with a thick red leather binding.

The corners of the pages are all tattered and, in spindly gold writing, the cover reads: *CREATURES OF THE GREAT STEPPE*. I found it in the palace library— perfect for my research.

I open the book on my lap, debating for a moment whether to turn to the centaur page—or the dragon page.

"Brought your library with you again, have you?" laughs Kirsty. "You should buy one of those fancy e-readers with your prize money."

I stare down at the heavy book. Kirsty might have a point.

I skip past the centaur page and instead, I read all I can about dragons.

Just in case.

CHAPTER TWENTY-TWO

www.WildeHuntTheories.com/forums/
PRINCESSEVELYN

Welcome to the Wilde Hunt Theories forums—
home of all Wilde Hunt discussion on the World
Wide Web. Rules are simple: no anonymous posting, no revealing any personal information, and no
unverified links. Mods' decisions are final. Thank
you—the WHT Mods.

   **Due to an overwhelming number of
requests, we've decided to open a subforum
devoted exclusively to PRINCESS EVELYN
OF NOVA. Please remember to respect our

rules and keep all discussions relevant. Happy Hunting!**

104,783 readers; 910 here now
14,013 posts; 1803 new since last visit

[STICKY POST] **NovaBlast says: WHO WILL PRINCESS EVELYN MARRY?** Welcome to the mega-thread devoted to the most likely candidates for Princess Evelyn's betrothed. If you are new to the thread, please use the search for your theory first so you don't end up repeating something that's been said a hundred times before. Will try to keep a running tally of the most popular options.

DAMIEN 7/2 *CURRENT FAVORITE*—Age: 24, Occupation: pop star. Been papped at the palace several times after the Wilde Hunt and he's due to perform at the Laville Ball. *ETA* His newest single is called "Crown Calling."

PRINCE STEFAN OF GERGON 7/1—Age: 22, Occupation: second in line to Gergon Throne. Frontrunner before the Wilde Hunt but has dropped off the radar since then. The sensible political choice. If spotted on Royal Tour, his odds may increase.

MYSTERY CRUSH 7/1—Age: ??, Occupation: ?? *DETAILS WANTED BUT BE PREPARED TO VERIFY SOURCE* Why all the secrecy? If he was a valid option, we would expect to see an announcement by now. One to keep an eye on.

ZAIN ASTER 20/1—Age: 18, Occupation: student. No longer single but still a likely choice if it comes down to the wire. Old friend of the princess.

1304 replies

CHAPTER TWENTY-THREE

AFTER HOURS OF DRIVING, THE BEAUTIFUL scenery in Runustan becomes monotonous, grass stretching as far as the eye can see, blue sky above us, like a catchy tune played over and over again until I beg it to stop. I close my eyes and try to sleep for the rest of the journey.

When Kirsty wakes me, I can tell we've arrived somewhere special. For one thing, there's a huge lake spread before us, glittering in the high noon sun. It's like an oasis, but instead of being in the middle of the desert, it's in the middle of the grasslands.

On the shore of the lake is also the first sign of human civilization we've seen—a circle of round tents, which Kirsty tells me are called *gers*—mixed with a few regular-looking brick buildings. "This is Lake Karst," Kirsty says. "And the village on its shores is called Karst too. It's quite a popular spot for locals on their holidays but off the tourist track. We'll stop here to meet my contact and to pick up gas and supplies on our way to the centaur herd. Who knows, if we're lucky they might be close by."

We'd demolished all our snacks on the journey, and as the smell of roasting meat drifts over to the car, my tummy rumbles. "I'm glad we're stopping—I'm so hungry, I could eat a horse!"

Kirsty laughs. "Well, you might be in luck—horse is a traditional meat around here." When I grimace, she tuts. "Hey, no one turns their nose up at you for drinking that synthetic sugar crap they put in your speciality coffee at Coffee Magic—at least this is all natural."

"I know, I'm sorry," I say. If I have to eat some horse to be polite, I will. Or just say I'm vegetarian.

Kirsty jumps out of the car first, and she's greeted by a young woman who has emerged from one of the tents. She's wearing a long cream linen dress, tied at the waist with a thick piece of black leather. A pop of color is provided by the intricately patterned scarf over her hair.

"Nadya!" Kirsty embraces the woman in a warm hug.

Zain and I share a look. "Does she know everyone, everywhere?" he asks me as we stand by the car waiting to be introduced. He lifts his sunglasses up into his dark hair, pushing it off his face. I grin as one of the unruly strands sticks straight up in the air.

"I think so," I say, reaching out to fix the wayward hair. "That must be her Runustan contact."

I stretch out my arms wide, taking a deep breath of the

fresh, cool air. The *gers* have all been set up to face the lake, and the water is so crystal clear it looks like the facet of a diamond. At the water's edge, some kids a bit younger than us are playing volleyball on a small stretch of beach, and there's a shack nearby offering all kinds of motorized water-sports adventures for adrenaline-junkies. "Want to join them?" Zain says with a wide grin. I shake my head. I'm so uncoordinated at sports, I might as well have two left hands.

"Come on . . . you're tall. You must be good at volley-ball."

"That's an unfounded stereotype and you know it . . ."

Kirsty finally ushers us over. "Nadya, meet my two traveling companions, Sam Kemi and Zain Aster."

"Sam Kemi? The young apprentice who won the Wilde Hunt?" Nadya stares at me, her brown eyes wide with surprise. "And I know you too," she says, turning to Zain. "The princess's . . . best friend?"

I blush under her gaze. "You know about us, huh?"

"We might be nomads, but we still hear the news! Can you give me any gossip about who the princess is going to marry?" Her eyes twinkle with mischief.

"I'm as clueless as you!" I say, honestly.

She frowns. "Don't you know it's very rude not to offer a Runu tribeswoman a piece of news as you pass through?"

"No! I . . ." *Agh!* I rack my brain furiously for some news to share.

Nadya and Kirsty burst into laughter. "There's no such

tradition, Sam," Kirsty splutters. "She's just being nosy."

I stick my tongue out and my stomach makes another loud grumbling noise.

"Now I'm the one being rude." Nadya smiles warmly. "Come inside and get something to eat. You have a few minutes to stop?"

"Where's Zain?" I ask, realizing he's not behind me.

"Oh, check out your boyfriend," says Kirsty, giving me an exaggerated wink. I follow her line of sight down to where Zain has joined the kids at the beach. He's stripped his shirt off and I blush at the sight of his chiseled abs.

After a moment, Kirsty gives me a little push in the small of my back and I stumble forward, following Nadya inside the *ger*.

"Wow, you're so tall!" Nadya says as she holds the curtain door open for me. "Make sure you duck as you come through."

"Thanks," I say, narrowly avoiding a bruised forehead as I nearly bash against one of the tent poles holding up the intricate roof.

"It's not like Kirsty to travel with so many others. Normally she's a lone ranger," says Nadya, who leads me further into her home.

"This is a special mission for her."

"Oh? I rather thought this was a special mission for you, seeing as it is *you* who is searching for something, no? Aided by the princess, no less . . ."

I stop in my tracks just inside the door of the *ger*. I don't know what to do—whether this stranger is threatening me or not. Kirsty seems to trust her, but what does she know? And where is she, anyway? I look anxiously over my shoulder but there's no sign of her.

"Tea?" says the woman, still smiling at me. "Don't worry about me knowing that the princess helped you get here—I have no one to tell but the wind and the grass. It was easy for me to put two and two together when she changed her plans to come here."

"You probably have high-speed Internet," I say, staring pointedly at the laptop in the corner. "You could tell the whole world. And . . . is that a transport screen?" Who is this woman anyway? I press my lips together.

"Well spotted. I applied for one not long ago and my request was granted, along with our own transport technician. I didn't get a chance to tell Kirsty and besides, it's not exactly registered on the official magic streams yet."

I can't keep the question in any longer. "Who are you again?"

She laughs. "You can trust me. I don't care why you're here . . . only that you don't cause any trouble." Then her voice turns serious. "They're not going to like your group, you know that . . . especially not those two accompanying you. A Talented and a Finder? Maybe if you were on your own, as the descendant of Grand Master Kemi . . . they might hear you out."

"You mean the centaurs?"

She nods.

"Have you heard of my great-grandmother then?" I take the cup from Nadya's hands, deciding that I might as well settle in and take advantage of the tea.

"Of course I've heard of her. She spent time in our village when she was a young woman, learning our ways. That was *long* before my time, but the memory of her visit remains. Most people from Nova who pass through here are looking to give *us* advice, not the other way around. But your great-grandmother . . . she was different. She cared about where the ingredients came from and the history and culture that nurtured them. She was an alchemist I admired. Not many come to learn anymore."

I frown. "I didn't realize."

"It's not the norm to do that kind of training nowadays." She shrugs. "Just like we move around far less than our ancestors did. Time moves on, traditions change."

"Sometimes for the better." I lower my voice. "I can't believe one of the teams in the Wilde Hunt back then killed a centaur for its eye."

"You can't believe it?" She looks at me.

"Okay, so maybe I can," I say, shifting under her intense gaze. What lengths would I go to for a great potion like an aqua vitae? It's a question I'm not sure I want to know the answer to.

"So why the urgency to meet the centaurs? Why

now? And why is the princess of Nova involved?"

I speak slowly, choosing my words with extra special care. I don't want to reveal too much, especially not to this stranger. "It's my belief that my great-grandmother Cleo left something behind in Runustan. Something really important."

"Oh?" One of Nadya's neat, sharply-threaded eyebrows rises in my direction.

"But I'm not the only one looking for it. There are others. That's why the princess is involved. We need to keep the fact that we're here as secret as possible. We don't think the other party knows we're looking yet, but it's better if they never find out."

"I understand," she says. "Well, I will try to help as much as I can."

There's a commotion behind me as Kirsty and Zain walk in. He's put his shirt back on (to my disappointment). "Hey, you haven't been corrupting my girl, now, have you, Nadya?" says Kirsty.

"Corrupting?" I ask with a frown. It's hard to imagine the beautiful, sweet-faced Nadya corrupting anyone.

"You haven't told her?"

Nadya shakes her head.

"This woman has a PhD in Advanced Synth Mixology from one of the top universities in New Nova. She's looking into how she can work with the communities here to develop new ways of administering synths now that there are almost no Runu alchemists left. She's a very important lady, don't you know."

My eyes open wide as I see Nadya in a new light. "You're like . . . my hero!" I splutter, and she laughs.

"Well, maybe when you've finished your studies, you can come back here and work with me." She must sense my hesitation because she adds, "You *are* studying, aren't you?"

"Well—" I begin, but Kirsty interrupts me.

"Her family don't exactly approve of the synth industry."

"My granddad especially," I add.

"But the son of ZA is your boyfriend, no? How do they allow that?" Nadya turns her dark brown eyes on me, and I feel stripped down. "Somehow, I'm not sure your great-grandmother would have felt that way about progress. Synths are the way of the future, and she was a woman well ahead of her time."

"Well, I can't exactly ask her to clarify that right now, and my granddad is dying so I'm not about to question him," I snap back, and immediately wish I hadn't.

"I apologize if I overstepped," she says.

"It's fine," I say. I know it's not fair, but I'm annoyed at Kirsty for talking over me and at Nadya for presuming to know more about my family than I do.

But what bothers me most of all?

The fact that she's probably right. But unless I can save my granddad—and my country—I'm not going to have any kind of life at all.

CHAPTER TWENTY-FOUR

THE CONVERSATION WITH NADYA LEAVES me feeling shaken. My family has always been my solid foundation. Even though everything could conspire to make me feel like a fish out of water: my mixed-race heritage, my old-world skills, my lanky frame, my obsession with grades—my family have always been a reassuring constant.

I'd known that my great-grandmother was different—and now her missing potion diary was a tiny chip in our family history that was threatening to turn into an enormous crack. Her portrait in the mountain lodge near Mount Hallah had been surprise enough. It had thrown into doubt everything that my granddad had told me about alchemists—how they were homebodies who only experimented in the lab, not suited to grand adventures. *Alchemy rewards the scholar, not the explorer.*

"You're quiet, Sam," Zain says, after we've been back

on the road for some time. I'm in the backseat this time.

"Just reading," I say, gesturing to the book on my lap.

"Well, you haven't turned a page in at least ten miles. So either that's a very complicated page or—"

I stick my tongue out at him, then I close my eyes. "Oh god, this drive is making me want to puke." The road around the lake is unpaved, and we've been juddering off potholes for the past half hour.

"Oh no! What about a game to take your mind off it?"

I roll my eyes. "Really?"

"Yeah, sure! It will be fun." His face brightens, and I can't help but laugh.

"I haven't seen you this excited since you heard the new *Talented Spy* movie was coming out."

"Correction: I haven't been this excited since I asked to take *you* to the new *Talented Spy* movie and you said yes. One day." He winks and I laugh.

"One day," I repeat. Then I throw my hands up, conceding.

Zain bounces in his seat. "Okay, let's play twenty questions. Kirsty, are you in?"

"Why the heck not? It's not like there's much else to do on this drive."

"You should be careful, Zain . . . I know you don't like to lose and I'm really good at games," I say with a laugh and a wink of my own.

"You're on. I'll think of someone and you guys guess," says Zain. "Okay, ready."

"Is it a woman?" I ask.

"No."

"Fictional?" says Kirsty.

"No."

"Oh, I have a good question!" I lean over the seat. "Am I going to meet them at the Laville Ball?" I ask in a husky voice, waggling my eyebrows.

Zain scowls. "Dammit, yes!"

"Ooh, that narrows it down," says Kirsty.

"Is it . . . Damian?" My first guess is the most famous pop star in Nova—if not the world.

"Nope!" Zain looks all too happy for me to be wrong, and I pout.

"Is it Carlos Remani?" Kirsty asks, referring to the prime minister of Espano.

"No—I think you guys need to ask some more questions. Maybe you're not as smart as you think."

"Stefan of Gergon?" I say.

Zain slaps the dashboard. "How did you do that?"

I smirk. "Just good at games, I told you!"

"And hey, you said *not* fictional. I'm fairly certain Stefan's crown is basically a joke now," says Kirsty.

"How would anyone know?" I say, shrugging my shoulders. Gergon has been a black hole for the past year. Almost no one goes in or out, and the royal family—with the exception of the youngest, Prince Stefan—have not been seen in public for months. The prince is a reminder of Gergon's former power: In pictures he appears handsome, strong, and intelligent, and he was on the list as one of Princess Evelyn's prospective suitors . . . but no one knows much more about him, and he disappeared following the Wilde Hunt.

"Well, that's what *I've* heard on the Finder grapevine anyway."

We play a few more rounds, and then Kirsty sticks on the only music disc in the car and we all end up singing loudly to Midwinter holiday classics—even though we're months away from the festive season. Something about the impossibly long car drive has driven us all loopy. The passing scenery has returned to its hypnotic monotony.

As the hours pass, even talking and singing lose their appeal. The sky has darkened so intensely that it's almost impossible to see beyond the headlights. Zain has now taken over the driving and we travel in tired silence. My head wants to nod into sleep, but I pinch myself to stay awake. If we miss the gathering, this whole journey will be for nothing.

We climb the sharp crest of a hill—I can tell by the way my stomach lurches that it must be a big one.

"Stop the car," says Kirsty.

Zain obliges, then kills the headlights. Kirsty opens the glove box in front of her and pulls out two black cases. She hands one to me. "Night vision binoculars. I'll head outside and see if I can see anything—you stand up and look through the sunroof. You'll have a better vantage point. Look for any source of light—like a campfire or a torch. It could be big; it could be small. The size of the herds has been unreliable for decades and there's no recent documentation on how big the gatherings are at the moment."

I take the binoculars from the case as Zain opens the sunroof. I stand up, the fresh air filling my lungs. The sky is full of stars. It's still something that always gets me whenever I'm in the Wilds—on top of a mountain, out in the middle of the ocean, or in the middle of the Steppe. On Mount Hallah, I felt close to the stars. Now, here, they feel incredibly far away—and I feel impossibly small.

Through the binoculars, the world takes on a greenish, alien tinge. I make out the rocky terrain, huge boulders seemingly out of place in the grassy plain. When I turn the glasses on Kirsty, her face is cast in greenish-gray. Only the whites of her eyes are bright, like the stars.

I lower the binoculars for a second, a shiver running down my spine. I look up at the sky, still slightly freaked out at the thought of dragons flying overhead. Here, with my head popping out of the sunroof, I'm perfect prey. It's similar to the creeping dread I feel when I go swimming somewhere if I can't see the bottom. Mum blames my book-fed imagination. But I can't help it: When I'm in water, my brain conjures up images of sharks with rows of pointed teeth, krakens with curling tentacles, jellies with stinging strands.

I only hope I don't develop quite the same fear of the sky, or else I might never be able to go outside again.

The dragon radar hasn't beeped in hours, I remind myself. *It's okay.*

I lift the binoculars back up again. Straight ahead of us, I spot the bright white flash of eyes. But they're not Kirsty's.

It's a centaur.

CHAPTER TWENTY-FIVE

KIRSTY'S BACK IN THE CAR IN A FLASH, AND I drop down into my seat. My fingers grip the edge of the leather, my knuckles turning white. I can just about make out the outline of the centaur, and it's a terrifying and unsettling sight. He stands well over seven feet tall. His arms are crossed so his huge biceps bulge, almost unnatural-looking in their bulk. His human-esque torso merges seamlessly with his bottom half, which is all horse. He must be young—his beard is not far grown off his chin. Apparently older centaurs have beards that run all the way down their front, like a mane.

When he stops a few feet away from us, Zain moves to put the headlights on. Kirsty stops him with a touch. "Just follow him—can you see well enough?"

Zain swallows and nods. I don't like it when he looks nervous too.

Kirsty leans out of the window. "We are looking for Cato. Are you of his herd?"

The centaur makes a sound that is somewhere between a grunt, a whinny, and a word. Kirsty's face blanches. "Is he speaking Kentauri? I haven't heard that in years . . ." She tries again. "I understand you don't want to speak our language, but if you speak more slowly, maybe I can understand you . . ."

The centaur repeats the sound as Kirsty puts her fingers to her temples and squeezes her eyes shut. "He's telling us to leave," she says, finally.

"Please," I say. "You have to tell him to take us to Cato."

Kirsty leans out again. "We come not as Finders, but to ask your advice and to seek your knowledge."

"We need to turn around," says Zain, sweat beginning to bead on his forehead. "This isn't safe anymore. Not that it was safe before. Maybe we should have brought Nadya . . ."

"What? We can't go home now, we're so close," I say.

But Kirsty looks between Zain and me, and agrees with him. "Sam, if they turn on us, we won't be getting home—ever. They might look like people, but remember the mermaids? They look like people too. But they're not rational. At least, not the way we know it. They don't understand mercy. They've told us we're not welcome. We can't press our luck."

"I know all that, but still . . ." Nadya's words echo in

my mind: *Maybe if you were on your own, as the descendant of Grand Master Kemi . . .*

"I really don't like the look of his arms. He's too tense," says Zain, his voice tight. His hand is on the gearstick, ready to move.

The centaur's nostrils flare. I can see the whites of his eyes, then he reaches around his back and quick as a flash, draws his bow and arrow. But this is no normal weapon. The bow is as tall as the centaur, and the arrow itself looks more like a javelin, and it could easily pierce through the body of our car.

"GO!" Kirsty roars. Zain slams the gearstick into reverse. It's now or never.

I decide it's now. I open my door and roll out.

Kirsty screams as I tumble out of the car. Hard thuds pound the ground around me, one after the other, dust and rocks flying up into the air. I hug myself into a ball until the sound stops, my arms covering my face and head.

When I think I'm clear, I slowly stand, my legs shaking. I am surrounded by a cage of arrows. The closest one has landed just inches from the edge of my steel-toe hiking boots.

"Please," I say to the centaur, blinking furiously now that I'm caught in the fierce headlights of the car. "My name is Samantha Kemi. I am the great-granddaughter of Grand Master alchemist Cleo Kemi. I know she passed through here many years ago, and she spoke to a herd.

In particular, to a centaur named Cato. It's a matter of life and death," I say. I have no other ideas, and I'm not leaving without answers—or at least, another clue.

A tense moment of silence hangs in the air. Kirsty and Zain's eyes laser into my back, but they're not who I'm focused on. All I can do is stare at the centaur and pray my gamble has paid off. I wouldn't forgive myself if I'd come all this way and not given it my best try.

He shifts, and I can see him better. His eyes are hypnotic. The longer I stare at them, the stranger they become. They're far more impressive than the replica in the ZA lobby. They look like golden stars—no, like galaxies, a thousand million stars and nebulas swirling in his irises. Like he has an entire universe within each one. I smell whiskey on the air, strangely, but I'm only vaguely aware of it.

All at once, the universes narrow into thin slits. "Fine. You may come with me," he says, his voice seeming to come up from the ground itself. It takes me a moment, but I realize he's spoken Novaen. I can understand.

He turns around and walks away. Before I know it, he's leapt forward into a gallop.

"Quick!" says Kirsty. She leaps out of the car, tugging arrows out of the ground so I can escape and join them. "Sam, you crazy, reckless weirdo."

"I got him to take us, didn't I?"

"Yes, but to what?"

We follow the great plumes of dust the centaur throws up behind him. Soon, we're not just following one. In fact, we are surrounded by hundreds. They ride along beside us, making the ground shake with their thunderous hooves.

"Are we about to give these creatures two barrels of whiskey?" I ask, eyeing the wooden barrels sloshing around in the back. The centaurs look wild enough already.

"Trust me, that's barely a significant offering," says Kirsty. "The centaurs like their drink—and they only get to indulge a few nights of the year. The festival of the Fire Horse being one of them."

"Yes," says Zain, "and we don't know if it was your plea or the fact that Kirsty opened up the cork on the top of one of the barrels that made him change his mind."

A shudder runs through me. "You mean . . . he might not have done this for me?"

"Hate to say it, but I think not. Did you see the way his eyes changed when he smelled the alcohol?"

"Then why the heck are we heading with him and not far, far away?" I say, suddenly losing my nerve.

"Because if they accept the gift, then they won't harm us."

For the first time all night, I breathe a sigh of relief.

"Holy dragons," Zain says. And I know what he means. A single fire has appeared on the horizon, a blaze of light—but it's no ordinary campfire. It's a full-blown bonfire, with flames shooting high in the air. All around it are hundreds—if not *thousands*—of centaurs. Both Kirsty and Zain look like they can't believe their eyes.

I'm amazed, but I'm not shocked. My ancient book said that herds could number in the tens of thousands.

"Sam, get my camera," Kirsty says, snapping her fingers at me. She grabs it out of my hands as soon as I fetch it from her bag on the backseat, and she starts shooting away. "I need to get a good shot of this or else no one will believe us. There are only supposed to be a few herds left. Heck, they're on the endangered creatures list! But this is not endangered. This is . . ."

"Thriving," Zain finishes. "I checked in with the national databases before we left. The status is definitely endangered. There should not be this many of them."

"Didn't your teachers ever tell you not to use online resources as your only source?" I say. "My book says this is normal."

"How old is that book again?" asks Kirsty. "Does it mention the blight—the mysterious illness that wiped out almost the entire centaur population? It's yet *another* reason they hate Finders. They think it was a disease *we* brought to their lands that killed so many, and then we went ahead and killed a centaur at a time when there were already so few remaining."

"I would hate us too," I say, my voice small.

Kirsty slams her foot down onto the brake, throwing us forward in our seats. Our centaur has come to a stop. We are closer to the fire now, and our car is surrounded by angry-looking centaurs. Or maybe they always look angry: the deep V of their eyebrows screams constant grouchiness to me.

"Come on, let's get this over with," says Kirsty, unclicking her seatbelt. She steps out of the car and walks around to the trunk. Zain and I quickly follow. She looks up at the centaur and says, "Do you have a name?"

He looks at her for a long moment then says, "I am Solon" in his broken and uneasy Novaen. I'm glad that the fire is so bright and smokey that it stings my eyes and blurs my vision, because I can't clearly see the pandemonium around us.

Zain and I move closer to Kirsty. As if the three of us could do anything to stop Solon if he decided to use that bow and arrow again.

"We have a gift," says Kirsty. "But we want an audience with Cato. Then we will deliver our offering."

"You come here and expect to bargain with us?" Another centaur steps out of the smoke. And if I thought Solon had been big and scary, he looks like a *foal* compared to this one. His Novaen is superb, as if he's spoken it his whole life—it has none of Solon's hesitation and broken syllables. He is incredibly old, if the length of his gray beard is anything to go by.

Kirsty lowers her voice. "That's Cato," she says. I swallow hard. This is the centaur who could tell me what happened to my great-grandmother. I want to bow or curtsey or *something* to show respect. Instead, like Kirsty and Zain, I stand stock still.

To Cato, Kirsty says, "Of course not," and she hurries to unlock the trunk of the car. "Here, please . . . accept our humble gift. We are honored that you have allowed us to join you here today."

"Good—I thought for a moment that the rumors were true, that all Finders had lost their manners." He nods at two of the centaurs either side of him, and they step forward to take the gifts. Kirsty looks relieved.

"Come, walk with me away from here. It is too loud to talk."

We follow him, and I grip Zain's hand tightly, glad to be moving further away from the main gathering. Most stories of centaurs portray them as gentle, introspective beings. Those historians probably never saw a gathering.

In my peripheral vision I can see centaurs wrestling, hooves and fists clashing together. They're lifting huge barrels of drink and downing it like they're at a university frat party. The ground vibrates so hard I can barely walk in a straight line. Gradually as we move away from the mayhem, my racing heart slows to a more normal pace. Cato comes to a halt and turns to face us.

"Samantha Kemi," he says, his eyes drilling into my

soul. Like Solon, his eyes are like galaxies—except where Solon's burned golden and red and brown, Cato's are deep blue and silver and purple. I read that centaurs can see along different spectrums to humans. Not just colors and shapes—but pasts, presents, and futures, dreams, intentions, hopes and fears. "Come."

I hesitate until Kirsty gives me a reassuring nod. Zain bites the edge of his lip, but he allows my hand to slip from his, squeezing my fingers at the last moment. I take a deep breath and step forward.

"Your ancestor was wise and foolish," he says.

My knees tremble as he speaks to me. "Did . . . did you know her?"

He tilts his head to one side, and I take that as a yes.

"I need to find her diary before it's too late. There's a woman named Emilia Thoth who is looking for it, and if she gets her hands on it then the consequences for Nova will be dire."

"I can see the desperation in you, child. It is written all over your skin, clear as the day. But it is not for Nova that you are desperate."

My eyes prick with tears. He's right. "It's my Granddad," I say, feeling as small as a mouse.

"Now these other two—their ambitions aren't nearly as pure. On him, I can smell chemicals and synthetics—it makes me sick. And her, I can see her calculating our worth in her mind, seeing the potential for profit."

I cringe, wondering if they can hear. "She's a Finder—that's her job. And he works in a synth lab. But I will listen to you alone if you would prefer." I turn back to Kirsty and Zain, summoning my courage. "You two need to go back to the car."

"No, Sam. You're going to need us. Centaurs can speak in riddles. He won't give you a straight answer," Kirsty says.

"He's been pretty straightforward so far. I have to try."

"I'm not leaving you," says Zain.

"You don't have a choice," I say back.

Eventually he nods and they return to the car. Kirsty keeps throwing glances over her shoulder, as if she expects me to be struck by an arrow at any moment. I watch them until they disappear into the smoke, and then I turn back to Cato.

He is looking up at the sky.

"What is it that you see?" he asks me.

I crane my neck up at the sky. "I see . . . inky darkness and bright stars . . . too many stars to count."

"Good, good." He closes his eyes. "I know the object you seek. And I can see where it is, right at this very moment."

"You can?" My voice squeaks with hope.

"Yes. It sees this. This sky . . ."

My heart sinks. "That's all? The diary is somewhere out there, in the open?" It doesn't help me at all. My mind starts racing. What kind of place is out in the open, but where a diary can be lost for half a century with no one finding it?

"There is one more thing," he says.

"Yes! What is it?"

"In that place, the stars spark on command, but the day is always night."

I take a deep breath, trying not to let frustration cloud my memory. "The stars spark on command, and the day is always night. So, not out in the open?"

"My role is not to interpret. Only to tell you what I see."

"The stars spark on command, and the day is always night." I repeat to myself. I repeat it until it's seared onto my brain.

"Now, I must ask you and your companions to leave. You have been here long enough."

"Please . . . is there nothing more? Can you tell me a city? A landmark? Anything?"

He stares at me, unblinking, until I get the picture. There's nothing else. Finally, I nod. My heart feels like it's been trampled on by hooves. I don't know what I expected—maybe that Cato would have my great-grandmother's diary tucked away somewhere in that enormous beard of his? I'm too full of despair to laugh at the thought. I've come away with one extremely cryptic clue and nothing else.

And I don't have much time.

CHAPTER TWENTY-SIX

"THE STARS SPARK ON COMMAND, BUT THE day is always night," I say as I slide into the backseat. "Write it down somewhere!"

"What's that?" Kirsty asks.

"Where the diary is."

"Wow, Sam . . . that's not a clue, that's a poem."

"I know, but can we talk about this later? I think we need to get out of here. For real, this time."

A snort grabs our attention, loud as gunfire. Cato and his followers have gone, replaced by a group who look far less friendly. The centaur closest to us drags his front hoof slowly along the ground.

Kirsty grips the steering wheel. "But which way do we go?"

The journey through the centaur camp has turned us around completely; I have no idea which is the way back to Nadya's village.

"Just drive," says Zain. "This looks bad."

Kirsty starts up the engine and steers away from the centaurs. I scan the horizon for the rock formation we entered at, but the bonfires (there are lots of them now, so we can't even use those as guides) are obscuring the scene with their smoke, making the dark seem even darker. The night-vision goggles are no help here.

"They won't hurt us since we've given them the gift, right?" I ask.

"That *was* the tradition. But traditions change."

The centaurs still follow us, backlit by flames. One grabs my attention more than the others, because his eye is glaring at me with as much hatred as it can muster. And the other eye is covered by a patch.

He comes to a halt. Then, he rears.

"Floor it, Kirsty!" I scream as the entire herd of centaurs picks up into a charge.

Kirsty's knuckles are white on the steering wheel, the car bouncing hard on the rocky ground as she pushes the car to its limits. Centaurs appear out of the darkness whichever way we turn. They appear to be channeling us out of the camp. We can only pray that we're going to escape—and not get driven off a cliff to our deaths.

"On your left!" shouts Zain, and Kirsty jams the wheel right to avoid being flanked by another set of stampeding creatures.

"What's got into them?" I scream.

"Whiskey!" Kirsty yells back.

"They're slowing—they're falling back," I say shakily, not daring to take my eyes off the back window in case there are more surprises.

"Good." Kirsty doesn't lessen the pace. As we rocket deeper into the Great Steppe, my view of the centaurs fades. Only one is still looking out at us. His face is disappearing into shadow but I can tell it's the one with the eye patch. And that he has a smirk on his face.

"Do you think they were directing us somewhere?" Zain says to Kirsty. "Why haven't they followed us? They could have easily caught us—they're supposed to have crazy amounts of stamina."

"Who knows. Maybe it was the final part of their game."

"Maybe they were leading us in the direction of Cleo's journal?" I ask, hopefully.

"I don't think so," Kirsty says with a dry laugh.

"Well, are we going the right way, do you think?"

"No idea. When we're further away, we'll pull over and set up camp for the night. We can check the compass then, too."

I nod. Sleep sounds really good right now.

We drive for another hour, then Kirsty stops by an outcrop of rocks, which will vaguely protect us from the elements. The sky is already beginning to lighten, and we won't have long to rest.

Zain leans over to me. "Sam, you can sleep in the car. It will be just as comfortable as the tents."

I don't complain—I'm glad to have the metal cage of the car around me. I brush my teeth, then settle down into my sleeping bag on the backseat.

"You take the first watch," I hear Kirsty say to Zain. "Then me, then Sam." Their tents are the kind you throw up in the air and they pop up fully formed. Kirsty crawls into her tent, and I'm glad she can get some rest.

Strangely, I'm not tired. The night sky is alive with stars, the kind of sky that makes me feel like a tiny dust mote compared to the vastness of the universe. In a weird way, it's comforting.

"Mind if I join you?" Zain leans up against the car.

"Course not," I say, shuffling away from the window, giving him space to get in.

"Can't sleep?" he asks. I lay my legs across his lap and lean back against the far window.

"Not really. Too many thoughts. I can't turn my brain off."

"Your granddad?"

"Yeah. And it's weird. I haven't mixed a potion in ages. Between the store closing and the travel . . ." *Next time you mix a potion, it will be to save Granddad,* I tell myself.

"You're lucky, you know that?" says Zain.

"What do you mean?"

"I dunno. The thing is, after watching you . . . I'm not

181

sure if working with synths is for me. Not even 'Synth-Natural Potions Studies.'" Something about the way he says it makes me think he's putting air quotes around the title.

I shift closer to him, grabbing his hand. "But what about your fancy office that's all set up?"

"Screw the office," he says with a ferocity I haven't seen before. "I want what you have. I want a passion. I want to be on fire about what I do. I want to get up every morning and run to work."

"Trust me, I don't run to the store every morning . . . sometimes I *definitely* prefer my bed."

He gives me a small smile. "No, okay, maybe not *every* morning. But Sam, when you're working on a mix, when you're hunting down a recipe, you light up. A fire burns in you that can't be put out. It makes you shine. And that's why I don't just love you. I'm in awe of you." He kisses me deeply and I shift my legs so I can cuddle up against him.

I lie there for a moment, happy. But something else niggles. I put my hand against his chest, feeling his heartbeat. "You don't have to have it all figured out. I know this might sound weird coming from me but . . . you're eighteen. I don't think you're supposed to know everything at eighteen."

"Maybe."

"You'll figure it out. You could do anything. You just have to keep your eyes open. Of all the people in the world, you are *not* one of the ones that needs to worry."

He laces his fingers between mine. "That's because I have you."

"*No,*" I say. "I mean, yes, you do have me—but that's not what makes you great. And besides, you make me better. I mean it when I say we're a good team."

He chuckles. "How come you're so wise?"

"I read . . . a lot," I say with a grin.

Sleep hits me as Zain's arms wrap around my shoulders. My eyes stay open long enough to see a shooting star dance its way across the sky and then I'm out like a light.

When I wake, it's because of a curious beeping. I'm disoriented and stiff from sleeping scrunched up against the door, and it's far brighter outside than when I closed my eyes.

I rub my eyes, just as my brain clicks into gear. *Oh crap.* I leap forward into the front seat and lift up the middle panel of the dashboard. The bright green radar screen is on and flashing. But there isn't just one dot on the screen. There are two.

I dive for the car door, fumbling with the lock.

"DRAGONS!" I yell at the two tents outside.

In one of the tents, there's a mad scramble. Zain emerges looking disheveled. He searches the sky, then a stream of expletives leaves his mouth.

Even though I've only had a handful of driving lessons, the adrenaline coursing through my veins gives me confidence. Luckily, Kirsty has left the keys in the ignition, so I turn on the engine and put the car into gear.

"Where's Kirsty?" I yell at Zain as he jumps into the car.

"She's not here?"

"Is she still in her tent?" I haven't seen a dragon yet but frankly, I don't want to. According to the radar, they are *very* close.

I lean on the horn, hoping to wake Kirsty.

"Don't do that!" Zain yells. "The dragons are attracted to the sound. It's how they find food out here in the plains."

"What? I didn't read that! Then how did they find us all the way out here . . . we didn't make a sound for hours after we left, did we?"

"We must just be very unlucky."

And yet, another answer leaps from the rocky alcove above us. Kirsty lets out a piercing holler that seems to split the morning sky in two. Zain and I both look up through the windscreen and see her launching herself off the tallest rock, wrapped in what looks like a bright orange blanket. But as she opens her arms, the blanket expands and catches her, like wings. She floats softly to the ground.

Then, the moment I've been dreading plays out in front of me. Swift on her tail is the dragon. At first, I don't recognize it. It's so lithe and sleek, it slips through the air like an otter in water. It's too graceful to be fearsome. But that's when it opens its mouth and lets loose a stream of blue-green flames.

The flames lick the edges of Kirsty's wingsuit as she hits the ground and starts to run. Luckily the flames don't quite reach her, but then she does the opposite of what I expect: she drops to the ground. She fumbles with her belt, where a large, flasklike container is attached to a long piece of knotted rope. She quickly unties the rope and lays it out on the ground. One edge of the flame catches the rope and the flame dances along it like a wick, straight into the flask. Kirsty jumps on it and puts the lid on.

"Is she . . . collecting the flame? Is she always this crazy?" Zain asks.

"You have no idea."

"The dragon looks young—maybe only a year old," says Zain hopefully.

But he catches my eye, and registers my terrified expression. "Though if it's a baby then that means . . ."

A dark shadow passes over our car, and I know it can't be the baby, which is still in sight, circling around Kirsty like a miniature bird of prey. No. When this one passes overhead, my stomach leaps into my mouth. It's a cloud passing in front of the sun.

The dragon that's above us is more what I was

expecting. No longer as sleek as an otter—this is a whale of the sky. It's a freight train in the air. It flaps its wings and the car shakes and our teeth rattle in our skulls.

I have to do something quickly. Kirsty is so Finding-focused that she might not notice the other dragon until it's too late.

"How do we get away from them?" I ask Zain.

"They're territorial. We just need to get out of their zone—they won't follow us beyond where they're comfortable."

"Come *on*, Kirsty," I say, mentally calculating how long it will take to drive to her, versus whether this is all part of some crazy master plan of hers and she doesn't want to be rescued.

"What are you doing?" yells Zain. "We have to go get her!" He reaches over, wanting to drive the car himself. But there's no time for us to switch. My eyes are locked on Kirsty and finally, *finally*, she lifts her gaze to meet mine.

I know what that looks means.

It means *go*.

I slam my foot down on the accelerator, ignoring Zain's cries.

The huge dragon is visible in my rearview mirror. I can see now that by racing to pick up Kirsty, I'm only going to spell her doom. I need to draw the dragon away from her. Dragons, I know from my book, have limited firepower. After one large burst, the dragon will need to go back up into the sky to recharge.

I spin the wheel, trying to throw the dragon off. But it seems fixated on Kirsty, even though we are moving much faster. Its body curls and stretches, moving like a snake through sand. I wonder if it has a deadly strike like a cobra, too. I can't think like that. I lean down on the horn.

"We can't outdrive the dragon!" Zain yells in my ear. His words are not helpful. I know what he's afraid of. The dragonfire will be so hot, it'll melt right through the bodywork of the car, vaporize the wheels, cook us in our seats . . . so much could go wrong. But there isn't time for logic. There's only time for instinct.

My instinct so far is spot on. By pressing on the horn, I've attracted the big dragon's attention—and that of the baby. Both of them are after us now, the baby riding in the mother's slipstream, the two of them writhing in the air.

I swerve in a zigzag pattern, hoping that will throw the dragons off. I've read that works against other reptiles, like crocodiles. But all it does is slow the car down. Zain grips the dashboard to brace himself against the movement of the car.

The mother dragon releases one small blast of fire that just misses us—a warning, I'm sure of it. But as I look back in the rearview mirror I can see that Kirsty is back on her feet and running toward the tents. She waves her arms frantically for me to come and get her. *Even with the dragon tailing us?* But I can't really think. I can only follow instructions. I slam on the brakes and turn the wheel, and we spin around in a sharp u-turn. The car stalls as the dragon's wings beat overhead, caught in the downdraught as it soars above us. I restart the car as quickly as I can, then race toward Kirsty.

The mother dragon's mouth yawns open, slow and steady—as if she knows we don't have a shot. The fire builds in her mouth, and I know at any instant she's going to release her fury. And she's going to get all three of us in one, if Kirsty doesn't do something quickly.

As I'm hurtling toward her, I see Kirsty pick up the tent and put something inside it. It's one of the fireworks from the boot. She points it directly above the car, then lights the wick and runs away. I change the direction that I'm driving to meet her. The firework shoots above our heads just as I brake to avoid hitting Kirsty.

I come to a stop and she jumps in the car. The distraction works: The dragons chase after the bright flying tent as it whistles through the air, and when it explodes into a bright sprinkle of red stars, the mother dragon unleashes her stream of fire. In the early morning light, the flames are so bright they make spots dance in front of my eyes.

"Go!" says Kirsty, pointing in the opposite direction.

"We'll have five minutes, max, to get as far as possible while the dragons recharge."

I floor the accelerator and drive as fast as I can while keeping the car under some illusion of control.

After half an hour of tense, flat-out driving, Kirsty finally taps my shoulder and says we're far enough away. I stop the car, get out, and dry-retch into the ground. I haven't eaten enough to throw up, but my arms and legs are shaking. I drop to my knees, tears streaming down my face.

Zain is next to me in a flash. "You did great. You saved us back there."

Kirsty pats my back gently. "He's right. If you hadn't taken that mother dragon for a bit of a walk, I wouldn't have been able to get back to the fireworks in time."

"*That* had been your plan all along?" I narrow my eyes.

She shrugs. "Standard dragonfire acquisition procedure."

Anger builds up inside me, then disappears. I'm too tired to be angry. "Did you get the dragonfire, at least?"

"Of course," she says with a smile. "No way I would let a trip out here go to waste." She must see the stricken look on my face, because she backpedals. "I'm sorry, Sam, but it's true. There's no way you're going to find your great-grandmother's diary based on that clue."

And even though I know she's right, hearing it feels like a centaur is trampling all over my heart.

CHAPTER TWENTY-SEVEN

"ANY LUCK?" EVELYN BARELY HAS TO GLANCE at us to know the answer. I'm slumped down in the airplane seat, my eyes rimmed with red and sunken into my face from lack of sleep. When I shut my eyes, I see dragonfire. When I'm awake, all I can think about is the centaur's riddle.

I repeat the centaur's words to Evie: *The stars spark on command, but the day is always night.*

After a moment, she shakes her head. "I'm sorry," she says. "Those words mean nothing to me."

I shrug. "Me neither." And I've tried. I've asked everyone. Nadya couldn't think of a place related to the riddle. My Internet search constantly fails me; trawling websites and chatrooms turns up nothing. I even debated putting the riddle up on the Wilde Hunt Theories forums—they seem to figure out anything else—but that's just a step too far. Evelyn promises me access to the Laville Palace library.

But rather than being excited at the prospect of all those books, I just feel numb. I can't save Granddad. I can't stop Emilia's quest for power.

"We won't give up, Sam," says Zain from the seat next to me. "We can always—"

"What can we do?" I interrupt him. "Search every book in every library for reference to 'stars that spark on command'? The centaurs were our best lead! And they obviously know something about the diary or else they wouldn't have given me that stupid riddle."

"Then we'll go back and ask them again. We'll bring ten times more whiskey. We'll beg them!"

"Go back?" The thought makes me weary, but I nod. It's probably the only way.

Zain puts his arm around my shoulders and pulls me tightly toward him. My side digs into the armrest, but I let myself lean into him. "There's nothing we can do today, anyway," he says.

"That's right," says Evelyn, ever the optimist. She puts her hands on her hips and looks down at me. "Today is the Laville Ball, and you *have* to go and at least have your picture taken there, so your cover story sticks."

I sit up a little straighter. "Then, after that, Zain and I will mix in the ark flower for your potion," I say. "And I'll follow up on my research for a more permanent solution."

"No!" Evelyn protests. "You don't have to do that."

"I do. Your well-being is just as key to Nova's safety."

"No," she says, her lips tight. "My problem has an easy solution, a solution that has worked for every one of my ancestors before me. I just don't want to face it. I appreciate what you're doing more than you know, but I have to face facts. And the other fact is that Emilia is still out there. You can't stop looking, Sam. She has your grandfather's memories. She is still ahead of you."

I shudder at the thought. "I know that. But if you're strong, then you can help me with Emilia. After the ball, Zain and I will get you the new, stronger mix, then we can head to Gergon."

Evelyn looks up sharply. "Gergon? Why Gergon?"

I allow myself a small smile. "Have you heard of the Visir School?"

"The old alchemist academy?" Zain asks, one eyebrow raised. I haven't had the right moment to tell him about my findings either.

"Yeah, exactly. It's a long shot but after I saw Da Luna's painting in your library, I remembered something I'd read a long time ago. Apparently, the alchemists there had been working on some kind of storage system for power. Basically, they wanted to use magic without having an actual Talented person present in the school . . . You know how ordinary alchemists feel about Talenteds," I say with an apologetic shrug.

Thankfully neither of them look offended. "Anyway, the school closed down years ago," I continue. "But there might be something there that I can use, some clues in the ruins . . ."

Evie looks both guilty and relieved. "You have an actual clue for a permanent solution for me? You're amazing! But if you want to get into Gergon, you're going to have to get special dispensation from the Gergon royals. They haven't been seen or heard of for months." She frowns, and then her face lights up. "But Prince Stefan is on the ball guestlist! If you can talk to him at the ball, maybe he will let you in."

"That would be perfect!" I say.

"Great. It's going to be another whirlwind when we land," Evelyn says. "You and I will be taken straight to the palace to get ready."

"What, straightaway?" I ask, unable to hide my disappointment. I was hoping to at least get a glance at the famous Tree of Lights—the main landmark in the city of Laville. And now that I had the riddle, I had planned to take up Evelyn's offer to explore the palace library . . .

"Straightaway," Evelyn repeats firmly.

Zain takes my hand. "Don't worry, Sam—I'll do some poking around in the library for another clue. Then I'll be there to escort you to the ball at six, *mademoiselle*." My heart jumps a little at the thought of going to the ball with Zain.

I nod. "Okay, but I want a full report of everything you find—no matter how small."

"You bet, boss," he says with a wink, then kisses me on the cheek.

"That's sorted then," Evelyn says.

Once we land in Laville, the princess is true to her word. I'm swept away from Zain and into the madness of Evie's entourage. A stretch limousine is ready and waiting to take us through the broad streets of Laville, past beautiful white stone buildings adorned with wrought-iron balconies. Trees, bold green and in full bloom, stand like sentries outside the houses, each one spaced a perfect distance from the other. The streets would be even more impressive if they weren't packed with people—all waiting for a glimpse of the princess. She touches the glass of the window nearest to her, and the glass turns from opaque to clear. She waves at the passersby, sending up cries of delight that follow us around the city, like the wake of a boat.

Yet nothing prepares me for my first sight of the palace: a building that looks like it's built from solid gold. They say that in full sunlight in midsummer, the glare from the sun shining on the Laville Palace can be seen from all over the country of Pays. It's their literal beacon of wealth and prosperity. I think sometimes that the Kingstown castle is a bit of a let-down: although it sits high at the top of a hill, it's pretty boring in its appearance, a functional square shape with only a few stone turrets and rounded towers on each corner. The floating Palace Great of Nova is invisible, so even though it's amazing, it doesn't really count as a landmark.

As we're swept through enormous golden gates, I can't tear my eyes away. We drive round to a set of steps polished to a mirrorlike shine and as we step out, I have to shield my eyes from the golden light that emanates from the building's every surface.

The inside continues the theme of pure Pays opulence: There's not one wall that's not covered in portraits of former Pays royals, great paintings of battle scenes or tapestries depicting ancient magical creatures. In the suite where Evelyn and I will be getting ready, I'm overawed by the shining gold brocade wallpaper on a rich crimson base and the deep navy carpet so thick, my low heels (apparently it's a must to wear heels in Pays, so my compromise was the tiniest kitten heels I could find) get lost in the weave.

Almost instantly, a pack of makeup artists and hair stylists surround us, whisking me in front of a mirror. They sit Evelyn in a chair next to me (although no mirror, as per her request). I always thought Evelyn just needed to dream up a look and she could create it with a touch of her power, but she says she still needs people with real artistic talent to perform the magic in order to bring out her best features.

"I would be useless at glamouring my own makeup," she says, making me cough. "It's true! Okay, maybe now and then I'll enhance what the makeup artist does. Or, as with my dress, I like to give it my own twist." She winks.

"Yes, and your twists will be the death of me one day!" says her hairdresser with a dramatic sigh.

"Now, Sam, you are going to get the full treatment as well," Evie says, ignoring her. "You're going to need it to complement your exquisite dress! I won't take no for an answer. And . . . don't hate me, but . . ."

"But what?" I say, narrowing my eyes in suspicion.

"I'm going to apply a glamour."

"What?!"

"Just a gentle one! Just a little silver to your gorgeous dark hair, to play off the metallic sheen of your dress."

The thought makes my skin crawl. "I dunno . . . everyone will know it's not *my* glamour, something I had to borrow for the evening . . ."

Evelyn rolls her eyes. "Don't be silly. Everyone *also* knows that you're my friend. No one is going to think less of you because you're an ordinary. Trust me, you will look far more out of place if you don't wear a glamour." Her expression softens. "Let me?" she pleads.

I shrug. Evie can be very persuasive when she wants to be. "Okay, fine. But if you keep ordering me about like this, I'm not going to want to hang out with you."

"Sure you will," she smiles. "You already love me, and I didn't even need to make you drink a potion. Now, we should just go over a few things."

It's hard to listen closely to Evelyn as the stylists start to tackle my hair and makeup. This is the first time I've been "styled" before—I never go to any of the fancy parties that Anita likes. She just about managed to convince me to attend our school's summer dance—except it got cancelled in lieu of the Wilde Hunt. Thank goodness. Even for the ceremony to announce the Wilde Hunt winner, everyone decided it would be best if I just looked like my normal self. I preferred that.

When we're close to the end, Evie comes and stands behind me, and cold drafts of magic embed themselves in my hair, braiding strands of it with silver to match my dress. I give her a small smile, surprised to catch her eye in the mirror. It looks so pretty.

"Oh!" Evelyn cries out. The delicate stream of magic flowing from her hands turns into a gushing waterfall.

I shout out in pain. The magic grips each strand of my hair like a vice, twisting it tighter and tighter. The stylists stand paralyzed with shock and stare at Evelyn. She can't stop. Her eyes are wide with panic.

I fall out of the chair, unable to stand the relentless flow of magic.

A guard bursts into the room.

"Don't touch me!" shouts Evelyn, but the guard ignores her. She grips Evie's wrists with one hand, while with the other she flicks the security cap off a syringe. With one swift movement, she jabs the needle into Evelyn's arm.

With a very un-princess-like grunt, Evelyn shuts off the magic flow.

"Everybody out!" shouts the guard. The stylists look all too happy to flee.

Evie's face is drenched with tears. "Oh dragons, Sam, are you okay? Are you hurt? Do you need to see a doctor?"

The pain disappeared when the magic stopped, so I gingerly touch my scalp. It's almost solid with silver, like a helmet. "I think I'm okay . . . but I'm gonna need help removing this glamour."

Evie reaches to hug me, but the guard stops her. "Wait, Your Highness, I need to run some checks."

For the first time, I get a proper look at the guard. She's tall, like me, but unlike me she has lily-white skin that stands out against her smartly tailored black suit. But it's her hair that's most striking: copper as some of our mixing pots, it sparkles with natural bronze highlights. Even pulled back into its tight, no-nonsense braid, I feel a pang of envy. It's stunning.

"Look at me," the guard says to Evie. I'm surprised by how casual the guard is around the princess—and equally by how meek Evie is in her presence. I don't think I'd have the courage to boss her around like the guard is doing, but Evie is obeying her every command.

I don't think I've seen that before.

The guard looks deep into Evie's eyes, scrutinizing her pupils. Then she lifts up Evelyn's hands and checks for residual magic. "Are you feeling in control?"

Evelyn nods. "I think so."

I breathe out a loud sigh of relief, then hang my head. I know exactly why the princess's magic is out of control:

because I haven't been focused enough to help her. After the ball it might be too late.

When I look up again, the guard is still holding Evelyn's hands, her thumb gently stroking the topside of her palm. Evelyn's eyes are closed, but when they snap open and she sees me looking, she takes a step away from the guard, pulling her hands away.

"Thank you for your service, Katrina. I feel much better now. That will be all."

Katrina doesn't miss a beat. She bows low in response, then turns on her heels and leaves the room.

My mind races a million miles a minute. "Wait, is that . . . ?"

Evie looks toward the door and smiles. "Maybe." She turns back to me, her eyes sparkling, and my heart lifts. Katrina the guard. Who knew? "I promise to tell you all about it after the ball. But I think I have to go lie down if I'm going to recover in time. I'll send the stylists back in—they have a deglamourizing shampoo they can use. I'm really very sorry again."

I nod. "No, sure—you need to rest. And you don't have to be sorry. I'm the sorry one. I'm your alchemist and I haven't made you the perfect mix."

"Then let's both be sorry, and let's forget about this for one night." Now she steps forward and kisses me on both cheeks. "I'll see you later. Zain will come up about half an hour before your entrance, so you can chat. Don't you and your escort get so smoochy that you forget to come to the ball, all right? I need you both there."

I blush. "I'll be there, don't worry."

"Well, good. Oh, and Sam—don't forget to eat something. You'll be grateful you did."

"Got it."

It's still another hour until the styling team are through with me, and even with the glamour removed, when they're finished I feel like a goddess. They've restyled my hair so it's as fun as my dress, plaiting it so that it falls into a fishtail braid over one shoulder, but they've curled some strands around my face in a way that hints to the same forties era that the dress plays on. For the first time, I'm wearing bright red lipstick, and my face has been smoothed by foundation so that it looks as if I don't have a single flaw, even though I know I have a smattering of spots near my forehead. I never expected that makeup could perform *this much* magic. I smile at myself, tentatively.

Once I'm primped, prepped, and zipped into my dress, finally Evelyn's entourage of people leave me alone in the room to wait for Zain. My heart feels like it's about to pound right out of my chest. I don't know why I'm so nervous. I run through the plan: There's going to be an indoor red carpet to walk, filled with celebrities—although thankfully the ball itself will be blissfully paparazzi-free. There are going to be several waltzes, and I need to accept invitations on my dance card, reserving the first and last for my escort. There's going to be lots of tiny finger food on trays that I'm going to have to *not* spill down my dress. Okay, I cut myself some slack. I know exactly why I'm nervous. It's the freaking Laville Ball.

At least every time I quake, my dress seems to move in a very fluid way. Maybe Evelyn helped me chose it especially for that. I need Zain to calm me. Once I have him by my side, I'll be ready to face anything.

I prep the little bag that Evelyn gave me to accessorize my dress, but it's so tiny I can barely fit a tube of lip gloss inside—let alone anything else. My old, battered leather cross-strap is lying on the table. It's big enough to fit the lipgloss, a pair of flats, my phone, *and* my potion diary. The bag doesn't exactly go with the dress, but by the time Evelyn sees me, it will be too late to change. I make an executive decision and go with my leather bag.

On the table next to my bag, a bright purple box catches my attention. It has my name engraved on it in gold foil. I pick it up and open it, and inside is a stunning silver bracelet, perfectly matched to the dress. I look a bit closer and I can see that it is inlaid with tiny jewelled carapaces of heart beetles (named unsurprisingly for their distinctive heart shape). Each one has a distinctive indigo or violet shimmer, elevating the bracelet from something ordinary into something really beautiful. I pick up the piece of white card that accompanies it.

You might not want one of my live beetles, but
I thought you should have something pretty
anyway.
Have a ball,
Kirsty xx

I smile, and slide the bracelet onto my wrist. It requires
a little persistence to get it over my hand but once it's on,
it looks perfect. I go to text Kirsty my thanks, when the
clock catches my eye. It's almost time. Zain is going to be
here at any moment.

Evelyn's last piece of advice for me was to eat. But I have
no idea how to call for food. In the corner of the room I spy a
half-eaten platter—obviously put there for the stylists—and
there's a stray sandwich lying abandoned in the corner, plus
an array of little pastries. I guess even the makeup artists
avoid fattening foods in this place. I have no such qualms. I
overlook the healthy sandwich and stuff my mouth with a
delicious, flaky pastry. This is Pays, the country of butter and
bakeries. The pastries here are insanely good.

Right on time, there's a knock at the door. My heart
lifts—and I say a little prayer of thanks that Zain is here.
I might have eaten my bodyweight in croissant otherwise.

I rush to the door, fiddling with the ornate handle. I
open the door but the figure I end up beaming at and
almost throwing my arms around isn't Zain.

It's Prince Stefan. The second prince of Gergon.

CHAPTER TWENTY-EIGHT

MY FACE SHIFTS RAPIDLY FROM A MASSIVE grin to confused frown. *Oh god, I'm frowning at a prince!* I bow my head to obscure my burning cheeks and subtly wipe my lips free of stray pastry flakes. I'm lucky that Stefan is tall too—at least a head taller than me, so the head-lowering trick works.

I shuffle back a few steps to let him into the room before I raise my head again. How do I address a prince of Gergon? I have no idea. I go with a curtsey and a slightly mumbled "Your Highness."

He seems to accept that, and an amused smile plays on his face. He bows to me. "Ah, so you know who I am?"

"Prince . . . Stefan?" I say with slight hesitancy, even though I'm sure it's him. Having seen him only in photos, I can't really believe my eyes. My first thought is that he is *much* more handsome in person than in the stern, serious pictures I've seen of him.

"*Enchanté*, Miss Kemi, it's a pleasure. May I come in properly?"

"Of course," I say, recovering my composure. "But, uh, Princess Evelyn isn't here. She's in a different room somewhere." I gesture back down the hallway.

He raises his eyebrows. "I'm not here for the princess Evelyn. I'm here for Miss Samantha Kemi."

"Oh," I say. Then it clicks. Evelyn must have set this up after I asked about getting into Gergon. That girl can move fast when she wants to.

"You do need an escort to the ball, correct?" One corner of his mouth lifts into a lopsided smile. He looks as confused as I feel.

"Oh yes, but . . . Well, I'm waiting for my boyfr—for Zain Aster. He was supposed to be my escort."

A tiny frown appears on the prince's face, but it's soon as smooth as silk again. "Oh no, I applied to be your escort as soon as I heard you were coming to the ball. I've really wanted to meet you, Sam Kemi."

"You have?"

He steps past me, striding into the room like he owns the place. He reminds me of Evelyn in that regard, but I have to remind myself that he is the *second* in line to his throne. He doesn't have the same kind of power that the firstborn royal does.

I find myself staring for a few seconds at his back, cloaked in a bright red military-style jacket. His clothing is ostentatious, reminding the world of Gergon's military strength, even though there hasn't been a war for half a century and there are plenty of rumors swirling around about Gergon's waning power. But the bright gold shoulderpads offset his wavy golden hair and I can't tear my eyes away as he walks. He spins around and gestures for me to join him on the small sofa.

"Of course I have! You are the world-renowned winner of the Wilde Hunt! You've brought glory back to the alchemists of Nova. I *had* to meet you."

I perch awkwardly on the sofa, only one bum cheek on the cushion. "Well, hi, I guess."

I look for the glamour. Evelyn said that everyone would be wearing extravagant glamours this evening, and if I didn't join in then I would look like the odd one out. I catch his gaze again, and that's when I realize it's his eyes. His eyes are golden too, and almost catlike in their intensity. Big-cat-like. But his pupils are an odd shape. They are little jewels, like sparkling topaz or tiger's eye.

Tiger's eye—a special gemstone with a silky luster, best for warding off prying minds, to conceal thoughts.

"Your eyes are beautiful," I say, rather without meaning to.

He laughs. "You're too charming, Miss Kemi."

I pull my gaze away from his eyes, blushing again. Where on earth is Zain? I look anxiously toward the door. I can hear the ticking of the clock on the wall beside me so loudly, I want to slap it to turn it off. I know nothing about this prince or his family except rumor and speculation. I shouldn't leap to judge, but I can't help but feel on edge. I force myself to relax. This is the opportunity I've been waiting for. "Actually, there is something I want to ask you . . ."

"Oh?"

"I've heard a lot about the old Visir School in my research and I really would love to visit, if it is at all possible."

He leans forward in his seat and his eyes search my face. He's like a big cat about to pounce on his prey. Did I mention that tigers are my favorite animals? An unwelcome blush creeps up my neck, my palms pricking with sweat.

"You *are* interesting, Miss Kemi! Your first meeting with me, the prince of Gergon, and you ask me for a favor, before even offering me a drink!"

My jaw drops in horror at what a terrible hostess I'm being. I scramble to my feet. "Oh dragons, can I get you something to drink?"

He laughs. "No, no, we will need to leave soon and there will be plenty at the ball."

"Right—some food?"

"Miss Kemi, I was . . . My Novaen isn't so good. I was teasing you. You are just very practical."

Heat burns in my cheeks. "That is one way to describe me," I say with a shrug.

"I'm sure we can arrange a visit to the Visir School for you."

"Can it be soon?"

"We can go tomorrow! But tell me, why the hurry? The school has been closed for almost a century . . . it will still be there in a few months, I'm sure. There are far more interesting places in Gergon for someone like you."

I don't want to give away too much to this stranger, even if he is a prince. So far, the palace has done well to keep a crackdown on leaks about Evelyn's instability— even the stylists today will have signed heavy NDAs— and I don't want to fuel any other fires.

"It's just been on my bucket list for ages . . ."

"And here I was thinking all alchemists were patient souls. But you are different, I can see that." As he says it, he lightly runs his finger down my arm. My skin tingles where he touches it.

Zain, think about Zain.

It's weird—Prince Stefan radiates a completely different energy to Zain. Maybe it's those tiger eyes, but the prince is all predatory charm. Zain never makes me feel like I'm his prey. In fact, even though he's got all the money and Talent in the world, Zain works for my affection and respect. As though he feels he still has something to prove. Prince Stefan has never had anything to prove. In that way, he's more like Evelyn. But Evelyn wears her royalty with warmth that endears her to people. Something about Prince Stefan makes me think he's stepped out of a world from a hundred years ago, when royals were far more powerful—and relished it.

Maybe that's why I'm drawn to him. Alchemists are like relics from another time too, after all. Nothing to do with his incredible blond hair and tiger eyes and broad shoulders . . .

I clear my throat. "I'm different probably because I'm not a fully-fledged alchemist yet. I'm still an apprentice."

He smiles. "We are very proud of our alchemists in Gergon. Did you know that once your great-grandmother came to train with us? Maybe that is where she learned some of her greatest recipes."

My ears perk up at that, but I try to keep my voice even. "My great-grandmother came to Gergon? I didn't know that."

"Oh yes, when she was just a young girl, not much older than you. We admire the Kemis very much. We, unlike the Novaens, have not completely gone over to . . . the dark side, as it were."

"What do you mean?" I say sharply. *The dark side? Does he mean Emilia?* All the rumors say that Gergon is still one of the few places where dark potions are mixed. Everyone says *that's* where the dark side is.

"The synths," he says. "I heard before you won the

last Wilde Hunt that your family's business, and that of others like you, was practically obsolete. That . . . what's that company's name . . . ZoroAster Corp," he says with a sneer, "had taken over almost complete production of your potions industry."

I relax. He only meant the synths. But then I frown. "How does it work in your country?"

"We don't believe that old methods should just give way to new technology. In Gergon, we believe that they must work together. Enhance each other."

"That sounds . . . eminently sensible," I say. I eye him with suspicion, even as I can feel my inner self turn toward him and say *Yes! Yes! That's exactly what I've been saying!*

"Well, unfortunately, neither alchemist nor synth have been working well for us." He casts his eyes downward, and his shoulders curl forward, as if he carries the weight of the world.

I frown in concern. "What do you mean?"

"When you come to Gergon, I will show you," he says with a sad smile.

I return an awkward half-smile of my own. Thankfully I am saved by the sound of trumpets, and it shatters the strange atmosphere that's built up in the room. The sound is bright, light, and full of celebration. Suddenly I'm too hot in my dress, and the thought of being announced in the spotlight makes me want to throw up.

Prince Stefan stands and offers his hand. He shakes off his sadness and his smile is as bright as before. "That is our cue. Shall we descend to the ball?"

I hesitate for an instant, and then take his hand. "Prince Stefan?"

"Yes, Samantha?"

"Thank you, for your generosity in offering to bring me to Gergon." I feel like I should curtsey or something.

He nods. "Well, maybe if all goes to plan, we will be seeing lots of each other soon." He guides my hand so that it nestles in the crook of his elbow and leads me out into the hallway.

I swallow down a small ball of guilt. He still wants to marry the princess. He still thinks he has a shot. But of course he does—that's the whole reason he's here. It's just that I want to go to Gergon to prevent that from happening. I sense that I should keep that knowledge to myself.

As we walk down the long corridors, we pass other couples on their way down to the ball. At the sight of the prince, they back up against the wall and bow their heads. There are members of other royal families here, but we are led past them all, to be introduced toward the end of the line—the hierarchy of power going from least at the front to most at the back.

We pass Zain and his eyes open wide as he catches sight of whose arm I'm on. I open my eyes wide and shrug my shoulders, hoping he'll catch the "I had nothing to do with this" expression on my face. Zain glowers at the prince, his blue eyes smouldering, but if Prince Stefan catches the gaze he does nothing to show it. I don't recognize the girl Zain's now been made to escort, and he doesn't seem to be doing a great job of showing her any attention. She's staring at her nails, clearly bored, as they wait in line for their turn to be announced. Every time one couple's name is said aloud, the whole group shuffles forward. Prince Stefan and I slot into place, seemingly at the end of the line. But I know Evelyn will come after us.

The bright lights of the ballroom get bigger and bigger as the moment looms closer.

"Shall we dance?" the prince whispers in my ear.

We step through the double doors and into the ballroom.

CHAPTER TWENTY-NINE

"PRINCE STEFAN OF GERGON AND MISS Samantha Kemi."

There's a tittering of the crowd as our names are announced, but it could just be my imagination. Prince Stefan holds my arm steady as we descend the staircase.

When we reach the bottom, he takes a step back and gives me a small bow. There are already couples waltzing round and round on the ballroom floor, and I lose my nerve. A couple of high school dance lessons are *not* going to cut it. Suddenly everything feels wrong: My dress is too short, my feet too big, my hair too loose.

He stretches out his hand and I tentatively grab it. But there is nothing tentative about his movements. He pulls me into a hold, gripping me firmly around the waist. My nerves calm somewhat—I'm clearly in the arms of an expert. He sweeps me into the rhythm.

Luckily, there's not much time for chat. Because we're

one of the last ones to be announced, the dance comes to an end quickly. I curtsey to his bow.

"It was a pleasure to meet you, Miss Kemi. You are every bit as remarkable as I hoped you would be."

I nod, smiling weakly, then I separate from him and move as quickly as I can to the edge of the room. I don't look to see if those tiger eyes follow me. The crowd is soon distracted by the announcement of Princess Evelyn, who is being escorted by her father. The king looks puffed with pride at having the beautiful Evelyn on his arm. That makes me worried. If her father is happy, that means Evelyn must have said something to reassure him about her lack of an engagement ring. I don't want her to do anything rash.

I scan the faces in the crowd for Zain. I spy him at the far side of the room and make a beeline, dodging party guests in their finery and waiters with teetering platters of sparkling wine and hors d'oeuvres.

"Zain!"

He smiles, pulling me into a big hug and kissing me on the cheek. "Sam, finally! Holy crap, you look gorgeous. I didn't recognize you at first."

I throw a punch at his arm and he winces gamely. "What the dragon's happened? I showed up to collect my escort card and it had some other girl's name on it! Turns out Prince Stefan had requested you as soon as your name appeared on the guest list!"

"Trust me, you weren't as shocked as I was when he turned up at my door!"

"Hmm, I suppose so. What do you think of this fancy shindig then?" he says, gesturing over the crowd. Now that everyone's been introduced, there's a lot of mingling going on. It's the first thing I notice about this kind of party. Even though people are talking to each other, they're always looking over each other's shoulders, waiting to see if someone more important and powerful passes by so they can try to talk to them. No one is just pleased to see each other.

I wrinkle my nose. "To be honest, I kind of hate it."

He leans in close. "I agree. Even though I'm used to it. Let's just show our faces for a bit and then we can sneak away."

"Sounds good. The sooner the better. But we have to talk to Evelyn first."

"We won't get close to her for ages—have you seen the size of the circle around her?"

"It's important."

"Okay, I'll make it happen. What's the urgency?" he says, raising one eyebrow at me.

I take a deep breath. "I need to talk to her about Prince Stefan."

His eyebrows knit together, casting a dark shadow over his eyes. "What happened?"

I look around. For some reason, people seem to have

moved closer to us, and I can't help but think that there are ears everywhere. "Not here," I say. "I'll tell you and Evelyn together."

He nods. "One circle of the room, one dance, then I can get us close to her." He places his hand on the small of my back, and a shiver runs up and down my spine. I let him lead me around one of the large columns, and he introduces me to one of his parents' friends, from another high-ranking synth corporation.

Now that we are finally together, I'm able to relax and take in my surroundings. The ballroom is enormous, with three diamond chandeliers hanging down the center line of the room, casting a delicate sparkling light over the equally glittering crowd. At the far end of the room, a tiered stage showcases a small orchestra playing traditional Pays music, and a touch of magic enables the music to be heard at the perfect volume no matter where you are standing. I wonder if magic also maintains and adapts the temperature in the room, because there are warm bodies everywhere, but I am as perfectly comfortable in my thin-strapped dress as the woman across from me is in her fur-lined bolero. I see plenty of men and women wearing one of Kirsty's glittered jewel bugs. I swear one woman has an entire skirt made out of the creatures, and as they move across the fabric their jewelled backs catch the light. It's both beautiful and incredibly creepy.

A waiter steps in front of me with a tray of drinks, and I gladly take one of the crystal glasses, filled with a beautiful pale gold liquid. I hold it to my nose and give it a sniff, delighting at the delicious green apple scent, then I smile up at Zain—though my happiness is quickly replaced with alarm.

He's offering me his arm. "A dance, my lady?"

I groan. "I thought I'd already got the dancing out of the way?"

"With the prince? Nah. Put it this way, if you dance with me, we can avoid talking to my dad—who is making a beeline for us as we speak."

I sneak a glance over my shoulder and I see that he's right—Zol is about three "hellos" away from us. If there's anyone I want to avoid at this party, it's him. I don't want to have to keep turning down his offer of a cure for my granddad.

There's nothing else for it. I put down my glass, reach out, and grab Zain's hand. "Take me for a twirl, then, fine sir," I say.

Zain grins widely and leads me out onto the dance-floor. He rests one hand on my waist, and holds my other hand out to the side. I place my fingers lightly on his shoulder. We wait for a few moments, and then we step in amongst the others.

Like Prince Stefan, it's obvious that Zain has done this before—not that he would have ever admitted that to anyone in high school. I don't seem to remember him twirling any girls around our high school gymnasium. I wonder what other secret skills Zain might have, that he's kept from me? Unlike with the prince, I feel comfortable in Zain's arms. My eyes roam the room.

"When did you learn to dance like this?" I ask him.

"I was Evie's practice dance partner when we were growing up. I think I was the only person who wouldn't laugh at her too much." My stomach clenches at this reminder of just how close they were growing up. But then I tell myself not to be so stupid. Like I didn't have male friends growing up too? Just look at Arjun—he might not have helped teach me to dance, but he did teach me to be good at algebra. In many ways, I think that might be *more* impressive.

The next face I catch sight of is Zol's, laughing with the king. Next to him is Zain's mother, the beautiful Zelda Aster.

If I marry Zain, I wonder if they'll make me change my name to Zamantha?

The thought makes me giggle, and Zain looks at me questioningly. I straighten my face.

I think about Zol's offer to join ZoroAster's prestigious Synth-Natural Potions Studies program. It seems like it's been designed especially with me in mind.

The trouble is, I can't quite bring myself to work for the enemy.

217

Poor Zol, I think. *No Zamantha, and no Zain in his program, if he gets any choice about it.*

Zain spins me elaborately, and all thoughts abandon me. I'm sure that my previously neat hair is now in disarray, but I don't care—I grin widely, wishing we could go faster and faster. Then I spot Prince Stefan staring at me from across the room. He's standing between two columns, his posture perfect. His eyes catch mine, and the corners of his lips curl upward. He winks at me, and involuntarily I squeeze Zain's hand tight.

"Ow!" he says.

"Oh, sorry . . . I got confused with one of the steps," I say, quickly pulling my gaze back to Zain.

A breeze tickles the back of my neck, and I realize that Zain has danced us across to the far side of the room. Here, a set of stunning glass doors, framed with (what else?) gold, is propped open to allow air to circulate in the room.

"This is our stop," says Zain. When the music ends, Zain bows to me and I respond with a half-curtsey. Then I take his arm, and we step outside, into the beautiful Laville night.

CHAPTER THIRTY

THE PRINCESS IS OUTSIDE TOO—AND ONE of her bodyguards steps forward to tell us to stay back, before realizing it's us and letting us pass.

She looks weary, her forehead lined with stress—the first time I think I've seen Evie look anything less than flawless. "I'm not sure this ball was a good idea, guys," she says to us.

"Are you okay?" I ask.

"Just tired. Really, really tired." Then her eyes flick up at me. "So did my ears deceive me, or did you come into the party with Stefan of Gergon?"

"So you *didn't* set it up."

"Nope."

"I thought maybe because of what I said about wanting to get into Gergon . . ."

"Even I'm not *that* fast. So how did it happen?"

"I kinda want to know that myself," Zain says. He

leans back against the stone railing of the balcony and raises his eyebrow at me.

"Basically . . . all he said was that he wanted to meet me. Someone who brought glory back to the alchemists of Nova."

"Wow, smooth. Are you sure that's all he wanted from you?" Zain asks, his hands balling into fists.

I touch his shoulder. "Hey . . . I don't think it's *my* heart that he's after. He's still desperate to marry you." I nod to Evie.

"It would be a good political match . . . ," she says with a shrug.

I grimace. "And what about Katrina?"

Zain's eyes dart between me and Evie. "Wait, who's Katrina?"

Evie shoots me a warning look. "Not now."

I fold my arms across my chest, but then I relax. It's not my place to tell. "What I mean is, Prince Stefan agreed to let me into Gergon tomorrow. Give me two days to see if my idea will work before you do anything you can't undo."

A smile tugs at the corners of Evie's mouth. "Okay, forty-eight hours are yours. No rings on my finger until then." The smile disappears. "It just won't be too long before the severity of my situation becomes public. Today in the suite was too close for comfort. Renel spent ages making sure none of the stylists would leak the news."

"What happened in the suite?" Zain asks.

I shrug. "It was nothing . . ."

"It wasn't nothing," snaps Evelyn. "I could have killed you." A deep, hacking cough almost bends her over double.

We rush forward, supporting her with one arm each. "Are you all right?" I say.

She waves us off. "I'm fine, I'm fine. Temporary blip. Oh dragons, I need a drink."

"Take mine," Zain says, passing her his glass of champagne. She downs it in an instant.

When she's finished, she looks revived. I'm always amazed at how Evelyn can pull together her poise. I'd need to go straight back to bed. "Speak of the devil, look who's next on my dance card. Prince Stefan. I guess I'd better get back to it. Zain, is this . . ."

Zain puts his finger to his lips to stop Evelyn and she nods, knowingly. I stare between them. "What's going on?"

"Ah. I'll leave you two lovebirds to it. Have fun, Sam," she says, before blowing a kiss my way and signalling to her bodyguards that she is ready to reenter the party. I'm sad when I notice Katrina isn't one of them this time.

"Follow me." Zain turns to me, smiles, and I have to take a moment. The light from the party shines against his tanned skin, emphasising his chiseled cheekbones. I return the smile. Prince Stefan might be handsome, but he can't hold a candle to Zain.

"Come on, this can't wait," he says.

"Just so you know, this running away stuff isn't that easy in these . . ." I gesture to my heels.

"We don't have far to go."

"No, wait one second . . ." I pull out the emergency pair of flats I'd stashed in my bag and slip them on.

When I finally look up, the view from the balcony is almost enough to stop me in my tracks again. The garden is spectacular. It stretches out in front of the stone steps, a series of water fountains drawing the eye down the length of it. These aren't ordinary fountains; the water hops in perfect curves between small pools, arcing over the guests strolling in the garden, all in perfect synchronicity with the music emanating from the ballroom. The sun is setting, tinting the sky different shades of blush pink and purple. It's all kinds of stunning, a view I thought I'd only ever get to dream about, and I just want Zain to wrap his arms around me and keep me in this moment.

"This place is breathtaking," I say, lagging back despite Zain's insistent tugging on my arm.

Zain doesn't even turn his head to look. "If we don't get a move on then we're going to miss it."

"Miss what? Okay, okay," I say, reluctantly turning away from the view. We hurry down the stone staircase that connects the balcony to the garden.

We leave the palace grounds via a small gap in the

otherwise impenetrable thick green hedges. Then, we're out onto the city streets. I feel like an actress in an old black-and-white movie, one where the characters only speak to each other in sweeping statements full of melodrama. In what other world would I be running through the streets of Laville, in the most expensive dress I've ever owned, following behind a handsome young man in a tuxedo? It doesn't feel real.

A deep voice sounds from behind us. "Halt! Stop there."

Zain and I stop in our tracks. One of the palace security guards jogs toward us, his heavy form lumbering across the cobbles. My first thought is that they should keep their security team in better shape. My second thought is: *Oh crap, we're in trouble.*

"Yes, sir?" asks Zain. He subtly steps in front of me, putting himself between me and the guard. I take a small step to one side and stand next to him again. Whatever it is, we're going to face it together.

"Are you planning on coming back to the party?"

"Yes, of course," says Zain.

"There's a strict no reentry policy. If you return with me now, I can get you back in."

Zain bites his lower lip. "Please, sir—we'll only be a few minutes. We'll come straight back."

The guard looks back over his shoulder at his partner, who's just visible in the dark shadow of the hedge. "Find me when you're ready. I'll help you get in." His change of heart takes us aback, but we don't question it.

"Thank you, sir—we'll be quick," Zain says.

He nods, and Zain grabs my hand. Excitement vibrates through his grip, and it transfers to me as if by osmosis. I want to know what's making him so pumped.

It's not long until we join a crowd, all heading in the same direction. My heart lifts. Maybe we're going to see the famous *L'arbre des lumières*—the Tree of Lights—the one place in Laville that has been at the very top of my bucket list. It's situated in a tiny part of Wild territory that has been preserved within the city's confines. But Zain is pulling me *through* the crowd, parallel to it, not joining it. We escape through the other side and I can't help the small frown that appears between my eyes. What can be more spectacular than the palace gardens, or the Tree of Lights?

"We're almost there," says Zain, and I'm glad that the sky has darkened so he can't see the look of disappointment on my face. He slows as we approach a bridge over the inky black waters of the River Calor. He pulls his phone out of his jacket pocket and looks at the time. "Oh good, I think we've just about made it."

We walk hand-in-hand until we reach the center of the bridge. Zain stops and leans on the gold-painted railing, staring down at the slow-moving water below. A stout, wide boat glides beneath us, the glass roof revealing couples eating by candlelight inside. It's the definition of romantic.

"Over there," Zain points.

Looking out over the river, I can see that there is a vast expanse of darkness on the shore, where all light has been extinguished. It's only visible now that we're in the very center of the bridge—otherwise, it's obscured by buildings. I can just about make out the silhouette of a tree, and I gasp. The tree is huge, its tallest branches disappearing into the night sky.

"Is that what I think it is?" I ask, breathless.

Zain nods. "The Tree of Lights. It's not the side that most people see it from, as you can tell by the lack of crowds. But I think this is so much better. Plus, we get it all to ourselves."

A familiar shiver runs up my spine, which Zain mistakes for a chill. He shrugs his jacket off his shoulders and wraps it around mine. He whispers in my ear, "Now, look up."

I do as he says—so far, he hasn't led me wrong. I look up and there's not much to see at first: the sky is dark, but there are no stars—the light pollution is too strong for that.

I'm about to look away, when it happens. A shooting star. Except—it can't be a shooting star, it's way too close for that. But it was a bright point of light, moving faster than my eye could catch it, leaving just a streak of golden glitter in the air. There's no sound, but I swear the hairs on the top of my head move ever so slightly in its wake.

"What *was* that?" I ask Zain.

He doesn't answer, just squeezes my shoulders.

Another, and then another light shoots overhead, until suddenly there are too many to count. They're all heading toward the Tree of Light.

The first light settles in the upper branches of the tree, and then it is joined by a swarm of others. They sparkle on the tree so that it looks on fire, the lights winking in and out.

In another breath, they change color, switching from brilliant white to a piercing red in perfect synchronization. But from our angle, I can see other things happening too. The crowd of lights above my head streaming toward the tree becomes thinner, so I can make out the individuals. They're fairybugs, magical creatures with incredible powers.

Fairybugs—drawn to sadness, or to those who are about to receive bad news, sometimes seen in the delusions of those who drink too much psychedelic liquid or who are under the influence of drugs. Said to be brilliant muses for creativity, if they can be caught. The bright lights that they carry, sometimes confused for will-o-the-wisps, can illuminate any dark places, if given freely as a gift. The dust trails they leave behind can also cause levitation, if acquired in enough quantities.

The fairybugs are making the utmost effort to create a dazzling light show. From this angle, I can see that every now and then, one of the fairybugs will exhaust itself, falling from its place on the tree, and another will come and take its place so that not a beat is missed from the display. The tired bug is collected by some of its friends, who carry it back, over our heads, to wherever it is that they've come from.

I turn to Zain. "Do you know that they think that this happens in other places in the Wilds? Just not on a regular basis. Can you imagine coming across something like this in the Wilds, without expecting it? That's why I'm so desperate to keep exploring. The Wilde Hunt just opened my eyes to all the wonders—and now I think I'm addicted."

"Sam, the great explorer," Zain says with a smile.

I grin back.

I've seen pictures of this phenomenon. I've even seen a docucast, which tried to bring it to life as vividly as possible. And yet, no medium can compare to seeing it with my own eyes.

Just as quickly as it begins, it's over. The tree turns dark again. I can imagine everyone on the other side of the tree starting to walk away, back to their homes or hotels, but Zain and I stay put. We watch the now-extinguished fairybugs fly overhead, swarming through the night sky, lit only by the dim glow of the streetlights.

"Thank you for bringing me here," I tell Zain. "How did you know about this place?"

"A lot of people know about it, but they want to see the main spectacle. They don't want to see behind-the-scenes, the hard work of the fairybugs. But for some reason, I thought you would feel the same way as me. Seeing how hard it is for them . . . I know you appreciate that the best things don't come easily."

"I do appreciate that. This is . . . this is beyond wonderful, Zain. I have no words."

If I lived in Laville, I would be out here, on this bridge, every night. How do people resist it? But then I think about all the wonderful sights in Kingstown, sights that people travel from all around the world to see. The mermaid gathering practically on our doorstep. The prancing kelpies in High Park. Do I really appreciate what's in my own backyard? I don't think that I do. We become immune to the wonders on our doorstep.

Some people even complain that the Tree of Light is too much of a distraction in the center of town. That magic performs strangely on the streets around it, so it's not always a safe place for Talenteds. They complain that's why they can't wear glamoured clothing, because if the stability of the magic drops for a moment, all the glamour could unravel, leaving them ordinary and boring at best, and naked at worst. I think it serves them right for wearing totally glamoured clothes in the first place.

"Wow, it's great that we can get into Gergon tomorrow," Zain says, when the last of the fairybugs has disappeared overhead.

"I know. I hope the princess sticks to her word. And I hope forty-eight hours is enough time."

"Yeah, it feels like a long shot. And besides, a marriage to Prince Stefan could be a good thing for her."

I pull back from him slightly. "What? I can't believe you're saying that. Evelyn doesn't *love* Prince Stefan."

"I know that . . ." He taps the railings with his fingers, deep in thought. "You haven't known the princess as long as I have, but she's known about this requirement her whole life. She's prepared for it. And yes, okay, she went to great lengths to avoid it, but it's kind of part and parcel of the whole "being-a-royal" thing. She's always known it was the price of her power. She's *lucky* to have you to help her stave off the decision with your stabilizing potion. I don't think she really recognizes how lucky."

"You're helping. She has you too," I mumble.

"She had me her whole life—I couldn't figure out a way to help her! No, *you* did that. She doesn't give you nearly enough credit. You can't help her forever. Eventually she knew she'd have to face up to this. That's not your fault."

"It is my fault. If it wasn't for Granddad, for Emilia . . ."

He shakes his head slowly. "You ask too much of yourself, Sam. You're the most amazing girl I've ever met.

Do you know that? But you can't always be saving the world."

Why not? I want to ask, but saying it out loud would make it sound stupid. I know I can't save the world. But I do want to do my best to help my friend.

He lifts his hands up to my face and draws me toward him, entangling his fingers into my hair. Our lips meet, and all the worries that have built up into tight knots between my shoulder blades melt away.

A kiss—if it could be bottled, it would be the most potent cure . . . for sadness, for worries, for tension, for despair, for anger . . . maybe that's the aqua vitae.

When we part, I look up into his eyes and smile.

"I love you, Sam Kemi," he says.

"I love you too, Zain Aster."

I turn away from him, afraid that if I keep looking at him I'm going to cry. I look down at the ground, breathing deeply, squeezing my eyes tightly shut. When I open them again, I jump back in shock. There's a fairybug fluttering in front of me.

And she's staring at me, her tiny hands on her hips, giving me the darkest glare I've ever seen.

CHAPTER THIRTY-ONE

SHE SPEAKS TO ME, BUT THE HIGH-PITCHED squeaks make little sense. I wish I knew what she was saying. It seems to be urgent, and she spins a frustrated circle. Eventually, she rolls her eyes at me. Then she turns, removes a small light that is attached to her waist, and hands it to me. She gestures impatiently for me to put it in my bag. I do as she says. Then she puts her finger to her lips.

That much I understand. She flies away, as quickly as she appeared.

A feeling of dread creeps over me, and I pull Zain's tuxedo jacket tighter around my shoulders.

Zain hasn't noticed a thing, distracted by the sight of a narrow boat floating underneath the bridge.

"Let's go back to the party," I say. I tug at his shirt sleeve.

Then my phone rings and I jump.

"What is it?" Zain looks alarmed at my reaction.

I fish my phone out of my bag, and swallow hard as I see the name on the screen. *Mum.* She knows I'm at the ball (or supposed to be). She wouldn't be calling unless it was absolutely necessary. *Fairybugs appear to those about to receive bad news.* I already feel my eyes prick with tears.

"Hey, are you going to answer that?" Zain asks softly.

I flip the phone open and try to keep my voice normal. It could be nothing. "Hi, Mum!" I say, as brightly as I can.

"Hi, Sam." Her tone confirms it. Bad news. The phone trembles against my ear. "I wouldn't call but . . . it's Granddad. He slipped into unconsciousness last night. We're not sure if he's going to recover."

Now the tears fall freely down my face. Zain grips my free hand tightly. "Oh, Mum, should I come home?"

"I think it would be best. I hope the princess doesn't think you're being rude . . ."

"She'll understand, I promise."

Zain squeezes my hand again, and I look up into his eyes. They're glassy too, as if he's attempting to hold back tears. But looking at him jogs another memory. "ZA," I say.

"What was that honey?"

"ZA, ZoroAster . . . they said they have a new medication that's just been approved that can help Granddad's symptoms."

"I don't know. He has the no-synth rule in place."

"The no-synth rule is for when there is a viable natural potions alternative. There isn't in this case."

Zain nods at me. It might just work. "My dad can get someone out there straightaway," he whispers.

"We can get Granddad the medication ASAP," I relay to Mum down the line. "At least mention it to his doctors. If we can do anything to help him . . . we should do it, right?" I'm speaking so quickly, I don't know if I'm making any sense.

"I promise I'll talk to the doctor about it," Mum says. Her voice has brightened a tiny bit, I'm sure of it. "We'll see you soon."

"I'll be there as soon as I can."

I hang up the phone.

Zain grabs my arm. "Come on, let's get back to the party. I can tell my dad to get ZA on the case and then we can arrange your transport back home."

I slide my arm around Zain's waist and pull him tight. He puts his arm over my shoulders, and wrapped up in each other, we speed-walk back toward the palace—and the party. We find the security guard, who helps us slip back in.

It's almost like we never left. Everyone is in a merry mood, laughing a little bit louder, their faces a little bit redder, eyes sparkling a little bit brighter. It seems like the ball is a great success.

"Come on, I see him," Zain says. Zol is never hard

ALWARD

to find, his imposing figure always surrounded by hangers-on.

The expression on Zol's face moves from welcome surprise to concern. "Everything all right?"

"Oh my, is this the lovely Samantha?" Zain's mum spins around on her heels, a wide smile on her face. It freezes in place when she registers my appearance. "Oh dear." Her hand flies to her mouth.

"Mum, Dad, Sam needs your help. Her grandfather has taken a turn for the worse and . . ."

"Say no more!" Zol says. "I'll have the medication out to the hospital this evening."

"Thank you," I stammer. It's not exactly how I pictured my first meeting with both parents, but I can't worry about what kind of impression I'm leaving. All I can think about is my granddad. "Now, I have to get home—"

Before I can continue, a waiter presses a glass into my hand, along with a little spoon. Then the entrance trumpets sound again, bright and cheerful, stopping me in my tracks. There's no chance of me slipping out now.

An old man in full military dress stands at the front of the room, his hands outstretched. At his side is a tall, slender woman, at least three decades his junior. It's the Pays president and his wife. She used to be a famous Pays actress—I've seen her in a few films from the time when Anita and I thought it made us uber cool to only watch movies in translation. It did expand our world view, but also taught us that bad movies can be made in *any* language. I want nothing more than to leave, but to do so now would just be to draw more attention to myself. I'm already getting evil glares just for breathing so loudly.

"Ladies and gentleman," says the president in a lightly accented voice. "Welcome to the Laville Ball!"

I can't stop fidgeting with the urge to get away. I put down my glass and clap, but the sound of my hands is out of place as everyone else tinkles a spoon against the edge of their glass, creating a delicate noise throughout the room. Much more refined. Yet another *faux pas* of mine.

"The Laville Ball has been a Pays tradition for centuries, and has always hosted many wonderful celebrations. Tonight is no exception. But not only are we here to celebrate the wonderful Princess Evelyn of Nova's life and health, but also . . . her happiness. And it is with great pleasure that I present to you, Princess Evelyn!"

There's more glass tinkling as Evelyn steps up to the stage and takes her place next to the president. She looks utterly radiant in her crimson-and-orange ombre gown that's glamoured to imitate the colors of a sunset. He gives her three kisses on alternating cheeks, before finally letting her have the floor.

"Thank you, President Lafleur," she says—first in perfect Paysan and then in Novaen. "It is a particularly special feeling to be here tonight, especially as it could easily have been a different story. So many of the people who have supported me throughout my life are here. And all of you will know I have never been one to let fate dictate what happens to me . . ." The room laughs along with Evelyn, but I feel a tightness in my chest that I can't get rid of. "And so tonight is a celebration of health and happiness. I want to clink my glass to the health and happiness of all here tonight—and to all our citizens across the globe."

The chime of glasses is so loud I'm surprised none of them shatters. Once the crowd settles down, Evelyn speaks again. "And now, how about some cake!"

On cue, an enormous gateau is wheeled out into the center of the ballroom. It's the most extravagant cake I've ever seen: a seven-tier, white-iced extravagance adorned with a thousand iced fairybugs that shine and flash with their own edible lights. It's a homage to the Tree of Lights, in patisserie form.

There's a snap as all the lights in the room go out simultaneously.

My breath hitches inside my chest, but I know this is just part of the spectacle.

But then there's a loud, piercing scream. The room lights up, but not with fake fairylights. Instead, there are blindingly bright flashes from explosions that shake the room with their force, the room filling with smoke that stings my eyes. Everyone shoves toward the exits, and I hear the tinkle of glass again—but this time, the guests aren't tapping their glasses, they're dropping them.

In the intermittent flashes, I see Evelyn's security storm the stage, grabbing her and carrying her away from the action. There are spells going off everywhere, trying to clear the smoke or get the lights back on—but whatever magic has been set off to cause this commotion is resisting any interference.

My eyes are streaming, each breath searing my lungs—this isn't magic at all, this is just plain old tear gas. Simple, but effective.

Someone yanks at my arm, so hard it feels like they're going to tug it out of its socket. At first I think it must be Zain, or one of the security team.

But then as a wad of cloth is stuffed into my mouth, I know that this isn't a friend. I struggle, throwing my arms out as wide as possible, and I drop down onto my knees. I cry out in pain, my voice muffled by the cloth, as my knees scrape against the broken glass on the floor.

"SAM!" I hear Zain cry my name.

I can't cry out through the gag. I can't respond. I taste the metallic tang of blood in my mouth as I cough my throat sore, trying to expel the gag and the smoke and the fear.

My attacker doesn't stop, wrestling my arms behind my back and binding them tight. I'm powerless to stop them, as they drag me from the room.

CHAPTER THIRTY-TWO

LEFT.

Right.

Right.

Down some stairs.

I try to keep track of where I'm being taken, but it's futile. I never thought I'd *want* to be knocked out, but being dragged—fully conscious but bound—through the dark, twisting passages beneath the palace is painful, disorienting, and terrifying.

Zain's voice screaming my name echoes in my ear, accompanied by the high-pitched ringing of tinnitus caused by the explosions. I wonder if my ear drums have burst. I'm in such pain throughout my body, I can't seem to isolate what's actually injured.

Just as we left the room, the security team hit the person pulling me away: I could feel the pressure lessen on the rope securing me, felt the ground shudder as they fell. I scrambled to escape. But someone else took up the cause, pulling at me even harder until it felt like my arms were going to be yanked from their sockets. They dragged me backward through a small hole they'd blasted in the palace walls. They folded me over like a pretzel, forcing me into an unnatural pose: backward, hunched-over, moving in an awkward half-run, half-crawl.

That's when I started to keep track of our direction. If there's any opportunity to escape, any chance to run, I have to be able to remember how to get back.

We run—or rather, they drag me—through a labyrinth. My eyes dart around, taking in the moss-covered, crumbling stone and the ancient-looking metal hooks that would have held torches before there was electricity. I keep waiting, praying that I will see Zain, or Katrina, or any of the other stern-looking security guards appearing in front of me, chasing my attacker down. But the noises from the party seem to be growing dimmer—I can't hear the cries of the crowd, muffled or not. Maybe they've all fled or fainted from the gas. Maybe others are being dragged down tunnels, similar to me. Or maybe they've forgotten all about me . . .

I twist in my captor's grip, attempting to see the face of the person who has taken me. All I can see is the black, ribbed fabric of the balaclava over his face. It is definitely a man though, judging by the bulk of his biceps and the rough, hairy skin on his arms. There's something eerily familiar about him, but I can't put my finger on it.

Straining my neck, I can just about see a couple of other figures scampering through the tunnels like rats ahead of us. They seem to know the palace tunnels well—they don't hesitate over which turns to take. Eventually it seems like we leave the palace grounds, because the tunnels take on an altogether more sinister appearance. I swear I see the flash of a skull embedded in the walls, and what I think is brick turns out to be bone. The catacombs. I've heard of these. They lie beneath the city of Laville, a whole generation of the dead forgotten, yet propping up the buildings. A ghoulish foundation.

The tunnels widen so that my captor stands upright, and that's when they blindfold me. The coarse fabric over my eyes blocks out every pinpoint of light. Without warning he wraps his arms roughly around my waist. I instinctively curl up into a ball like a hedgehog, compressing my middle around his forearms. I kick out with my legs, trying to make some kind of contact, but he ignores me, lifting me up and tossing me unceremoniously into a small box or a crate.

I find out the hard way just *how* small—I kick my feet out and they hit solid wood. The force of it pushes my head up and it cracks against the top of the box. My wish to be knocked out is almost granted.

Now is when the panic really settles in. I've never been good in tight spaces, but this is claustrophobia times a million. Lying on my back, the gag presses deeper into my mouth, choking my air supply. The blindfold is still firmly attached but since my head rings with pain, starry bursts explode in front of my eyelids.

The box lurches along with my stomach, and the ringing in my ears clears enough for me to hear water lapping up against a hard surface. Rock, maybe. Stone. Bone.

I'm in a boat.

To distract myself from the fear that is threatening to engulf me, I force myself to remember what I know about the geography of Laville. There's the River Calor, which snakes through the city center. But it doesn't pass through the palace—or even near it—that I know of. This must be an offshoot, a tributary. An underground river that doesn't show up on any maps.

The reminder of being underground freaks me out even more.

I can't breathe.

I can't see.

I don't know if my captors want me alive or dead, but if they don't let me breathe without a gag then they won't have much choice in the matter.

Strangely, there's only one face that rises to the front of my mind, as my heart races and my breaths become increasingly shallow.

Molly.

Who's going to be a big sister to her?

My eyes roll back inside my head.

The thrashing of my limbs slows until I'm still, no energy in my muscles left for a fight. I can't get enough air to move.

I hear a distant grunt, feel rough fingers on my cheek. Someone pulls the gag out and I roll onto my side and cough until my lungs feel like they're about to fall out.

Melling bee honey and hot Lethe water—for extreme bouts of coughing. What's the likelihood of them having a potion on board? A weird, twisted urge to laugh comes over me, but it disintegrates into another hacking fit.

When I'm done, I open my mouth and scream.

Nobody stops me.

And, if they're letting me scream, that must mean they think that no one can hear me. That I'm alone.

They let me scream until my voice is raw. They wait for my brain to catch up and realize that the screaming is futile. Which it does, eventually.

"Search her," I hear a gruff male voice say.

I'm pulled up to a seated position and I gasp down the fresh air—grateful that I don't have to bear the fug of fumes from the boat's engine anymore.

My bag is roughly pulled up and over my head and someone empties it out on the floor. I hear the thud and crack of my phone, the flutter of the party invitation, the tube of lip gloss, my party heels. That all seems incredibly frivolous right now. Lastly, they unzip the lining of my bag and my stomach lurches. Someone shakes the bag to get it out, and I hear the last thing drop.

It brings tears to my eyes to hear it. The slap of the leathery skin on the wooden boards.

My potion diary.

You shouldn't have brought it, Sam, you idiot, I think to myself.

I whimper when I hear another sickening sound—something being lobbed overboard. My things. Several splashes in the water. "Please," I say, tears now streaming down my cheeks. I picture my diary, sinking in the river. The leather chain unravelling, the pages spreading like wings, the ink blurring . . . until it settles at the bottom, never to be seen again. My life's work is going to drown. A resting place shared with old bones. "What do you want from me?" I hate how pleading my voice sounds.

A voice speaks so quietly, I can barely make out the words. "No, not that," the person says. "Give that to me."

Someone takes a few steps toward me and the boat tilts. My shoulders tense.

Something drops in my lap. It's my bag. But it feels weighted down by something inside. I fumble with the clasp, my fingers clumsy with desperation.

When my fingers touch leather, I can't contain my relief. My diary is there. And it's intact.

"No alchemist should be without their diary, now, should they?" the voice says.

I'm so overcome with happiness that my eyes are shut when my blindfold is yanked down. When I open them, I blink furiously. It's still dark, and it takes me some time to clear the starry bursts from my vision. But when they disappear, I finally recognize my captor. It's the security guard from earlier. The one who helped Zain and I return to the party.

I don't understand. Why would he want to kidnap me?

And then his eye starts to sag. My first instinct is to feel concern for him—it looks serious—but as the rest of his face follows suit, sliding down his neck like melting wax, I'm not worried for him anymore. I'm terrified for me.

Because the figure who emerges from beneath the wax is the one person I least wanted to see.

Emilia Thoth.

CHAPTER THIRTY-THREE

"SAMANTHA KEMI." EACH WORD SOUNDS like it's being dragged out of her mouth over hot coals, raspy and thick.

My first thought is how *monstrous* she looks. Even though I saw her not long ago in the Zambi Wilds, at the end of the Wilde Hunt, it looks as if she's aged fifty years. The black veins visible beneath her skin seem even blacker, her fingernails curved and sharp like claws. The golden luster of her hair, which once resembled Princess Evelyn's, is now a dirty white.

Changeling potion.

I dry heave onto the wooden boards as I realize that *Zain and I* must have been the ones to let her into the party. The other guards had seen us leave—they wouldn't have questioned our returning with a guard as an escort. It had been Emilia all along.

I shudder.

The boat is one of those long houseboats unique to Laville. While most of them are brightly painted, in the dim light this one looks neglected: The paint is peeling and patchy, the shiny lacquer dulled with age. We're out in the open now, but I can't see much to indicate our location through the darkness. There aren't many lights on the riverbanks, so we must be far out of the city.

"You must be starving. I know they barely feed you anything at those royal parties." Emilia snaps her fingers at someone inside, a loud click that makes me wince. A man emerges from the cabin, strides over to me, and pulls me up roughly by the arm, out of the box. When I reluctantly stumble to standing, he pushes me forward. With my arms still tied behind my back, the muscles in my shoulders ache like crazy.

"Come on, Ivan," Emilia says to the man. She strides ahead of us, her small frame engulfed by the security guard's oversized clothing. The man grabs my head and forces it down to avoid the doorframe. The door is shut behind me, and Ivan pushes me onto a low bench. I grimace as I jam my wrists against the back wall, not able to get them out of the way in time. He leans over and, with a couple of slashes of his knife, cuts away the ties around my hands. I shake them out, trying to bring back blood to my hands and feeling to my fingers. There are angry, deep red grooves where the rope has bitten into my wrists.

Emilia disappears behind another door, so I focus on my second captor. Ivan is a big abominable of a man with a bald head, pale as milk, and engorged muscles that bulge out of his black T-shirt. It's as if he's been plucked from a design-a-muscle-man book. Dutifully following Emilia's instructions, he stands over a small stove and ladles a big spoonful of beige, lumpy gruel into a bowl. He thumps it down on the table and slides it across to me.

I stare at it, still holding my sore wrists, and even though my tummy is rumbling like crazy, I'm not hungry. Up close, I can see the gruel is made up of mashed-up beans. Plenty of bean varieties have magical properties. Who knows what Emilia might have concocted for me?

Jack's beans—known for gigantism and contain the power of growth. There is one variety rumored to be able to age you in an instant—a cruel punishment sometimes used in the middle ages.

"Eat." Emilia reappears at the door. Her voice is softer than before, her throat recovered from the extreme body morph. She's swathed in a long black dress and a cowl-like hood, also black. Instinctively I push backward on the bench, trying to create as much space as possible between her and me.

"Still so afraid, Samantha Kemi?" She leans forward so that her face enters the circle of light from the oil burner hanging on the ceiling. I'm shocked at the depth of the wrinkles that crisscross her face. Maybe she has been eating too many beans. "They're not poison," she says. "Just food. Plain, ordinary food. Surely even you can tell that."

My eyes flick down to the bowl of beans again. They do look normal. I still don't want to eat them.

"Suit yourself, but it's going to be the only sustenance you have for a while." Her voice trails off.

My eyes dart around the boat's cabin, trying to search for something—anything—that will convince me that I haven't just been trapped and kidnapped by Emilia Thoth.

Unfortunately, her presence is kind of a good reminder.

"Why have you taken me? Why not just . . . kill me?" I finally manage to choke out.

"Kill you? My, my, Sam, you don't understand me at all. I have no desire for your blood—unless it's useful for a potion, of course." She chuckles, but I don't find it funny. "I merely have a favor to ask you."

I narrow my eyes.

"It has come to my attention that once again we share the same goal. We both would like to find your great-grandmother's missing potion diary. Isn't that right? Isn't that why you've been jetting off here, there, and everywhere?"

I bite down on my tongue. I'm not going to dignify her questions with an answer.

"Yes, well." Emilia drums her nails on the table,

which sets my already fragile nerves on edge. "My initial attempts to find it have also proved fruitless."

"You mean by *poisoning* my granddad!" I spit out.

"Ah, so you figured that out, did you? Clever girl. Alas, your grandfather's memories are incomplete and he is a stubborn man. He doesn't appreciate my intrusion. But you are of his blood. Maybe there are things his memories will reveal to you that I cannot see. The sooner we find the journal, the sooner you can save your grandfather's life."

"You mean the sooner you get to take Nova's throne."

She laughs, and the sound is like tires over gravel. "You think I am the real danger? Look at me. I cannot be Queen looking like this. I am a pawn. Well, perhaps more of a knight. But that doesn't change the game. I need that journal but it's not for me."

For a moment, I wonder what it must be like to be so deformed by potions you can't interact with society. She looks upset. But wait a second—am I *pitying* Emilia Thoth? She didn't have to choose that path.

And as I think of another hole in her story, all the hatred returns in full force. "I don't believe you. You want the aqua vitae to give yourself some kind of sick makeover!"

She shakes her head. "You misunderstand, but you will see in time."

I lift the bowl of beans to my lips, then in a fit of rage,

I throw it at her head. She dodges it smoothly, the bowl shattering against the far wall, gross bean paste dripping off the surface.

Ivan is on me in a second, pinning my arms back and tying them again with the rope. I struggle, wriggling against the bench, but he is so much stronger.

"My family isn't just going to forget about me. The princess will send her people to look for me!"

Emilia's dry, cracked lips spread into a grin and then she gets up slowly from the table, her limbs protesting against every movement. But I can see the strength in her eyes.

"I hope my employers do come, because then you will truly know what is at stake," she says, leaning on the table so her face is terrifyingly close to mine. "And unless you help me get what they want, I'll make sure you won't remember your family at all."

same picture that's been photo-altered from when she was there a couple of days ago? False leads are NOT HELPFUL. Latest police reports think she's still somewhere in Pays—since that's where Zain is, probably worth assuming he's following up on the most relevant leads. Her family have been advised to stay in Kingstown in case she returns there. They'll be making a public plea for her safety tonight at 6 p.m.

MOD NOTE Since this thread is moving so quickly, please check your lead hasn't been disproved already before posting. Anyone blatantly posting misleading and false information will be banned from the forum permanently. A girl's life is at stake here.

Ushuanado says: I know the news is all about Samantha Kemi right now, but did anyone see the reports that a ZA van showed up at Kingstown General Hospital yesterday, allegedly to treat Ostanes Kemi? Surely that is HUGE.

www.WildeHuntTheories.com/forums/
PRINCESSEVELYN

CHAPTER THIRTY-FOUR

www.WildeHuntTheories.com/forums/
THEKEMIFAMILY

[MOST RECENT POSTS]

OrdinaryLover3000 says: NEWSFLASH: EXPLO-
SION AT THE LAVILLE BALL, one dead, twenty-six
badly injured. SAMANTHA KEMI and one security
guard reported missing. My question is: where is
Samantha Kemi?!

154 replies

Castillione says: NO. She's definitely *not* in
Runustan—can we please stop sharing that

[MOST RECENT POSTS]

RoyalRuiner says: Has anyone considered the possibility that the explosions at the Laville Ball were caused by the princess's out-of-control power? She hasn't been seen in public since the explosion. We all predicted something like this was going to happen. Just lucky it happened in Pays and not Nova, right?! It's about time our government cracked down on this. DON'T LET THE PRINCESS BACK INTO NOVA.

CHAPTER THIRTY-FIVE

THEY LEAVE ME IN THE CABIN, ALONE. A tiny part of me registers that it's nice not to be crammed into a tiny box at the back of the boat, bound, blindfolded, and gagged. But the rest of me is a numb, empty shell. I want to curl up into a ball and hide away from reality.

I don't think I've moved an inch when they come back for me. I'm taken from the boat to the back of a pickup truck. We barrel down an empty gravel road, deeper and deeper into unknown territory.

At least they didn't make me sit within touching distance of Emilia. I might've tried to bite her. Do I have anything to lose?

Will Emilia ever let me see my family again? Even I'm not so stupid as to believe that she'll just let me go, whether she has the power to alter my memories or not.

She wants you for a reason, I tell myself. But even that isn't a comfort. Because whatever she wants me for, I'm not going to give Emilia the satisfaction of getting it.

Just accept it. You're a dead woman. And now I can't help the tears that prick up behind my eyes. I think back to only an hour before the kidnapping. Was I really staring at the Tree of Light with Zain, thinking about how beautiful and precious the world was?

Did Stefan, the handsome prince, who seemed so charming, if a little predatory—did he know about what was to come for me?

I think of Zain. How one day might never come, and we might never get to go on that proper date. I think of Granddad—unconscious, in hospital. I might not even get the chance to say good-bye. And I think about my family—I've given them yet another thing to worry about, just when it didn't feel like things could get any worse. I've messed everything up.

It's all too much for my brain. The darkness, combined with the steady motion of the truck and the ache in my bones, sends me into an uneasy sleep.

I have no idea how much time has passed when I wake—I only know that we have finally stopped. The sharp sound of slamming car doors takes me from drowsy to wide awake. They're coming for me.

Ivan jumps up to the back of the truck. He throws a blanket over me, bundling me up like I'm a baby.

There's a wall of trees in front of us, huge great

evergreens that leave a carpet of brown needles on the ground. Behind me is rolling green countryside, dotted here and there with the odd farmhouse and barn. I know that we're going to head deeper into those dark, foreboding woods—a twisting road seems to disappear inside it. I feel like I'm about to enter into a fairytale land, but not a nice one with happy endings. One of the terrifying ones, that end up with a young girl's bones being crunched by ogres.

I don't recognize it from pictures, but I know we must be in Gergon. Not because of the scenery—it could also belong to nearby Prussia or even certain northern parts of Nova (I should be so lucky). I know we're in Gergon because we're about to swap the pickup truck for a horse and wagon.

They taught us in history class that there are some parts of Gergon so anti-technology, they refuse to use anything powered by electricity. Some of us thought it was quaint, but secretly we couldn't imagine our lives without it. And now, here I am.

I'm loaded up onto the back of a wagon, where I sit down on a hay bale. Ivan chains me to the wagon—as if I'm going to do a runner into the woods.

Emilia goes ahead of us, in a black carriage, pulled by a pair of black horses.

The horses that are pulling our wagon are less elegant—more like farm horses drafted in for the role. I prefer them. They don't look like they're going to gallop while I'm chained in the back.

Ivan lumbers up into the front and grabs the reins of the horses. He looks back at the truck, a wistful look on his face. It's interesting to note that not everyone in Gergon is happy about the lack of motorized vehicles.

My chains give me enough slack to lie back on the hay bales, and my eyes threaten to drift closed again. I pinch myself to stay awake. Pretending it's all a dream is not going to help me.

I stare out into the maze of trees. There's something weird about them, and it takes a few moments of looking before I realize what's bothering me. An area of trees this big feels like it should be Wild land—a haven for magical creatures. If I came across this wood in any other place, I would fear dire-wolves stalking me between the trunks, or fierce brown bears in the clearings. But instead, there is something a bit too manicured about the area. The trees are planted in neat rows, paths carved through the forest in a way that shouts human interference. No, not *human* interference. Talented. This is not so much a forest as it is a garden, like the one at the palace in Laville. It's just that some parts of Gergon tastes run toward the sinister and dark, rather than the neat and pristine. So they've created a terrifyingly perfect dark wood.

I lose track of time, listening to the bumpy, monotonous rhythm of the cart, and the steady clip-clop of the horses' hooves on the stony ground. Despite the darkness of the forest, the sky overhead is perfectly blue—and totally not in keeping with the way I'm feeling at the moment. Storm clouds, flashes of lightning and pounding rain would be a better match. At least the rain might soothe my aching wrists. They're still burning like hell.

I need a salve to heal them—something for severe rope burn.

Juice from a prickly pear cactus, crushed and mixed with mermaid tears—perfect for curing burns.

Staring up at the sky reminds me of Anita. She and I used to waste away hours lying on the grass in High Park, trying to decide the perfect name for the color of the sky above us. Blue just didn't seem enough. Each season it seemed to change—from the pale, powdery blue of winter, to the murky and cloud-filled azure of spring to the piercingly bright lapis of summer and the rich, smoky cerulean of autumn. Anita always preferred the brightest blues, and for her sixteenth birthday I spent all winter in the lab trying to perfect a mix that would shine just as powerfully as the sky on a hot summer's day. It was worth it for the look of delight on her face when she saw the tiny vial of blue, which I had fixed to a gold necklace. Then, even on the grayest day, she had something to make her smile.

I sit up as soon as the tops of the trees disappear from view. The woods clear, and across the countryside I get my very first glimpse of where we're headed.

It takes my breath away.

It's a castle built into a vertical cliff face of a huge mountain, clinging to its side like a barnacle on a ship.

I count at least three round towers, with conical roofs which are a faded burnt orange—the only part of the castle that's not made of pale white stone. It contrasts against the dirty gray of the mountain, a white stain on the cliff. It looks like a place a dragon would guard.

I'm not wrong about that last bit. As we pass beneath the gates that lead up toward the castle, I spot a half-broken insignia of a dragon wearing a crown. The symbol of the Gergon royals.

I curl my legs up into my chest. Is this where Emilia has been hiding this entire time? Who is giving her access to a castle? *I am a pawn. Well, perhaps more of a knight.* That's what Emilia said. If that's the case, then are the king and queen of Gergon behind this? I wish I'd paid more attention in my world history class—then maybe I'd know.

I don't know the facts, but I do know some of the legends. There are many famous tales that have sprung from the darkest reaches of Gergon. Some of them are beautiful—tales of princesses living in elaborate castles, being rescued by handsome princes who slew dragons in their honor. As a child, my favorite Gergon tale had been of two children who were able to turn anything they touched into sugar. They lived in a house of candy and sweets.

I even had a picture book of the story at home, with the most amazing illustrations. The tale had another benefit too: It taught me to be nice, to play with others, to share—and not to eat too much candy.

Well, *that* version of the tale did anyway. In the public library near our house, I once found an old hardback collection of Gergon fairytales. It told the candy story as it had originally been written—in this version, the two siblings got greedy and started fighting each other. At the very end, the sister turned her brother into toffee and ate him. Nice.

The thought draws my eyes back up to the castle. I wonder whether a gruesome fate awaits me inside— whether I will become a character in one of those stories. The apprentice alchemist who became an ingredient in a new potion, maybe, my fingers and toes ground up in the name of mixing?

Goosebumps crawl up my arms, even though the air is warm. I'm really not helping myself.

I peer over the wooden slats that surround the cart. There's a small village at the base of the castle, though I can't see anyone about. It looks like one of those plastic villages I've seen in theme parks, depicting life as it might have been hundreds of years ago. I can see evidence of people—a small wheelbarrow full to the brim with apples, still rocking; the mewing of a cat outside a closed door, desperate to be let in; the twitch of a curtain. So there are people here.

I crane my neck to look inside the windows. It's

getting dark but there are no lights on—not even the flickering of a candle—and there's no telltale flicker of a television in sight either. *What do these people do for fun?* I wonder.

There are no telephone wires, no landlines, no cell signal. Unless they're sophisticated enough to have the technology running underground (which I strongly doubt), that means I have no way of getting a message out even if I do escape. How will I call for help? Messenger pigeon?!

I turn from the village to the castle itself, which looms ahead of us. It's hard to see where the castle ends and the mountain begins, as if the mountain itself is spewing out towers and conical roofs and turrets. I wonder who built it—who had the audacity to try to carve a home out of a cliff.

A grim thought crosses my mind. Once I'm inside that place, it will be even harder to escape. I tug on my chains, pulling until my wrists and ankles are sore. But they don't budge.

I fall back onto the hay. As we trundle through the main gate, I watch as its spikes pass above my head, and as the gate falls back down, missing the back of the cart by mere inches, my last hope falls with it.

CHAPTER THIRTY-SIX

"COME ON NOW, QUIT DAWDLING."

I could not hate Emilia any more right now. My legs are refusing to function properly, my left foot burning with pins and needles that flared up once the ankle chain was released. I hobble inside.

My first instinct is to look up. It might once have been an impressive entrance hall, but most of the decorations have been stripped from the walls—or maybe looted. High above me, I can see where a gold frame has been hacked off a painting, the dour face of an old man in a long cloak still visible on the canvas. He does *not* look happy about being vandalized. The only remaining sign of opulence in the entrance hall is a gold chandelier— too high up to be reached easily. Whoever used to live here must have had long poles to light it with. Curling up the chandelier's chains to the ceiling are two golden snakes, their eyes bright red jewels.

I frown. The intertwining snakes are an old alchemical symbol, representing the opposing forces alchemy attempts to balance: life and death, illness and health, ordinary and Talented. It also cautions us about the nature of our work—that the mixes we create can either help or harm.

This version of symbol gives me the creeps, the eyes glinting as we pass underneath. No wonder Emilia chose this place to settle. Its creepiness suits her right down to the ground.

"Take her upstairs, Ivan. She can rest while I get things set up."

"I'm not going to give you ANYTHING!" I try to shout the last word, but it just comes out like a rasp.

"Oh, and get the girl some water. I need her to be able to talk."

Ivan roughly shoves my shoulder until I reach a staircase. He thankfully leads me *up* not down. At least it means I'm not being thrown in a horrible dungeon.

We head up five flights of stairs, before he nudges me down a hallway with several closed doors. He opens the third door down, then gestures for me to go inside.

I obey, too tired to do anything else. There's a sink in the corner, and he fills up a clay jug that's beside it. He puts the jug in my hands and gestures for me to drink.

"Don't you ever say anything?" I ask him.

He moves to force the water down my throat.

"Okay, okay, I'll drink it!" It does feel good not to be parched. As soon as I'm done, he grabs the jug and takes it with him. Damn. There goes my plan to hit him over the head with it.

I hear the lock turn in the door. Now that I'm alone in my "new room," I check around for any potential exit routes, weapons, ingredients, anything I can use to help me get out of here or communicate with the outside world. But out of my tiny window is a completely sheer drop to the ground below, past several spiky-looking rocky outcrops that would be pretty painful to fall on. Besides, the window is too small for me to fit through even if I managed to make some kind of rope. This is bad.

The room is small—if I stretch my arms out I can reach the sides—and there is only a small single bed and the sink. It reminds me of the pictures Arjun sent to Anita of his university dorm room. Maybe this castle was once a university of sorts. Or a monastery: It's so bare.

There's not a single plug socket in any of the walls—or anything to charge a device even if I had my phone on me. I know I shouldn't be shocked—so far, I haven't seen a trace of electricity—but each time I realize there's not even the *capability* here, it scares me. I know it's sad, but my phone is my life.

I count my blessings. At least I have a bed and sheets for comfort, a sink to wash in, water to drink—and hopefully, I pray, there's a proper bathroom and I don't have to use a bedpan. There's a pair of plain cotton trousers and a t-shirt to change into on the bed, which is good because I'm still wearing my ball dress—not practical for any escaping I might need to do.

Once I've changed, I hug my bag like a lifeline. The bed creaks as I sit down on it, and dust rises, as if it hasn't been used in years. I carefully place the bag down and remove its sole contents: my potion diary. I can't really believe they let me keep it.

"What would Kirsty do?" I say out loud. I need to fill the silence.

She'd keep her eyes open at all times, I think. *She'd remember everything, in case it became useful.* I try to think back over my journey. There were piles of broken glass outside the castle walls, and a bonfire of rubble, still smouldering. If I didn't know better, I'd say someone was doing some building work. Then there was the mysterious pair of snakes I saw on the way in. If I can figure out where I am, maybe I can get a clue as to how to get out of here. Or, if I have the chance to send a message, then someone will be able to find me.

Next, I examine my bag. Can I use the straps in some way? They're not very long. Throw my diary at someone's head? It's quite heavy, but probably wouldn't do any lasting damage—except to piss them off.

Maybe there's a stray hairpin that I could use to pick a lock . . .

It's more wishful thinking, but I rummage through the bag anyway. The front pocket turns up nothing but lint. The main section is empty too, apart from a small hole in the lining.

I have no idea what silk lining could be used for, but I bet Kirsty would have some ideas.

Then my fingers grasp something else. I think I'm imagining it at first, as it's more of a jolt to my senses, like a static shock. But no, there is something between my fingertips. It feels like I'm holding a marble of air—firm but soft.

I remove the object from the bag, holding my breath. It glows in my palm, its brightness dazzling my eyes. It's the light the fairybug gave to me—the perfect gift I had already forgotten. I finally have time to examine it a bit more closely. It's a delicate light, about the size of a single crown, that glows gently in my palm. When I enclose my hands around it, it glows even brighter. When I take my hands away, it returns to a gentle shine.

This is the first glimmer of hope I've had since the party. I enclose the ball of light in my fist. It's small enough that I can tie it around my neck with one of the long strands that dangled from my ball dress. Maybe they won't notice if I tuck the light beneath my t-shirt.

Now that I've exhausted every escape option, I lay down on the bed, struggling to sleep. I have to admit: I'm pretty scared right now. My eyes feel like they're being held up by tiny needles, and as much as I want to close them and fall into oblivion, I can't.

This is nothing like the fear I felt during the Wilde Hunt. There's no adrenaline rush—this is sadness that's keeping me awake.

I know there's probably a hunt out there for me now. My parents must be searching. What about Zain? Evelyn? Unless others were taken too, to a different place than me. But why? I'm the one Emilia wants. I wonder if Evelyn has some kind of super monitoring system where she can find me. What if they think I'm already dead? Did Granddad get his medicine, or have they been distracted by me?

My thoughts keep jumping from place to place. But before I can think any more, the door is thrown open.

"Come with me," Ivan says, in rough Novaen.

CHAPTER THIRTY-SEVEN

I DON'T WANT TO FIND OUT WHAT IT IS Emilia wants with me. But I'm never going to escape if I don't get out of my tiny cell.

I follow Ivan out into the hallway, turning the opposite way to how we came up, and to my relief he doesn't blindfold me. We walk past a large window and I look outside to take note of my bearings. We must be in one of the circular towers, as the wall is curved. The vast forest we drove through spreads as far as the eye can see, broken here and there by small wisps of smoke that rise from hidden dwellings. Apart from the little village right at the base of the castle, there's no other town or village in view.

Ivan gives me a grunt that means I've been lingering too long.

"So, where are we going?" I ask, not expecting a response but tired of listening to nothing at all—even my own voice is better than silence. "Who are you, anyway? Are you, like, Emilia's lapdog or something?"

He grunts again and I sigh. He leads me down a narrow circular staircase that seems to spiral down for an age. Every time we cross a landing, I crane my neck around the corners to see as much of the castle as possible.

We creep past the fifth landing when I realize something is odd about the castle. I've been comparing it to the palaces in Nova and in Laville when it strikes me— there are doors everywhere here. If this castle belonged to the Gergon Royal family, they wouldn't need to have so many doors—I've seen Evelyn pass through walls with barely a blink. Even the less powerful nobility tried to replicate the fashion—hiding doors behind huge paintings or tapestries. Anything to give the appearance of extreme magical power. But here, there's none of that pretending.

We finally exit the staircase two levels below ground.

My jaw drops. We're no longer in a castle. We're in a cave so big you could fit the rest of the castle inside it.

Stalactites drip from the ceiling, sharpened to a point so the cave looks like the inside of a monster's mouth. I wrap my arms around my body, trying to ward away the shivers. My eyes dart around, my heart racing every time I think I see a menacing face in the dark recesses of the cave. *It's just your imagination*, I say to myself, as I shy away from what looks like a giant bat hanging from the ceiling. *Just a weirdly shaped stalactite.*

Something that isn't my imagination is the giant hole in the center of the cave, leading down to a whirlpool of rushing water.

Ivan pulls my arm and I stumble forward. My legs don't want to move—there's nowhere to go except that steep drop into the water—and who knows what sharp rocks lurk underneath. *Is this how I'm going to die?*

My brain is so unhelpful.

As we get closer to the hole, I see there's a narrow path running around the outside. I'm not going to die this time. As we edge our way along the path, I look down, into the abyss at my feet. My head spins with vertigo and I snap my eyes back to the path. I'm not normally afraid of heights but this drop freaks me out. Thank the dragons for my big feet—at least they keep me stable.

Fortunately, once we're on the other side, the ground widens again. The cave splits into several smaller "rooms" and the ceiling slopes down to normal height.

The man leads me into one of the rooms. I flinch as I see who is waiting for me. Emilia has her back to us. Even *that* radiates evil, her shoulder blades as sharp as scythes, visible through the thin material of her dress.

In front of her is a blackboard, and behind are rows of desks. A classroom in a cave? Things keep getting weirder and weirder.

Emilia stares at the board, hands on her hips. If I didn't know better, I'd say she was looking at a problem she didn't know how to solve. But the blackboard is completely blank.

"Sam, take a seat."

She gestures to one of the desks. I don't want to, but Ivan pushes me forward. Eventually I give in, curving my body around the protruding desk. He speaks a few words into the air, pointing his baton at me. Chains jump up around my wrists, confining me to the desk. I grimace.

"These are the Vul caves—do you know them?" Emila spins round on her heels.

I shake my head before I can stop myself, then silently curse. So much for not giving anything away.

She tuts loudly and the sound echoes off the cavernous walls. "Do they teach you anything in school these days? I thought a Kemi would have heard of the Visir School of Alchemy."

"But that's in ruins! It doesn't exist anymore!" I blurt out.

"Doesn't it? Look around, Sam. I'd say it exists. Think how many amazing potions were discovered here. It honestly is a wonder."

The Visir School? So we are in Gergon. And the school isn't just famous, it's *legendary*. "It doesn't look anything like this . . ." I've seen photos of the Visir School. It looked like a normal school, in the center of Gergon's capital, Byrne. That's where I expected Prince Stefan to take me. Not here.

Emilia smirks. "The pictures you have seen are a ruse. All the better to maintain the anonymity."

I frown. The Visir School might have once been legendary but now it's irrelevant. It belongs to the middle ages, along with tallow candles, chainmail armor, and messenger pigeons. The school closed its doors officially over a century ago, but it had been dying a long, slow death before that. Sure, it might have once been the place for an alchemist to study, but that was what— two hundred, three hundred years ago?

Suddenly things begin to slide into place. All those doors—they were to classrooms. The piles of broken glass outside—old beakers, flasks, and test tubes, no longer needed. The twin snakes, signifying alchemy. *Now* I recognize it.

The Visir School may have officially closed its doors, but there's at least one person still making use of its vast resources.

Emilia stares at me with an intensity that turns my stomach.

"I've brought you here for a reason. There's only one of these boards in the entire world, and it was developed right here at the Visir School. They say that all the innovating is now done in synthetics labs. They forget what true artistry looks like . . ." She sweeps her arm over the board.

True artistry? To me, it looks like a plain old, boring blackboard. It's been freshly painted, sure: The black is so dark my eyes can't seem to focus properly. But then something shifts within its black, inky depths, and I involuntarily shoot back in my chair. Maybe there is something to it after all.

"Why am I here?" I can't cross my arms because of the chains, so I let them hang by my sides, fists clenched.

"I need your help. *Nova* needs your help."

I raise my eyebrows. "Now you're telling me you're helping Nova? I don't think so."

"If we are quick, yes. But we must hurry before . . ." She shakes her head. "If I say his name, it will summon him."

I would laugh if I wasn't so terrified. "As if I would believe you. I'll never help you."

"Even if it brought back your granddad?"

I shift in my seat and my stomach twists. "That's why you want me to be quick. Because he's dying."

Emilia rushes forward to my chair, so close to me I can smell the evil stench of her breath. I recoil but I can't really get away. "You should consider yourself lucky it was I who found your grandfather first and not one of the others."

"He is in hospital because of you." I narrow my eyes and force myself not to quake in front of her. "You attacked him, stripped him of his memories, and now you say I should be thanking you? You're out of your mind."

"We are wasting time," she repeats. "How about I just show you what I want from you, and you can make your mind up on your own."

She walks over to a tall cupboard at the far side of the classroom. The cupboard stands out against the gray cave walls—it's a rich, burnished mahogany inlaid with an intricate, swirling ivory pattern. Another indication of how rich the school once was. When she opens the doors, I see several rows of test tubes hanging from an built-in rack. Some have red caps on them, others white. She selects a white-capped vial filled with an impossibly dark liquid, inky black like the blackboard. But I also catch flickering colors within, the way gasoline looks when it catches the light.

She swirls the bottle around three times and apprehension settles in the back of my throat, making it hard to breathe. She uncorks the stopper, then approaches the blackboard from the side and tips the bottle onto the very top of the board.

The liquid is thick and viscous like honey, and it drips down the surface with agonizing slowness. As it makes its way down to the bottom, the liquid spreads until it covers every inch.

My hands shake as an image forms in the liquid, and I recognize it. It's flickering like an old film on pause.

Emilia takes the blackboard and drags it on its wheels until it is right in front of my face. She grabs my hand and forces me to reach out and touch the image—and I am sucked into the board.

CHAPTER THIRTY-EIGHT

I KNOW INSTANTLY WHERE I AM: BACK AT Kemi's Potion Shop. For a second I wonder if I've transported back home through the blackboard, but everything feels wrong. The world is blurry around the edges—if I look too closely, details start to slip and fade. The counter looks different—our cash register is gone. Or rather, it's been replaced by the old-fashioned kind with brass flags and spinning wheels. I think I've seen it in the basement of the store, gathering dust.

The view shifts totally and moves from the shop into the lab. I'm disoriented, confused, and scared. What is this? I feel like I'm in one of Arjun's video games—I almost expect to put my arm out and see a weapon in its place. I try to move my body but I can't. I'm limited to a single point-of-view. I wonder whose eyes I'm seeing through.

Standing there, her back hunched over a desk, is my great-grandmother. At least, I think it's her—I've only ever seen her in photographs.

"Cleo?" I try to ask. No sound emerges.

The point-of-view moves in front of a mirror, and I can finally see my "host." It's a boy about my age. His thick black hair is a mess on top of his head, and his eyes have bags underneath like he hasn't slept in days.

"It's no good," the woman I think is Cleo says, throwing her arms out wide and knocking a half-mixed potion off the counter. "I can't do this."

"Please, Master," says the boy. "You have to. If there's no master in Kemi's Potion Shop, then we will have to close. We can't let that happen."

"This way of life is doomed. You read the news. The newfangled synths will be taking over."

The boy's eyes shut, but I can feel his rage—and his fear. He's shaking with it. "That can't happen," he splutters out. His eyes open again. "It won't happen. Please, Master, we just have one more hurdle to pass, then we can go to the council and apply for my permit."

"The council? Who are they?" The woman's eyes glaze over. "Why do you call me Master? I am your mother."

"Mother, Mother." The boy grabs the woman's hand and strokes it. There's so much tenderness in that touch, but there's also desperation. "You remember the alchemical council. The ones who govern our profession? You were the president last year?"

The woman frowns, then shakes her head. "Let me go and make some tea," she says, and she gets up from the bench and disappears into the kitchen. The boy's eyes close again for a moment.

That couldn't have been Cleo, I think, although a sick feeling has settled in my stomach. The woman my grandfather always told me about was fiercely intelligent, bordering on cold—always expecting the very best from her son, always insisting that he call her Master while she was in the lab.

Didn't I tell you to get out? A voice roars, shaking through my core. I'm disoriented—did that voice come from my mind? From the illusion Emilia has caught me in? I'm still looking through the eyes of the boy and he hasn't reacted.

Then I feel a shove in my mind, and for a moment my vision doubles—I see both the inside of the potion lab and the classroom I'm sitting in with Emilia. I struggle to get out of the weird vision and into the classroom completely, but Emilia pushes me back into the lab. I'm caught in a twisted tug of war.

Get out, get OUT, GET OUT! The voice yells again.

"I'm trying!" I cry out.

Then the voice changes. *Wait, who is this? Are you another one of that woman's goons? I won't speak to ANY OF YOU. GET OUT OF MY MEMORIES.*

I recognize the voice. I know I do. "Granddad?" I say, tentatively.

Samantha?

"Granddad!" my mind cries out. I can't believe it. Now I understand. I'm inside my granddad's memories. The boy in the vision kneels to the ground to clean up the spilled potion. In the inky black liquid, I can see his face. It's the picture of concentration. Is this my granddad but . . . young? There is something about the set of his jaw, the determined frown lines criss-crossing his brow . . . it could be him. He looks so old before his time. Then I notice it. The small scar on his eyebrow from catching a pox as a child. Before Cleo developed a mix to vaccinate him from it . . . and the rest of the world. It *is* him.

"Granddad, it's me? Hello? Are you there?" I panic now. I don't want to lose him—even his voice.

The memory continues. Once young Ostanes has cleaned up the potion, he takes a piece of paper from the desk Cleo had been sitting at. It's a letter of recommendation from a master alchemist, saying that his apprentice is ready to be made a practicing alchemist. It's a letter I hope to get one day too. Except, as I keep reading, I see that this letter says not only to make the apprentice a practicing alchemist, but a *master* alchemist. The apprentice in question? Ostanes Kemi. And the master? Cleo. Except it's unsigned at the bottom.

The boy puts the letter down, then pulls a small vial out of his pocket. He seems to hesitate, before finding his nerve and drinking the potion. He waits a couple of moments, then picks up a pen and signs the letter, *Grand Master Cleo Kemi*. Now I know what the potion is for. It's to disguise the fake signature against any fraud checks. It's a smart and complicated potion. Even though he's faking the letter, he *is* clearly ready to be a master.

I always knew the legend about my grandfather—that he became the youngest master in Nova, one of the only apprentices ever to skip the long years of experience and trials required to make the leap from practicing alchemist to master. But if what this memory is showing me is true, that means that he lied his way to his position.

All to keep the store open.

Sam, is that really you?

"Granddad?"

But, how are you here? Is she with you? Don't tell me you're working with her.

My eyes well up with tears. I haven't heard his voice in so long, especially not sounding so coherent. The sensible part of my brain knows that I should be wary, in case this turns out to be one of Emilia's tricks. But the rest of my brain and my heart want to believe this is real. "Is that really you? I . . . I'm not working with anyone. I'm here against my will."

Is she with you? I only sense one of you in here.

The voice sounds frantic, and I can hear it echoing all around my head. "No, it's just me, I think. But Emilia is watching. She's on the other side." I don't know how else to describe it.

Oh thank the dragons. We won't have much time. Sam, you are inside my memories. The ones that were taken from me.

"So these are real?"

Shh, don't talk. Just listen. I'm here because when Emilia took my memories, I managed to send most of my consciousness with them. I've been protecting those memories from her. I don't know what's happened to the rest of me.

"You're being cared for, but you're sick. You're in the hospital. No one knows what happened. They've shut down the store," I tell him.

No!

"I'm trying to find Cleo's diary so that I can save you—so that I can bring you back."

No! You must not. Leave it alone. It's too dangerous.

I cut him off before he can continue. "So it is out there?"

Bloody Kemi stubbornness.

"I'm not having any luck, though. I've already been to Runustan, where she was last seen. Nothing but riddles."

Good. May it stay that way. Listen, Samantha—Emilia will force you into my memories and you will learn many secrets about me. Things you should forget. She will attempt to break you. Don't let her.

"Granddad, you don't need to worry about your secrets. They're safe with me."

Suddenly I feel a tug, and I can sense that the memory is fading and Emilia is trying to pull me out. I push back against her, suddenly not wanting to leave the security of my granddad's memories, the sound of his voice.

"Granddad!"

Let her take you! You'll be back. The memories can't play for more than a few minutes at a time. Don't tell her anything. She will have you back here soon.

"Okay," I say. "Granddad—I love you." I let myself be dragged back into the real world by Emilia.

CHAPTER THIRTY-NINE

WHEN I'M BACK IN THE CLASSROOM, I SLUMP
down onto the desk.

"Well?" Emilia asks. "What did you see?"

After a few moments to catch my breath, I lift my
gaze up to meet hers. Having the conversation with
Granddad—knowing that he's not gone completely,
only . . . displaced, has given me strength. "You know
what I saw. My grandfather, as a young man."

"And?"

"And the potion shop. And my great-grandmother."

"Did your grandfather speak to you?"

I hesitate for a moment, but I know there is no point
in lying to her. I nod.

"I knew he would talk to you. Tell me you found out
something."

"Not a thing," I say, honestly. "Something happened
to my great-grandmother when she came back from the

hunt. She was a different person. Maybe it was too much pressure. Maybe it was some other kind of trauma. Who knows." I frown.

"I forget that you are a young and inexperienced alchemist. Your great-grandmother's condition has only verified for me that she must have made that potion. To make a single dose of an aqua vitae, you must be prepared to lose all your alchemical knowledge and skill. It becomes the very last mix you ever make. That's why most alchemists aren't even willing to try. The risk is too great—even for the most powerful potion in the world."

That does seem to describe what has happened to Cleo . . . I wonder if Emilia could be right. As much as I'd hate that.

"If it's so risky, how come you're doing it?"

Her dark eyes flash. "It's an exchange. Business, let's call it. But I'd rather do business with you. If we find the diary, I'll make the potion—a drop for me, and a drop for your granddad."

I laugh. "Someone has hired you to make an aqua vitae, but now you're prepared to double-cross them too? And you expect me to trust a word you say?"

Even as I fight with her, my brain whirrs. What would someone pay for a mix to cure all illnesses? For prolonged life, free of disease—to live until accident, murder or old age takes you?

I think of the riot in our store. The desperation I've seen at the mere hint of such a cure.

"You'll regret not trusting me. And you don't have much time until that option expires."

"The option is gone already! Just like my great-grandmother's diary! Face it. She probably destroyed it."

"Pah! That's where you're wrong. Like any true alchemist, it would have killed your great-grandmother to know that she would have all those recipes but not the knowledge or the skill to mix them. So she hid the diary. She wouldn't have destroyed it. Would you be able to destroy yours?"

I know in the space of a heartbeat that the answer is no. She reads my face. "Exactly. So it's out there."

I narrow my eyes. I can't believe I'm having this conversation with Emilia. It makes me sick. I can't look at her, so I stare back at the blackboard. *Granddad.*

"Remarkable invention, isn't it?" Emilia follows my gaze. "It's coated with a specially mixed paint that simulates the mind's eye, allowing us to enter and view the memories as if they were on a reel of film. Developed right here at the Visir School by a *very* talented alchemist. Very top secret. And how about these vials? These are some of my best creations, if I do say so myself. I adapted it from an old recipe of theirs that they created to help them store magical energy. Now it's perfect for preserving memories. A mix of ancient Kauri resin, bacopa flower, and my own little secret ingredient."

Kauri resin—not used in traditional potions as it is too thick to be ingested easily, often used for aesthetic reasons to encase and preserve pressed flowers for jewellery.

Bacopa flower—thought to boost brain power and increase resilience to stress.

Two thoughts run through my mind: one, that it *is* an incredibly impressive alchemical achievement. Two, that if she's telling me, it means she isn't planning on letting me go.

And what about the blackboard paint mix?

Maybe midnight squid ink, for reflection? Definitely some kind of silver ore, and then there is the board itself—it would need stickiness, maybe sable tree sap?

And it needs stolen memories to feed it. I switch off my runaway alchemy brain immediately. The blackboard paint is a *dark* potion. It needs an ordinary mind to feed on in order to work. I can't hide my disgust.

"See? Maybe you can't stomach it, but sometimes the dark can be brilliant too."

I bite down on my tongue. Emilia can read me a little too well—I must be giving so much away. I wish I knew how to control the expression on my face; I'm like an open book. Despite myself, I'm intrigued and she knows it. I thought that the only innovation in our field came from working with synths. I studied alchemy for the love, for the tradition, but not for the innovation. I followed and tweaked recipes, yes, but I didn't develop completely new ones until the princess. Why would I, when there were labs with big, expensive, complex technologies to do that? But this . . .

Her eyes flash. "What did your grandfather tell you?"

She wants something from me, so I'll give her something. A dead end. "Something about . . . centaurs," I say through gritted teeth, squeezing my eyes tightly shut.

My bonds loosen and I relax. Maybe she bought it.

But then I'm lifted up and out of the chair. I fly through the air until my back slams against the rocky classroom wall, pinned there by magic. The back of my head throbs and I cry out in pain. "LIAR!" Emilia screams, her wand pointed directly at me.

"I don't know anything," I sob.

I drop to the ground, landing hard on my knees. I don't feel strong anymore. I don't feel like a winner of the Wilde Hunt, an experienced adventurer. I feel like a kid who just wants to go home.

"What is the meaning of this?"

I look up, not daring to believe my eyes.

Standing in the doorway of the classroom, his golden hair shining even in the dim light, is my rescuer. Someone has finally found me.

Prince Stefan.

CHAPTER FORTY

I'M STILL CURLED UP IN MY LITTLE BALL, and I don't relax until I feel the prince's comforting hands on my back. "Come, now, Samantha."

"Home? Can I go home now?"

"Hush, hush. Come with me."

I let him help me to my feet, gripping the sleeve of his shirt. I'm not letting go. I'm not letting Emilia take me again. When I dare to look at the front of the classroom, both Emilia and Ivan are gone. "Emilia—it was Emilia Thoth who kidnapped me. Did you see her?"

"I saw her all right. She's done a very bad thing. Let's get out of here."

I give him a grateful smile. "Thank you. Thank you, thank you, thank you. How did you find me?"

"I know everything that goes on in my country." His eyes narrow. They're still the same tiger-striped shade as before. Maybe it wasn't a glamour, after all. "Or at least,

I thought I did. No matter now, I've found you."

"Do you have a cell phone? Can I send a message to my parents?"

"Not from in here. As soon as we're out of this region, we'll get signal again. It's very traditional here, as you've seen."

"Okay."

I can't believe my luck. Even the caves don't seem as scary now that I'm crossing them on my way to freedom. The prince speaks comforting, soothing words to me for the whole walk back via the Great Hall.

Outside, there's a horse and carriage waiting for us. The horses are grays, their coats shiny and bright, with none of the menacing qualities of Emilia's black stallions. Stefan gives me a boost into the carriage. This is much plusher than the hay bales I was sitting on before. The seats are covered in crushed red velvet and the curtains covering the windows are made of purple silk.

Stefan gets in after me, shutting the door. I hear the crack of a whip and the horses pull forward. I breathe out a long sigh of relief. Home, at last. I'll get the princess to send the NSS to secure my granddad's memories and they can recapture Emilia and . . .

"You must be tired," the prince says. "That's quite some ordeal you've been through. Do you want to sleep?"

I shake my head. "I don't think I could. I'm just so glad to be leaving."

"I'm glad to have found you." He gives me a small smile, then he turns and looks out the window.

The goofy grin I've had plastered on my face slips a little. Even though every fiber of my being prays that this is a rescue, one tiny voice slips through and whispers, *But how did he find you so fast?*

"Did you know Emilia was using the Visir School as her base? When I asked you if I could come here . . . did you know?" I try to keep my voice casual.

"I'm sorry that this is what you've seen of Gergon. I think you would like it very much. In fact, do you mind if we make a detour? I have something to show you that I think you'll find *very* interesting." He doesn't wait for my answer, but turns around and opens a small hatch in the front of the carriage. He shouts something to the driver in a language I don't understand.

"I'd rather just go home, if that's okay with you."

He smiles, but it makes the hair on the back of my neck stand up on end. I know I'm just being paranoid—being kidnapped will do that to you—but I shiver despite myself. "It will only take a few minutes," he says.

I don't really have a choice, so I just smile back.

We take a different route to how I came in, skirting around the dark woods rather than through. The castle disappears from view as we follow the base of the cliff. *Please let this be a faster route home. Please.*

"I'm taking you to my favorite village in Gergon. It's

called Botsani. The people here still live life as they did a hundred years ago."

"Is that a good thing?" I ask.

"That depends on whom you ask. I think so. As a prince and representative of my country, I need modern things . . . a cell phone, computer, transport panels, etc. But how much freer would life be if I didn't have them? Ah, look . . ."

I lean out of the window to see where Prince Stefan is pointing. Down in the valley below us sits a picture-perfect village, with tiny colorful houses topped with thatched roofs. The hills stretching up from the valley are covered in funny looking hay bales the shape of upside-down ice-cream cones. Under any other circum-stance, I would be utterly enchanted.

"Is that a shepherd I see?" Our carriage creaks past a young boy, a piece of straw dangling from his mouth, with one kid goat under his arm.

"Yes—except look a little closer."

I blink and look again. "Oh—it's not a goat at all. It's a satyr."

"Exactly!" Prince Stefan grins like he's just told me I've won the lottery. But I don't get it. My brain just isn't functioning properly—all I can think of is *home, home, home*. He leans forward, his amber eyes locked onto mine. "Don't you see? The people here live in harmony with their Wild and magical creatures. Just like it used to be in Nova, a long time ago."

"That's true," I say, and his smile returns. I turn back to the window as the boy puts down the satyr, who runs around his ankles and gently head-butts his knees. They do look happy.

There used to be way more magical creatures in Nova, especially near Kingstown. There was a big uproar when the bones of an entire kelpie colony were found buried underneath one of the luxury spas just outside the city. It was a reminder of how far we'd buried the memory of the Wild creatures that once called our city home.

As we enter the village proper, people leave their houses to watch the carriage pass by. It's not that different to traveling in the limousine with Evie, except that no one is snapping selfies out here. Once again, I'm struck by the total lack of mod-cons—no cars or mopeds outside the houses, no satellite dishes, no electric lights.

"This is the best part," Stefan says. He raps on the carriage wall closest to the driver and we pull up to a stop. He opens the door, jumping down to the ground, and helps me out too.

There's a queue of people standing patiently in line outside a store. There's a woman with a baby in her arms, the baby staring at me with her gorgeous blue eyes, framed by long lashes. I give her a small wave. She buries her face in her mother's chest, then looks back at me shyly.

The people don't seem to know what to do with the arrival of the prince. They step back, pressing against the wall of the shop. Some of the men attempt a small bow, but Stefan waves them up.

I look up, reading the name of the store. *Andrej Alchemistik.*

"The local alchemist is at the center of village life here, just as it should be. Come in and meet Andrej. He's a legend."

The queue parts to let Prince Stefan and me through.

As soon as I'm in the store, I feel at home. It's amazing how similar the interior is to Kemi's Potion Shop—the wall of ingredients, the recipe books scattered on the counter and the brown paper bags filled with prescriptions.

"Andrej, meet Samantha Kemi," says Prince Stefan. When Andrej steps out from behind the counter, I'm surprised by how young he is. Well, comparatively. He looks about my dad's age, with a head of thick dark hair and a deep tan.

I take his outstretched hand and shake it. There's a slight twitch in Andrej's eyebrow at the mention of the name "Kemi." "Nice to meet you," I say. Then he puts his hand on his heart and shrugs apologetically.

"He doesn't speak Novaen," Prince Stefan explains.

"Thank you for letting me visit your store," I say, and the prince translates. I turn to him. "Can we . . . go now?"

"Sure, sure," he replies. He says something in rapid Gergonian to the alchemist, who replies with wild, flailing arm gestures. I get the distinct impression that all is not well in the alchemist's world, despite what Prince Stefan is trying to show me.

Once we're back in the carriage, my curiosity gets the better of me. "I hate to ask but . . . what were all those people waiting for? It looked like half of the village was waiting for a potion. It's good for an alchemist to be busy, but not *that* busy."

Prince Stefan nods and, as the carriage pulls away, he draws the curtains tightly shut.

"I'm sure you're still wondering why I took your boyfriend's place at the ball."

Really? I think. *I've been kidnapped, bound, gagged, and imprisoned since then.* I bite my lip even as alarm bells are ringing in my head. "But I was telling you the truth when I said I had to meet you. You see, I need your help."

"Well, you rescued me from Emilia. What can I do for you?" I say, a little stiffly.

He tilts his head to one side and for a moment, he's not a tiger—he's a kitten. "How much do you know about my family?"

I raise my eyebrows. "Almost nothing, I guess."

"That's good. That's how they want it. Because if the truth came out . . ." He leans his head against the door, swaying as the carriage rocks along the road. "You've been around the Novaen royals a little bit now, so you might have a good understanding of how royal magic works, as opposed to Talented."

"I know a little." My pulse picks up.

"Something has been happening to my family. A rot. A disease. It started with my father. It happened so quickly . . . One day, he was fine, the next? His power was drained. He couldn't do a single spell. My mother had to break a hole in the wall of their chambers so he could leave. But then she started to weaken too."

The blood drains from my face, but luckily he's so wrapped up in his story that I don't think he's registered my expression. If what he's saying is true . . . it's terrible.

"My brother made the decision to close down the borders—to stop anyone seeing what was happening—and to stop anyone getting out to tell the tale. He was infected too—at a slower rate than my parents, but the disease is certainly progressing. Every Talented in Gergon is affected to some degree. Only I have managed to stave off the worst of the symptoms—thanks to a special serum that an alchemist here has developed. So my family have been channeling their remaining power to me. I am what remains of Gergon now."

He looks up at me and I swallow, hard. "Prince Stefan . . . I'm so sorry. Other than power being drained, are there any other symptoms?"

He nods. "A vicious cough. Weakness in our limbs.

You can be assured that our very best alchemists have been on their own Hunt for the cure—even Andrej was involved—but of course, we couldn't make it a world-wide event like Nova. Not when the entire royal family was affected."

"No, of course not . . ."

"It is spreading to common Talenteds now. We are dying, Samantha." He reaches out and grips my hands, so fast he's like a viper. "I thought I had a hope," he says, his tiger eyes searching my ordinary brown ones. "I thought if I could only marry the princess . . . then her power would flow through into me and I could save my family—save my country. But she has refused me—once, before the Wilde Hunt. And once at the Laville Ball. I am running out of time, and out of options."

"If you told her, maybe—"

"No, don't you see? Nova and Gergon have been rivals for centuries. Although things have been peaceful now, if the truth came out about how weak we are . . . I cannot take that risk."

I'm so moved by the prince's story, tears prick behind my eyes. "I don't know how I can help you, but if I can . . ."

"I've seen the lengths you're willing to go to, to save your grandfather. Even the lengths you're willing to go for your friends. I hope you understand the lengths *I* am willing to go, for my country."

He draws back the curtains in a lightning-quick movement. "Now, your aqua vitae is my only hope. Find it for me."

I drop my head into my hands. We're back at the Visir School.

And Emilia is standing there, waiting for me. She throws back her head and laughs.

CHAPTER FORTY-ONE

I WAKE IN THE DARKNESS OF MY CELL. IT doesn't matter what this place was before—to me now, it's a prison. I can't remember much after the carriage ride, my mind shutting down at the prospect of being trapped here for good after being *so close* to freedom. Or the illusion of it, anyway.

Prince Stefan and his family had been behind this the whole time, willing to do anything to preserve their power.

I don't know how long I've been out, but it's still light outside. Maybe I slept all through the night and now it's morning? Maybe I was only passed out for a few minutes? My stomach growls. I ignore it. I roll over on my bed and pull the blankets up over my head. Sleep was oblivion. I prefer it.

A sharp rap on my door makes every muscle in my body tense. The door swings open. "Wake up, Samantha. Time to go."

"Make me," I say. The petty defiance barely makes me feel any better, and I swing my legs off the bed despite my words. The only fraying string of hope I have in this place is speaking to my granddad again. I follow Emilia, making sure to keep my distance. Ivan is nowhere to be seen. Now that Prince Stefan is here, she must feel more comfortable to be alone with me. She knows I'm hardly a physical threat.

I sneak glances at her back as we walk. It's actually eerie how much she resembles Princess Evelyn from this angle, where I can't see her face or any bare skin. Her hair is long, like Evelyn's, wrapped in several bands down her back. She carries herself with the same self-assured confidence, her head and neck straight as if she were wearing a heavy crown that required balance.

But Emilia will never wear the crown. I understand now. The Wilde Hunt had been her golden opportunity to take the throne; now she's back to being a pawn in Gergon's political game.

We don't head straight down to the caves. Instead, we walk back through the main hallway and I get more of an impression of what the school must have once been like. It's incredibly creepy to be walking down the cavernous hallways, our footsteps echoing off the high ceilings. There are dusty paintings of old teachers on the wall, grim-looking portraits of such miserable-looking people that, frankly, it gives alchemy a bad name.

I wonder how long Emilia has lived here. Is this how she got her alchemical training? I wonder how long the Gergon royals have been prepping her for just this sort of occasion. Someone who hates Nova and who will do anything to get back at them. Someone who's willing to take dark potions and ruin her body. Someone who would sacrifice her alchemical skill to make the aqua vitae—because what does she have to lose?

"They say that at its peak, the school had over two thousand students. They even had some students from Nova. One of them went on to be a teacher here. Do you recognize that name, Sam?" She's stopped underneath one of the portraits.

I reluctantly look up, and catch sight of the name: *Helena Kemi.*

Another ancient ancestor, my great-great-great-too-many-to-mention-grandmother. I've seen her diaries on our shelves.

"Did you know it was at this school that they perfected the isolation and preservation of patches of Wilds—like the famous one they have in Laville, which I'm sure you saw . . ."

For the first time, Emilia seems almost wistful for Laville. I wonder if she misses having a normal life. She would have been offered so many privileges as the daughter of royalty—just not the one she always wanted. As the second child, she would not have been as powerful as her brother, the king, or as Princess Evelyn is. But she maybe would have won the opportunity to join a first family and increase her power, like Stefan wanted to do by marrying Evelyn. Why would she squander that for this life of loneliness and dark potions and covert operations?

My curiosity gets the better of me. "How did you come to be here?"

She pauses in the hallway, forcing me to stop too. A beam of light streams through one of the tall windows, catching one side of Emilia's face. For an instant it over-exposes her skin, blanching it so that I almost can't see the horror beneath.

She sighs and steps sideways, out of the light, shaking her head as if it burned her. "I hate what Nova has become." Bitterness laces her every word. "My brother loves it. He has all the power . . . and for what? So he can live in his floating palace with his empty-headed queen, throw extravagant parties and attend the openings of hospitals and primary schools? That's not power. That's a waste. He is a neutered puppy when he should be a wolf. He rolls over and plays dead when he should be leader of the pack." Quicker than I thought possible, Emilia whips her wand from its holster and blasts a hole in the wall of the Great Hall. The ground shakes with her power, and I shake with it. Thank the dragons that anger wasn't directed at me. This time.

The bonus is, she looks calmer afterward. A little. "Gergon is different. They showed me what true royal power is like, that there would be, could be, a different path for Nova. I just needed to be strong too. Stronger than the rest of my family. I owe them everything. And now I owe them the ultimate potion. Then, my time will come."

I've never been more afraid of Emilia than I am right now. Her determination is so fierce, it's like she's forgotten I'm there. She's like a time bomb on the edge of explosion. The more I understand her, the more freaked out I am by her.

She looks up into the ceiling, her eyes roaming the crumbling brick, the cracked chandeliers and the peeling frescos. "And although the school is in ruins, some of its protections remain. The special magic of the building means that I can't be traced in here. Nobody can. Just in case thoughts of rescue had crossed your mind."

"No, you and the prince have made it pretty clear that rescue is not going to be possible." I try to stop myself from shaking. I had suspected that there was something like that going on, but I didn't actually want it to be true.

"Good. Now, what do you think of this?" She walks a few steps forward, then passes through a thick wooden door, which I have to really heave to push open. Heat blasts my face and the brightness causes me to squint.

When my eyes adjust, I see that I'm in a kind of greenhouse.

I recognize many of the plants—lots of them extremely dangerous and potent.

Purple nightshade—the deadliest of poisons and also virtually untraceable.

Speckled conium leaf—if ingested, can cause almost instant, though temporary, paralysis.

Skeleton flower—a key ingredient in potions to alter appearance—can be used to replace chameleon scales if required.

My mind whirls. It's like a Wilds designed solely for alchemists. Arjun and Anita have a greenhouse in their backyard, but it doesn't compare to this. This has multiple levels—and the treasures extend up, over and around each other. Emilia walks down the central aisle, her fingertips lightly brushing the plants as she passes. It's the first time I've seen her look at anything with an expression that resembles love.

One plant sidles up to her, a tendril unfurling in her direction and I jump back against a table, knocking a plant pot to the ground.

"Ah yes, eluvian ivy," Emilia says, allowing the plant to wrap itself around her forearm like a snake. "I forgot you were well acquainted already. Don't worry, you're too emotionally unstable at the moment to interest it."

I bend down to clear up what I've just knocked off.

While Emilia's distracted, I slip a single leaf into my pocket. *Speckled conium leaf.* I have no idea how or when I'm going to use it, but it makes me feel better to have it with me.

Emilia's head snaps up, as if some kind of alarm has gone off in her mind. "The board is ready. Let's go."

The visit to the greenhouse has revived me in a way I wouldn't have believed possible. I can't give up. I won't.

CHAPTER FORTY-TWO

WE CROSS BACK OVER THE CAVERN WALKWAY and I keep my eyes wide open. It pays off. I spy what looks to be the decaying remains of an old ladder clinging to the side of the cave wall. Maybe once upon a time, people went down to the water. That means potentially it leads somewhere.

Somewhere . . . like escape?

I snap my eyes away from it, in case Emilia turns around and sees me looking. But she doesn't. We enter the classroom.

Prince Stefan is already in the room. He's wearing a military-style uniform: tan trousers and a tan shirt adorned with dark red lapels and polished brass buttons. Emilia is still in *her* idea of a uniform: a long black dress overlaid with a black shawl. They look like a really twisted couple. But even I can tell that being someone's subordinate does not sit well with Emilia. I wonder if Stefan can see that too, or if he is blinded by what she can do for him.

"Remember what's at stake, Sam," he says to me. "Your granddad's life. Your family's future. If you succeed, I'll make sure you never want for anything under my rule."

"Go die in a fire," I snap.

He looks as if he's about to hit me, but then he doubles over in a coughing fit. He turns bright red with effort, covering his mouth with his sleeve. But when he stands up again I can see a smattering of a powdery white substance over his arm, some of it collected into strands like a spider's web.

"I have your serum, Your Highness," Emilia says. Stefan gestures for her to approach. She takes a small pill box out of one of the pockets of her cloak, then—without even waiting for Stefan to compose himself—takes one of the pills and pushes it into his mouth. I can half-read the name on the side of the box. It says *FELIP*. I shudder. It must be a medicinal potion made from King Felip's waning power.

The potion appears to take immediate effect. Stefan throws his head back and breathes deeply. When he looks at me again, his eyes sparkling, he seems even taller and stronger than before. The pill really worked wonders on him.

"My dear Sam," he says, reaching out and placing his perfectly manicured hand on my cheek. I want to cower, but I won't give him the satisfaction. I keep my expression neutral, and stare at him straight in the eyes.

"You see? My alchemist helps me keep my condition under control. If only the princess of Nova was so lucky. Instead, she was stuck with you. Now, when I am finally strong again, the princess won't have a choice. She will *have* to marry me. Or we will take Nova by force before she destroys it completely."

Nova's not yours yet, I think. *Not if I can help it.* I block out his smarmy presence.

"I have the next memory," Emilia says to Stefan, holding up a glass vial.

"Good. I want to see this in action."

She pours it onto the blackboard.

I don't hesitate. I reach out and touch the paint.

"Granddad?"

Sam! His voice is full of excitement. *You're back. How long has it been? I have no idea of time.*

"Not long, I don't think. It's only been one night since we last spoke." I look around the memory. This seems to be an ordinary day in the store. Sixteen-year-old Granddad is at the till, serving customers in old-fashioned outfits coming through the shop door. I feel like I'm in a play.

Good, but time is of the essence.

"I know. Prince Stefan has arrived."

Prince Stefan? Of Gergon? What is he doing here?

"He and his family are behind this. There's some strange disease or sickness that has infected their entire family.

That's why they really need the aqua vitae. Emilia doesn't want it for herself after all."

What does Emilia look like?

I describe her appearance to him.

Hmm. You would do well not to trust a word she says. Too much changeling poison. Emilia is a master at potions to change her appearance—remember that. What are the ingredients for her changing potion?

"Changeling skin, a pinch of Talented blood . . ."

Talented blood. Exactly. An ordinary cannot be impersonated but neither can ordinaries take a changeling potion—another reason why we are so well trusted. Such dark potions are for those with dark blood. If you escape, you cannot trust anyone Talented. Remember that.

"Granddad, I need to have something to give Emilia and the prince—a clue or a decoy. Otherwise they won't keep me around."

I know, my heart. I think I have found a clue here, in this memory. It's only a small thing, but it's important. I hadn't been paying much attention at the time, but Cleo kept mumbling about a lake of stars.

"A lake of stars . . ." I repeat. It means nothing to me, but it matches what the centaurs said. Where stars appear on command . . . Unfortunately, it's still not a clue I can use.

Sam, I have tried to protect you, but I know I have failed. If Emilia and a prince of Gergon are going to these lengths to find the diary, then there is a chance they will succeed. They cannot. You must escape from her. You must find it first, and then you must promise me one thing. You must not make the aqua vitae.

"What?"

When you find the recipe, you must destroy it. It's not worth it to save me. The cost is greater than you could ever imagine. In the wrong hands, the damage will be catastrophic. Not to mention that it would destroy your life. You will lose all your skill. Kemi's Potion Shop will never run again.

"It might never run again anyway," I say. "I need to save you. Or else . . ."

You must find it. But you must not make it. You have to destroy the recipe. That's your mission in finding the diary. Promise me, Sam.

"I promise," I say, my throat tight.

Good.

Then another thought strikes me, and panic washes over me. "Why are you telling me this now? What's changed?"

There's a long pause. The silence is terrifying. *As you are my apprentice, I owe you the truth. My body won't last much longer without my consciousness. I'm surprised I have lasted this long already.*

I could tell him about the synth now, but I can't. This is what I've been afraid of: that it was only a temporary cure. "I understand," I choke out.

Now go. Do what you can. Don't worry about me—do not let Emilia get her hands on that diary.

Now that we've spoken, I notice the memory itself. I'd been so wrapped up in talking to Granddad that I hadn't realized the change of location. I take a look around, and the room feels eerily familiar, even though I don't immediately recognize it. The door, the positioning of the windows . . . then I realize: It's my room. Just with none of my decorations on the walls and none of my furniture. In fact, the bed has been moved to the middle of the room, whereas I prefer to sleep with my back up against a wall, underneath the window so I can turn and look at the stars. My desk with my computer is missing. Instead, there is only sparse furniture—except for a large trunk on the floor, covered in place stickers.

Someone stirs in the bed and they must be really thin, because I had mistaken them for scrunched up bedclothes. Cleo. I wonder if a few years have passed since the last memory, because she looks so much older than before. White has appeared in her hair, and there are more lines on her face. Even in sleep, she looks weary, and much older than her early fifties—which is how old she should be.

I look back at the trunk, because something has caught my eye. At first, it was the sticker of Mount Hallah—I'd recognize that anywhere. This must be Cleo's trunk. I scan over it for clues as to other places she might have been, when I spot a sticker for a place called Lake of Stars. The lake Granddad mentioned. In the picture, it has the same shape as Lake Karst by Nadya's camp. Could they be the same place? *Where stars appear on command.* Could it be a coincidence? My heartbeat quickens. Maybe the answer is right here, in front of my face.

When I catch young Ostanes' face in the mirror, I realize no time has passed at all. Through my granddad's sixteen-year-old eyes, I watch as he cools Cleo's forehead with a damp cloth, whispering soothing words. Cleo aged since the last memory—more rapidly than is at all natural. How could that be possible? Could making the aqua vitae really have such an effect? And if Cleo did make the potion, what happened to it, if she didn't use it to win the hunt? I'm angry on her behalf. That all this was in vain.

My love for Granddad expands in my heart. He took care of his mother and the store at the same time. It gives me newfound respect for him. No wonder he is so hard on me: He had to endure so much more.

"Mother, the letter came through from the council," young Ostanes says. "They're willing to make me a master, but you have to make it to the ceremony. I know you can do it."

She turns her face toward him, but her eyes are empty—devoid of any warmth or intelligence or understanding. My heart breaks for him.

Now you know why you cannot make the potion, says my grandfather's voice.

"I promise," I say.

CHAPTER FORTY-THREE

THE VISION FADES, AND I DON'T RESIST the pull. Now that I have a destination in mind, I'm ready to move. I just need to get out of here first.

"What did your granddad reveal?" Emilia asks as soon as I'm back in the classroom.

"The terrible cost of the aqua vitae. I told you he knows nothing about where my grandmother's diary is! She was a shell of her former self when she arrived back after the hunt."

"She's lying," says Prince Stefan, and I look up at him sharply. He's staring at me through narrowed eyes. "She knows something. I can see it in her face. If you can't get her to talk, make her."

My palms are slick with sweat. What does he mean, *make her*? Will they use torture? Or Ivan's heavy fists? "I don't know where it is, I swear! Maybe a few more sessions, some other memories . . ."

"We know you already traced the centaurs and it was a dead end. We're all running out of time here." When I offer him nothing, he turns on Emilia. "You said that this was a guarantee. If we could get Samantha here, then you could break her. This is what we've been working for! If she knows something about the diary, we must find out *now*. Use the truth serum."

I stiffen in my chair. Truth serums are terrifying, but I'm prepared for this. As part of my alchemist apprenticeship, Granddad made me ingest several variations of truth serums to test them—so that I can recognize when someone is trying to potion me. Truth serums can *normally* only be applied under the direction of a Talented lawyer (although I've violated that rule a few times in my young potions career). Obviously they're not going to care about that here.

But I know how to respond to a truth serum—even if I can't lie when I'm under the influence. Some people crumble at the mere thought of taking one, but I am more confident. I know they can only ask three questions before the serum starts to wear off. After that, they can't be certain of its effectiveness. I will speak the truth, but the bare minimum.

"I have some serum prepared for this occasion," says Emilia. "I will return shortly."

It's funny seeing Emilia in the same room as Prince Stefan, because she becomes a different person. She loses her natural swagger. I suppose she's a woman under pressure. I wonder if it galls Emilia to have had to jump from one domineering family's ship and landed straight on the deck of another.

I'm left alone with Prince Stefan, although he is standing and I am still strapped down to the desk. He doesn't question me further—but why would he, when he knows the truth serum is on its way?

Instead, he goes up to the blackboard and runs his hand over it. There's no danger of him being sucked in—there's no memory on the board at the moment.

Stefan walks over and examines the rows of vials containing the memories. He picks one up and twirls it around in his hand. It makes me sick to think that part of my granddad's mind is contained within those tubes. Prince Stefan raises his hand and runs it through the front of his hair. I can't believe my eyes . . . he's using the inky black, glassy surface to check his reflection! How impossibly vain can you get? His real self is coming out now. He's unreal.

That's his weakness, says a voice inside my head. The beginnings of a plan formulate in my mind.

Emilia returns much quicker than I expect, the truth serum in hand.

"Ready?" She walks over to me. As used as I am to taking potions, I can't help but feel uncomfortable. "Are you going to make this easy, or are you going to make

Ivan come over here and force it down your throat?"

I shoot her a dark glare, then I give in, because I don't fancy having my mouth forced open when the outcome is going to be the same either way. I just have to trust in Granddad's training. He's never taught me wrong before.

I tilt my head back and open my mouth. She pours the truth potion in.

It tastes disgusting: bitter and gritty, and it burns the back of my throat as it slides down. Already the natural barriers in my mind fall down. The trick to getting around a truth serum is to redirect the mind, rather than attempt to lie. I need to keep calm, breathe, and not fight the process.

After the serum has had time to settle, Emilia begins her questioning.

"Has your grandfather told you where your great-grandmother's potion diary is?"

"No," I reply, and it's the truth. He's only hypothesized. One question down. Maybe I'll get through this.

"You're being too specific," says Stefan.

Emilia nods. "Do you know where the diary is?"

Thankfully, this is another question I can answer truthfully. "No."

"This is the last question," says Emilia. Prince Stefan groans.

"Let me try. Samantha, tell us where you would go next to find your great-grandmother's journal."

I swallow before answering, trying not to reply directly. But there's no way out of it, and the truth serum is pushing out the answer before my brain has a way to stop or redirect it. "The Lake of Stars," I say, through gritted teeth.

The serum then makes me drowsy, and I slump down over the desk. Emilia nods, her mouth in a firm line. "Come on, then. Let's secure her and we can get going."

She grabs my upper arm and yanks me to my feet. "I'm coming, I'm coming," I say. Emilia quickly gets frustrated with me and walks out through the door. I follow behind, my feet falling over each other. I just about catch myself against the doorframe.

Prince Stefan reaches out and grabs my arm before I fall completely. I slip the leaf I stole out of my pocket and put it in my mouth, pushing it into my cheek—careful not to break it. I flop about, exaggerating the weakness in my limbs. "Woah there, be careful," he says. "Don't want you falling down into that pit of despair." He whispers in my ear, "We might still need you yet."

I stand up straighter, leaning against the doorframe. "You're very handsome," I blurt out, then I slap my hands over my mouth.

"Truth serum effects are lingering, are they?"

"Something like that." I try to put on my best flirt, biting my bottom lip and fluttering my eyelids at him. I'm sure I look ridiculous—I feel it—but I know that if

315

this is going to work, I need to play to his overinflated ego. "You're right, you know. I wish Nova was more like Gergon. I wish alchemy was more respected."

"It will happen again, Samantha. I promise you." He grips my hand and stares deep into my eyes. I stare right back.

I lift my hand to his face, stroking his jawline. "If I could do what I really wanted to right now . . ."

"What do you want?"

"I can't . . . I can't tell you—I have a boyfriend," I say, lowering my eyes so I look coy.

"I won't tell if you won't." I know that Prince Stefan has no real interest in me, but I'm sure the fact that he would be getting one up on another guy plays right into his vanity again. He wants something to brag about. And I need to give it to him. I need this to go exactly right—or else it could end up a total disaster.

"I just want to kiss you," I say. I need him to believe it, so I lean in a bit. I flick my eyes up quickly and see that Emilia has already crossed the cavern and is back in the main part of the castle.

"Well, I don't see the harm in a kiss," says Prince Stefan. "Your dreams are going to come true—getting kissed by the handsome prince."

That's almost enough to break me—the thought is so disgusting, I can't believe he's said it out loud. But I only need to hold on for a tiny bit longer.

He leans in. As his lips press against mine, I bite down on the leaf. Then I open my mouth to kiss him deeper and press the broken leaf inside his mouth. I pull away.

"What the—" is all he has time to say before the leaf's natural sap takes action. His lips stop moving midsentence, and his body stiffens like he's been turned into a statue. I know that I'm only going to have a minute—if that—of a head start before the effect wears off and he comes after me. I grab his bag and the vial of memory from his hand, then run away from him as fast as I can.

I go against my instinct and run to the gaping hole in the floor. I swallow back the vertigo, find the remnants of the ladder, count to three, and swing my legs over. It's a long climb down to the river, and the sound of running water rushes in my ears. I'm barely a few feet down when the rung I'm on cracks and breaks.

I half-slide, half-fall down the rest of the rungs, my hands raw with rope burn, smashing the rotting rungs with my feet. I hit the cavern floor hard, my knees buckling. I break my fall with my hands on the slimy ground. The ladder is completely destroyed. At least they won't be able to follow me that way.

I crawl to the edge of the underground river, and it looks far more fast-flowing than it had from up above. Not only that, but where I'd assumed the water flowed into darkness, there's a thick rock wall. It's not a river; it's a whirlpool.

I'm trapped.

There's a shout above me. Stefan must already be moving. Dammit, I thought I had longer.

Rock explodes above my head as Stefan launches a spell at me.

"SAMANTHA!" Emilia shrieks, and I know I only have one choice.

I loop the straps of the bag tightly around my arms, jump in the pool, and let the current pull me under.

CHAPTER FORTY-FOUR

TOSSING, TURNING, TUMBLING. I SPEND several terrifying moments trapped in the swirling current. Luckily for me, it is an underground river after all, and I'm pulled through a tunnel of rock.

Just as I think I won't be able to hold on any longer, the tunnel opens out and I break the surface of the river, my lungs burning. It's absolutely pitch black and I take a series of ragged breaths in the darkness. My legs flail but I can't touch the bottom. Then, the current slows enough for me to feel like I've some control. I swim to one side and pull myself out of the water and onto a rocky ledge. I could kiss it, I'm so glad to be on land.

I don't kiss it, but lie there breathing heavily. One side of my head throbs from where I bashed my head on the entrance to the tunnel. My hands are tender and my knees are wobbly. But I'm alive.

I fumble around my neck for the fairybug light, praying

that it didn't break off in the whirlpool. Thankfully, it's still there. I balance it in the palm of my hand and it emits a small glow. What it shows me is not comforting. Cave, cave, and more cave. I can reach up and touch the damp roof with my hands, and beyond my toes is the rushing river. I'm cold, wet, and shivering.

Still, I'm so grateful to have that tiny bit of light, enough to illuminate the space around me, that I burst into tears. I need to get it out before I bottle it all back in. *Pull yourself together, Sam.* I need to take stock. I swing Stefan's bag off my back. In it, I find his cell phone and a wallet with money in it. To my relief, the phone powers on. Of course, as a royal, he has the very latest model— fully waterproof and capable of holding a decent charge. Unfortunately, there's no signal down here. Thank the dragons for waterproof money too. I take half a second to feel bad for having robbed someone—until I remember that he is responsible for kidnapping me, holding me hostage, injuring my granddad, and generally being a jackass. A bit of robbery is the least that he deserves.

I need to get somewhere I can use that cell phone.

I'm pretty reluctant to get back in the water, so I crawl as far as possible along the bank. I keep bashing my head and knees on jagged rocks, but I keep moving. Sometimes, I see remnants of human presence—like initials carved into the rock (what is it with students wanting to leave their initials everywhere?). I linger over where someone has carved "Z" into the rock, my fingers tracing the indent.

I crawl further until the bank ends. Now I have no choice but to get in the water. I brace myself, then jump in again. The cold water wraps itself around me like a blanket. The current moves swiftly enough that I don't have to swim to keep moving—I drift onto my back and float feet-first, so that my head isn't the first thing to collide with whatever obstacles are ahead. I'm able to lift the fairybug light above the water and in fact, it becomes rather peaceful.

I tilt my head back and look up into the roof of the cave. To my surprise, it's not completely pitch black. In fact, there are little pinpoints of light dangling from the ceiling—only one or two at first, and then hundreds of them. It's mesmerizing. I enclose the fairybug light in my fist to get an even better view. The lights dangling from the ceiling are a pale blue and soon the strands grow so thick, it's like I'm traveling underneath a canopy of stars.

Glow-worm thread—for shock and for daydreaming; to root the potion taker to Earth. Especially helpful if they are away in the clouds. Can also be used to make objects such as gloves.

Thinking about the ingredient calms me down.

The sound of rushing water interrupts my feeling of tranquillity, and I notice that I'm speeding up. I open

my palm, urging the fairybug light to even greater brightness. I wish I hadn't. All I see is the river in front of me
tumbling off into somewhere unknown.

It's too late for me to stop or scarper to the side; the
current is too strong to swim against. Before I know it,
I've reached the waterfall's edge and all I can do is angle
my body to make sure I go over feet first, squeeze my eyes
shut, and take a really, really deep breath.

When I dare to open my eyes, I've washed up ashore
not far from the base of the waterfall. Water pounds at
an outcrop of rocks at its base and I can't believe I'm still
alive and no worse for wear. I stagger to my feet. There
are more positives to being down at the base of the
waterfall, like finally being able to stand up straight and
see natural light. That can only mean one thing: an exit.
There are two other openings as well, but they're each
as dark as the place I've come from. I choose the light.

"Samantha!" I hear my name from high up above my
head. It's Emilia. *Already?* I thought I had more time. I
sprint to the exit.

"Wait!" she says. She jumps from the top of the waterfall, using her magic to break her fall.

I've only taken two paces when a spell hits me and
I fall to the ground. When I look up, she's next to me.
She grabs my upper arm and yanks me to my feet. "We
don't have long," she says. She opens my palm and
presses something inside. It's a large envelope, with bulky

contents. She closes my fingers around it. "Inside is an emergency transport panel and something else you can use to find the diary before Prince Stefan can find you. I know you have no reason to trust me, but you must. I can't get away from them. I'm in too deep. They want the cure, then the Novaen throne, and if you don't get to your great-grandmother's diary first, they're going to take it. Now, there might be light but this is not the exit. Take the left-hand tunnel and follow it until you think it's a dead-end. Just above your head will be a mailbox-size opening: You can get through it. Then do what you need to do. I will delay them as long as I can but you won't have much time. He knows about the Lake of Stars now. I know you don't trust me, but think about your experience here. I've been trying to help you at every point along the way, including giving you all the tools you needed to make your escape. I brought you to the greenhouse so you could pocket that leaf. Think about that."

There's noise above us. "Go, go!" she says.

I don't want to trust her. I don't know how I can, but then something in me snaps. I don't have to have all the answers now—I just need to get through each moment alive, one at a time. Even if trusting my worst enemy is my only option.

I dive into the dark left-hand tunnel but I don't completely follow her directions. I find a large rock on the floor with a jagged, pointed edge, and I put it into Stefan's backpack. I then crawl into a crevice near the entrance. If Emilia betrays her word and sends the prince after me, I'm going to come out swinging.

There are four more blasts of wind. Stefan, Ivan, and two more heavyset men I don't recognize come flying down the waterfall. "Quick, she went this way," Emilia says, pointing toward the light.

"What are you standing around for then? Let's move," says Stefan.

They run down the tunnel, leaving me alone on the left-hand side. I still can't shift the feeling that this is some kind of trick, but the longer they run in the opposite direction, the more chance I have of getting away. I dump the rock from the bag and sprint down to the end of my chosen path. As Emilia said, it looks like a dead end. But above my head is a tiny gap that looks far too narrow for my body.

I hoist myself up. *Okay, legs first.* I clutch the bag tight to my stomach, then inch my way through the opening. It's working! The rock closes in around my face, so I can feel the heat of my breath reflecting back at me. I focus on the tiny movements of my body, every millimeter a success. Claustrophobia claws at my skin, panic licking at the rational corner of my brain. Then, just as it threatens to be too much, my hips are through, and then the rest is easy.

Now there's light here. Sunlight streams through a hole in the ceiling, dark green creeping into the cave. I pull on a tree root to help me up and clamber out into the day.

I lie there, delirious with cold shivers from my still-wet clothes, and let the sun warm my face. I count down from fifteen, then I sit up, grab the phone, and dial the only ordinary person in the world I know who can get me through this.

Kirsty answers. "Stefan?"

CHAPTER FORTY-FIVE

I IMMEDIATELY HANG UP THE PHONE.

I sit there in shock for a few seconds.

That can only mean that Kirsty has Prince Stefan's number. But why would that be? I don't have time to think about it. But if she's somehow connected to Prince Stefan . . . I can't trust her either. Now I need to pick someone else to call. I desperately want to call Evelyn or Zain but Granddad's words ring in my head. *Only Talenteds can be impersonated by changeling potion.* What if Emilia tricks me again? I need people I can trust implicitly, who will help me no matter what, who won't question me when I ask them to join me on this crazy ride. And they need to be ordinary.

Nervously, I dial another number. After a few rings, the person I've been waiting for picks up.

"Hello?"

"Anita? Don't freak out. This is a Molly-and-the-unicorn level emergency. Do you hear me?"

There's a mad scramble and I hear a door lock shut. "Sam?" Her voice chokes as she speaks to me. "But I thought . . . the news says . . ."

"I know. But I'm okay. I promise I can explain everything. But first, I need you to listen. I need your help."

"Anything," she says without a moment's pause, and my heart explodes with love and gratitude.

"I was kidnapped by Emilia, but under the order of Prince Stefan."

"What?!" Anita screeches down the phone. "Where are you?"

"Right now, I don't exactly know. Somewhere in Gergon. I'm outside the Visir School—tell Arjun, he'll have heard of it."

"Does this mean I can bring Arjun in on this too?"

"Yes," I say. I trust Anita's brother Arjun as much as I do Anita, and if I won't have Kirsty's Finding skills to draw on then his are the next best thing. "But no one else. We can't trust anyone who is Talented. Emilia is a master at changeling potions and that makes anyone who is Talented a risk."

"Okay," says Anita. "So what can I do? How can I get you home?"

"I can't go home yet. I've been hunting for my great-grandmother's potion diary. I believe that she hid the recipe for an aqua vitae in it." I hear Anita gasp, but I keep going. "I need you to get to Runustan as quickly as you can—to the village at Lake Karst. There's a woman there called Nadya Ivanov. She has special dispensation for a transport screen—the only one inside Runustan at the moment. She can help you get there quickly. Tell her I sent you. Can you do that? I'll meet you there."

Anita's teeth are chattering down the line, a sure sign of her stress. "Sam, I don't know . . . your parents are devastated; Zain's transporting all around the world looking for you; the royal family are in a state of panic. They haven't stopped searching for you—and they're properly freaking out. If you're safe, why don't you just come home and then we can figure all of this out from here?"

"I'm safe, but my family isn't. Heck, *Nova* isn't. If I go home now, I'll be putting everyone at risk." My voice rises into a high-pitched squeak. I keep looking over my shoulder, fearing that at any moment Emilia or Prince Stefan is going to come bursting out of the woods behind me. "If you don't help me, I'll do it alone."

"Okay, okay!" She takes two deep breaths, then continues. "Sam, how are you going to get to Runustan?"

"Let me worry about that." Do I trust what Emilia has given me? Once again, I don't think I have a choice.

"Sam, I love you. Be safe. We'll make up an excuse and meet you there."

"I love you too." The words choke me. Then I hang up and throw the phone down into the water before I can change my mind, in case it has a tracking device. I pull out the emergency transport panel and fold it out on the ground. Its mirrored surface reflects back the top of the trees that surround us. It looks harmless, but I know it's not. I swallow hard. Will I be able to transport over this huge distance without it killing me?

I stand up and step away from it, not able to build up the courage straightaway.

I take the other strange object out of the envelope and examine it in my hand. I'm not quite sure what this is. It feels like it's made of glass, or maybe some kind of crystal. Inside, there's another object, but I can't quite make out what it is in the darkness. I bring it out into the light of my fairybug.

Then I almost throw it away.

Encased in the crystal is a swirling galaxy. It's filled with stars, with streaks of crimson and violet and indigo running through it. It's unmistakable. It's a centaur's eye.

An eye encased in the glass.

Take this and use it to find the diary, Emilia had said. Use the centaur eye?

Centaur eye—the first synth ingredient ever made. Key ingredients in potions to aid seizures (especially those with accompanying visions) or to help find things that are lost.

My head swims with potions. But even though it could possibly give me all the answers I need, I can't use the eye now that I've met the centaurs. They might have tried to kill me—but it didn't make me less in awe of them.

This eye needs to be returned—so they can bury it with the centaur who died to provide it. It wouldn't feel right to use it.

I wonder why Emilia hasn't used the eye to find the diary already. But then I remember: Centaurs can sense intention. Maybe that goes for the eye too? If it can sense Emilia's evil plans for the diary, it might attempt to thwart her—rather than help her.

I place the eye inside Prince Stefan's backpack. Then I take a cautious step back toward the transport screen. I try to think how I've seen others do it. I put my hand on it and say, "Nadya Ivanov, Lake Karst."

Within a moment, Nadya's face appears on the screen. Her eyes widen as she recognizes me. "Your friends weren't joking when they said you didn't want to waste any time."

I feel a rush of gratitude at Anita for moving so quickly. "Nadya, can you help me?"

"Of course," she says. "I'll grab one of the techs." For a moment, I hesitate. Nadya's transport technicians are *also* Talented. But can I really be suspicious of every Talented person in the world? Emilia couldn't have got to all of them. *If you escape, you cannot trust anyone Talented.* My brain flip-flops on the decision. "If you come through now, your friends will follow shortly," says Nadya.

The tech pushes his hands through the screen. I decide to take the leap, give him my hands, and am pulled through the glass.

CHAPTER FORTY-SIX

"I AM ONLY HELPING YOU BECAUSE YOUR friend made it clear that this is an emergency." Nadya's arms are folded across her chest, her dark brown eyes narrowed.

I'm bent over double, my hands on my knees, attempting to calm my jagged nerves.

"I see you didn't bring Kirsty with you this time. She didn't want to come and see the damage she's done in person then? Sometimes I wonder if the grand adventurers are actually the biggest cowards. Typical, arrogant Finder."

Now it's my turn to frown. "I don't understand . . ."

But she hasn't finished. "First the dragons, then an influx of heavies making demands of the centaurs and the people of the village. Is Nova going to help us sort out this mess? You're displacing this entire village and they have nowhere to go; they have to start all over again . . ."

"Displacing the village?" I ask, shocked.

She adjusts her headscarf, which has come loose with her anger. "We all have to move."

"But why?"

"You think you can rile up a dragon like that and get away with it? We've lived peacefully for decades and then three outsiders come along and mess it all up. The centaurs are suffering from the dragon's anger and they blame us for it. The centaurian envoy, Solon, came by and said we either move away or they will drive us out. They want this territory now."

"You're kidding."

"No, I'm not. So to be perfectly honest, I'm not sure that you are going to be all that welcome here. I don't think I can help you."

"Please, Nadya. This isn't just for me, it's for everyone."

"Pah, everyone. You Novaens act like you're the center of the world, like the sun and stars revolve around you. You've been squabbling with Gergon throughout the centuries—your monarchies rise and fall—and yet in Runustan we do not notice. Our sun still rises and sets and our stars still shine. Your concerns are not ours."

I nod slowly. We do make Nova the center of the world on all the maps, and I'm ashamed to be so Nova-centric. "Well, I should thank you anyway. You have already helped me by bringing me here."

There's a slight crack in her serious façade. "Sam, I don't think you understand. I feel for your grandfather and what you're going through, I really do, but I don't have time to drop everything and rush to your aid. If there's more damage done to the village, no one will forgive me. They won't let me back in, and all the work I've done here will be lost."

"I understand if you don't want to help me but if it's the village's relationship with the centaurs you're worried about, I can help *you* with that. I need one meeting with a centaur. With Cato."

She waves her hands dismissively. "That will change nothing."

The weight of the centaur's eye is heavy in my pocket. "Nadya, you have to trust me. You said that my great-grandmother was the only one who cared about learning not only where the ingredients come from, but the history and culture that nurtured them. That she was an alchemist you admired. On my honor as a Kemi—as Cleo Kemi's great-granddaughter—I give you my word."

She searches my face and I don't shy away from her intense gaze. "Fine. I'll give you one chance. But Sam, if you mess up with these centaurs . . . that could be the end for these villagers and their way of life. This is a rift *you* created."

"And I can fix it. I know I can," I say, with all the confidence I can muster. "And if I don't, then there could be worse things coming your way. Worse people. People who really *won't* care about what happens to you."

"Fine. I will call Solon. But you had better be

prepared. The centaurs might take less kindly to you than the villagers—and you already know they don't share the same forms of justice as we do." She runs her hands over the front of her dress. "I had better set off straightaway. The technician is on alert for your friends. They should be through soon."

"Thank you," I say.

She nods, then disappears from the tent.

I pace around Nadya's *ger*, waiting for Anita and Arjun to arrive. I throw my portable screen straight in the fire. As an acrid smell rises from the flames, I pray to the unicorns that there wasn't a tracer on it.

I drop down onto one of the cushions and wrap my arms around my knees. My foot starts tapping on the ground.

I don't have to wait long. Not even an hour passes before the tech rushes in, helping Anita and Arjun through the transport one at a time. I hug Anita so tightly she winces. But then when I let go, she squeezes me back again just as hard. "We thought you were dead," she whispers in my ear.

"I'm still here," I whisper back. Arjun is next.

His hug is briefer but no less comforting. Worry mixed with relief blazes in his eyes. "Sorry it took us so long." We wait for an awkward moment in silence as the Talented tech confirms that the link is closed and heads back outside. He seems in a hurry. I think back to what Nadya said about the whole village being displaced. Hopefully I can help them a tiny bit.

But first: the diary.

Once we're sure the tech is gone, Arjun continues talking. "We had to think up a rapid-fire excuse to tell my parents *and* I had to put together an emergency Finders kit *and* we had to get to a transport terminal. Luckily it's like the whole world is looking for you, so our parents weren't surprised when we finally told them we were joining the hunt ourselves."

"Wait, you *told* your parents you were coming to find me?"

"Only in a general sense!" Anita assures me. "Everyone thinks we've gone to Crane Beach in New Nova because . . . don't be mad, but I've been on the Wilde Hunt Theories forums too. I did a quick bit of photo doctoring and made out that you've been spotted there."

"Why would I be mad? That's genius!" I say.

"I know how you feel about those forums."

"Anything we can use to throw people off the scent is good."

Anita shrugs. "Well, I'm not sure if it worked. I don't think Zain believed it. All I can say is, thank dragons he could only chat online and not in person . . . he probably would've seen right through me. He's actually still in Pays, near the Gergon border. He's with the princess petitioning to gain access to Gergon to search for you."

"We got here, like you asked," says Arjun. "Now you tell us—why *are* we here?"

I swallow and nod. "I've been here once before. To meet a herd of centaurs who live nearby."

"Back up a sec . . . ," says Anita. "*Why* did you meet centaurs?"

Super-speedily, I tell them what Emilia did to my grandfather and how important finding my great-grandmother's diary is. To their credit, they both listen without interrupting. Aware that time is ticking, but also that they need to be armed with the facts, I fill them in on my last visit to Runustan, the mystery of the centaur's riddle, and I summarize what I learned while under Emilia's captivity. The only thing I leave out is the gift that Emilia left me, and I imply that I stole the transport screen—just like I stole Prince Stefan's phone. I don't want them to have the same confusion about Emilia that I do.

"What was that riddle again?" Anita asks. She loves a good puzzle, and with her brain on this, we might stand half a chance.

"A place where day is always night but the stars spark on command."

"And you have no ideas?" Arjun asks.

"I'm not sure. But I saw that Lake Karst was nicknamed Lake of Stars on a sticker on Cleo's trunk."

Arjun taps on his phone. "A quick search says it's because on certain nights it is so flat and still that the reflection of the night sky makes it look like the lake is filled with stars."

Anita frowns. "That doesn't really fit the 'day is always night' part though . . . Could it be an indoor location somewhere? Maybe where they can turn lights on and off? That's the only way I can think of how stars could appear 'on command.' Is there an observatory or something near the lake?"

"Maybe, but there's nothing like that here. It would be a brilliant place for an observatory. But there are a few buildings with electricity . . . maybe it's one of those?"

"Well, if you had asked me about that before now, I wouldn't have said it was in Runustan. There's a really famous lake known by that name in Bantu, near Zambi, that's called the Lake of Stars because it's so high up in the mountains that when there are meteor showers, it looks like the stars fall into the lake."

"I've heard of that too," I say. "But that can't be it. The sticker on my great-grandmother's trunk most definitely depicted this place."

"Hang on—what did you say the Runu name for the lake is?" asks Anita.

"Lake Karst," I say.

"I *have* heard of it." She takes out her phone and pulls up a scrapbooking app. "I use this to keep track of all the places in the world that I want to travel to after university. Hang on a second. I knew I'd saved a picture of Lake Karst. It's known for having this bioluminescent algae."

"Biolumi-what now?" I ask, confused.

The biology geek in Anita surfaces. "It's this specific type of algae that emits a bright light when disturbed. It's a rare natural phenomenon that occurs in special places all around the world—just some places are more distinctive than others. Like here, look, there's a beach on an island in the middle of the ocean where the waves light up at night because of the algae washing up on the shore." She shows us the photo on her phone and she's right—it looks stunning and otherworldly. The waves are lit up like the Tree of Light in Laville. "Anyway, Lake Karst in Runustan is known for having this phenomenon too. But it's so far off any other normal tourist trail that not many people come here.

"It's also really hard to photograph the algae here, so there are no spectacular photos like that island. But it could be an explanation for the riddle: stars that appear on command. If you snap your fingers or clap your hands underwater then this algae sparks up like fireworks!"

"And it would be dark as night under the water too," I say. "Anita—you're a genius! Do you think that could be it?"

"It's worth a try," says Arjun.

For the first time, I feel a surge of optimism. I'm here with two of my best friends in the entire world—who also happen to be the smartest people in the world—and I know that if anyone can figure this out, it's going to be us.

CHAPTER FORTY-SEVEN

WHEN WE STEP OUTSIDE, KARST LOOKS completely different. Half the *gers* have been taken down and the villagers are frantically running around, loading their worldly belongs into flatbed trucks. It's a far cry from the calm, peaceful village I knew.

I swallow hard. Did Kirsty, Zain, and I really do this? I hadn't realized that my actions—and subsequently Kirsty's—could have such terrible ramifications. Did she know, and act anyway? I wonder how much dragonfire costs. Probably a *lot*.

But it's not worth this.

And still not as much as a centaur's eye.

My lips press together. Kirsty and I have been through so much, but that means I know exactly how ruthless she is. She'd probably make me use the centaur's eye. Use it—or sell it.

Anita puts her hand on my shoulder and I tilt my head so my cheek rests on her hand.

"Look, over there." Arjun points at a plume of dust rising from around the edge of the lake. As it comes closer, I can see it's Nadya in her 4×4. We run down to the water to meet her.

"I've spoken with one of the envoys: Solon. He said Cato would not meet you."

"What? But—"

She holds her hand up to stop me. "I stressed how insistent you were about the importance of this meeting and so Solon agreed to meet you and me alone. You, so that you can offer him whatever it is you think will change the centaurs' minds about our town. And me, so that I can negotiate the terms. It is a glimmer of hope."

It's not Cato, but it's a step forward. "Great. Is there a way for us to explore the lake?"

Nadya points to the small shack down by the lake's edge. "That's the water sports center. Unfortunately for you, all the young people who work there have abandoned the village and gone back to the main city. They want to try their luck elsewhere before this place becomes food for the dragons . . . literally. But most of the equipment is still there—they haven't had time to move it yet. And there's a boat. I'll make sure the owner knows."

"I'll take a look at it, Sam," Arjun says.

"Are you sure?"

"Yes, I've taken diving courses in my Finder's training—

I can at least check the equipment and see whether it's safe for us to use."

"I'll take a look online and see what I can find out about the algae in this lake," says Anita. "Maybe it can help us narrow down the location. It's pretty massive, after all." I follow her gaze out toward the lake. It *is* massive, the far side of the shore looks to be at least a mile away. It's only because the sky is so bright and clear that we can even see that far at all.

I've never loved my friends as much as I do in this very moment. "Thank you so much for doing this for me."

"Thank us when you're back," Anita says, her fingers flying across the keyboard.

I give them both big hugs. "If all goes well, I'll be back here in a couple of hours, okay?"

"We'll be ready for you."

I jump back in the car with Nadya, my fingernails bitten down to the quick. I'm grateful that the centaur wanted to meet me, but nervous at the same time. What if he wants payback for what we did to his herd?

When I see Solon standing at the edge of the water, a lump appears in my throat. He's alone, his body a dark silhouette against the sky. We park a short distance away, then Nadya and I approach. Once again, Nadya whispers to me out of the corner of her mouth, "You had better have a good plan."

Once we are within speaking distance of Solon, I bow my head. "Hello, again."

He doesn't say a word back to me—only stares with his golden eyes, his arms folded across his chest. He doesn't need to speak to me. I'm the only one who needs to say anything.

"I am deeply sorry for what happened to you and to your herd. I'm sorry that this was brought about by my visit. I assure you that I never had any intention to hurt you, or to anger a dragon. I have only come here to try to find my great-grandmother's missing potion diary. I know that she came here, and I thought it was my best chance to follow in her footsteps."

Solon interrupts me, anger distorting his voice. "You have done more than that. Your ancestor would have never been so reckless. You have provoked the dragon's ire and now she is hungry. She won't be satisfied until she has tasted flesh—centaur or human. It is all we have been able to do to protect ourselves and our young. She won't cross to the other side of the lake, and that is why we need the humans to give up their territory until the dragon is vanquished."

"Is there nowhere else you can go?" I plead.

"No. It must be here."

I nod my head, slowly.

"You said that you have something of great import-ance for me?" Solon asks, scraping his hoof against the ground, impatient now.

"Yes, I do. And I'm not going to use it as a bargaining

chip. I won't ask for anything in return." I turn back and look at my companion. "I'm sorry, Nadya. It has to be this way. I won't withhold this from the centaurs."

Her eyes harden. "You are just going to give freely something you could use to save us?"

"Yes," I repeat. "It was given to me by someone who thought I would use it to further my own goals. But I can't do that. I'm sorry that I deceived you."

I unloop the chain from around my neck, pulling the eye out from underneath my shirt. As soon as Solon sees it, he rears backward until I can see the whites of his eyes, and he shouts in Kentauri. He reaches back and draws his bow. Then he seems to remember himself and he says in Novaen: "Where did you get that?"

Even Nadya leaps away from me. I, by contrast, take a few steps toward Solon. I kneel down on the ground and hold the eye out in the palms of my hands, trying to ignore the fact that there's an arrow pointed straight at my heart. "I know that this belongs to your herd. Please take it and return it to the rightful family, so that they may bury it with whomever had to give it up because of an alchemist's greed and ambition."

I keep my eyes lowered to the ground, because I can't bear to think what might happen if he doesn't accept the eye—or if he decides that I'm the one who deserves to be killed for its theft.

I feel more than hear his hoof-steps coming toward

me, and I close my eyes in anticipation. There's a gentle pressure on my palm as he lifts the eye out of it. As soon as the eye is gone, I stand up and stumble backward away from him. He is holding the eye up to the light, examining it as I have done. "I know a certain centaur who will be very happy to have this back."

"Wait—the centaur who lost this eye . . . he's *alive*?"

"Indeed. And I believe you may even have seen him? He chased you out of the herd."

I swallow and nod. The centaur with the eye patch.

"We forbade him from killing you outright, which is what he wanted. We offered you that courtesy as the descendent of Cleopatra Kemi, who provided a great service to our herd in their time of need."

I decide to try my luck. "Will you allow these villagers to continue living by the lake?"

Solon shakes his head. "I'm afraid we have already seen that this is what we must do. There is no other way. You will have until tomorrow nightfall to vacate your camp before the first centaurs move in. And they won't show mercy like me."

"Why are you showing us any mercy at all?" I ask, not really expecting an answer.

"Because I remember what your ancestor did for us better than anyone."

"What did she do?"

He doesn't answer, but encloses the eye in his fist and gallops off, away from the lake.

I stare after him as he leaves. Reluctantly, I turn back to Nadya. Surprisingly, there isn't as much hatred in her eyes as I expected. Her shoulders are rounded, her eyes downcast, resigned to her fate. We walk back to the car.

"I'm sorry that I wasn't able to change the centaur's mind," I say, after the silence becomes too much for me to bear. "It didn't feel right to bargain with the eye. Or to use it to save Nova. It belonged to them."

There's another long period of silence as she turns the car around and begins the drive back to the village. After a while, she clears her throat. There are tears in her eyes. "I understand what you did. And I understand why you didn't tell me about the eye. I might have tried to convince you to do something different. But what you did was right. I at least must respect you for that. But I can't help you any further. This has sealed our fate. I must help the last of the villagers with their packing, and discuss where we should go next."

"Will you find somewhere to go?"

"We always do," says Nadya. "It's just the fewer elders there are, the fewer people there are who know how to live successfully like we do, in the old ways. So many of the young ones want to make their fortune in the city, and who can blame them? It's what I did. I've come back here educated, privileged. Life moves on. At least now you have paid your debt to the centaurs. Maybe one day they will let you learn more of their secrets."

"I don't know what the point of that will be. If I don't

find the cure soon, my grandfather might . . ." I can't even finish the sentence; I choke up. "I might not have a mentor, a store—heck, I might not even have a country to go back to! Not as I know it."

"Don't give up yet," says Nadya. "You still have the lake to search, remember?"

We are driving along its shores and I look out over the vastness of the water. "We're looking for one tiny journal in this immense lake. How will we possibly find it, even if it's there? This is just a hunch."

"From what the Wilde Hunt showed, your hunches often turn out to be right. That's no longer called luck. That's called brains."

"And I might have to give them all up to save my granddad . . ."

"What was that?" asks Nadya.

"Oh, nothing. I'm just terrified what the cost might be to make the aqua vitae, if indeed I find the recipe."

"Whatever the cost is, I'm sure it's not more than your grandfather's life. You know that."

I smile up at her. "I do."

CHAPTER FORTY-EIGHT

NADYA DROPS ME OFF AT THE SHACK BY the water's edge, when Arjun emerges with two large oxygen tanks over his shoulder.

"I have to leave you here," Nadya says. "I'm sorry that I can't be more help. Good luck to you, Samantha."

"Thank you. I understand."

She gives me a small smile and then heads off in her 4×4. Dust clouds rise up in the wake of her vehicle. The volleyball court beside us has been taken down hastily, the bottom of a net pole still sticking up out of the sand. My heart aches, but I know I will never be so casual about dropping in on a community again. I will come back here and make right what I've destroyed.

Anita comes up behind me. "You couldn't have known."

"Couldn't I? Things always seem to go wrong in my pursuit of potions. My sister almost died when I tried to produce the love potion . . . And now a whole village is gone. And it still could all be for nothing."

"Let's make sure it's not for nothing," she says. "Come on, I've been doing some good research."

I head inside the shack and it looks like a typical diver's hangout: lots of bright, bold stickers on the wall, postcards of beautiful ocean vistas and coral formations. There are also pictures of the different type of fish that can be found in the lake—with some varieties that are unique to this region. There thankfully aren't any big lake creatures for me to fear—and definitely no sharks. There are also charts on the wall. Lots and lots of charts, covering the room like wallpaper. Anita has spread one of them on the floor—all the other furniture has been taken away.

"Arjun? Are you ready? Sam's here . . ."

"Yeah, coming."

Arjun emerges, his brow covered in sweat. "We found a few full air tanks out the back along with wetsuits, snorkels, and fins. I think they were planning on taking all the equipment tomorrow. We can pay them for the air we use and the petrol for the boat—I negotiated a deal. But no one is willing to stay to help guide us."

Panic grips my chest at the thought of heading out into the lake without any local knowledge whatsoever. "Do you think we'll be okay?"

"Well, I have *some* diving experience—I should be able to show you the ropes. Hopefully it will be enough," he says.

"Hopefully," I say. I hadn't actually given the whole

searching underwater part much thought before the moment arrived. I've known a few people who have dived without any training though, and thankfully I know how to swim. It was one of the first skills that our mum had us learn. She had always struggled in the water, and she didn't want Molly and me to ever have that same issue.

"Okay, so I've taken a look at these charts, and it seems that the algae really likes to clump in a few locations," says Anita. "It *does* drift around a fair bit, so if the centaurs said that the diary was looking at the algae about a week ago, that gives us a good idea of which part of the lake to search. I've highlighted three areas . . ."

At the same time, Arjun is writing down a dive plan. "We won't have much opportunity to waste. You should normally only go diving twice in one day, but if we don't go too deep we can maybe stretch it to three."

"The water is quite deep in some of these locations," Anita says, pointing at the charts.

"We'll just have to do what we can. If we can't find it now . . . maybe we can come back and search with a proper dive master?" Even saying it out loud, I know that would be impossible. For one thing, the area will soon be swarming with centaurs. They're not exactly going to appreciate a bunch of divers in wetsuits coming to break up their party.

"So do we know how to get to those locations by boat?" Anita asks.

"Yes, the boat has a GPS system on it. We can input

the coordinates and make sure we're searching the right areas."

"Okay, well then, let's suit up and go," I say, with more confidence than I feel. Is it even possible that a diary could survive underwater for so long without dissolving into mush? I try not to think about it.

Anita hands me a swimsuit she found drying in the back room, and I change into the black one-piece. Then I try to get the wetsuit on. It's cold and slightly slimy, and I hate the feeling of it enclosing my body. But it's better than being out in the cold—and I definitely wouldn't survive being at any depth in the water without it. I have to jump a few times to get the wetsuit up over my hips, and then I tug at the long string attached to the zipper to get it done up all the way. Just before I close it off completely, I slip the fairybug light out of the backpack I took from Prince Stefan and put it on around my neck, tucking it beneath the tight collar of my wetsuit. I hope I won't need it, but the riddle "day is always night" suggests darkness that maybe even a flashlight can't brighten. Then I join Arjun and Anita on the boat. Arjun is also suited up.

"Wait, before we get too far offshore, you need to practice a few things in the water," he says. He helps me into the vest, with the airtanks strapped onto my back. He tosses me a whistle as well, which I put around my neck. "You're going to need that in case we surface away from the boat. Now, put your regulator—that's the thing that you breathe into—in your mouth, hold it tight to your mouth with your hand—and follow me." He rolls off the boat and into the water, and I reluctantly follow suit. I let out a little shriek as the cold water seeps into my wetsuit.

Slowly, though, the suit warms up, and I start to feel more confident. Arjun shows me how to inflate and deflate the vest I'm wearing so that I can sink, checks my air supply, and then gets me to put on a weight belt. I learn how to empty my snorkel mask in case it fills with water or gets knocked off my face while I'm under, and how to retrieve my air regulator if it gets separated from my mouth. He also teaches me a series of hand gestures we can use underwater to communicate. We descend to a small distance, and I learn how to equalize the pressure in my ears. Once he's satisfied I know the basics, we clamber back into the boat. Anita inputs the coordinates, and we're off.

Arjun and I sit together in the back of the boat, while Anita focuses on navigating us to the right spot. Arjun grabs my hand. "You know, Sam, you don't have to try and fix everyone, all the time."

The words are enough to make me shake with fear and worry. He pulls me toward him and hugs me. "You know you are like a sister to me," he says, when I finally sit back up again. "But you don't have to do this alone. I'm glad you called us. What you went through with Emilia . . . that must have been terrifying."

I wipe my eyes, willing my tears to stop, and let out a

hiccup-laugh. "I don't think I've really processed it yet," I say with a small shrug.

"No, I don't think you have. What happened to you is a huge deal. But we'll look for this diary today—and then we'll let the professionals handle it, okay? I'm sure Evelyn can get teams of divers to search this entire lake. We'll find your great-grandmother's diary. And if we don't? We'll make sure that Emilia and Prince Stefan can't find it either. We'll find a way to make your granddad well again."

"Thank you," I say, smiling gratefully. I love his optimism, but deep down I know this is our only shot.

"Okay, we're at the first spot," Anita says. "Stay safe down there. I'll be counting for you—you're allowed twenty minutes, tops, okay?"

I nod, unable to talk now that I have bitten down on the regulator with my teeth. I give Arjun a thumbs-up, then tip back into the water, holding onto my snorkel mask with my fingers.

I hit the water, but at least the cold isn't so much of a shock this time. Anita has dropped the anchor and there's a bright orange buoy attached to the top to act as our reference point. Arjun makes me hold onto the anchor line as we descend, so that I can get my bearings without panicking. I'm grateful to him as we descend, and my head is slowly swallowed up by the lake water.

We're diving. We're actually under the surface.

This is unreal. We descend to about twelve meters

according to the gauge on my suit. I'm surprised by how clear it is underwater, and I can see the bottom of the lake rising up beneath me. It's a relief to be able to see the sandy floor, as I was worried we might not be diving deep enough.

I look up at Arjun. He's brought a long stick in order to overturn rocks or dig in the sand if necessary. He's gesturing at me, pointing first at my eyes and then at his. He's telling me to watch him at all times—or, at the very least, to be mindful of where he is and not to drift too far away. The current doesn't feel very strong, but there's no telling what we might find underneath the water—and I could find myself adrift from him in the blink of an eye. I give an "okay" sign with my thumb and forefinger to show I understand. I follow just behind Arjun and to his right. We scan the bottom of the lake, but here it seems far too empty.

Arjun points toward another section of the lake, which looks like it's covered in a forest of kelp: perfect for concealing something for over five decades. I nod and swim over to it, brushing the scalloped edges of the seaweed aside to search. There are far more fish swimming around once we are inside the kelp forest. They seem completely undisturbed by the fact that we're in their midst.

As I push another weed aside, one strand of it loops its way around my arm. Even though it's completely harmless, I have a flashback to the eluvian ivy, and panic grips my heart. I launch forward with my other arm and manage to grab Arjun's flipper—and at the same time, his attention.

My instinct is to swim straight to the surface, but Arjun is by my side with a few strong sweeps of his arms. He is calm as he unwraps the kelp from my wrist and takes me up above the weed. He looks me deep in the eyes and brings his hand to his mouth and then back out again, simulating a breath. I try to follow him. Breathe in, breathe out. Breathe in, breathe out.

My heartbeat returns to normal. Arjun looks concerned, his dark brown eyes magnified by the mask. He gives me a thumbs-up, but I know what he means: He's asking if I want to surface. I check my air: I still have plenty. That means we can't have spent our twenty minutes yet. We still have so much lake to search. I shake my head and nod to continue. He holds me there for a few moments, then nods back. He gives me an "okay" sign, and we continue.

I feel silly for having panicked, as it really is so peaceful beneath the water. Because the fish don't seem bothered by our presence at all, it's almost like we're not there. I've always loved heading to the local aquarium to watch the fish swim past—and this is like the up-close-and-personal version. I'll have to do this again, under different—less stressful—circumstances.

Arjun indicates that he's going back down to search the kelp by hand, but that I should float above and see what I can spot with my eyes. I wish I had the courage to go back in there, but I also know I'll be less than helpful if I panic again. I wish I hadn't been so traumatized by the ivy, but it remains the most terrifying experience of my life. Even more so than the abominable snowman—the thing that brought me and Zain together. The thought of Zain makes the chain of guilt rattle once again. I wish I could have called him after my escape.

When our twenty minutes are up, Arjun gestures for us to head up to the surface: another thumbs-up. I nod, and we ascend until we're only a few meters away. Then I hold onto the anchor line as my body adjusts. When we've stopped for the allotted time and allowed our bodies to readjust to the depth, I climb back up the anchor to the boat.

"Any luck?" Anita asks as she helps me back into the boat. I take off my mask and shake my head.

"'Fraid not." My mouth feels dry from the compressed air, so I take a large swig of water.

"Nothing down there except a lot of seaweed and a *lot* of fish," says Arjun. "That was kind of wild, huh? I've never done any lake diving before."

I nod, but my heart is tight within my chest. "It feels even more like a lost cause when we're down there," I say.

"Let's move on to the next place," replies Anita. "It's almost right in the middle of the lake. Are you happy to go again?"

"Yes, let's do it," I say.

"We'll have to rest for at least an hour before we can go under again," says Arjun.

"Seriously, Arjun? Aren't we going to run out of day-light by our third dive?"

"Okay fine, forty-five minutes rest. But I'm not budging on this. There's no point if we find the diary only to die of decompression sickness."

"I suppose," I say.

But the next dive is no more fruitful than the first. Arjun dives a bit deeper than I do, but he finds nothing. We even get to explore a cave, which excites me as that could fit the brief: somewhere where it is always dark, but stars can appear on command. Unfortunately, there's no sign of *any* human objects down there—let alone a journal. I do come face-to-face with an eel though, which is slightly more than I bargained for. Luckily for me, it just opens and closes its mouth, gaping like a child on Midwinter morning. I feel deflated, like someone who hasn't received the presents they wanted. I haven't even seen a sign of this bioluminescent algae that Anita was going on about. I keep trying to snap my fingers and clap my hands, but nothing happens.

"Okay, this next location is a bit closer to the shore, but according to the charts, the shoreline drops quite steeply underwater, so it's still pretty deep. I also won't be able to drop an anchor here," says Anita, once we're back on the boat.

"Are you sure there isn't somewhere with a great con-centration of algae—where it's more likely to be?"

Anita frowns. "That's exactly how I'm choosing them: These are the top three algae locations."

"I know," I reach out and grab Anita's hand. "Thank you. I'm sorry I'm being grouchy. It's just that . . . I really *really* need this to be it."

We wait the allotted hour, and watch as the sun heads steadily toward the horizon. It's amazing how fast the sun sets here—it seems to fall through the sky. Something about the flat landscape and our proximity to the equator makes the twilight shorter.

"I don't know if we should do this," says Arjun, looking up at the sky. "Diving in the daylight is one thing, but at night? That's for advanced divers."

"Well, we'll have flashlights with us, right? We can use them to search as much as possible. Then as soon as you feel uncomfortable, I'll come up. I promise."

He hesitates, so despite the fact that I hate having to force him to make a decision, I leap off the boat so he has to follow me. Inside my flippers, I try to cross my toes, just like I'm crossing my fingers. This needs to be the time we find it.

It has to be.

CHAPTER FORTY-NINE

WHEN WE DESCEND THIS TIME, IT'S noticeably darker. Luckily, the flashlights illuminate the darkness, though only for a few feet. It's much eerier down here in the twilight. The water that was once clear becomes murky, and even though I know there are miles of lake all around us, I can't help but feel enclosed.

I can tell that Arjun is annoyed at me through his body language: the sharp, curt hand gestures and the snap of his fins. I hope that he will forgive me one day, because it seems like he might have been right. Searching in this semidarkness, which is getting darker by the second, is stupid. The bottom of the lake is just sand, sand, and more sand—and then a steep drop that leads down deeper into the lake. There are more plants down here opening in the darkness, huge flowers unfurling their large petals—and I might have been able to appreciate their strange beauty under different circumstances—but now all I feel is frustration.

Arjun has better eyes than me, because he spots a large object sitting on the lake bed a few meters from where we are. I follow him, when all of a sudden I let out a squeal under the water.

Arjun looks like he's shooting light from his flippers. I wave my flashlight frantically at him and he spins around under water. I swim forward a bit, then clap my hands. Light explodes around me. As I move my arms, disturbing the water, it's like the light is dancing with me. It looks like when we use sparklers on New Year's Day and write our names with the light.

We can hardly believe it. Arjun does a somersault in the water, the sparks surrounding him. Is this what it feels like to be Talented, to be able to cast a magic spell? My heart wants to burst with the beauty. And also the hope. *Where stars appear on command*, the centaur had said. I snap my fingers and stars appear in the water. *On my command.*

This has to be where the diary is.

We swim over to the large object, which is teetering on the edge of the shelf of sand before the bottom drops down sharply into a black abyss. I'm shocked to see that it's an old-fashioned car. Most of it looks rusted and broken, but it's still unmistakably a car. Fish swim in and out of cracks in the bodywork, and all the windows have been smashed in—whether caused by the crash or some other pressure, I don't know. But it's exactly the type of car my great-grandmother might have driven in her adventures.

Then, the worst thing I could imagine happens. My flashlight flickers and turns off and I am plunged into darkness.

And Arjun's does too.

I do the only thing I can think of, and I clap my hands. Arjun is by my side with a few swift kicks of his fins. He wants us to go to the surface, and he tugs my arm. But I tug back. We need to search the car, and I have one last trick to try.

The fairybug light.

It's been hanging around my neck. I take it out from underneath my wetsuit and I pray for it to come on. Arjun won't be able to see it, but I can. He's just going to have to trust me.

I give his hand a squeeze, but I don't let go.

The fairybug light brightens just enough for me to be able to see the car again. I can also see the fear on Arjun's face and I know I have to be quick. I grab his other hand and place it on the car's frame. I press it against the frame, hoping he understands that I want him to hold on while I search the car.

I let go of his hand and swim through the front window. I sit down in the front seat, hooking my flippers under the wheel to anchor me down. I pull open the glove compartment first, thinking that would be the most logical place for it: but there's nothing. I reach under the seats, but still my hands come up empty.

I drift up from the front seat and swim around to the back. I can see Arjun watching the flashes of light I'm making, and I know I can't leave him much longer. The darkness is claustrophobic enough as it is. I just need to check the trunk, and then I'll be done.

I tug at the handle, but it won't budge. I curse my stupidity. With the window busted, I can just reach in. I shift aside a piece of blanket that has been covering the contents of the trunk, getting the shock of my life as dozens of fish are disturbed and swim up into my face.

Underneath the blanket I see a spare tire, a box of tools, the normal things you expect to find in the trunk of a car. I put my hand inside the center of the tire and feel around.

My fingers grasp something hard, and I lean in to try to tug it loose. When it finally comes free, I see that it's a locked box of some kind. It's extremely heavy. I try to open it, but it's no use underwater. I'm going to have to take it with me. I make a frantic gesture to Arjun, sending off sparks of light in different directions. He lets go of the frame and swims toward me. Then, the car shifts forward without warning, sending up a cloud of sand that even the fairybug light can't penetrate.

I shoot my arm out and Arjun grabs it. He then grabs

the other side of the box. With several big kicks, we drag it out of the trunk, just as the car tips off the side and begins to freefall into the abyss.

We surface slowly, my fairybug light the only thing guiding my way. I'm so unbelievably proud of Arjun for completing this in almost total darkness.

When we surface, the lights of the boat are shining across the lake. We shout and wave, while clinging desperately to the box. Anita swings the boat around and drives it toward us. Then she kills the engine, leans over and helps us lift the box into the back of the boat.

"I was so worried for you guys—it got dark so quickly and you were down there for ages," says Anita.

"Our flashlights went out," said Arjun. He grabs a towel to wrap around himself. He's shivering, and I can tell that being underwater in total darkness has rattled him badly. "That box better be worth it."

"I had this," I say, bringing the fairybug light out into the open. It seems almost spent now. "But I'm the only one who can see the light emitted from it," I say.

"Well, that's good for you but I thought I was going to have a panic attack." I sit close to him and give him a hug. I know he's not too mad, because he leans into me and accepts my warmth.

Anita drives the boat back to shore, then we drag the box off the boat and onto the dock.

"Wait!" says Arjun, putting his foot in front of the box

CHAPTER FIFTY

"ANITA, GET BACK IN THE BOAT." USING strength I didn't know I had, I haul the box almost single-handedly back on board, pushing Anita in as well.

"Sam! You're all right!" Zain shouts. He runs toward the dock but I stand shoulder-to-shoulder with Arjun and hold out my hand, palm facing out. Arjun holds the stick horizontally in front of us.

"Zain, stop there!" I shout back.

A frown flits across his forehead, but he slides to a stop. "What are you doing? Sam, it's me!"

Kirsty walks more slowly toward the dock. My eyes dart between the two of them. My heart pounds, my head a confused mess of excitement and fear and worry and relief. I stare at Zain: Does he look like the Zain I know? His hair is a mess, his face looks more drawn and gaunt than normal—but that could be worry. Would I know if Emilia was impersonating him? Would it be obvious?

to prevent us from moving it any further. "Look—
inside the shack."

"Someone's inside," I say.

"Get ready," Arjun says. Anita and I crouch,
gripping the handles of the box, ready to haul it
into the boat and make a getaway. Arjun picks u
long stick he'd used for digging in the lake, ho
tightly in his fist, and takes a few steps toward the s
"Hello?" he calls out. "Anyone there?"

There's a bit of commotion from inside the shack
an outside light is switched on. The door opens an
familiar silhouettes run out: It's Kirsty and Zain.

Kirsty looks exactly the same. She walks with her hands at her sides until she's shoulder-to-shoulder with Zain. We're in a strange kind of standoff, with Anita in the boat behind, ready to take off with the box.

"How did you find me?" I ask, the words catching in my throat.

"I've been searching for you everywhere!" says Zain, his hands out in front of him, his blue eyes begging me to trust him. "Then Kirsty said she saw Anita and Arjun take off in a hurry and realized it had something to do with you . . . she got wind that they were heading to Runustan but we had to fly here rather than transport. She got in touch with me as soon as she could to follow her hunch."

"I thought you were still in Pays . . ."

"I was! But I wasn't getting anywhere with the Gergon border. I knew Kirsty might have a genuine lead. I know how close you guys are. Please. We've been so worried about you. Why didn't you get in touch straightaway?"

"I couldn't," I say. "Emilia is too strong; I didn't know whom to trust. And Kirsty, how could I possibly trust you?" I shake my head, my body exhausted from the exertion of the diving, my mind tired from trying to extract the strand of the truth from the web of betrayals. "When you answered Prince Stefan's phone, it sounded like you knew him! Are you working for him?"

"Sam, I swear, I didn't know what he wanted when

he hired me to send you a bracelet. I didn't realize his intentions . . ."

"This bracelet was really from Stefan?"

Kirsty nods miserably. "It probably has a tracer inside."

Fear grips my throat and I try to tug the bracelet off my wrist. It won't budge.

"That's how he found me so quickly. How could you not realize he was bad news?" I shake with rage now.

She shrugs in apology. "He paid good money . . ."

"It's always about the money with you, isn't it? How much has he paid you this time to find me and bring me back?"

Now her face turns from apology to horror. "No, Sam, I would never! When I heard you'd been kidnapped I was devastated, and I asked my Finder friends to keep their ears to the ground for word about you. I brought Zain here because I know he can help you with the potion . . ."

I turn my attention from Kirsty back to Zain. Kirsty might be motivated by money, but at least I know she is who she says she is. I want nothing more than to run into Zain's arms but I have to test him first.

I rack my brains for a question to ask him, something that only he would know. Then I have a spark of inspiration. "What did you write to me in a coffee cup in Mount Hallah?"

Zain pauses for a moment. Then he smiles wide. I feel my body relax—I would know that smile anywhere: the dimples that form in his cheeks and the small creases that appear at the corner of his eyes. "You are special to me, Samantha," he says. His voice is little more than a whisper, but I hear him so clearly.

I hesitate only for a moment more, then I run forward and throw myself into his arms. There's a moment of surprise from him, then he hugs me tightly back. When we separate, I even hug Kirsty—she came looking for me, and I can't begrudge her too much for acting exactly as she normally would. "Thank you, guys."

"A little help back here?" calls Anita.

"Come on . . . we might have found something." I gesture for Zain and Kirsty to help grab the box off the boat, while Arjun heads into the shack and emerges with a heavy mallet. We move the box directly under the light so that we can see it clearly. It's definitely some kind of trunk.

"Ready? One, two . . ." On three, he hits the mallet and the rusty lock snaps in two. "Sam, do you want to do the honors?"

I swallow hard and nod. I open up the lid of the trunk, not knowing what to expect.

Miraculously, the inside is dry. I run my fingers around the edge, wondering if it's amazing workmanship or some sort of magic glamour to protect its contents. The next thing I notice is that this trunk definitely belonged to my great-grandmother. There's a photograph tucked into the lid in one of the far corners, a faded black-and-white image turned yellow at the edges, of Ostanes as a young boy.

"Is that your granddad?" Anita asks, looking over my shoulder as I take the photograph carefully between my fingers.

I nod, tears welling up in my eyes. I place the photograph carefully down on the table next to me. Then I sift through the other contents: some clothes, a blanket, a pair of shoes.

Then, there's a sharp intake of breath from us all. At the bottom of the trunk, the one thing I've been looking for this entire time. A pale brown leatherbound journal, wrapped many times around with a strip of leather rope.

My great-grandmother's potion diary.

I've found it at last, and I can finally save my grandfather.

I collapse onto the floor, my friends standing around me. It's like they don't know what to do now that I have the diary in my hands. Eventually, they sit down around me. I look up, catch Zain's eye, and he gives me a small nod. His eyes are wide with excitement.

I unwrap the leather ties, my hands shaking. I open the cover, and read the words written in neat penmanship on the inside:

The Potion Diary of Cleopatra Marie Kemi
Grand Master Alchemist
#34

"It's real," I whisper.

I turn the page, my breath held in anticipation. The diary starts in midflow, her words moving seamlessly from the last potion diary to this one. The pages that follow are endless lists of complex alchemical compounds, some scratched out and rewritten, others surrounded by hastily scrawled question marks. I recognize the franticness of her handwriting as an alchemist on the point of a breakthrough.

"Do you recognize it? Is it the start of an aqua vitae recipe?" Anita asks me.

I shake my head. "No, these are all formulas for potions, but I've never seen them written out like this before. This is . . ." I stop to breathe out sharply. This isn't what I've been looking for, not yet, but even so, it could change everything. "Look, she was trying to figure out the formula for a synthetic version of an ingredient."

"Wait—you're telling me that a Kemi grand master dabbled in synths?" asks Anita, shocked.

"I don't think she just dabbled in them," I say. "I think she *created* them. Right, Zain?"

He nods, but his face looks pale.

"Woah, woah," says Arjun. "That's a bit of a leap from a few scrawls in a journal, don't you think?"

"It's not just a few scrawls in a journal," I admit. "Zain told me when we were up in the mountains in Bharat that his grandfather stole a synth formula that my great-grandmother created." I look at Zain. "I didn't believe you at the time, not one hundred percent, but this might just prove it."

"Will your family believe it? Your grandfather?" asks Anita.

"I have to cure him first," I remind her.

This is fascinating, but still not what I'm looking for. I flick through every page of the diary, simultaneously trying to be quick, thorough, and not destroy the diary any further. This needs to be preserved back in the Kemi archives when I'm finished with it.

I reach the last page, and I swear my heart almost stops.

"Did you see anything?" asks Zain.

"No . . . nothing even closely resembling an aqua vitae formula."

"Maybe you missed it?" says Arjun.

I go through it again, even slower this time. Then I come across something that almost breaks my heart. Two pages have been ripped out, their edges blackened. Burned right down to the stitching, but not so close that it damages the integrity of the book. I sniff it and get an odor I recognize.

Bookworm powder—dissolves the pages of any book.

I know these pages weren't simply torn out and handed to someone else. They're gone for good. And I can only guess at what they might have contained. The pages either side give absolutely no clue that a recipe for an aqua vitae might have lived inside there.

But whether it did, or didn't, it doesn't matter. Because it's not there now.

A sob escapes my lips, and Anita wraps her arms around me. "At least Emilia can't get hold of it, or the Gergon royal family . . ."

Zain stands up and sighs, his head falling into his hands. "How can it not be in there? Everything indicated that it was . . ."

I stand up with a fierceness that breaks Anita's hold on me. "No . . . no . . . this is not the end! If my great-grandmother can figure out a recipe for the aqua vitae, then so can I." I pace around the room. "Maybe I'll go to Zhonguo, I can ask the monks that live there . . . and I can search Pays for the waterfall. I still have . . . a few days . . . until . . ."

Anita stops me. "Don't worry, Sam. We'll get through this."

I can't believe I've come all this way, and the recipe isn't there. My heart feels like it's broken into a million pieces. All I can think is that I'm going to have to start the hunt for the recipe all over again.

CHAPTER FIFTY-ONE

AS THE OTHERS LOAD UP THE CAR, I REST my chin on my knees and hug my legs. I don't want to look at anyone, and I don't want to talk to anyone.

The others wouldn't let me do anything more last night. They rightly pointed out that there was nothing productive that *could* be done—the transport technicians had left, I'd burned the other screen, it was too dark to travel now with the centaurs roaming about . . . We searched for a phone, but the signal booster has also been dismantled and taken away. We hunkered down in sleeping bags for an uneasy night's rest.

And I had to face the facts. Time had run out for me anyway. The only comfort was that it was running out for the Gergons too. If I didn't have the recipe, neither could they.

Oh how disappointed Emilia and Prince Stefan would be.

It's a small comfort. My mind feels like it's been separated into jail cells, certain thoughts being locked away so they can't rattle my sanity any further. Thoughts like my grandfather, lying in hospital . . . the cell bars rattle. I turn away from those thoughts again.

This morning, Zain looks tired and twitchy. I know he wants to ask me tons of questions about where I've been since the Laville Ball, but I haven't been up for that yet. I woke up with a crushing headache that threatened to turn into a migraine. My plan last night to continue searching for ingredients for an aqua vitae just seems stupid in the harsh light of day.

For one thing, my parents aren't ever going to let me out of their sight for as long as Emilia is still at large.

Kirsty is driving, Arjun is next to her, and I am squished between Zain and Anita.

"Can you imagine how happy your family will be to see you alive and well?" says Anita, trying to inject a touch of optimism. "And although they've tried to keep the news about what happened out of the media, it's going to be a crazy time for you."

"Not making me feel better, Anita," I say. I wish I could keep the whining tone out of my voice, but I can't. I feel like the ultimate failure. I feel like I've failed everyone: my family, my grandfather, my great-grandmother, Princess Evelyn, Zain, Anita, and Arjun. Literally everyone I have ever cared about.

ALWARD

"You'll make it through this, Sam," Anita says. "Come on, you solved the riddle of your great-grandmother's journal all on your own! That's not nothing."

"It has come to nothing," I say, retreating into the tortoise shell of a scarf I have wrapped around my head. Anita puts her hand on mine, then stares out of the window.

"Hey, what's that up ahead?" says Arjun.

There's a great cloud of dust on the road, blocking our way. Kirsty slows the car down to a crawl.

"Maybe some of the villagers who went before us have run into some problems?" says Anita.

My heart jumps into my throat as I think of Nadya. "I hope everyone is okay," I say.

But then a figure begins to emerge from the dust, and it's not human. A hoof appears first, the size of my head. It's Cato. And he's followed by not one, but many others. The entire herd. I can see Solon behind him, and behind him the centaur with only one eye. He still only has one eye, the other one dangling around his neck on a much nicer chain than the makeshift one I'd made. They are still wearing angry stares, the great V shape of their eyebrows locked in a permanent and terrifying frown. Cato points at me, then beckons me toward him.

"Is that what I think it is?" says Zain, his voice suddenly dripping with ice. "Samantha—what did you do?"

I frown. "What do you mean?" I haven't told Zain about

374

the centaur eye. But maybe that's not what he's referring to. "I want to hear what they have to say. If they wanted us dead, they would have fired their arrows at us already."

I step out of the car.

"Well then, we're all coming with you," says Arjun, unclicking his seatbelt. The others follow close behind—although Zain comes up to stand beside me. He radiates energy, his hands balled up into fists.

"Please," I say to Zain. I take his hand. "Don't antagonize them. We've done enough damage."

But I don't have time to say anything else, because Cato steps forward.

"Samantha Kemi. We have not been friends to humans for a long time. Even lately, you have brought more destruction to us and our herd."

I nod my head and swallow. I don't want to have the burden of any more news for Nadya and her community—especially not the news that things are just about to get worse and worse. But the responsibility is being laid at my feet again, and I will accept it.

"But, now that you have returned the eye to us," he continues, "we are in your debt. None more so than Valu himself, from whom the eye was taken."

"You did *what?*" says Zain beside me, and I shoot him a sharp look. I blink several times, because something about Zain seems to be shifting. I'm not sure if my eyes are behaving properly.

Cato's words draw my attention back to him. "In return, he wants to give you something. We know that what you have been asking for—the diary—was not truly what you've been looking for. You want the aqua vitae."

"Yes, more than anything," I say. I know my intentions must be telling him that as well. It's what I want with all my heart.

"You are correct that Grand Master Cleo found the recipe for the aqua vitae. She made it. She did it to save our herd when we were in our darkest hour. She chose to help us, above and beyond her quest in the Wilde Hunt to save her queen. She single-handedly ended the blight that could have wiped out our species, but in doing so, she lost her alchemical skill. It is the sacrifice required to make the aqua vitae. She said we would no longer have as many humans coming to our herd for ingredients, since she had found a way to replicate the properties in another format. She was a prophet as well as an alchemist."

Synths. Cleo had created synths to spare another centaur from losing another eye.

Cato continues. "She managed enough quantity of the aqua vitae for us to distribute amongst the herd, before it became too much for her. We survived, thanks to your ancestor."

For a moment, I am speechless. But I still have so many questions. "And then she destroyed the recipe. Why?"

"She knew it would be dangerous if it fell into the wrong hands—and the cost of such a recipe is too high."

"Selfish," snaps Zain.

Valu steps forward, every hoofstep heavy. He looks even more fearsome with his second eye hanging around his neck—both eyes seem to stare at me. "To repay my debt to you for returning the eye, I would like to give you something in return." He reaches into the side bag where he carries his bow and arrow. He pulls out a tiny vial, filled with a thick crystal-clear liquid. He gestures toward me with his head. "Hold out your hand," he says.

I do as he asks. He places the vial in my upturned palm and closes my fingers over it. I've never been this close to a centaur before, and I'm shocked at how warm his skin is. He feels like he is on fire. For the first time, I look up into his eye and I don't see anger there. I see . . . gratitude. My own cheeks burn.

"This is our last drop of the aqua vitae," he says. "Use it to heal your grandfather."

CHAPTER FIFTY-TWO

ZAIN LETS OUT A PIERCING SCREAM.

He contorts his body into an extreme angle, his back bent, his fingers curled over his face like he's trying to rip it off, the tendons of his neck popping.

Anita scrambles behind me while Arjun rushes over to Zain. "Are you okay, man?"

Except by the time his hands come down from his face, it's not Zain at all. It's Emilia. A more haggard, wretched Emilia than I have ever seen before: her skin sagging off her face, her hair so white as to be practically translucent, her body almost skeletal. She must have poured herself into her magic to hold such a transformation for so long, and now she is paying the price. How did I not see? How did I not know?

A violent urge to be sick overwhelms me, and I dry-retch into the ground.

I *kissed* Emilia-as-Zain.

Despite the amount of magic she must have exhausted, she is still lightning-quick.

With one hand and overwhelming strength, she pushes Arjun away while lunging forward toward me, snatching the vial from my grasp. Anita and I both swing at her, desperate to do anything to stop her, as the centaurs all draw their bows at once and point their arrows at her.

But she unstoppers the vial and downs the potion in seconds.

It works almost instantly. Her skin plumps and thickens, turning from translucent to milky white. The dark veins beneath the skin disappear, her eyes returning to the same striking blue as Evelyn's and her hair regaining its natural golden sheen. When the transformation is finished, it's as if she could be Evelyn's sister, not her wicked aunt.

She looks down at her hands in awe, their delicacy no longer showing the age and wear of a few moments ago. She is reborn—beautiful, strong, and really freaking dangerous.

The sight wrenches my heart out of my body and stamps on it.

"What have you done?" I shriek in agony. *What have I done?* is what I scream internally. How could she trick me like that? How could I be so stupid? What was it that Granddad had told me? Trust no Talented. And I ignored him.

The centaurs shoot their arrows but she throws up a barrier that glances them aside like they are swan feathers.

I hear a sharp, metallic double-click and spin around to see Kirsty unloading a shotgun from the back of the 4×4. She shoots at Emilia, but not even bullets can penetrate when Emilia is at her full power. She points her wand at the gun and shouts a spell.

"Kirsty!" I yell.

Luckily, she has the sense to toss the gun away and leap for safety. The spell hits the gun and twists it, turning it into a heap of smouldering metal. Still, some of the spell residue blasts into Kirsty and I see her take a bad fall, her head ricocheting off the ground. "Kirsty!" I shout again, but my feet are rooted to the ground. I beg Kirsty to move. I see a twitch of her hand and hear her groan, and breathe a sigh of relief.

From beneath the glowing light of her barrier, Emilia's eyes sparkle like stars. "I knew that I could count on you to find the potion, Samantha. Somewhere, somehow, I knew you would find it. That's what makes you such a great alchemist."

Even her voice sounds different—smoother, less like she drank an entire glass of gravel and more like it's been coated in silk. "I've never felt so . . . alive! Thankfully your little boyfriend was very easy to capture, all alone as he was on the Gergon border. Now look at me!" She turns to Cato, her eyes narrowing. "This is a human matter. Not for centaurs to get involved. Do you under-stand?"

"I'll KILL YOU," I scream, even though I have no way of backing up that claim. "Shoot her again!" I tell the centaurs. "She is evil incarnate. She was the one who had the eye to begin with. The one who kept it and prevented Valu from healing properly. It was her fault."

But Emilia's right. The centaurs don't interfere in human matters. Cato stares at me with what I think is a hint of sympathy, but he doesn't move a muscle. Instead, he turns and signals the others to leave us. Their hooves hammer the ground as they pick up into a gallop.

Emilia stretches and then walks toward the car. "I'm afraid I'm going to have to borrow this now. I have a country to take over."

"What about Prince Stefan?" I say in a last effort just to keep her talking until I can figure out a plan.

"What about him? He found out about my little ruse with you and fired me. What do I care. You found me the aqua vitae. That's what I wanted all along. And now, when your Princess runs out of time . . . I will be the one waiting in the wings."

"It's too late!" I say. "Princess Evelyn's not stupid. She'll marry before she lets her power destroy her."

Now Emilia smiles at me, all her teeth neat and white. It makes me shiver. "Married, unmarried, who cares. It doesn't matter anymore. I have the only antidote to the illness that is destroying the Gergon royals. Wouldn't it be a shame if it started attacking the Novaen royals too?"

"You're disgusting," I tell her. She laughs, then turns away from me and gets in the car.

Anita falls to her knees, sobbing, and Arjun goes to comfort her. I have a plan, but it's a foolish one. I just can't think of anything else. All I can think—and hope—is that maybe all the shouting has already started the process.

I rush over to them and put my arms around them both. "Arjun, I have a plan. Give me your phone."

"We can't call for help, there's no signal out here!"

"I know! Set your alarm on your phone as loud as you can, for two minutes from now. I'm going to distract Emilia, but I need you to get it ready as quickly as possible." I pull out the whistle that I wore for diving. I haven't taken it off. I blow as hard as I can, making a shrill noise.

"What are you doing?" shrieks Anita, tears staining her cheeks.

I take the whistle out of my mouth for a moment to answer. "Just don't move a muscle, no matter what you see," I say.

I blow the whistle again and again, blowing so hard my cheeks start to burn. I beg for it to work. *Please work. Please work.*

Finally, I hear the sound I've been waiting for. The flapping of wings in the sky.

"Oh my god, what is that?" asks Anita, her head tilted up to the sky.

"You don't want to know," I say. I grab the phone, which Arjun has just finished setting up, and launch into a sprint toward Emilia. She's already started up the engine, and she needs to draw her wand to reach me before she can get in properly. She also catches sight of what is now in the sky, which delays her by a crucial second. She blasts a spell at me—but it's an awkward angle around the body of the car. It's easy for me to dodge and roll. She curses me and slams her foot on the accelerator, ready for a speedy getaway. Just as she does, I toss the phone in the backseat, and then I sprint in the direction away from Anita and Arjun.

They barely take any notice of me. Everyone's attention is focused on the sky—on the great swirling, slithering dragon in the air above us. It's the same one that chased me last time—bright red scales glinting in the midmorning sunlight. At first, I think she recognizes me: I'm the one that called her, after all, with my screams and the blasts of my whistle. Does she remember how I antagonized her last time, how I tricked her? I don't know whether dragons carry the notion of vengeance within them. I wish that had been covered in one of my books—then again, I had never planned on making an enemy of a dragon.

My plan had better work—otherwise I'm going to be served up on a dragon barbecue. Arjun kneels by Anita, his hand covering her mouth, whispering furiously in her ear. I hope he's telling her to be quiet and stay still.

The dragon circles me, ignoring Emilia—who is speeding off in the car. I suddenly realize the massive flaw in my plan: The car is going to move out of the dragon's territory before the alarm has time to sound.

I've just condemned myself to one heck of a fiery death. At least it's going to be over quickly.

The dragon opens her mouth, the fire building inside. And then, like a miracle, I hear the alarm blast. It's like a foghorn piercing the mist: the only sound that can get Arjun out of bed.

Within seconds, the dragon passes over my head—and there's no sign of fire. I keep deathly still in my crouched-down position as the dragon undulates her way over to Emilia. My face is pressed against the ground by the down-draft of her wings and I end up eating a mouthful of dirt.

The car starts swerving frantically as Emilia reaches behind and tries to shut the phone off, and I worry that it's going to be enough to throw the dragon off the scent.

But the dragon is far too smart for that. She's angry, she's hungry, and if she recognizes me, she might also recognize the car as another source of her ire. Whatever she thinks, she opens her mouth and yawns wide, and out pours a stream of fire—right down on top of the car.

The car screeches to a halt: Emilia's attempt to avoid the flames.

But I see her as she escapes the burning car—her hair and clothes aflame. Water is pouring out of her wand, but it's not enough. As she screams, it attracts the dragon even further, and it swoops over her for another pass.

This time, Emilia can't get away. The dragon lands, followed by her baby, and on the ground, they do what dragons do best: they finish off their prey.

After a few agonizing seconds, the mother dragon lifts Emilia's corpse in her mouth and flies back toward the inner mountains of Runustan: her original home and territory.

Arjun comes rushing over to me. Anita is by Kirsty's side, and I'm pleased to see the Finder sitting up, although sporting a nasty-looking cut on her forehead.

"Did that just happen?" Arjun asks.

I nod, shell-shocked. "I think Emilia is dead."

CHAPTER FIFTY-THREE

ONCE THE CENTAURS SAW THAT THE dragons had returned to their original territory, they were happy to allow the villagers to return as well. Arjun rushed ahead to tell them the news. As soon as Nadya arrived back, I begged her to get the transport up and running. Even though Emilia was dead, the danger was far from over. I still needed to warn the princess about Prince Stefan. And I needed to make sure the real Zain was okay.

Back inside Nadya's *ger*, Arjun says: "Emilia would've had to keep him alive in order for the spell to work."

"I know. But I'm so worried . . . ," I reply.

"I can't believe Emilia's actually gone," Anita says, rubbing her temples. "And I can't believe you summoned a dragon on purpose."

"I couldn't let her get away . . . I . . ." It still hasn't really hit me that my direct actions caused Emilia's death. And yet, it also hasn't sunk in that the last chance I had of saving my grandfather—the drop of the aqua vitae—was stolen away by her before I even had a chance to savour it.

My only consolation is that now I know what it looked like, the possibility of my being able to make it again has increased.

No matter what my grandfather made me promise.

"Oh no, I know that look," says Anita. "We're going straight back to Nova this time. I'm not allowing you to take any detours."

"Her diary . . . everything . . . is gone again." There's no chance that it would have survived the dragon's fire. The car was reduced to ash. Even though potion diaries were built to be virtually indestructible, there are some forces that are just too powerful.

"Now, no one will know the truth about who made the first synth," I say.

"*You* will know," says Arjun. "And you can tell your family."

"I know," I say with a small smile. "It just won't be the same.

There's a small cough from behind us, and Nadya is standing there. "The transport is almost ready. But, um, Kirsty would like a word before you go?"

"Of course." I leap to my feet. Kirsty can't travel with us because of her head injury, but she's been seen by the local village doctor and she's going to be okay. When I see her, she looks worse for wear. Her head has been shaved in order for the doctor to stitch up her head, but Kirsty can pull it off. If anything, it makes her look even more badass.

She grins at me as I come in. "This haircut is going to be hella practical for Finding—not sure why I didn't do it sooner."

I return her smile and sit down on the bed next to her. "Thank you, for all your help."

To my surprise, Kirsty scoffs and pulls a face. "For my help? You mean bringing that devil into your midst in the form of Zain. I should have had my suspicions when he found me so easily—I knew he was supposed to be in Pays. But my instincts must have been off. I am *sorry* about that. I would never do anything on purpose to hurt you—"

"I know," I cut her off. "Of course I know. You don't need to be sorry. You couldn't have known. She had me fooled too, and I'm supposed to be in love with the guy."

"Good luck," Kirsty says. "And if anyone can find the way to save your granddad, it's you." We hug each other and then she ushers me away. "You have work to do. Go, go!"

I enter the transport room, and I see Anita is biting her fingernails. "What's wrong?" I ask.

"We can't seem to get in touch with the princess. Apparently she's been rushed to a top secret location until they can confirm that the threat from Emilia is gone. We can't even get any messages to her in case there's a security breach. They're sending agents here right now to confirm Emilia's death. They need to clear you before you can talk to the princess."

"I can't stay here! Can they clear me from somewhere else?"

"They say no."

"But—"

"Don't worry . . . I've got you covered. But you need to leave now. Your family is waiting for you."

"You got in touch with my mum and dad?"

"Of course! They're in Kingstown General Hospital."

"What are we waiting for? Let's go now!"

"Arjun and I will wait here to deal with the royal security when it arrives."

I frown. "Oh." Then I throw my arms around her and hold her tight. "Thank you. For *everything*."

"You're always welcome, you silly goose. Now go . . . go and see your family!"

The transport takes me directly into Kingstown General. As soon as I'm clear through the screen, Mum and Dad are all over me, pulling me into the biggest hug that I've ever received. Mum eventually pushes Dad aside, planting kisses all over my face until I try to wriggle out of her grip.

"Mum, Dad, I'm fine. I'm okay," I say.

"We've been so worried about you!" says Mum when she's finally finished. She still holds onto me tightly, as if she's worried I'm about to disappear out of her grip.

"I've been . . . it's been . . ." I don't even know where to begin.

"Start at the beginning, young lady," Dad says. "And

don't even think about missing out a single detail."

When everyone—Mum, Dad, and Molly—are sitting together in the little private area outside Granddad's room, I give them the story right from the start: from the moment I found out about Emilia's plan, to chasing down the diary in Runustan, getting kidnapped in Laville, seeing Granddad's memories in Gergon, and the final showdown with Emilia. They are an attentive audience— gasping and crying out in all the right places. But I can see their disappointment when they learn that I haven't been able to get the aqua vitae.

"Can I please see Granddad now?" Just telling the story again makes me desperate to see him.

Mum and Dad exchange a look, and then finally Mum nods. "He's sleeping right now. You can go and see him but then I want you to come straight back here. We have a lot more to discuss."

"I will," I say. I gently push the door open, not wanting to disturb Granddad. I pad over to his bedside and sit in the hard plastic chair that has been placed beside him. One of his wrinkled hands is lying outside the covers. I slide my hand until it fits underneath, then I grip it tight and kiss it gently.

"I'm so sorry, Granddad," I sob. *I've failed you.*

I feel a small hand on my shoulder. I look up, my eyes bleary with tears, and see Molly standing behind me. She in turn gives me a big hug. "I'm sorry I got mad at you on the phone," she says. "I thought . . . when you were gone . . . I thought that might be the last thing I ever said to you."

Her voice begins to break, so I grip her hand too. Between Molly, myself, and my granddad, we are a trio of sufferers. The sadness of it slightly makes me want to giggle. We're all okay, though, because we're together.

I let go of Molly's hand and wipe my eyes. She moves over to the other side of the bed and puts on the unicorn-tail gloves she left on the bedside table. "I've not been able to make much progress," she says with a small frown. "The synth has helped stabilize him, but his mind is still missing pieces."

"I almost had the aqua vitae that could have saved him."

Molly looks up at me. "You tried as hard as you could."

I want to nod, but I feel empty. I'm sure there was more I could have done. Trying my hardest and failing is not an outcome I'm used to.

Molly continues to talk, her forehead creased in concentration. "I feel like I could heal him if I had those missing memories. Maybe then I could edge them back into his mind?"

Suddenly a lightbulb explodes in my head; I can't believe I've been so wrapped up as to have forgotten about it. "I have one of the memory vials," I say. "I stole it from Emilia and Prince Stefan before I left the cave."

"You do? I can see if I can plug the gaps in Granddad's memories."

"Are you sure you can do this? Should we call one of the doctors?"

Her eyes open wide. "With these gloves, I can do it. I don't think Granddad would let anyone else other than family mess with his memories, do you? You know how stubborn he can be—even with some of his mind missing."

I nod. None of the other doctors has been able to see what Molly sees. If anyone has a chance at this, it's going to be her. I can't help but feel my insides warm with pride. She's going to be an amazing doctor.

I fetch the memory vial from inside the backpack. Thank goodness I basically kept it attached to my body at all times. Even touching the dark vial gives me the shivers but this is our opportunity to get Granddad back.

"How are you going to get the memories back into Granddad's mind?" I ask as my sister adjusts her gloves.

She frowns. "How did the memory board work again?"

"Emilia poured the memory onto the blackboard surface and when I touched the board, I was sucked into the memory."

"Well, that's it then. It must react to human contact. So I'll see if he can reabsorb it through his skin, and I'll use the gloves to kind of . . . guide it into place. I can't really explain what it feels like to use the gloves, but you'll have to trust me on this."

"Of course I trust you." I hand over the vial.

She unstoppers it and, very gently, pours it onto

Granddad's forehead. It gathers in a pool on his skin. He takes a deep breath as it touches him, which shocks us both. But Molly regains her composure first, touching his temples and closing her eyes.

After a few moments, with Molly muttering words I can't quite hear underneath her breath, the memory disappears completely from view, sinking into Granddad's skin and . . . hopefully . . . his mind.

When Molly opens her eyes again, I ask her, "Do you think it worked?"

But it's Granddad who opens his eyes. "It did," he said. "I can remember, I just . . . not quite everything." He frowns. Then he smiles. Molly collapses on top of him, hugging him tight, and I fall on top of her—though gently, so as not to crush Granddad's lungs.

He holds us tight, with strength that surprises me. Then he lets go, and slowly his eyelids droop until he's asleep once again.

"We need the rest of the memories," I say, my pulse racing. "I need to talk to the princess. She'll know what to do."

There's a thunderous pounding on the door to the waiting room.

"Sam?" comes Mum's call.

I take one look at Molly and we rush back. Mum has opened the door, and standing, silhouetted in the doorway, is Renel. And he looks mad.

CHAPTER FIFTY-FOUR

"WE WERE EXPECTING YOU IN RUNUSTAN. You should have waited for us there."

"I'm sorry," I say, but I keep my head held high. "I believed that seeing my family was my first priority."

"Be that as it may, we believe that you know where the deceased enemy of the state, Emilia Thoth, has been hiding out—and the potential location of hostage Zain Aster."

"Yes!" I say. "The old Visir School in Gergon."

"Impossible!" says Renel. "That school has been shut down for years."

"It's where I was held, and that's where Zain will be."

"Right, thank you. These guards will take your statement."

"Wait!" I say, before he can leave the room. "I want to go with you. To the Visir School."

"This is going to be a raid, Miss Kemi, so that would be entirely inappropriate."

I pull myself up to my tallest height. "There are items being held at the Visir School that belong to me. Plus, I have intelligence on the location of the castle," I try to speak as much like a security operative as I can manage, "which could be invaluable to your rescue effort and save you time."

He stares at me for a few long seconds. "Okay, fine. But we need to leave right now to extract the hostage as quickly as possible."

"Now, hang on a second," says Dad. "You only just got back. I'm not having you jetting off back into danger, into enemy territory no less."

"I'm sorry, Dad. This isn't a matter of giving them a map and telling them where to go. Zain's life is at stake. And there's Granddad. There might be something there that can save him."

I don't give my parents a chance to protest—this is something I'm doing, with or without their approval. Dad can see the determination in my face and he relents.

"Go get him," Mum says, giving me a kiss on the cheek.

In another room, Renel gives me a special uniform to put on: a close-fitting black shirt and trousers, a spell-and-bullet-proof vest overtop. When I emerge, he hands me a pair of wraparound sunglasses and gives me my briefing.

"We're going to have to do a moving transport—are you comfortable with that? The principles are the same, but we have to transport into a jet that is flying above the Visir School, then parachute in. Once we're there, we can set up a temporary screen in order for you to transport back."

I nod, setting my jaw. "I understand. Can I see the location of the Visir School?"

He shows me the map, pointing at Byrne. I shake my head. "It's not here. It's in an old castle, with this symbol on the front." I draw them a picture of the dragon with the crown.

Renel nods. "We know that place. Good. It's in Northern Gergon. You'll be tandem parachuting in with one of our agents."

"No problem," I say, and it isn't. I've faced down a centaur, scuba-dived in the dark night, and summoned a dragon. What's scary about jumping out of a plane after all that? "I need to speak to Princess Evelyn first."

"You can't," says Renel. "She is still in her secure location. We cannot risk a breach until the hostage is secured."

It's frustrating, but I know I don't have much of a choice. Saving Zain has to be the priority for now.

As a gaping hole appears in the airplane, metal giving way to a rush of air and bright blue sky, I suddenly change my mind about the safety of skydiving. But by then it is too late. The man I'm strapped to takes a flying leap and all of a sudden we are tumbling through the air toward the Visir School. I can't believe that I'm participating in a covert Novaen mission. But we all have a job to do. The briefing was clear: get in, get Zain, then get out as quickly as possible, without alerting the Gergon government to our intrusion.

Because of the way the castle is built into the mountain, we land on the top of a small ledge and rappel down, entering through the windows and down the twisted stairs of the highest tower. I recognize the floor I was kept on, and I point them toward my former cell. Could it have Zain in it?

There's no sign of Ivan or Prince Stefan—thank goodness. It's only been a couple of days since I escaped (was it really so recent?) and I hope that Zain is okay.

"Zain!" I shout.

"Sam?" I hear a weak cry from behind one of the other doors. I rush down toward it.

"Zain, are you there?" My fists pound on the door. "It's me. Renel is here with the security team."

To my surprise, he shouts, "No! How do you know he's the real Renel? Emilia, she's a master changeling . . ."

"Emilia's dead, Zain! I promise you, everyone is real." The agents swarm past me, carrying battering rams. "Get back from the door, Zain!" I shout, and I hope he's smart enough to listen.

With three sharp cracks of the battering ram, the door

breaks open. One of the agents uses the ram to make the hole wider, then another jumps through the gap and grabs Zain. His skin is pale as milk, his hair shaggy across his face. He looks like he hasn't eaten in days. He stumbles as he steps through the remnants of the door, and I catch him as he falls. "You're okay!" I kiss him on the lips, gently at first, but he presses back harder.

"I'm okay," he says. "She took my blood . . ."

I grimace. "I know, trust me."

"But I found this." He holds up my potion diary, which I'd left in the room. "And that gave me hope that you were here . . . and alive. Don't worry—I didn't read it." He gives me a small smile. My heart swells and I know I couldn't love him any more right now. I throw my arms around him and kiss him again.

Renel pushes me to one side. "Get this boy a medical evac, stat," he says to one of the agents. "Now, let's move."

The agents rush past me, but I stand my ground.

"Come on, Samantha," Renel says.

"No," I reply. "There's one more thing I need to get."

"We don't have time for anything else!"

But I don't listen to him—I don't even give him the time to refuse. I spin on my heels and I start to run. "Follow her!" I hear Renel shout behind me.

I run down the stairs to the cave, my knowledge of the castle giving me an advantage over the agents. I dash across the narrow passageway, careful not to look down to where I made my escape. I enter the little room where the memory diving occurred and I'm thankful to see all the vials still intact. The blackboard, on the other hand, is not. It's smashed into pieces on the floor. I wonder if it could ever be recovered, but for now I don't feel like explaining what it is that the board can do.

"What is this?" says one of the agents who follows me.

"I need these vials," I say. I swing my backpack off my back and start loading them in. I need to make sure I get every single one and none of them go to some secret Novaen security vault somewhere that can't be accessed.

When all the vials are loaded up into my backpack, I turn to the agents. "Okay, now we can go." They nod, and we head back up the stairs to the top of the castle as quickly as we can. We've been inside for maybe fifteen minutes, tops. When I reach the roof, there's already a transport screen that's been set up to take us home. I grab the arms that are ready to guide me through and, safely carrying my grandfather's missing memories, I step through the mirror and back to Nova. I never want to set foot in Gergon again.

CHAPTER FIFTY-FIVE

BACK AT THE HOSPITAL, I RUSH TO MOLLY and my parents. I carefully hand Molly the backpack, and then we drag our parents into Granddad's room, not giving them a chance to protest.

Molly restarts the process of feeding Granddad's memories back into his mind and my parents are gobsmacked. Only one of the vials—the final one—is different. It doesn't have a memory in it—only the strange inky black liquid that Emilia used as storage. I keep that one, sliding it into my jeans pocket. Their jaws don't leave the floor until she is done, when slowly, ever so slowly, Granddad opens his eyes.

"I thought we'd lost you, Dad," says my dad. He sits on the bed and gives his father a hug.

Granddad hugs each one of us in turn, then turns his attention to Molly and me. "Thank you both. For everything you've done to bring me back."

"There was no other way, Granddad," I say. "It required both of us to do it. Both of our skills. Both of our talents."

He rubs at his eyes, and the familiar twinkle is back. He looks around the room, seeing it all properly for the first time. He takes in the vast array of flowers, the balloons, presents, and cards that have been sent to him wishing him a full recovery. Although he's never been one to be sentimental, I can tell that he's touched. His eyes settle on the shoulder bag he was carrying when he was attacked. He frowns. "Has anyone been in my bag?"

I can't help myself—I chuckle. The first thing Granddad does when he wakes up is worry about his privacy being invaded.

"No, of course not, Dad," says my dad.

"Bring it to me," he says. Molly does as he asks, laying the leather bag on top of his lap. "The morning that I was . . . attacked," he said, "I had a particular journey to make. It's probably what gave Emilia the time to find me." He smiles ruefully. "I had to pick up a letter. I wasn't sure, then, if I was going to tell you right away. But having spent this time trapped in my memories . . . remembering what my own mother stood for . . . what I had to go through . . . I know now that I have been holding you back. And I don't know why.

"Sam Kemi, I believe your work in the Wilde Hunt, not to mention what you have gone through over the past two weeks, has made you eligible to become a proper alchemist. I had submitted all the documentation to the guild at the end of the Wilde Hunt and I was on my return trip from the council with their decision, when I was ambushed. I'm afraid that my mind was not capable of passing on the news to you. But the news has sat in this bag ever since. I would like you to have this." He hands me a large envelope, which feels padded with lots of paper.

My pulse speeds up and my mouth feels dry. For once, I am genuinely speechless. I carefully take the envelope from his hands, sliding my finger beneath the seal.

I pull out the stack of paper and unfold the letter that sits on top of the other sheets:

Dear Grand Master Ostanes Kemi,
We have received your application to make your
apprentice, Miss Samantha Kemi, a fully fledged
alchemist.
We have examined the evidence that you presented
to us, including the samples of several brews that the
apprentice has mixed completely free of interference
or guidance from her master. In light of the evidence
presented, we find there to be sufficient proof that
Miss Samantha Kemi, daughter of Mr. John and Mrs.
Katie Kemi, apprentice of Grand Master Ostanes
Kemi, of Kemi's Potion Shop, is not only worthy
to be named an alchemist but a Master of Alchemy

in the town of Kingstown, Nova, and anywhere
else worldwide where the profession of Alchemy is
recognized and performed.
We invite Miss Samantha Kemi to a ceremony
confirming this pronouncement at Castle Nova on 31
July this year. Please note that Samantha Kemi cannot
practice as a Master Alchemist until she has attended
this ceremony with you, and pledged her vow of safe
practice in front of the Guild.
Our sincere congratulations, and welcome to the
Guild of Alchemists, to Samantha.
Mme Slainte

The rest of the papers are the returned evidence that my grandfather sent in.

My hands shake as I put the paper down on the white hospital bed sheets. When I think about all the times I doubted myself—all the times I thought I would never get to practice this profession that I knew and loved . . . All the times I agonized over the decision making of my future. And here it is, handed to me on a silver platter . . . or, rather, an aged piece of vellum. Granddad covers my hand with his own. "Well done, my girl," he says. I think I spy a little tear in his eye.

"Granddad?" I swallow hard. The next words are not going to come easily.

"Yes? What is it?"

"After Emilia took your memories . . . your mind became unstable. You were unconscious."

His eyes don't leave mine for a moment. I take a deep breath and go on. "Don't blame Mum or Dad, it was my decision. But, the truth is, I authorized the use of a synth as part of your medication to help you get better. And it worked."

His lips purse in a thin line. "Well, as long as nobody knows . . . ," he manages to say.

That's when things get worse. I grip his hand. "ZA are going to put out a press release, saying they helped cure you. And they *did*. They just—aren't going to keep quiet about it. So to make it easier on us, I've made a decision about what I'm going to do next year. I'm going to join the ZA Synth-Natural Potions Studies team they're putting together. I want to work on cures that will help everyone, no matter what their circumstances."

For a moment, my heart stops as Granddad lowers his eyes. I'm sure that any pride he had in me has now evaporated.

I stand up and shuffle slowly to the door.

"The Kemi-ZA Synth-Natural Potions Studies program," he says, and I spin around on my heels. "Make sure Kemi is first."

I run back to the bed and throw my arms around him. Granddad's back. And I'm never letting him go again.

CHAPTER FIFTY-SIX

www.WildeHuntTheories.com/forums/
THEKEMIFAMILY

A MESSAGE TO ALL HUNT-OBSESSED

Unfortunately, owing to the misinformation disseminated via this forum about the whereabouts of Miss Samantha Kemi following her kidnapping, leading to the false arrest of an innocent citizen in New Nova and the storming of a home in Runustan, these forums have been shut down permanently.

It's been fun while it lasted.

Your WHT Moderators

EPILOGUE

"I CAN'T BELIEVE THIS IS HAPPENING TO you!" Zain says, squeezing my hand tight. He's come with me to the room in the Grand Alchemist's Lodge where I'm being held until I'm called up for the ceremony— and to take the oath that all alchemists must abide by.

"What, you can't believe I'm being made a Master Alchemist before you even graduated university?" I joke, lightly punching his shoulder.

"No, that I *can* believe. You're the youngest Master Alchemist that the Guild has ever known. You've beaten your own grandfather's record. And now, you're going to be the bridge between our two worlds."

"I'm glad you have faith in me."

"I'm not the only one," Zain says, jumping to his feet.

"What do you mean?" I frown and spin around, following his gaze.

"Samantha! Here you are!"

Princess Evelyn walks into the room, looking radiant. She sweeps me up in a warm embrace and kisses me on both cheeks.

"Evelyn! You came!" I can't keep the squeak of excitement out of my voice. "I've been trying to get in touch with you for days . . ."

"I know—I've practically been in exile since what happened at the Laville Ball! I am *so* glad you're okay!"

"I need to talk to you urgently."

"Can't it wait until after the ceremony—you're about to go on!" She winks at me, and spins in her long floaty dress. "I'd better go out and watch you! I hope you don't mind that I brought some of the media with me. I have to be very present now to reassure the nation that everything is okay."

"Evelyn, I . . ." I reach out and grab her hand.

"Sam, we'll talk when you're finished and ordained, or instated or whatever it is they do to you alchemists." She shakes free of me and turns to walk out of the door.

"Please," I say, unable to keep the desperation out of my voice. "I just need to tell you one thing. I've figured it out. I've worked out a system so you can store your excess power! Turns out there were magic-storing potions left in the Visir School. You don't have to get married after all!"

Evelyn's jaw drops. "But Sam . . . you're too late."

"What? What do you mean I'm too late?"

"Your forty-eight hours were up over a week ago. I couldn't wait any longer."

My eyes open wide. I look at Zain, who looks as confused as I do.

"Are you engaged?" I ask. An engagement can still be undone.

"It's a long story," she says, then she stumbles. "Oh, forgive me, I'm feeling a little weak. Maybe I'm coming down with something." We rush over to her side, helping her regain her balance. As I grab her hand, I feel something new on her fingers. Not just one ring. But two. My heart stops. "I'm fine," she says with a smile.

She coughs, and a powdery white substance leaves a trail on her sleeve. I gulp. I've seen this once before. The Gergon illness has entered Nova. And I think Evelyn may have caught it from her new husband.

ACKNOWLEDGMENTS

FROM FIRE-BREATHING DRAGONS TO BIO-luminescent algae . . . this book has been incredibly fun to write and has been inspired by so many cool real-life places, creatures, and experiences. As always, I owe a huge debt of thanks to so many people who allow me to live my dream of writing and adventuring.

Rachel Mann of S&S UK and Zareen Jaffery of S&S BFYR are my intrepid editors, with me every step of the way of this book's journey. Their endless patience and insightful comments make them the perfect companions on the road to publication! Thanks to the Simon & Schuster teams in all corners of the globe for bringing my books to life—especially Liz Binks and Hannah Cooper in the UK and Shannon Vaughan and Adria Iwasutiak in Canada who have all worked so hard on my behalf. Emma Young, my copyeditor, never misses a beat. And Juliet Mushens, my agent, whom I trust implicitly and who never ceases to amaze me with her publishing prowess—she's my guardian angel (and also one of my best friends).

Outside of the business of publishing, huge thanks to Kim Curran and Laura Lam for their close reads and unwavering support! Speaking of support both near and far, I have to thank Juno Dawson, Laure Eve, Sarah J. Maas, James Smythe, and Zoe Sugg for being the most inspiring friends a writer could ask for. Your books and talent keep making me want to up my writing game! Sarah Woodward, Sophie McCulloch, Angus McCulloch, and Maria McCulloch, thank you for reading and encouraging me when I doubted myself. I can't express to you how much your enthusiasm and belief in me helps keep me going through the good times and the tough.

Lastly, I have to thank Lofty—every day of our lives is a grand adventure, and I wouldn't have it any other way.